Acclaim for *New York Times* bests‌
and her captivat‌

THE THIRD W‌

"Jewell's last few novels have been a revelation—emotionally sophisticated and complex—and this latest, which gradually rewrites the history of a 'perfect' family, is a fine follow-up. . . . Taut pacing and complicated characters shape this rich examination of the modern family."

—*Kirkus Reviews*

"Jewell excels at juggling multiple perspectives to slowly peel back the layers of supposed domestic bliss. Like Liane Moriarty, she manages the perfect blend of women's fiction and nail-biting suspense, throwing enough red herrings in the reader's path to keep the pages turning."

—*Booklist*

"A great choice for readers seeking a mystery with a blended family twist."

—*Library Journal*

"*The Third Wife* is a summer gem. The story is complex . . . the many characters well drawn. . . . Readers of Donna Tartt and Tana French will recognize Jewell's pacing for what it is: essential."

—*NY Journal of Books*

"*The Third Wife* explores complicated family dynamics in a genuine way that is witty yet realistically nuanced."

—*Shelf Awareness*

"Lisa Jewell presents us with yet another emotionally intelligent, brilliantly plotted and beautifully written examination of a very modern family that will keep you gripped to the end. . . . Take this to the beach, or indeed anywhere—I promise you won't regret it."

—*Daily Mail* (London)

THE HOUSE WE GREW UP IN

"A dramatic look at siblings, parents, and hoarding."

—Redbook

"Jewell cleverly frames the destruction of the Bird family."

—Booklist

"Jewell keeps the reader engrossed with her characters' winding, divergent paths."

—Publishers Weekly

"Jewell delivers with this latest tale of loneliness and the lure of beautiful things."

—Kirkus Reviews

"You will be desperate to find out what messes this family up so badly."

—Sophie Kinsella, author of Shopaholic to the Stars

"Lorrie is one of the most vivid—and complex—characters I've read in years."

—Jojo Moyes, New York Times bestselling author of Me Before You

BEFORE I MET YOU

"Jewell unfolds each detail . . . with impeccable timing."

—Publishers Weekly

"Jewell keeps the pace steady, the plot intriguing, and the characters highly relatable. Family dynamics, the search for love and personal meaning, and the simple yet evocative daily motions of each woman keep the pages turning."

—Booklist

"Heartbreakingly good."

—Marie Claire (UK)

THE MAKING OF US

"An engaging tale of choices made and not made, families lost and families gained, this should appeal to fans of Jewell's work as well as such authors as Jodi Picoult."

—*Booklist*

"Compelling and entertaining. . . . Jewell's moving novel immerses readers in the lives of these unique characters through the universal themes of family and a search for belonging."

—*Publishers Weekly*

"Odd and lovely. . . . Filled with heart and humor."

—*Kirkus Reviews*

"An irresistible read. . . . Anyone who has ever pondered the nature of family or imagined finding a long-lost sibling will be captivated."

—*Shelf Awareness*

AFTER THE PARTY

"Flipping between their perspectives and illuminating their desires, fears, and sometimes clumsy actions, *After the Party* entertainingly marches its characters along the path to finally growing up."

—*Booklist*

"Jewell's easy prose and storytelling ability make for a pleasant trip. Engaging."

—*Kirkus Reviews*

"Jewell writes, as ever, with wit and verve."

—*Guardian* (UK)

THE THIRD WIFE

WIFE

A Novel

LISA JEWELL

ATRIA PAPERBACK

New York London Toronto Sydney New Delhi

ATRIA PAPERBACK

An Imprint of Simon & Schuster, Inc.
1230 Avenue of the Americas
New York, NY 10020

Copyright © 2015 by Lisa Jewell

First Atria Paperback edition February 2016

ATRIA PAPERBACK and colophon are trademarks of Simon & Schuster, Inc.

For information about special discounts for bulk purchases, please contact Simon & Schuster Special Sales at 1-866-506-1949 or business@simonandschuster.com.

The Simon & Schuster Speakers Bureau can bring authors to your live event. For more information or to book an event, contact the Simon & Schuster Speakers Bureau at 1-866-248-3049 or visit our website at www.simonspeakers.com.

Manufactured in the United States of America

20   19   18   17   16

Library of Congress Cataloging-in-Publication Data is available.

ISBN 978-1-4767-9218-7
ISBN 978-1-4767-9219-4 (pbk)
ISBN 978-1-4767-9220-0 (ebook)

This book is dedicated to all my friends on the Board

PART ONE

1

APRIL 2011

They might have been fireworks, the splashes, bursts, storms of color that exploded in front of her eyes. They might have been the northern lights, her own personal aurora borealis. But they weren't, they were just neon lights and streetlights rendered blurred and prismatic by vodka. Maya blinked, trying to dislodge the colors from her field of vision. But they were stuck, as though someone had been scribbling on her eyeballs. She closed her eyes for a moment, but without vision, her balance went and she could feel herself begin to sway. She grabbed something. She did not realize until the sharp bark and shrug that accompanied her action that it was a human being.

"Shit," Maya said, "I'm really sorry."

The person tutted and backed away from her. "Don't worry about it."

Maya took exaggerated offense to the person's lack of kindness.

"Jesus," she said to the outline of the person, whose gender she had failed to ascertain. "What's your problem?"

"Er," said the person, looking Maya up and down, "I think you'll find you're the one with the problem." Then the person, a woman, yes, in red shoes, tutted again and walked away, her heels issuing a mocking clack-clack against the pavement as she went.

Maya watched her blurred figure recede. She found a lamppost and leaned against it, looking into the oncoming traffic. The headlights turned into more fireworks. Or one of those toys she'd had as a child: tube, full of colored beads, you shook it, looked through the hole, lovely patterns—what was it called? She couldn't remember. Whatever. She didn't know anymore. She didn't know what time it was. She didn't know where she was. Adrian had called. She'd spoken to him. Tried to sound sober. He'd asked her if she needed him to come and get her. She couldn't remember what she'd said. Or how long ago that had been. Lovely Adrian. So lovely. She couldn't go home. Go home and do what she needed to do. He was too nice. She remembered the pub. She'd talked to that woman. Promised her she was going home. That was hours ago. Where had she been since then? Walking. Sitting somewhere, on a bench, with a bottle of vodka, talking to strangers. Hahaha! That bit had been fun. Those people had been fun. They'd said she could come back with them, to their flat, have a party. She'd been tempted, but she was glad now, glad she'd said no.

She closed her eyes, gripped the lamppost tighter as she felt her balance slip away from her. She smiled to herself. This was nice. This was nice. All this color and darkness and noise and all these fascinating people. She should do this more often, she really should. Get out of it. Live a little. Go a bit nuts. A group of women were walking towards her. She stared at them greedily. She could see each woman in triplicate. They were all so young, so pretty. She closed her eyes again as they passed by, her senses unable to contain their images any longer. Once they'd passed she opened her eyes.

She saw a bus bearing down, bouncy and keen. She squinted into the white light on the front, looking for a number. It slowed as it neared her and she turned and saw that there was a bus stop to her left, with people standing at it.

Dear Bitch. Why can't you just disappear?

The words passed through her mind, clear and concise in their meaning, like a sober person leading her home. And then those other words, the words from earlier.

I hate her too.

She took a step forward.

2

"According to the bus driver, Mrs. Wolfe lurched into the path of the bus."

"Lurched?" echoed Adrian Wolfe.

"Well, yes. That was the word he used. He said that she did not appear to step or jump or run or fall or slip. He said she lurched."

"So it was an accident?"

"Well, yes, it does sound possible. But obviously we will need a full coroner's report, a possible inquest. What we can tell you with certainty is that her blood alcohol reading was very high." DI Hollis referred to a piece of paper on the desk in front of him. "Nought point two. That's extraordinarily high. Especially for a small woman like Mrs. Wolfe. Was she a regular drinker?"

The question sounded loaded. Adrian flinched. "Er, yes, I suppose, but no more so than your average stressed-out thirty-three-year-old schoolteacher. You know, a glass a night, sometimes two. More at the weekends."

"But this level of drinking, Mr. Wolfe? Was this normal?"

Adrian let his face fall into his hands and rubbed roughly at his skin. He had been awake since three thirty a.m., since his phone had rung, interrupting a fractured dream in which he was running about central London with a baby in his arms trying to call Maya's name but not able to make a sound.

"No," he said, "no. That wasn't normal. She isn't . . . wasn't that kind of drinker."

"So, what was she—out at a party? Doing something out of the ordinary?"

"No. No." Adrian sighed, feeling the inadequacy of his understanding of the night's events. "No. She was looking after my children. At my house in Islington . . ."

"*Your* children?"

"Yes." Adrian sighed again. "I have three children with my former wife. My former wife had to go to work today. Sorry. Yesterday. Unexpectedly. She didn't have time to organize child care so she asked if Maya would look after the children. They're on their Easter holidays. And, obviously, Maya being a teacher, so is she. So Maya spent the day there and I was expecting her home at about six thirty and she wasn't there when I got home and she wasn't answering her phone. I called her roughly every two minutes."

"Yes, we saw all the missed calls."

"She finally picked up at about ten p.m. and I could tell she was drunk. She said she was in town. Wouldn't tell me who with. She said she was on her way home. So I sat and waited for her. Called again from roughly midnight to about one o'clock. Then I finally fell asleep. Until my phone rang at three thirty."

"How did she sound? When you spoke to her at ten p.m.?"

"She sounded . . ." Adrian sighed and waited for a wave of tears to pass. "She sounded really jolly. Happy drunk. She was calling from a pub. I could hear the noise in the background. She said she was on her way home. She was just finishing her drink."

"Often the way, isn't it?" the policeman said. "When you've reached a certain point of inebriation. Much easier to be persuaded into staying on for that one more drink. The hours pass as fast as minutes."

"Do you have any idea who she was with, in that pub?"

"Well, no. For now, we're not treating Mrs. Wolfe's death as suspicious. If it becomes apparent that there was foul play involved and we need to investigate Mrs. Wolfe's last movements, then yes, we'll talk to local publicans. Talk to Mrs. Wolfe's friends. Build up a fuller picture."

Adrian nodded. He was tired. He was traumatized. He was confused.

"Do you have any theories of your own, Mr. Wolfe? Was everything OK at home?"

"Yes, God, yes! I mean, we'd only been married two years. Everything was great."

"No problems with family number one?"

Adrian looked at DI Hollis questioningly.

"Well, second wives—there can be, you know, pressures there?"

"Actually, she's . . . she *was* . . . my third wife."

DI Hollis's eyebrows jumped.

"I've been married twice before."

DI Hollis looked at Adrian as though he had just performed an audacious sleight-of-hand trick.

And now, ladies and gentlemen, for my next trick I will confound all your preconceptions about me in one fell swoop.

Adrian was used to that look. It said: How did an old fart like you manage to persuade one woman to marry you, let alone three?

"I like being married," said Adrian, aware even as he said it how inadequate it sounded.

"And that was all fine, was it? Mrs. Wolfe wasn't finding it difficult being in the middle of such a . . . *complicated* situation?"

Adrian sighed, pulled his dark hair off his face and then let it flop back over his forehead. "It wasn't complicated," he said. "It isn't complicated. We're one big happy family. We go on holiday together every year."

"All of you?"

"Yes. All of us. Three wives. Five children. Every year."

"All in the same house?"

"Yes. In the same house. Divorce doesn't have to be toxic if everyone involved is prepared to act like grown-ups."

DI Hollis nodded slowly. "Well," he said, "that's nice to hear."

"When can I see her?"

"I'm not sure." DI Hollis's demeanor softened. "I'll talk to the coroner's office for you now, see how they're getting on. Should be soon." He smiled warmly and replaced the lid of his pen. "Maybe time to get home, have a shower, have a coffee?"

"Yes," said Adrian. "Yes. Thank you."

✑

The key sounded terrible in the lock of Adrian's front door; it ground and grated like an instrument of torture. He realized it was because he was turning the key extra slowly. He realized he was trying to put off the moment that he walked into his flat, *their* flat. He realized that he did not want to be here without her.

Her cat greeted him in the hallway, desperate and hungry. Adrian glanced at the cat blankly. Maya's cat. Brought here three years ago in a brown plastic box as part of an endearingly small haul of possessions. He wasn't a cat person but he'd accepted her cat into his world in the same way that he'd accepted her bright floral duvet cover, her wipe-clean tablecloth and her crap CD player.

"Billie," he said, closing the door behind him, leaning heavily against it. "She's gone. Your mummy. She's gone." He slid slowly to his haunches, his back still pressed against the front door, the heels of his hands forced into his eye sockets, and he wept.

The cat approached him curiously. She rubbed herself against his knees and she issued a vibrato warble. He pulled the cat towards him and he wept some more. "She's dead, puss. Beautiful, beautiful Mummy. What are we going to do? What are we going to do?"

The cat had no answers to offer. The cat was hungry.

Slowly, Adrian pulled himself to standing and let the cat lead him to the kitchen. There he searched through cupboards and shelves for something to feed the cat with. He never fed the cat. He had no idea what the cat normally ate. He gave up in the end and gave the cat tuna meant for humans.

The sun was out, flooding this spartan, unpretty, east-facing room with unaccustomed sunlight. It picked out the grubby honey tones in the floorboards and the dust in the air. It picked out the whorls of black fur left wherever the cat had settled for a sleep and the circular sticky patches on the coffee table where Maya had rested her morning smoothie. It picked out the damp bubbling behind the wallpaper and the cracks in the plasterwork.

Such a rushed decision, this flat. Maya's flatmate had found a replacement who wanted to move in that weekend, and as civilized as Caroline had been about his still living in the family home three weeks after his telling her he was leaving her for another woman, he'd known it was time to move on. They'd looked at three flats in one morning and chosen the worst one in the nicest street.

It hadn't mattered then. It hadn't mattered to either of them. Because they were in love. And ugly flats look pretty when you're in love.

He watched the cat pecking at her tuna fish. The cat would have to go. He could not have Maya's cat without Maya.

Then he pulled his phone out of his jacket pocket and he stared at it for a while. He had phone calls to make. Terrible phone calls. Phone calls to Maya's dry, unsmiling parents; phone calls to Susie in Hove, to Caroline in Islington, to his young children and his grown children.

And what would he say to them when they asked him why Maya was walking drunk and alone around the neon-lit streets of the West End on a Wednesday night? He really did not know. All he knew for sure was that his life had just come off its rails and that for the first time in his adult life, he was alone.

3

MARCH 2012

The woman in the pale gray coat stood on the other side of the post office, looking through a carousel display of greeting cards. She spun the carousel slowly around and around, but her gaze was not upon the cards, but on the gaps between the cards. It was on him. Over there. Adrian Wolfe.

He was wearing a big tweedy overcoat, black jeans, walking boots and a burgundy scarf. Tall and slim, from behind he looked about twenty, from the front he looked middle-aged. But he was distinguished, almost handsome, with his mop of dark hair and spaniel eyes. His looks had grown on the woman over the weeks, as she'd followed him from place to place.

She watched him pull something from his pocket. A small rectangle of white card. He said something to a member of the staff, who nodded and pointed at a blank area on the community noticeboard. Adrian Wolfe pulled a thumbtack from the board and then punctured his card with it. He stood back for a moment and regarded it. Then he put his hands into the pockets of his big tweedy overcoat and left.

The woman scooted from behind the carousel and walked to the noticeboard, where she read Adrian Wolfe's card:

Good Home Wanted for Mature Cat

Billie is roughly eight years old. She is a black and white moggy
with a sweet temperament and very few annoying habits.
I am going through some personal changes and am no longer
able to care for her as well as she deserves.
If you'd like to come and meet Billie and see if you hit it off,
please call me on the number below.

She looked from left to right, and then from right to left, before pulling the card from the noticeboard and stuffing it into her handbag.

"She sheds a bit."

Adrian glanced in the general direction of the cat, who was looking at the strange woman as though she knew that she was here to offer her the chance of a better life.

The strange woman, who was called Jane, smiled and ran her hand firmly down the cat's back and said, "That's fine. I have an Animal."

Adrian narrowed his eyes at her. In his mind's eye he saw her sitting on a sofa with a tiger at her side, or possibly a horse. "An animal . . . you mean another pet?"

She laughed. "No, sorry, I mean one of those vacuums, you know, for people who have pets. That suck up hair."

"Aaah." He nodded knowingly. But he did not know.

"So. Why are you getting rid of her?" She picked some fur off the palm of her hand and let it drop to the floor.

Adrian smiled sadly and let the next words fall as lightly as possible from his tongue. He was practiced by now in the art of making the unpalatable bearable for other people.

"Ah, well, Billie was my wife's cat. And my wife passed away. Eleven months ago. And every time I look at Billie I expect my wife to walk into the room. And she doesn't. So . . ." He shrugged. "There you go. Time to say good-bye to Billie." He looked fondly at the cat although he felt no fondness at all towards her. But he didn't want this strange woman to see this side of him, the dead-inside part that could feel so antipathetic towards a mere cat.

The woman looked up at him, her eyes filled with pain. "My God," she said, "I'm so sorry. That's terrible." Her blond fringe flipped across her eyes and she moved it back with delicate fingers. All her movements were perfectly executed, like a trained dancer or an Alexander technique student. Adrian noticed this at the same time as noticing her waist, small and neat inside a highly pressed blue shirtdress pulled in with a belt, and her earrings, tiny bulbs of blue glass hanging from silver hooks, the shade a perfect match for her dress. She was wearing tan leather ankle boots with a scattering of silver studs across the toe and a small heel. She was immaculate. Almost unnervingly so.

They both turned to look at Billie once more.

"So," said Adrian, "what do you think?"

"I think she's lovely," she said. Then she paused and looked at Adrian. He noticed with a start that her eyes were mismatched: one gray-blue, the other gray-blue with a chunk of amber. He caught his breath. There it was, he thought, the imperfection. Every woman he had ever loved had had one. A scar across the eyebrow (Caroline). A gap between her teeth (Susie). Bright red hair and a violent patterning of ginger freckles (Maya).

"But," she continued, "I'm not sure you're ready to let her go."

He gazed at her curiously, interested to hear the theory behind her opinion.

"How long have you lived with Billie?" she asked.

He shrugged. "Maya brought her with her. When she moved in with me. So, I guess, nearly four years."

He saw her rapidly working out the dates, behind those mismatched eyes. A wife who'd moved in and then died all within the space of four years. Tough stats to absorb. Unlikely and tragic, like a bad movie. But it wasn't a bad movie. Oh no, indeed. It was his Real Life.

She shook her head and smiled. "She is lovely," she said again. "But . . ."

Adrian watched her forming her next words.

"I'm not quite feeling it."

"You're not quite feeling . . . ?"

He stared at the cat, looking at her objectively for the first time. He'd never been a cat person and he assumed that they were all much of a muchness. Four legs. Whiskers. Triangles for ears. Roughly the size of a briefcase. None of the endless, glorious variations of the dog form: ears that mopped the floor, ears that reached for the moon, flat snouts, pointy snouts, size of a squirrel, size of a small pony.

"The connection."

He rubbed the point of his chin between his fingers and thumb and tried to look as though he could see her concern. "Right."

"Can I think about it?" she said, hoisting the strap of her neat little oyster-gray handbag up onto her shoulder.

"Of course! Of course! Yes, you're the only person who replied to the ad so the ball is firmly in your court."

She smiled at him. "Great. Can I come back? Maybe tomorrow? Meet her again?"

Adrian laughed. What a strange girl. "Er, yes. I should

think so. Although I'll be out and about a lot. Have you got my number? So you can call?"

"Sure." She gave him her hand to shake. "I'll call you mid-morning. See what we can arrange."

"Good." Adrian followed her towards his front door, opened it up for her.

"Wow," she said, looking at his whiteboard, nailed to the wall above his desk. "This looks pretty boggling."

"Yes. Boggling is the word. A little like my life. This"—he gestured at the chart—"is all that stands between me and total existential chaos."

She paused, a smile playing on her lips, and ran her finger across the words *Pearl 10th Birthday. Strada Upper St. 6:30 p.m.* "Have you got her present?"

He started at the question. So intrusive, yet so reasonable.

"Yes," he said. "Actually I have."

"Well done!" she said. "Very organized. Right. Well, I'll call you tomorrow. And thank you. Thank you for giving me time to think about it. Very important decision. Not one to be rushed."

"No, no, absolutely not."

He closed the door behind her and felt compelled to lean heavily against it, almost as though she'd taken his center of gravity with her when she left.

⌘

The whiteboard had been Maya's idea. Maya was one of those people who saw straight through to the core of the issue and sorted it. And the issue was that even though all he wanted was for everyone to be happy, he kept doing things that made people unhappy. And he wished he didn't care. He wished he could just shrug and say, Well, you know, that's life, nobody's perfect. But every time he forgot a child's birthday or an arrangement to watch a theatrical performance or to attend an awards ceremony, he was filled with seething self-hatred. His sprawling, unconventional family was a product entirely of the decisions he had made and therefore it was up to him to make sure that nobody felt the aftershocks. But still they came. Bang: a crying daughter. Crash: a disappointed son. Boom: an irked ex-wife.

"Poor Adrian," Maya had said one day after he'd had a terrible phone call with Caroline about a parent–teacher meeting he'd forgotten to attend.

Adrian had sighed and laid his head upon Maya's shoulder and said, "I'm a disaster zone. A human wrecking ball. I just wish I could show the children that even though I'm a disorganized fuckwit, actually I'm thinking about them every minute of every day."

And she'd unveiled this thing. They'd called it the Board of Harmony. The whole year mapped out and color-coded: children's birthdays, ex-wives' birthdays, ex-mothers-in-law's birthdays, who was spending Christmas where, who was starting big school or leaving university, the half-terms and holidays of three school-age children and the travel arrangements and job interviews of two adult children. If he spoke to a child and they told him something about their life, no matter how inconsequential, he would write it here: *Cat looking at flats this weekend*. That way, the next time he spoke to Cat he would be sure to remember to ask her about it. It was all there. All the tiny minutiae of the lives of the families he'd created and vacated.

Adrian had never intended for his life to get this convoluted. Two ex-wives. One late wife. Three sons. Two daughters. Three houses. And a cat. But more than that, not just those direct connections, but all the other countless people who'd been drawn into his world through these temporary families:

the boyfriends and girlfriends of his children, the mothers and fathers of their best friends, the favored teachers, the mothers- and fathers- and sisters- and brothers-in-law, these people who were his beloved children's aunts and uncles and grandparents and cousins. People who had once played a huge part in his life and continued to play a huge part in the lives of his children. People he couldn't just stop thinking about and knowing about and caring about purely because he was no longer in love with their daughter/sister/aunt.

And there it was. The sharp needle of tragedy, in the softest part of his belly, as he thought about Maya. Who'd left nothing. Not really. Parents whom he'd barely got to know, a brother he'd never met apart from briefly at their wedding, a brittle best friend who appeared to hold him responsible for her death. And this cat. This cat who had just failed to make a connection with a beautiful young woman called Jane and who, consequently, was still here, curled up like a sleek apostrophe in a shaft of sunlight.

He walked across the room and sat beside the cat. He observed it for a moment. Maya had babied this cat, talked about it all the time, bought it expensive treats and toys it never played with. He'd watched her, bemused. And then one day, a few weeks before their wedding, and although she'd never asked, he'd told her he could afford one more baby. "Just a small one," he'd said, holding his hands a few inches apart. "One we could keep in a box maybe. Or a pocket."

"What if it grew?" she'd said.

"Well, we'd squash it down a bit," he'd said, miming patting down the sides of a small baby.

"So it would need to be quite a spongy baby?"

"Yes," he'd said. "Ideally."

He put one hand onto the cat's back and it jumped at his touch. As well it might. He rarely touched her. But then it softened and revealed its belly to him, a cushion of thick black fur, two tufted rows of pink nipples. He placed his hand against it and left it there, feeling the comforting sense of warm flesh and blood beneath his palm. The cat pawed at his hand play-fully, and for a moment Adrian felt something human towards the animal, the "connection" that the girl called Jane had mentioned. Maybe she was right, he pondered. Maybe he did still need this living, breathing piece of Maya in his life. Then, as the thought passed through his grieving mind, he squeezed the cat's front leg gently and recoiled with a pained cry as the cat pierced the pale, thin skin of his inner wrist with one tiny hooked claw.

"Ow. *Shit*." He brought his wrist to his mouth and sucked it. "What did you do that for?"

The cat sprang to its feet and leaped from the sofa at the sound of his raised voice. He stared at his wrist, at the tiny pinprick in his skin, darkly black-red, but not bleeding. He continued to stare at it, willing it to bleed, willing it to yield something human and hot and bright. But it didn't.

4

It was Saturday night. Again. The forty-seventh Saturday night since Maya had died.

They didn't get any easier.

Adrian wondered idly what his family was doing. He pictured them lined up in front of the television watching whatever show was currently the big Saturday night thing. What was it the kids had made him watch last weekend when they were here? Something with Ant and Dec in it. He could barely remember. He was just grateful it wasn't one of those gruesome talent shows with people crying all over the place.

As the shadows grew long upon the pavement outside and a light shower of rain started to patter against the windowpanes, Adrian poured himself a glass of wine and pulled the laptop towards himself.

He had not realized until Maya had died and left him on his own for the first time since he was nineteen years old that he had no friends. He'd had friends in the past, but they'd come as part of the package of his two former marriages. The friends he'd had in Sussex with Susie had stayed in Sussex with Susie. The friends he'd had with Caroline had taken her side entirely in the aftermath of his affair with Maya. Or rather, the sides of their wives. And he and Maya hadn't made any friends because they'd been too busy keeping everybody happy.

Some odd-bods had popped up after Maya died, people he'd never expected to hear from again: the slightly sinister deputy head of the girls' school that Maya had taught at, with whom he'd once had a long and very strained conversation at a fund-raising evening; the ex-husband of a friend of Caroline's, whose nasal voice he and Caroline had taken great joy in impersonating behind his back; the rather bellicose father of Pearl's friend, whom Adrian had only ever met in ninety-second bursts on their respective doorsteps when delivering and collecting children. They'd forced him into pubs and even on occasion into nightclubs. They'd poured alcohol into him until he looked as though he was having a good time and then they'd tried to get unsuitable women to talk to him. "This is my friend Adrian. He's just lost his wife."

There'd also been a swarm of women in the wake of Maya's death. Mainly mothers of school friends, the very same women who'd looked at him in such disgust when they heard that he'd left Caroline, now circling him with wide, caring eyes, bringing him things to eat in Tupperware boxes, which he'd then have to wash up and return with words of gratitude.

He hadn't wanted them then. He'd wanted to stay inside and cry and ask himself why why why.

Now, eleven months later, he still didn't know why but he'd given up asking.

～

The girl called Jane came again the next day. This time her honey hair was down, blow-dried into loops that flipped off her collarbone, her fringe parted in the center and hanging either side of her face, as though she was peering through stage curtains. In the moments before her arrival Adrian had done things that he did not wish to consider too deeply. He had taken Maya's hand mirror from a dark corner of his flat to a bright corner of his flat and he had examined his face in great and unedifying detail in the light from a west-facing window. Maya had been thirty when he met her and he'd been forty-four. He'd seen himself as a young forty-four. A full head of dark brown hair, bright hazel eyes, upturned smile lines, still the face in the mirror that he expected to see there.

Time and grief were cruel at any age, but particularly at this middle point of physical flux, when the face became like a flickering image in a pretentious video art installation, in and out of focus, young-old, young-old, young again. At some point in the moments after Maya's death, the image had stopped flickering and there it was. Static. The face of someone older than he'd ever thought he'd be. He had not looked in mirrors very much these last few months, but now he wanted to know what he looked like. He wanted to see what Jane would see.

In minute detail, he saw that his jawline had begun to collapse; he saw folds and crenellations in the skin of his neck that put him in mind of the wild, tide-creased beaches of north Norfolk. He saw yellowish pillows of flesh beneath his eyes; he saw that his skin was dry, his hazel eyes were faded and his hair had achromatized, from rich dark brown to something like the color of a wet pavement.

Once this process was complete he'd got into the shower and done things to his face with the contents of tubes and bottles left there by Maya. He had washed his hair twice, until it squeaked clean beneath his fingertips. And then for possibly the first time in his life he put conditioner on it. He did not ask himself why. He just did it. Then he ironed himself a shirt. A green shirt that Maya had once said brought out the hazel of his eyes. And he used Maya's hair dryer on his hair, running his fingers through it, teasing it into something sleek and fragrant.

He cursed himself silently as he watched the clock turn from 11:22 to 11:23, seven minutes before her appointed arrival. "*You fool*," he muttered under his breath. "*You total and utter ball sack.*" He filled the kettle and he pushed things around the kitchen counter to make it look more welcoming. *"Forty-eight,"* he muttered to himself. *"You're forty-*eight. *You're a widower. You're a tosser."*

And then there she was, curiously ageless, at his front door, with her mismatched eyes and her disingenuous fringe, smelling of jasmine and clean clothes. Her neat little bag was clutched at stomach level with both hands and she was wearing a soft gray coat, fastened with one single oversized button.

"Come in. Come in."

"I'm really sorry," she said, striding confidently into the hallway. "I know you must think I'm mad."

"What? No!"

"Of course you do. It's like I'm *dating* your cat. You know, *courting* her. Next thing I'll be asking if I can take her out to dinner."

Adrian looked at Jane and then laughed. "Be my guest," he said. "She has impeccable manners. And doesn't eat much."

Jane headed towards the cat, which was in its usual spot on the back of the sofa by the front window. The cat turned at her approach and offered itself to her with a smiling face. "Hello," said Jane, cupping the cat's face inside her hand and appraising it affectionately. "You sweet girl."

"Can I get you a tea?" asked Adrian. "A coffee? Water?"

"I'd love a coffee," she said. "Bit of a night last night."

Adrian nodded. She did not look as though she'd had a *bit of a night* last night. She did not, in fact, look like she'd ever had a *bit of a night* in her life. "Black?"

She smiled. "Black."

When Adrian returned with the coffee he found Jane sitting on the sofa with the cat on her lap and a framed photograph of the little ones in her hand.

"These children are stunning," she said, turning the photo to face him. "Are they all yours?"

He glanced at the photo. It was Otis, Pearl and Beau, in sou'westers and galoshes, knee-deep in a creek somewhere in the West Country. Behind them the sky was gunmetal gray, below them the water was steel and their brightly colored clothes burst through the dreary background almost as though the children had been cut out and glued on. Beau had his arm around Pearl's waist and Pearl had her head in the crook of Otis's shoulder. It was a happy photograph; all three children were smiling evenly and naturally with open eyes and relaxed mouths. Maya had taken it. The children had always smiled for Maya.

Adrian handed Jane her coffee and she put it on the tabletop. "Yes," he said. "They are all mine."

"What are their names?"

He glanced at her. He'd flossed his teeth for this woman—he could hardly be surprised if she wanted to ask him personal questions.

"Well," he said, running his finger across the photograph. "That's Otis, he's twelve; that's Pearl, she's . . ."

"Nearly ten."

He looked at her from the corner of his eye. She looked back at him playfully.

"Yes. She's nearly ten. And this little munchkin is Beau. He just turned five."

"Adorable," she said, putting the photo carefully back on the table and picking up her coffee cup. "And they don't live with you?"

"You're very inquisitive," he said, sitting himself down on the armchair opposite her.

"I'm nosy," she said. "You can say it. I don't mind."

"OK then. You're nosy."

She laughed. "Sorry, I just find other people's lives fascinating. Always have."

He smiled. "That's OK. I'm the same." He inhaled and ran his hand down his freshly shaved jaw. "No," he said. "They don't live with me. They live with their mum. In a five-story Georgian town house in Islington."

"Wow." Jane ran her eyes around the cramped living room, a silent acknowledgment of the fact that Adrian's ex-wife had pulled the long straw.

"It's fine," he said quickly. He would hate for anyone to feel sorry for him, not for even a moment. "It's good. There's room for them all to squeeze in here every other weekend. Beau shares with me, Pearl and Otis in the spare room. It's good."

"So, you and your late wife, you didn't have any children?"

"No." Adrian shook his head. "Sadly not. Although, Jesus, I'm not sure what I'd have done if we had had a baby. I mean . . . I'd have had to give up work. And the whole precarious edifice would have come crashing down."

"The big house in Islington . . ."

"Yes. And the cottage in Hove."

She raised an eyebrow at him questioningly.

"Ex-wife number one," he replied. "Susie. Mother of my two eldest children. Here . . ." He got to his feet and picked up another framed photograph. He passed it to her. "Cat and Luke. My big ones."

She stared at the photograph with wide eyes. "You make very special children," she said. "How old are these two?"

"Cat will be twenty in May. Luke is twenty-three."

"Grown-ups now?"

"Yes. Grown-ups now. Although sometimes it doesn't feel like it."

"And do they live in Hove? With their mum?"

"Luke does. Cat's in London now. Living with Caroline."

"Caroline?"

"Yes. Caroline. Wife number two."

Jane looked towards the door into the hall. "I totally understand that thing now," she said. "The whiteboard."

"Yes. The Board of Harmony. Thank God for it. Thank God for Maya." He blew out his breath audibly, to hold back a sudden wave of tearfulness.

Jane looked at him compassionately. "So, if you don't mind me asking, how did Maya die?"

"Well, technically, she died of a blow to the head and massive internal bleeding after being knocked down by a night bus on Charing Cross Road at three thirty in the morning. But, officially, we have no idea how she ended up being knocked down by a night bus on Charing Cross Road at three thirty in the morning." He shrugged.

"So it wasn't suicide?"

"Well. The verdict was accidental death, but people like Maya, sensible, moderate people, don't tend to *accidentally* get so drunk they can't stand up and then fall in front of a bus on Charing Cross Road at three thirty in the morning. So . . ."

"A big question mark."

"Yes. A very big question mark."

"God, I bet you wish you knew."

Adrian exhaled. "I sure do. It's hard to move on, without answers."

"Do you have a theory?"

"No," he said. "Nothing. It was completely out of the blue. We'd just got back from Suffolk, from a family holiday. We'd had a lovely time. She'd spent the day with my children." He paused, pulling himself back from the dark place he always went to when considering the last inexplicable hours of Maya's life. "We were happy. We were trying for a baby. Everything was perfect."

"Was it?"

He glanced at her curiously. It sounded like an accusation. "Yes," he said, almost harshly. "It really, really was."

Jane let her hand fall slowly from her collarbone and onto her lap. "So young," she whispered.

"So young," he echoed.

"Tragic."

"Yeah."

"Awful."

"Yeah."

And there it was, like a cold draft, right on cue. The Awkward Silence. Maya's death was a conversational cul-de-sac. It didn't matter whom he was talking to, eventually there would come the moment when there was Nothing Left to Say. But it was Unseemly to Change the Subject. It happened much sooner with strangers.

"Right," she said brusquely, springing to her feet. "I'd better get on."

"Oh," he said, taken aback. "Right. And what about Billie? Are you feeling more of a connection today?"

"Yes," she said, "I am, actually. But I'm not going to take her. I'm going to leave her. With you. I think you need her."

He looked at her. And then at the cat. And he knew she was right. "Thank you," he said. "Yes. You're right. I do."

She smiled knowingly at him. "Good," she said.

"I don't know what I was thinking, really. I think I thought it was a positive thing. Moving on. You know."

"Ah," she said, picking up her handbag. "Moving on is something that happens to you, not something you do. That's what people don't realize. Moving on is not proactive. It's organic. Be kind to yourself." She smoothed down the skirt of her knitted dress, shook her blond hair over her shoulders and collected her coat from the arm of the sofa.

Adrian stared at her. *Moving on is not proactive*. Why had

no one ever said that to him before? Why did everyone keep telling him what he should do to make himself feel better? *Get away for a while. Join a dating site. Have some therapy. Move house. Throw things away.*

And he didn't want to do any of those things. He did not want to move on. He wanted to stay exactly where he was. Subsumed and weighted down by the sheer hell of grief. "Thank you," he said. "Yes. Thank you. I will."

She glanced again at the Board of Harmony as he saw her off at the door. "What did you get her?" she asked.

"Er . . . ?"

"Pearl? For her birthday?"

"Oh," he said, taken aback again by her familiarity. "I got her ice skates."

Jane nodded. "That's nice."

"I get her ice skates every year. She's an ice-skater. Been skating since she was tiny, five or something. She's quite brilliant . . . she wins things . . . cups and trophies. Spends all her spare time up at Ally Pally, training."

Jane's eyes widened. "Wow," she said. "That's impressive. At such a young age. To have a focus. Unusual, in this day and age."

"Yes. Indeed. I don't know where she gets it from. When I was ten I just wanted to sit in trees throwing things at people."

Jane smiled, but did not laugh. "Right," she said, "well, it's been nice to meet you, Adrian. And your sweet cat. I hope it all works out between the two of you."

"Yes. I think it might now. Thanks to you."

She took his hand in hers and shook it. Her hand was cool and slick. Adrian felt a sudden swell of panic as she loosened her grip on him, something primal and base. He wanted to say: *Don't go! Have more coffee! Ask me more questions! Don't leave me here!*

Instead he patted her shoulder, felt the downy softness of

her immaculate woolen coat beneath his fingers, and said, "Lovely to meet you, Jane. Do take care."

"You too, Adrian. Good luck with everything."

He closed the door behind her and went immediately to the window to watch her leave. He shared the back of the sofa with Billie, watching as Jane turned left and then stopped and, quite unexpectedly, pulled from her neat handbag a packet of cigarettes. He watched her take a plastic lighter from another section of the bag and light a cigarette with it, inhale, replace the lighter, shut the bag and walk away briskly towards the high street, a ghostly shadow of smoke trailing behind her.

5

In the context of Adrian's many children Beau was very, very small, but striding out of his classroom door, towering over his classmates, he looked like the tallest boy in the world. Adrian scooped him up from his feet and squeezed him hard before depositing him back onto the tarmac.

Beau looked behind Adrian. "Is it just you?" he asked, passing Adrian his schoolbag.

"Yes. Just me."

"Are we getting Pearl, too?"

"Yes, of course we're getting Pearl, too. It's her birthday!"

"Where are we going?"

They squeezed themselves through the crowd of children and parents blocking up the infants' playground. Adrian smiled at the occasional familiar face. He had Beau's hand inside his, small and dry, like a good-luck charm. "It's a surprise."

"For Pearl's birthday?"

"Yes. For Pearl's birthday."

"Is Otis coming?"

"No. He's doing something at school. So it's just you, me and Pearl."

Beau nodded approvingly.

Pearl looked haughty and regal, as she always did, standing tall among her classmates, her hands in the pockets of her padded coat, peering disconsolately from under her big bear-shaped furry hat across the sea of heads, as though she couldn't think what she was doing in this place. But as her gaze caught his, her face softened and she skipped like a small child across the playground towards his open arms.

"Daddy!" she breathed into his overcoat. "What are you doing here? Mum said Cat was getting me. She said you were busy, that you were coming for dinner later."

"We were both lying," he said. "So that I could surprise you."

Pearl smiled.

"Happy birthday, baby girl." He kissed the top of her head.

"Thank you," she mumbled, smiling embarrassedly at a passing friend.

He walked his two youngest children to the bus stop outside the school.

"Where are we going?" said Pearl.

"We are going to the cinema. To see something called *We Bought a Zoo*. And then Mummy, Cat and Otis are going to come and meet us for dinner."

Beau punched the air and Pearl smiled enigmatically.

"Is that nice?" he asked.

"Yeah," said Pearl, brushing her arm against his affectionately. "It's good."

Adrian smiled with relief. In the language of Pearl, "good" was equivalent to any number of superlative, multisyllable adjectives and he basked momentarily in the warm glow of her approval. They sat on the top deck of a bus that crawled through the school-run traffic heading south down Upper Street. Adrian held Pearl's bear hat in his lap and stroked its ears, Beau stood up at the rail watching the road below and Pearl sat upright, as she always did, as she had since she was a tiny child, staring imperiously at the shops, answering Adrian's questions politely and kindly, but without enthusiasm.

Adrian stared at her profile, during a lull. She looked so like Caroline: all beauty without any pretty, all lines and angles and carpentry. She'd never been a chatty child, not like Luke and Otis, his big boys, who used to wake each morning with a dozen fully formed questions spilling from their just-opened mouths, who would talk through films and stories and car journeys and not stop until they fell asleep. Cat, his oldest girl, had been more mercurial; sometimes she'd be open and conversational and other times she'd be closed. Beau was just your regular five-year-old. He and Caroline used to say that he was the one they'd bought off the shelf after doing extensive research. The perfect textbook baby and now the sweet, uncomplicated child. But Pearl—she was not like the others. She was the ice queen. Maya used to call her the Empress. Even as a baby she had held herself back from the heat of intimacy and affection, as if it might burn her.

"I can't believe my baby girl is ten," he said.

She shrugged. "I know," she said. "It feels like I was only born, like, six years ago."

"You're all getting so big."

"I'm the biggest in my class," said Beau.

"So am I," said Pearl.

"No, I mean so old. So not babies anymore."

"I don't feel like I ever was a baby," said Pearl.

"No," said Adrian, smiling. "No, I don't suppose you do."

❧

The film was gentle and moving. It featured a dead mother. This brought a lot of commentary from Beau about the fact of Maya being dead, and how maybe they too should buy a zoo, even though Maya hadn't been his real mummy. Pearl sat pensively through the sad bits and Adrian watched her for clues to her true feelings about Maya's death less than a year ago, because Pearl had never really talked about it. But she was inscrutable, as ever, steely even, her attention never wavering from the screen.

It was darkening when they left the cinema, the sky full of vivid purple veins. Adrian took Beau's hot hand in his and began to lead his children back up Upper Street to Strada. And it was there that he saw her, walking towards him, her arm hooked through the elbow of a good-looking man in a suit and overcoat, a single rose held in her other hand. Her blond hair was fixed into a bun high on her head, like a ballerina, and she was wearing the same soft gray coat with the big button that she'd been wearing when she came to see the cat. She looked taller than he remembered and Adrian saw that she was in the sort of heels that he could not fathom, with a platform sole and a four-inch spike, in leather the color of skin.

He was prepared to walk by without acknowledging her. She was on a date. He was with his children. But she saw him, and her face, already soft and animated in that way of people's faces on early dates, brightened a degree again with recognition. "It's you," she said.

Adrian arranged his face into an approximation of delighted surprise, pointed at her theatrically and said, "Yes. And it's you!" He sounded bizarre, even to his own ears.

"How are you?" she asked.

"I'm good," he said, his voice too loud, his tone too forced. "Just er . . ." He looked at his children, who were staring at Jane curiously. "Birthday treat."

Jane's eyes widened. "Yes! Of course! Pearl's birthday. And you must be Pearl."

Pearl nodded, mutely.

"Happy birthday, Pearl. Did you get what you wanted?"

Pearl looked nonplussed and Adrian intervened. "Pearl, this lady came to my house last week, to see if she wanted to adopt Billie. Her name is Jane."

"Sorry, I should have said. Yes, I'm Jane. And this is Matthew."

The man called Matthew nodded and smiled tightly, in a

way that suggested that hanging around on Upper Street in the cold talking to an old man and his kids was not part of the master plan for a night that had begun with a single red rose.

"And she saw my whiteboard," Adrian continued.

"Yes." Jane addressed the children: "I am a terrible nosy parker. I ask too many questions. Forgive me." She put a hand to her chest, her fingers brushing against the big button. Adrian stared at the button. He felt suddenly as though it were a part of him, that button. He could see the coat as it had looked draped casually over his armchair, in the relaxed intimacy of a Sunday morning, with no men called Matthew, no children.

"Don't be silly," he said, finally restored to a sense of his own usual self. "Well, we'd better get on."

"Yes," she said. She smiled and linked her arm back through the crook of Matthew's. "Off you go. Have fun, all of you. And happy birthday, Pearl."

Adrian was about to walk on, to slip back into the smooth passage of his evening, when she stopped, tugged Matthew back by the arm and said, "Oh, by the way, how are you and Billie getting on?"

"Really well," he said. "Really well."

Her smile changed then, to a smile that matched the familiarity of their previous encounters. "That's great," she said. "Just great. Well, have fun."

"Yes," said Adrian. "Yes, you too."

His face felt flushed as they walked on. There was something about that woman. Something that both unsettled and comforted him.

"Why are you giving Billie away?" said Pearl.

"I'm not."

"But that woman said she wanted to adopt her."

"I know. But I changed my mind. That woman made me change my mind."

Pearl thought about this for a moment. "Good," she said. "I'm glad. You can't give Maya's cat away. You can't."

"I'm not going to, Pearl."

"That woman reminded me of her."

"Of who—Billie?"

"No!" Pearl did not appreciate jokes that were not on her own terms. "Of Maya."

"Really?" Adrian asked this cautiously. Pearl frequently saw women she thought were Maya. Sometimes she'd tug his arm and point: *Look, Dad, look, it's her!* Only to find herself pointing at a red-haired stranger bearing no similarity to Maya whatsoever, her face already falling with disappointment. "I can't see it myself."

"No, I mean, this isn't that thing that I do, when I think I see her. I know it's not her. I just think there's something about her that's a bit like Maya."

Adrian brought his arm around Pearl's shoulders and squeezed them. She shook him off, gently.

"I really miss Maya," said Beau with a sigh. "I really, really do."

"Oh God," said Adrian, stopping and staring down into Beau's guileless gray eyes. "Oh yes. So do I. So do I."

⌒

When Adrian returned home alone, three hours later, his flat greeted him with shadows and empty spaces. He unfurled his scarf, unbuttoned his coat, hung his things on his coatrack. There was Maya's coat, just as she'd left it, on the warm spring day almost a year ago when she'd gone out to Caroline's house and never come back. It was a simple black thing, padded with down, with a fur-trimmed hood and a belted waist. He thought of her face peering from the hood on snowy days, her hands tucked in her pockets, snowflakes sitting on her copper fringe, her blue eyes full of mysteries.

And then he thought of Jane. His mind blew about with images of her glowing face, the rose in her hand, the button on her coat. She didn't look like anyone he'd ever known before. He had never gone for glamour. Glamour in women tended to throw him off course, like a driver coming towards him with their full beams on. He'd always gone for earthy but sexy women, women with strong features, good legs, throaty voices, thick hair, women happy to leave the house in oatmeal socks and an old fleece. Vikings, he called them, the type of women he liked. Maya had not been a Viking, but she had been low-key and natural, her hair a no-nonsense, coppery bob, jeans and a cardigan, makeup only after dark. He liked the sort of understated beauty he could feel he'd discovered, a secret between just the two of them. But Jane: she glimmered and gleamed. Every bit of her looked as though it had been dipped in gold dust. She was not a Viking, she was a princess.

The cat appeared as he walked into the living room. He fed it and unloaded the dishwasher. All his movements were accompanied by a kind of inaudible echo, like rocks being dropped down crevasses. He had never lived alone like this before. Co-habiting with Susie at twenty. Married to Susie at twenty-four. Divorced from Susie at thirty-five. Living with Caroline at thirty-five. Married to Caroline at thirty-six. Divorced from Caroline at forty-four. Living with Maya at forty-four. Married to Maya at forty-five. Widowed at forty-seven. Like an abrupt end to a really good book, frantically thumbing through the pages to see if he'd missed a bit, bewildered and rudderless.

He thought of Caroline, bundling back through the dark Islington streets to her cozy town house with their three babies in tow, with Cat by her side and her weird little dogs and the fire in the kitchen waiting for her. He thought of her turning off lights, wishing each child sweet dreams, climbing into her bed with the sounds of her family around her, the creak of floorboards, the breathing of the weird dogs, the insulation of other lives being lived alongside her, even in her sleep. He'd walked away from that four years ago, amicably and reasonably cheerfully, and into this other kind of life; a quieter life with one woman and her cat. He'd missed the noise and the clutter at first, the doors slammed, the shoes abandoned, the school-bags slung, the morning screams. And then he'd got used to the elegance of a life shared with just one person, where a five p.m. cocktail didn't seem out of the question and newspapers were a real possibility and no one ever looked at him as if he was an idiot. And just as he'd got used to that, it had gone. And he couldn't get used to this. He really, really couldn't.

He sat on his sofa, pulled a cushion into his lap and held it there. And then he looked at the armchair and once again he was struck by the memory of Jane's coat slung across the back of it. He picked up his phone and he opened up the text conversation that had started with Jane two weeks ago:

"Hi, this is Jane, the lady about the cat. I'll be near you on Saturday about 11 a.m. Would it be OK for me to pop by then?"

"Yes, sure. My address is Flat 2, 5 St John's Villas, NW1 1DT. I'll see you then!"

"Great. Thanks!"

"Hi Adrian, I'm just leaving a kickboxing class in Highgate. I can be there in half an hour. Is that OK?"

"Sure Jane, I'm here until lunchtime so see you then."

He switched off his phone and sat it on the sofa. What was this he was feeling? What kind of twisted anticipation was building in his gut? It was hot and overwhelming and it hit him that for the first time in almost a year he was feeling something stronger than grief.

He picked his phone up again, tapped out a text and pressed send before his brain sent a message to his gut to tell him he was making a mistake.

"Hi Jane. Lovely coincidence bumping into you just now. Hope you're having a great evening and thank you again for being so wise about the cat. And everything. It has been a pleasure meeting you."

Adrian rested the phone in the palm of his hand and stared at it, picturing suddenly and quite against his own will the handsome man called Matthew coiled naked around Jane, possibly with the single red rose clenched between his teeth. He placed the phone on the table and then he jumped in his seat as something vibrated near his thigh. He chased the vibration around the sofa with his hands until he found the source. A phone, tucked into the innards of his sofa. He switched it on and immediately saw his own text message.

His aging brain took a second or two to make sense of things. And then, of course, *her phone*. She'd left her phone. Jane had left her phone.

In his house.

6

Adrian met Cat for lunch the following day. Rather fortuitously, they both worked within a few streets of each other in Farringdon and tried to meet up for lunch at least once a week. Cat worked part-time for an animal charity. The rest of the time she was Caroline's unofficial au pair, paid in bed, board and a hundred quid a week.

Adrian owned an architectural practice called, imaginatively, Adrian Wolfe Associates. He'd started the practice in a room above a pub in Tufnell Park when he was thirty-five, just him, two friends and a secretary. Now he employed thirty-eight people and occupied two floors of a converted Farringdon factory building. Most of their business came from social housing contracts, and really, these days, he was not much more than a genial figurehead. He had his pet clients, the ones he'd brought with him over the years, and he still liked to sink his teeth into a nice little bijou urban-dwelling project. But after more than a decade of being a filthy, caffeine-dependent, sleeping-on-the-sofa, missing-the-kids'-nativities workaholic, the death of Maya had forced him to take a step away from the business and he'd been amazed to see that the ship had kept on sailing without him at the helm. Instead of feeling disempowered or out of control, he'd taken it as a sign to slow down. Take a backseat. Let the young people whom he paid very generously take the strain.

Cat was sitting at a window table in their regular restaurant, her rather dramatic blue-black hair twisted into two fat buns over her ears. From a distance he'd thought she was wearing earmuffs, and had wondered why she would do so on a relatively warm March afternoon. The way his eldest daughter dressed alarmed him occasionally. It all seemed designed to draw attention to herself. Too much makeup, in his opinion. She'd even taken to wearing false eyelashes lately. And her body: Cat was all tits and bum and bumps and curves and appeared to want everyone in the world to know about each and every one of them. It wasn't that Cat looked tarty, she just looked—to Adrian's possibly unobjective eye—a little try-hard. And it pained him to say it, but he sometimes felt embarrassed being seen with her in public, in case people thought she was his girlfriend. The problem was that she didn't look enough like him for it to be obvious that they were related. She didn't look like her statuesque, straight-up-and-down, mouse-haired mother either. She was the image of Susie's crazy Portuguese grandmother, whom Adrian had met a few times at the beginning of their relationship and who had once referred to Adrian as "a bit grubby and too thin."

"Hello, darling," he said, leaning down to hug her briefly.

"Hello, hello. You look like crap."

"Yeah, thanks for that." He pulled out his chair and took a seat. "Always so charming."

"Yeah, right. Whatever, let's order. I'm starving."

Cat was always starving these days. Cat was always eating. If Cat carried on like this, he observed worriedly, she would probably be the size of a house by the time she was forty.

She ordered herself a big bowl of carbohydrates and a full-fat Coke. Adrian ordered himself an antipasti platter and a glass of water. Then he pulled Jane's phone out of his jacket pocket and put it on the table between them.

"Why've you got such a shit phone?" she said, dunking a bread roll into a bowl of olive oil.

"It's not mine," he said.

"Right," she said, reaching out to pick it up.

"There's this girl . . ."

She groaned. "Oh God, Dad, no."

He looked at her askance, slightly taken aback by her reaction. "No, no. Just a girl. She came to look at the cat. Remember, I put that card in the post office a few weeks ago?"

"Yeah. Yeah. Right." She'd finished the first bread roll and was on to the second.

"Anyway. She came and looked at the cat, talked me into keeping her, stayed for a cup of coffee, really nice girl. Woman."

"How old?" There was a hint of displeasure in the way she formed the question.

"I don't know. About thirty? Maybe even forty. Hard to tell." He kept his reply as neutral as he could, sensing something antagonistic in Cat's demeanor. "Anyway. She talked me into keeping the cat and then I bumped into her last night on my way to meet you lot at Strada. We stopped. Had a chat. She was on a date. It was all of a minute. Went to Strada. Had dinner. Came home and then . . ." He glanced at the cheap phone. "I found this tucked down the side of the sofa. It's hers. I've had a good look at it but I think I must be doing something wrong because all I can find on it is my number and the texts we sent to each other. There doesn't seem to be an address book, a call history or anything. And that can't be right, surely? So I thought what with you being a *young person* and all, you might be able to winkle something useful out of it."

Cat stuffed the last hunk of the second bread roll into her mouth and picked up the phone. "Hm," she said after a few minutes. "This is weird. I mean, basically, she must have got this phone with the express intention of using it to contact you. I mean, it is literally *devoid* of anything else. How totally weird. Oh Jesus." She rolled her eyes. "You don't think she's in love with you, do you?"

Adrian snorted derisively. "No! Don't be ridiculous! Of course she's not."

"Then—what?" She held her hands palms up.

"I have no idea. No idea whatsoever."

A waiter brought Cat's vat of pasta with salmon and cream sauce. She beamed at it. Then she looked at Adrian's elegant wooden board of finely sliced meats and said, "Ooh, that looks good. Can I have some of your chorizo?"

"No!" said Adrian. "Eat your own food!"

She looked at him wickedly and stole a piece anyway. He pretended to slap the back of her hand and then groaned as she dropped the whole slice into her mouth in one.

"You are quite incredible," he said.

"I know," she said, picking up her cutlery. "So, the big question is: if you bumped into her in the street last night and she left her phone in your flat on Sunday, why the fuck didn't she ask you about it?"

"I know. I know. Exactly."

"It's almost as though . . ."

"She wanted me to have it. Yes. I know. I thought that. I thought that already."

"So what are you going to do about it?"

"I don't know." He shrugged. "The thing is . . ." He fixed his gaze upon a small whorl in the wooden tabletop. "She was . . . I felt . . ." He wanted to tell her. He wanted to tell Cat that for the first time since that awful night last April, he was feeling open to the possibility of moving on. He wanted to tell her that this woman had opened a sealed-up door deep inside him and that he was almost euphoric with the possibility of having someone in his life again. But there was something in his daughter's face, in her turn of phrase, that made him stop.

"Obviously," he began gingerly, "this woman is not in love with me. But there is something going on here. Something strange. Do you think I should pursue it?"

Cat shrugged. "That depends what you're 'pursuing,'" she said.

Adrian smiled. "The mystery," he said. "Just the mystery. But listen, Cat, it has been a year, you know. I mean, at some point I am going to be thinking about moving on. You don't want me to be on my own for the rest of my life, do you?"

She shrugged again, picking something out of her teeth with a long fingernail. "Well. It's not that I want you to be alone. Of course I don't. But you probably shouldn't be rushing into anything. I think it's good for you to be by yourself."

"Do you? Really? Don't you worry about me?"

"No," she said. "You're a grown-up. You'll get through this. You've got enough people worrying about you. I'm just waiting for you to shine." She made ironic jazz hands to accompany this pronouncement.

He laughed drily.

"And you don't need a woman to do that. IMO."

IMO. Adrian smiled.

"But," she said, curling creamy pasta around her fork, "if it's just the mystery you're pursuing and you haven't got any dirty-old-man intentions towards this woman, I'd def be up for helping you to track her down."

"Would you?"

"Yeah. Love a good mystery." She turned on the phone again and used the side of her thumb to scroll through the messages while she deposited a forkful of pasta into her mouth with the other hand. "Here. This one." She turned the phone towards him. "She said she was coming from a kickboxing class in Highgate. I could do some research into kickboxing classes. If you like?"

"That would be great, thanks, Cat."

"No probs." She smiled at him. "But no romance, Dad. No more bloody wives. Please."

⌒

Adrian walked back to his office after lunch. He took the long route through the back streets of Farringdon, noticing for the first time that it was properly spring, that the restaurants had put their tables out onto the pavements and opened out their windows, that people were wearing sunglasses and girls had on open shoes. He felt the inside pocket of his jacket for last year's sunglasses. They weren't there. He had no idea where they might be. He could not remember if he'd even worn sunglasses last summer. He couldn't remember last summer at all.

A young woman walked past with a tiny baby in a sling. The baby was fast asleep, its head flopped at ninety degrees. He smiled at the baby. Then he smiled at the mother. She smiled back at him and Adrian went on his way. Something was shifting inside him. Something that had been lodged in his gut for months. It was the grief. It was starting to melt around the edges, like a tub of frozen ice cream left on the counter, the mass of it still there, hard and cold, but almost soft enough to be able to scoop it out without bending a spoon.

7

"I think that woman came to see me when I was skating."

Adrian turned from the hob where he was heating tomato soup and looked at Pearl. "What woman?"

"That woman we saw on my birthday. Jane."

Adrian felt his color rise a little at the mention of her. "Hmm," he said, turning down the heat as the soup started to boil.

"I knew you wouldn't believe me."

He gave the soup one last stir and turned to face her. "I didn't say I didn't believe you."

"You said 'hmm.'"

"I just meant, when? How? I mean, are you sure?"

Pearl scratched at the wood of the tabletop with her fingernails. "No," she said, "I'm not sure. She was just sitting there, in the bleachers at Ally Pally, and it was like she was watching me. And I turned round and when I looked back again she was gone. And then we saw that woman, on my birthday, and I realized that it was the same woman. From Ally Pally." She stopped and looked at Adrian anxiously.

Adrian pulled out a chair and sat down opposite his daughter. "How sure are you?"

"I don't know. About seventy-five percent sure. Roughly."

He nodded.

"Do you believe me?"

"I don't know. Why are you only bringing this up now?"

"Cat told me about the phone. That's what made me think

I wasn't being mad and that I could tell you." She looked at him with those frosty blue eyes of hers, challenging him to disagree with her. "Why is she following us about?"

"She's not following us about. She's disappeared."

"OK, then why *was* she following us about?"

"I don't think she was . . ."

"So"—she looked at him pityingly and counted points off on her fingers—"first, she turns up here to look at a cat she doesn't want, *twice*. Second, she's watching me at skate training and third, she weirdly just *happens* to be there the night of my birthday dinner—"

"Coincidence."

"*Not* coincidence, Dad. It's written on the whiteboard."

Adrian half opened his mouth to respond and then closed it again. He got to his feet and walked into the hallway. How had he not noticed? There it was, in red pen: *Strada Upper St. 6:30 p.m.*

He came back into the kitchen and sat down heavily. "OK," he said, "you're right. This is weird."

"Stalker," she said, folding her arms conclusively across her chest.

"Disappearing stalker," he replied.

"Probably just as well." Her eyes drifted over his shoulder. "That soup is boiling, Dad."

Adrian leaped to his feet and turned off the heat under the soup. Then he poured it into two mugs and handed one to Pearl with a bread roll. This was their special thing: once a week, after skate training, Adrian picked her up and brought her here, gave her tomato soup and a bread roll. He did the same with the boys too; each had their own night. Another idea of Maya's. One-on-one time, she'd called it.

"Are you going to try and find her?"

Adrian tore off a corner of his bread roll and held it suspended above his soup. "I don't know," he said noncommittally. "Maybe. I've bought a charger. For her phone. I'm going to keep it charged, in case she tries calling."

"What's she like? Is she nice?"

"Oh, really, I hardly know her. I mean, we literally had three very short conversations."

"Maybe she was stalking me to see if she'd like me to be her stepdaughter?"

Adrian laughed. "I doubt that very much."

Pearl dropped her gaze to the floor and sighed. "I don't know if I want another stepmother."

"Oh, Pearl, darling, you really don't need to be thinking about stuff like that. Honestly. Three wives is enough for one man in one lifetime I think."

Adrian rested his spoon in his bowl and closed his eyes. After his spiky lunch with Cat he was aware that he needed to handle this subject with a deft touch. "You know, all the women I married, I married because they were absolutely the right person for me to be with at the time I was with them. I had no doubts about any of my marriages; I went into all of them wide-eyed with love and hope. And maybe that will never happen to me again. Maybe I'll meet women and I'll think they're nice but they won't be right for me like Susie was, like your mum was. And like Maya was."

Pearl studied him intensely. "You will get married again," she said. "You're a love addict."

Adrian swallowed back a smile at the sound of Caroline's words being funneled through his youngest daughter. "Well, whatever happens, I promise I won't do anything to make you unhappy."

"You can't promise that," said Pearl, shaking her head. "You totally can't promise that."

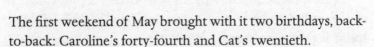

8

The first weekend of May brought with it two birthdays, back-to-back: Caroline's forty-fourth and Cat's twentieth.

Adrian arrived at the town house in Islington holding the rope handles of two gift bags and a carrier bag full of champagne. It was a beautiful day: cool on the street, but red-hot in the sun trap of Caroline's south-facing back garden. Susie was already there, looking incredibly old for a woman not yet fifty, her skin the wind-beaten hide of the seaside-dwelling gardener, her clothes not quite right for a birthday party: floppy canvas trousers and a rather worn-out muslin camisole which showed her bra. But her fine bone structure still took the eye, and her brilliant blue eyes.

"Hello, Suse," he said, approaching her and kissing her lightly on each cheek. "You look great."

"No, I look awful. I wanted to see what would happen to my hair if I stopped dying it. And now I know."

The smaller children were on a large trampoline at the bottom of the garden and Cat and Luke sat side by side on a blanket, staring at Luke's smartphone.

"Luke," he said in greeting.

Luke looked up at him and started to get to his feet.

"Don't get up. It's OK."

But Luke ignored him and approached him with open arms. Adrian felt vaguely alarmed by him. Where Cat was bursting out all over the place with lumps and bumps and only-just-controlled fat, Luke was like a wraith. Taller than Adrian by two inches, thin from every angle, he had Susie's coloring and Adrian's physique. And his eyes, the narrow, almost glacial eyes that had looked so extraordinary in his childish face, looked oddly unsettling now that his features had set.

"Dad," he said, wrapping his Mr. Tickle arms around Adrian and squeezing him. "It's really good to see you."

Adrian smiled in surprise. Luke had been an affectionate child, but for the last year or so he had become distant from his father, almost hostile. "Absence making the heart grow fonder?"

Luke put his hands into his trouser pockets and smiled. "Well," he said, "it has been six months."

"Jesus Christ," said Adrian, "has it really?"

Luke smiled at him from under his slightly fey fringe. "It sure has."

"God, I'm so sorry. What was it then, Christmas?"

"No, not even Christmas. I was away over Christmas. It was my birthday."

"November, then?"

Luke gave him a slow clap and then sat down again next to his sister. "Don't tell me the Board of Harmony is letting you down?"

"I think I might need to update the Board of Harmony," he said, sitting down in a chair that had been pulled across for him by Caroline and smiling his thanks to her. "It's not good enough. Six months . . ." He shook his head.

The small children had cottoned on to his arrival and Beau and Pearl threw themselves off the trampoline and hurtled towards him crying, *"Daddy!"* Pearl climbed onto his lap and Beau held his small arms around Adrian's neck. They both smelled of scalp and sun cream. Across from him Caroline sat down and pulled up the sleeves of her jersey dress. She looked radiant, her dark blond hair cut in a flattering style that showed off her cheekbones, long, toned legs in leggings, and wearing a dress decorated with flowers. Caroline rarely wore dresses. And certainly never ones decorated with flowers.

"You look beautiful," he said.

"Thank you," she said, accepting his compliment graciously. "You look worn-out."

Adrian frowned. "Thanks a bundle."

Luke had opened one of Adrian's bottles of champagne and passed him some in a plastic flute. "Cheers," he said, holding his own out towards the center of the group. "Here's to birthdays. To Cat." He turned and waved his flute towards his sister. "And to Caroline." He turned to his stepmother. "And to family. It's been too long."

Otis finally approached and smiled shyly at his father. "Hello, Father," he said. He'd never called Adrian "Father" before. Adrian took it as a thinly veiled expression of disenchantment.

"Hello, son," he said, and grabbed him round the middle. Otis was his best-looking child. He absolutely should not have been able to discern such a thing; he should have been blind to the variances in his children's physical attributes. But he wasn't. He himself had been one of those unfortunate products of the early sixties who spent his seventies boyhood in mustard knitwear, sporting hair that looked like a wig. He'd had crooked teeth and freckles, and studio photographs of him at the time showed him to be a slightly heartbreaking work in progress. Like every other boy of his age. Otis on the other hand looked as if he should be plastered to young girls' bedroom walls in poster form. His face was perfectly symmetrical, his eyes mocha brown, half his face full of lips and dimples, the other half full of eyelashes and cheekbones.

Adrian took a sip of his champagne and looked up briefly at the back of the town house. He could barely believe that this had once been his home, this beautiful white building with its tumble of windows, its garden of ancient fruit trees and frothing bushes of spring blossom. There was a white spiral staircase connecting the first-floor living room with the garden and Caroline had strung it with dozens of crystals and fairy lights that shone through a tangle of white climbing clematis. The house was enchanting—but he hadn't appreciated it when he'd lived here. He'd spent far too much time worrying about how to pay for it all and looking for ways not to be here. And now, well, he felt as if he'd won a competition just to be invited here for the afternoon.

He knocked back the rest of his champagne in one gulp and let his gaze fall to the floor.

"So," said Caroline. "Adrian. You have to tell us all about this mysterious girl with the phone."

The mystery of Jane had grown, exponentially, from his own tiny sliver of a secret into a slightly wider secret shared with his two daughters, and now, as the weeks had passed, into a big juicy anecdote passed around to each member of his sprawling family like a cookie tin.

He held his empty glass out to Luke, who was doing refills.

"What's this?" Luke asked, looking at his father with those unnerving, colorless eyes of his.

"Oh God," said Adrian. "It's nothing."

"A lady came to see Maya's cat," Pearl began. "Just before my birthday. And then I saw her at skate training. And then—"

"I put an advert in the post office window," Adrian broke in, wanting to take some kind of adult responsibility for the dissemination of the facts. "A couple of months ago. I thought I should rehouse the cat. Maya's cat. Anyway, this woman called me and we arranged for her to come to the flat and she came but said she didn't think I should get rid of the cat. She said she thought I needed the cat. Shortly after that Pearl *thinks* she saw this woman watching her at skate training—"

"I did! I did!"

"Maybe. Anyway. Then on Pearl's birthday we bumped into her again on Upper Street. On the way to Strada."

"Which she totally did on purpose because she'd seen it written down on Daddy's whiteboard."

"Maybe, Pearl. Maybe. And she was with a young man, on a date. We had a very quick chat and then I got home and found her phone down the back of the sofa. And when I switched it on I found that mine was the only number in it, that I was the only person she'd ever texted." He stopped and caught his breath.

"How bizarre," said Susie. "It's almost as if . . ."

"She was looking for Daddy," finished Pearl. "On purpose."

"And then she found him," continued Caroline.

"And then totally disappeared," said Susie.

"She was really, really pretty," said Pearl. "Daddy went all red and his voice went all funny."

"Oh God," said Luke, "don't tell me you're casting about for the fourth Mrs. Wolfe. God help us all . . ."

"Luke!" Susie admonished.

"What?"

"Totes inappropes," said Cat.

"Oh my God," said Luke, his hand held against his heart. "London is turning you into a cretin. *Please* tell me you didn't just say *totes inappropes*."

"I totes did," she said with a grimace.

"I barely know my own sister," Luke said theatrically.

"I was being *ironic*."

"Yeah. Sure you were."

"Anyway," interjected Adrian. "It's all irrelevant. Unless Jane reappears out of the blue to claim her phone we will never know what her intentions were."

"But we could make a stab at what yours were, eh, Dad?"

"Stop it, Luke!" said Cat.

Adrian sighed. "She was just a very nice woman," he said.

The distant sound of the doorbell chiming broke the momentum of the conversation and Caroline got to her feet. "That'll be Paul," she said.

"Who's Paul?" said Adrian.

"Mum's new boyfriend," said Otis with a groan.

Adrian felt his gut wriggle as he watched his ex-wife moving towards the back door and he reappraised the floral dress and the soft skin and the air of youthful buoyancy. Caroline had been steadfastly single since he'd left her, had constantly made pronouncements on the joys of single life: the empty bed, the lack of various male stenches, the spare drawers and folded towels.

"Paul's not her boyfriend," said Pearl crossly.

"Yeah he is," Otis retaliated. "I saw him touch her face."

Pearl tutted, put her hand out and stroked Otis's face. "There," she said, "I touched your face. Does that mean I'm your girlfriend now?"

He backed away from her in horror. "Oh my God, Pearl. You're such a sick weirdo." He rubbed her touch from his face and headed back to the trampoline, moodily kicking a football ahead of him.

Paul was in the garden now. Adrian looked up at him and blanched. He was at least ten years younger than Adrian. He looked away and unthinkingly pulled the small, hovering figure of Beau up onto his lap, almost like a talisman, or a kind of credential for being here. Beau burrowed his hot body against his father's and Adrian felt it then, a little bubble of yearning for the compactness of babies, the baby he and Maya had never had.

"Everyone," Caroline was saying brightly, "this is Paul Wilson. Paul, this is my ex-husband, Adrian, and this is Adrian's other ex-wife Susie, who's come up from Hove for the day. And this is my stepson, Luke, Cat's brother."

Adrian gave Paul Wilson what he hoped was the smile of a man confident and comfortable in his own skin, while also using body language to explain the fact that he would be unable to get to his feet because he had a child on his lap. "Good to meet you, Paul."

"So these are all your kids?" said Paul, his nice face opening up in awe.

"Er. Yeah. At least, so I've been told."

Paul laughed. "You've been busy."

"Well," said Adrian, giving Beau a little squeeze, "it's been a long-term project. I got started on it quite a long time ago."

"Christ," said Paul. "I'd better crack on myself. I'm forty next year."

Adrian swallowed down hard on his impulse to suggest that Paul also better "crack on" with a younger woman if babies were his aim.

Caroline erected another fold-up chair for Paul and Luke poured him out a plastic glassful of champagne.

"This is pretty amazing," said Paul, looking keenly from person to person. "All of you, getting together en masse like this. Nobody killing anybody."

Caroline and Susie exchanged a glance and laughed.

"No, I mean seriously. What's your secret?"

"We all just like each other, I suppose," said Susie.

"And we all like Adrian, which helps," said Caroline.

"Wow," said Paul, nodding in wonderment. "That's quite a testimonial. Honestly, I've known a few broken families in my time; in fact I am the product of one. And I've never heard of a family getting away with it before. You know. The messy aftermath." He shook his head from side to side and smiled. "Carrie tells me you all go on holiday together, too?"

"Well, we try," said Adrian, starting to feel oddly defensive. "At least once a year. For the children. Helps them to bond when they don't live together."

"Wow," said Paul again. "Amazing. Makes you wonder though, you know, *what lurks beneath*. Who's got the secret voodoo dolly." He mimed someone sticking pins into a doll and laughed extra loud to ensure that everyone knew he was joking. Caroline squeezed his knee in a cautionary gesture and Adrian eyed him uncertainly.

"Oh," Adrian said lightly, "I think you'll find there're no dark secrets buried here. I think you'll find we're all very open with each other."

Paul smiled at him and nodded. "Good for you," he said, "good for all of you."

Over the top of Beau's shaggy mop of hair, Adrian observed Paul and Caroline closely. She had always been the most beautiful of his three wives and he had imagined her living out her life in elegant, just-so singularity in this enchanted house, pruning her fruit trees, walking her dogs, tending to the needs of her family. And as he thought of Caroline's dogs, one of them appeared from where it had been sleeping under the table and made its way giddily towards Paul and Caroline. Paul put out his hand and the dog wagged its tail. He waited for Caroline to greet the dog—she'd bought the pair as puppies about two years ago and called them her "husband substitutes." She fussed over them like babies and talked about them constantly as though they were human beings—but she did not seem to notice that the dog was there. Instead her gaze rested upon Paul, her body lean and erect, her stomach, he could see, held in tautly.

He lowered his gaze into Beau's scalp and let the realization sink in that he wasn't the only person moving on.

⟡

Once again, Adrian's flat slapped him fully around the chops when he arrived home alone a few hours later. The sun had fallen behind the horizon and he hadn't left any lights on, so the four rooms of his home were dark and shadowy. The cat appeared at his feet like a murky phantom. He leaned to stroke her, more out of a sense of altruism than anything else. She leaned into his touch needily and he sighed. He switched on some table lamps but his flat still felt dank and lonely. He poured himself a glass of wine from the end of a bottle he'd opened the night before and he took it and Jane's mobile phone out into his backyard (he could not call the eight-foot square of concrete outside the kitchen door a garden, however many potted plants he put out there).

There was still some warmth in the air, but because his yard got only two hours of sunshine each day, it felt damp and mossy out here. He thought for a moment of the house in Islington, the soft sun-kissed garden with its flora and greenery, its children's clutter and gamboling dogs. Then he thought of Susie's house in Hove, the sweet Arts and Crafts cottage just off the main road full of the furniture they'd bought together in their student years from what used, in those days, to be called flea markets and junk shops: the bits of 1960s and '70s tat that were now worth hundreds of pounds. He thought of his odd moody son and his fragile air of entitlement and of beautiful Otis and his bee-stung lips. He pictured Susie in her scruffy gardening clothes and Caroline in her sexy floral dress with her new young lover. And the others: little Beau with his warm, malleable body; cocky Cat and her insatiable appetite for everything; and cool, inscrutable Pearl with her focus and her commitment. They had all belonged to him once: the houses, the wives, the children. And yet now he had nothing. A crap flat, a weird cat, a stranger's phone. For nearly five decades he had lived with an unshakeable belief in the decisions he made. Every morning for forty-eight years he had woken up and thought: *I am where I want to be right now.* And now he was not. He did not want to be in this flat, with this cat and this phone and this feeling of cold dread. He'd made a bad choice somewhere along the line but he didn't know where.

He drank some wine and stared at the cat and drank some more wine. Then he switched on Jane's phone, just as he'd done every few days for the past two months, and sat bolt upright when he saw a little envelope icon showing on the screen. And the words: *You have 1 new message*.

He clicked on the icon and a message came up.

"Hello it's Mum. Just checkin in. I havent heard from you in a while. Give us a call if you can."

The feeling of cold dread dissipated for just one moment as he read these words. He put down his glass of wine and formed a response.

9

The woman was called Jean and had a thick West Country accent and sounded as though she had no teeth. She lived around the corner from Adrian in Tufnell Park and said she'd be happy to meet him for a coffee. "There's a place by the station. Does proper porridge. Can't remember what it's called now."

Adrian walked a full circle around the station at Tufnell Park before he found the place she'd described, a putrid-looking place he'd seen a thousand times before without ever noticing it. It was called Mr. Sandwich.

The woman called Jean was sitting at the first table he passed. He knew she was the woman called Jean because she was eating porridge. And because she had no teeth.

"Adrian?" she said, rising to her feet. She was extraordinarily thin, wrapped up in an Aztec-knit cardigan that fell to her knees. Her hair was dyed henna red and tied back in a ponytail.

"Hi," he said. "Jean?"

"That's me. Take a seat. I didn't order for you, but I would strongly recommend the porridge."

Adrian pulled out a torn vinyl-topped chair and sat down. "I've had my breakfast. Thank you." Instead he ordered a cappuccino and an egg salad sandwich.

"So," said Jean, noisily scraping the last layer of porridge off the sides of the bowl. "You've ended up with my daughter's phone?"

Adrian nodded. "It appears so."

"And do I really want to know how?"

Adrian sighed. "Well, there's no story really. Your daughter came to my flat to see a cat I was trying to get adopted."

"What, Tiff? A cat? Are you sure? Doesn't sound like her kind of thing." She pushed the emptied bowl away from her and sat back in her chair, her chin tucked into her chest, hands deep in the pockets of her cardigan, scrutinizing him with tired brown eyes.

"Tiff?"

"Yeah. Her name's Tiffy."

"Tiffy?"

"Short for Tiffany."

"Tiffany." He absorbed this. The woman who'd come to his flat did not look like a Tiff or a Tiffy or a Tiffany.

"Tiffany Melanie Martin. To be precise. Though I think she might have changed her name when she got married."

"Changed it to . . . ?"

She shrugged. "No idea. Wasn't invited."

"Right."

"Why? What did she tell you she was called?"

"Jane."

"Jane! Well, that's exactly the name you'd say you were called if you were lying, isn't it? What the hell is she up to?" She groaned and leaned forward again. "Listen," she said, "there's a lot of shit under the bridge between Tiff and me. I wasn't the best mum in the world. I wasn't a mum at all, truth be told. She was brought up in care. I didn't see her from when she was eight until she was twenty-six." She sniffed and leaned back again. "So, there you go. We're more like strangers than mum and daughter."

Adrian sat back to allow the delivery of his sandwich to the table, slices of radioactive yellow egg on thick white bread, fat discs of cucumber and tomato and lots of salad cream. "When did you last see her?"

"About a year ago. Roughly. She came for her brother's fourth birthday. Would have been around July time."

Adrian tried not to let his shock at the fact that Jean was young enough to have a four-year-old child shine too clearly from him. He'd subconsciously placed Jean at mid to late fifties.

"And have you been in touch since? Recently?"

"No." She shook her head and laughed drily as though the idea were preposterous. "It's not like that with me and her. I only sent her that text last night because I was feeling guilty. You know. Coming up for a year since I'd seen her."

"So, what was she up to, last time you saw her? She was married?"

Jean broke off from the conversation to order herself a cup of tea. "Yeah, that's right. Newlywed she was. Looked like she might have done all right for herself. Brought Harry a lovely present, a computer thing, must have cost a bit. And was all tanned, from her honeymoon. Where'd she been? Maldives? Malta? Something like that. Yeah . . ." She sighed and stared into the middle distance.

He paused, wondering if what he was about to say was entirely appropriate. "She didn't seem to me to be what you'd call *married*. I mean, no ring. Well, not that I was looking, but I certainly didn't notice one. And the third time I met her she was . . ." He paused again. "She was on a date."

Jean laughed out loud, and then began spluttering; she held her hand against her chest. "Sorry, sorry. Stupid cough. Well. There you go then. Never did think she was the marrying type."

Adrian wiped a dribble of salad cream from the corner of his mouth and said, "So, the question is, do you have an address for her? A number?"

"Nah." Jean shook her head slowly. "Nah. That number." She nodded at the phone. "That was all I had of her. So," she said, drawing herself back to the present. "How was she? How'd she seem? When you saw her?"

"Well, you know, I only met her a couple of times, really. And as strangers. So I don't really know what she's normally like. But she seemed like a normal, happy person."

She nodded approvingly. "And how did she look? Did she look good?"

"Er, yes, I suppose. Nicely dressed, beautifully turned out, long blond hair."

"No no no. I think we're at cross purposes here, then. Tiffy wouldn't have blond hair. Never."

"Well, you know, it was probably dyed."

"What, really?" She shuddered. "Can't imagine it." She looked faintly appalled. "Don't think Afro hair really takes to bleach, you know. Goes sort of yellow, doesn't it?"

Adrian blinked at Jean and said, "What? What do you mean, Afro?"

"Well, you know, hair like Tiffy's. That curly hair."

"The woman I met did not have Afro hair. Her hair was straight and blond."

"Oh God, she's relaxed it, too! Not sure I'd recognize her!"

"No. I mean, the girl I met wasn't black. She was white."

"Well, Tiffy's quite light skinned. More of a café au lait. Her dad was only half and half, you know, so she's hardly black at all really."

"Right. No. This girl was properly white. She had blue eyes. Well, blue with a bit of gold in one of them."

Jean shook her head then and blew out her cheeks. "Nah then," she said. "Nah. We're talking about different girls. Definitely. Looks like your girl got hold of my girl's phone somehow. Nicked it off her. Most probably." She sniffed and smiled knowingly at Adrian, looking quite happy with her theory.

Adrian was about to say, No, not the girl I met. She was far too classy to steal a phone. But then he thought about the way she'd taken those cigarettes out of her smart handbag as she left his flat that first time, and had lit one inside cupped hands like a man. So he didn't say anything. Instead he said, "Yeah. Probably," and smiled.

"By the way," he said as he stood up to leave a few seconds later. "Your daughter. Tiffy. You say she was brought up in care. Where was that? Was that in London?"

"No. She was in Southampton. That's where she was born. That's where I met her dad. She went in when she was eight or so. Funny. Can't imagine it now. Now I've got Harry." Her gaze lingered on a spot just beyond the café window. "Can't imagine how I could have let her go." She looked up at Adrian sharply, as though he'd just accused her of something. "I was too bloody young, that's what it was. Too messed in the head. I'm doing it right this time. I was forty when I had Harry. And I'm doing it *all right* this time. Do you hear me?"

She looked angry and Adrian decided to end the encounter before it escalated into something unpleasant. He smiled at her, reassuringly, paid for his egg sandwich and for her porridge and headed home.

10

Cat changed into joggers and a tank top, pulled her dark hair back tightly into a ponytail and pouted at herself in the mirror. She jabbed at her reflection with bunched-up fists, bambam-bambam, and then high-kicked at herself. She laughed. What an idiot she looked. She turned to check her rear view. The joggers were low-rise with the word HOT spelled out across her buttocks. They were kind of *2008 called, they want their trousers back*, but they were the only vaguely athletic item of clothing she owned and no way was she going to spend actual money on clothes to do sports in. She stared at all the new bits of herself that seemed to arrive daily, the flesh that spilled from between her bra strap and the armholes of her tank top, the swell of her belly—someone had asked her the other day if she was pregnant—and the meaty squash between her thighs. She sighed and decided to love them. She had to love them. If she didn't love them she'd have to go on a diet. If she didn't love them she would not be able to wear trousers with the word HOT on the bum.

This was her third kickboxing class in as many weeks. She was aching and hurting and elements of her interior physiology felt as though they were on fire even when she was sitting down. There were a surprising number of kickboxing classes in the Highgate area. Six in total, at various locations and times. The last two classes had uncovered nothing beyond the fact that she was almost fatally unfit. No women with mismatched eyes. No women called Jane. No women called Tiffy. But still, two down, four to go, she was getting closer every week.

She aimed one more kick at her reflection, checked her shoulder bag for her travel card and deodorant, put on an extra layer of mascara and headed to Highgate.

∽

The class was held in a community center in the heart of a sprawling estate. It was the kind of place where a grasp of the martial arts probably came in quite handy, Cat thought, clutching her big bag against her body. A group of young boys in baggy clothes approached. She tried looking like the kind of girl who'd been brought up on an estate instead of the kind of girl who'd been brought up in a cottage in Hove. The four boys swiveled around as she passed, taking in the pure everythingness of her, making appreciative noises with their tongues and their teeth.

"Hot," said one, reading from the back of her trousers. "That you are. *That you are.*"

She turned and said, "I'm old enough to be your mother."

"Ha, yeah, if your boyfriend was a *pedophile.*"

The boys laughed and so did Cat. She walked away, backwards, holding up a hand in what felt to her like a very street kind of gesture. The boys blew her kisses. Then she smiled, feeling the love again for her own flesh, turned round and walked straight into the path of a blond woman carrying a gym bag. "Sorry!" she said.

"No problem," said the woman.

Cat looked at the woman curiously. There was something about her. Something that seemed familiar. And then she inhaled sharply at the realization that the woman had one blue eye and one blue and amber.

"Jane?" she gasped.

"Sorry?"

"Are you Jane?"

"No," said the woman. "Sorry. My name is A . . . Amanda."

"Oh," said Cat. "Right. Sorry. Are you going to the kick-boxing class?"

The woman looked at Cat and then at the hall behind her. She nudged her gym bag slightly so that it disappeared behind her back. She cleared her throat and said, "No. No. I'm not."

And then she walked away. Cat stood still for a moment. She felt torn between conflicting urges: the urge to chase the woman and shout into her face that of course she was Jane and why was she lying about it; and the urge to stay where she was and let this perfectly innocent woman called Amanda walk to her destination in peace. Then she saw the middle-ground option. She could follow her. At a discreet distance. She was dressed for it, after all. She pulled her mobile phone from her hand and dialed in her dad's number, holding it to her ear as she walked.

"Dad," she whispered. "I've got her! I'm following her!"

"Who?"

"Jane, of course! She was just about to walk into the hall where the kickboxing class was. I bumped into her. She had the eyes, like you said! She told me her name was Amanda. But it's her. I know it is!"

"Where are you?"

"God, I don't know. Some estate in Highgate." She was approaching the same group of teenage boys. They smiled as they saw her and one of them shouted out, "She just couldn't keep away! Come and talk to us! Come on, Miss Hot!"

She smiled and waved at them apologetically and they cat-called after her as she hurried by.

"Who was that?"

"Just some boys."

"Christ, Cat, be careful."

"They're just kids, Dad. Look, I'll call you when I find out where she's going!"

Cat followed the blond woman through the estate and back through the metal gates onto Archway Road. Then she saw the woman begin to run, her gym bag bouncing up and down urgently against her back. At first Cat thought she was running from her. Then she saw that she was running for a bus which was already letting on the last person in the queue. Cat touched her fingers against the edges of her travel card and began to run too. Cat didn't do running as a rule. Generally she would rather miss the train, miss the bus, than turn herself into a jelly on legs, but this called for a change of style. And she was, at least, wearing a sports bra. She saw the blond woman leap onto the steps of the bus just as the driver had been about to close the door. She pushed herself harder. She could feel the meat of each individual buttock lifting and dropping with every stride. She tried to catch the driver's eye as she got closer. But it was too late. The doors hissed and folded, the bus changed gear, and by the time she got to the bus stop it was nothing but a belching, farting box of fumes hurtling away from her down the bus lane.

11

On the weekend after his meeting with Jean, Adrian got a phone call from Susie in Hove.

"Darling," she said. He couldn't remember Susie ever calling him Adrian. "I need to talk to you. Are you free today? For a chat?"

He put down his coffee mug and said, "Yes. Sure. What's up?"

"I'd rather not talk on the phone, darling. Can you come down? To the house?" Both his ex-wives referred to their homes as "the house" as though theirs was the definitive one.

"Today?"

"Please. If you can. Bring a child if you need to."

"No, they're away this weekend. I'm unencumbered."

"Good. When can you come?"

Adrian considered the time and his state of readiness and said, "I could leave in about half an hour. Actually, I could leave now."

"Oh. Good. Thank you, darling. You are such a good boy. I'll see you in a couple of hours."

⌦

Adrian arrived at the house in Hove just before lunchtime, carrying a bunch of lilac stocks. The sky was a uniform blue and the sun was high, casting brightly off the stucco buildings and the shingled beach. Moving down here had been Susie's idea. She, like Adrian, was a Londoner, but unlike Adrian she had no emotional tie to the city and couldn't get used to living there after three years at Sussex University. She'd secretly taken the train down to Brighton twice a week after she'd discovered she was pregnant. Apparently she'd seen more than thirty properties. And then one day, about seven months into her pregnancy, she'd brought Adrian down to the coast for "lunch with friends" and walked him briskly away from their friends' house in Brighton, along the seafront to Hove and right up to the front door of the little Edwardian cottage where they'd lived for the next ten years. Adrian had mixed feelings about the area now. This was the place where he'd become a father, the trendy young dad, carrying his fat babies along the beach in a sling, pushing them along windswept pavements to nurseries and childminders. This was where his grown-up life had started. But it was also where he'd felt stifled and wrong-footed. Where he'd woken each morning thinking: When did the party end? Why am I here knee-deep in nappies living with a scatty, badly dressed woman who calls me "Daddy"? And what happened to London? Yes, for most of his ten years in Hove, Adrian had dreamed of London. And he still wasn't sure whether it was Caroline he'd fallen in love with when he was thirty-five, or whether it was the promise of a return to his beloved city.

But still, he thought, as he turned the familiar corner to the house he'd once lived in, it had been a golden time in many ways. It was hard to look back on the early years of living with any of his children without being filled with a sense of wonder and awe. And it was such a pretty house, the prettiest on the street. He paused to admire Susie's hard work in the front garden, a little parterre area in the middle, beds of campanula and amaryllis around the sides, a laburnum tree in full weighty bloom growing lasciviously over the entire front of the house.

"Darling," Susie greeted him on her doorstep wearing a droopy sundress and Velcro-strapped sandals, her graying hair tied back with a scarf. Susie had been like a mannequin when he'd met her. He'd felt compelled to touch her, just to confirm that she was indeed flesh and blood. But she'd never been comfortable with her flawless beauty and had begun covering it up within weeks of getting together with Adrian. She'd more or less embraced the degradation of her body brought about by pregnancy and childbirth and was happier now in these early stages of middle-agedness, the color leached from her hair, the lines riven through the plastic-perfect skin, the general falling apart of herself like a vacuum-packed bag of rice punctured with a knife.

She took the stocks from him with an extravagant display of appreciation and led him into the room at the back of the house that they'd always called the sunroom, even when it was dark.

She had tea set out in anticipation, and a bowl of fruit salad. The doors opened out onto the back garden, another riot of tasteful planting and heavy late-spring blossom. Everyone had told him he should sell this place when he and Susie had split up. Split it half and half. Take back what was rightfully his. And even though Susie had admitted to sleeping with half of Hove during the last year of their marriage, she'd only done that because she was being neglected by her husband, who was too busy fantasizing about an unattainable statuesque blond window dresser from Islington called Caroline to pay her any attention at all. It was the garden that had stopped him. Susie's garden. He couldn't take that away from her, too. So he and Caroline had lived in a house-share for two years, saving for a place of their own, the "oldest flatmates in town" as they'd called themselves.

"Where's Luke?" he asked.

"God knows," said Susie, pouring them both tea. "I haven't seen him all week. I need to talk to you about him. Actually I need to talk to you about you, too. I've been thinking about you a lot since Cat's birthday at Caroline's. I've been worrying about you."

Adrian stopped spooning fruit salad into a bowl to groan. "Oh God, Suse. Please don't. I can't bear being worried about."

"Bollocks," she said, taking the spoon from him and putting fruit into her own bowl. "You're a big baby. You love being worried about."

"No, you see, that's where you've always been wrong. I hate it. I'm actually a big grown-up man and I can do all my own worrying for myself."

"Hm," said Susie, unconvinced. "Well, whether you like it or not, you're worrying me. You're thin."

"I've always been thin."

"And you've got no sparkle in your eyes."

He groaned again. "Can we talk about Luke instead?"

"No," said Susie. "I want to talk about you. What's going on, Adrian? I mean, obviously you've been grieving. But there's more, I think. More to it."

"I honestly have no idea what you're talking about, Susie."

"Well. You never call anymore. You always used to call. Cat says you're distracted and weird. Luke says he can't remember what you look like. Is it that guy? Caroline's new man?"

"What!"

"I saw the way you reacted when he walked in. You went all sort of small." She made a small shape with her hands.

"Small?"

"Yes. You looked gutted."

"Oh for God's sake, I did not."

"Oh whatever, darling. I don't think it'll last, for what it's worth."

"I don't care, Susie. I don't care if it lasts or not."

She looked at him skeptically. "You've never had to experience this before. You've never had to properly relinquish a woman. You've always been able to keep them there." She made the same small shape out of her hands. "In stasis. As you left them. Even Maya."

Adrian flinched at the sound of Maya's name.

"Sorry, darling, but it's true. You've been able to stride out into your future knowing that the past is as you left it. When you chose to leave it."

"I didn't *choose* to leave Maya," he snapped.

"No, no. Of course not. But neither have you had to deal with her moving on."

"Oh Christ, Suse, you have no idea what I've been through these last months. What I've been dealing with."

"No. I don't. I've never lost anyone in that way. But I do know that this is a new one on you—Caroline's toy boy. On top of what you've been through with losing Maya. And I know you don't really have anyone to talk to. Your wives have always been your best friends."

Adrian sighed. This much was true.

"Anyway," she said, spearing a piece of pineapple onto the end of her fork, "I just wanted to say I know I'm a bit silly and a bit far away and we've kind of lost each other over the years, but you can talk to me. If you're having a hard time."

Adrian looked at her. She was smiling warmly and sincerely at him. For a moment he could see her: the waxy-skinned beauty he'd first laid eyes on nearly thirty years ago; the girl he'd lain on the beach with at night looking for constellations in the starry sky; the girl he'd sat outside pubs with on warm summer nights drinking pints, bare feet rubbing together beneath the table; the girl he'd married in a cheap rented suit in Camden Town Hall when he was almost the same age as their son was now. "Thank you," he said, "that's very lovely of you."

"I know," she said. "But you deserve it. You're a good man. Underneath it all. You need someone to look out for you. You're all alone."

"So are you."

"Yes. I am. But I'm really good at it. You suck." She

laughed, hard, revealing teeth that needed an appointment at the hygienist.

Adrian laughed, too.

"What about that girl?" she asked. "The one you were telling us about at Caroline's?"

"Another girl is not the answer to everything."

She laughed again. "It is for you, darling!"

"Well, anyway, as far as girls go, this is about the most elusive one I've ever come across. It turns out that the mobile phone she left behind at my flat belonged to a mixed-race girl called Tiffany."

"Who I assume is not . . . ?"

"No. Not the same girl. And Cat managed to track her down to a kickboxing class in Highgate this morning and she lied about her name and ran away from her. So. Brick wall."

"But if you found her, what's the idea? *Is* she going to be the fourth Mrs. Wolfe?"

Adrian leaned back into the rattan chair, recalling the disapproving words of both his daughters. "No. No, I don't think that's in the cards. Well, not for a long time at least."

Susie put her empty fruit bowl down on the table. "Ah well," she said. "Fate will sort it out for you. If it's destined to be, you'll find her again. I can't wait to find out why she's so interested in you. It's quite fascinating. A whole story just waiting to be told."

"Yes indeed." Adrian gazed past Susie and out at her beautiful garden. He saw ghosts of old afternoons out there, the shadowy echoes of small children, the shrieks of dips in icy paddling pools, the twang and thwack of a ball going round a swing-ball post, half-melted snowmen, barbecue parties that went on into the early hours, failed attempts at handstands, the sand that had sat year after year getting filthy in a plastic trough full of dead leaves and broken toys. Its energy was all still there, hiding among the manicured bushes and shrubs. "So many stories," he said, bringing his gaze back to Susie. "She was brought up in care, you know, the girl whose phone I've got. Tiffany. I met her mum. She didn't see her from when she was eight until she was twenty-six. She's married now, this girl Tiffany. And her mum doesn't know what her surname is. Or where she lives. Can you imagine, Suse? Seriously? Making babies and then not taking care of them . . ."

Susie looked at him pensively as though she was going to say something profound. But then she shook her head. "No," she said. "I truly can't. But listen, talking of babies. Your biggest one . . ."

"Ah, yes. Luke. What's going on?"

"Well, that's the real reason I asked you to come down. *Nothing* is going on with Luke. That's the problem. He's just such a . . . *waste of space*. He won't get a proper job. Goes from shop job to shop job without ever staying long enough to be promoted. He hasn't had a girlfriend in over a year. I've banned him from the Internet at home because that's all he was doing all day. So now I have absolutely *no idea* where he is all day. Probably in a café. Or staring at himself in a mirror. Doing this . . ." She prodded at her hair with her fingertips and sighed. "Remember we used to think that Luke would be prime minister? He was so focused. So driven. And now . . ." She broke off to consider her next move. "Listen. I need you to step in. I've given up. I've gone as far as I can and I've hit a wall. I want to send him to London. To stay with you."

"But the little ones—I haven't got the space . . ."

"I've spoken to Caroline about it. She's said you can move into Islington on your weekends with the kids. She'll . . ." She looked at him warily. "She'll go and stay with that boy, what was his name?"

Adrian felt his chest tighten. Things had been manipulated behind the scenes, pulleys and levers subtly rearranging the stage set of his life. This visit wasn't such a last-minute, sunny-morning affair after all.

"What do you think I can do for him that you haven't managed to do?"

"A change of scenery, for a start. And maybe a job?"

"A job?"

"Yes. At the firm. Just something basic."

"Oh God." Adrian ran the palms of his hands down his face. He thought of the way his son had looked at him in Caroline's garden the last time he'd seen him. The emptiness behind his eyes. And then he thought of toothless Jean sucking up her porridge in Mr. Sandwich, saying, *We're more like strangers than mum and daughter*. He suddenly felt very tired. "Yeah," he said. "Sure. Of course. But how are we going to do this?"

"E-mail him," she said. "It's the only sure way of knowing you'll get through to him. I'll help. We can do it now, if you like, here, together?"

Adrian smiled and saw again the nineteen-year-old Susie he'd once been enthralled by. "Sure," he said. "I'm not in a hurry. Let's do it now."

◦○◦

Finding himself on the coast, his day already shot to pieces, Adrian borrowed Susie's car (it was still technically his car and he was still insured to drive it) and set off to Southampton. He'd done some research earlier in the week, meaning to make some calls, but he'd been too busy at work. There was, it transpired, only one children's care home in Southampton and it was called White Towers Castle. He put the postcode into his smartphone and set off with a roast-beef sandwich and a bottle of organic lemonade on the passenger seat, courtesy of Susie.

His expectations were low. In a world where the safeguarding of children overshadowed everything else, he assumed that nobody would be allowed to give him any information worth having. But still. It was Saturday. The sun was shining. He had nothing better to do, miserable, lonely bastard that he was.

～

The care home was a folly, an actual castle with crenellations and towers, all painted over with thick, custardy paint. The wooden doors were painted heavy brown gloss and CCTV cameras stood on brackets at various angles, watching Adrian suspiciously. A woman who introduced herself as Sian opened the door to him when he explained his situation. He followed her into a small room off the hallway with the word OFFICE on the door and took a seat as directed in front of a small desk. Sian sat herself on the other side of the desk and said, "So. Tiffy."

"You remember her?"

"Yes. I do remember her. I've been here since I was twenty-one. For my sins."

"Well, like I said, I don't know Tiffy. But I have ended up with her phone. And I have met her mother."

Sian raised her eyebrows. "Really," she said flatly. "That's more than any of us here ever did."

"Yes," said Adrian. "She said. And, well, I have no idea what you are or aren't allowed to do, but I was wondering if there was any way you could get in touch with Tiffy. Assuming you still have contact details for her. Let her know that I have her phone. See what she'd like to do about it."

Sian was already pushing buttons on her computer before Adrian had even finished the sentence. "Any excuse to talk to one of my old ones," she said, smiling for the first time. "Let's see, right, yes, we do have fairly new details for her. She got married," she said, mainly to herself, smiling again. "That's nice. Right. OK. Let's try this number and see how we get on."

A moment later she looked at Adrian and nodded. "Oh hi, Tiffy. This is Sian. From White Towers. How are you, love?

Yes, I'm good. I'm fine. We're all fine. And I hear you got married? Wow, that's great. That's so great. Congratulations! Listen, strange one. I've got a guy here, called Adrian, he says he has your phone? That he met a woman and she left it at his flat. Any of this ringing any bells?"

The voice on the other end asked a question. Sian looked up at Adrian. "She wants to know how you know it's hers?" she asked of Adrian.

"Her mum rang me. Well, texted. Her. Tiffy I mean. And I met her. Her mum."

"He says your mum called on it. Yes. Which Mum?" she asked Adrian. "She has a birth mother and a foster mother."

"Jean," said Adrian. "No teeth."

"Jean," repeated Sian, "no teeth. Right. OK. Well, what would you like me to do, love? I can give you Adrian's number? Let you sort it out with him? Or I can post the phone to you? Or maybe you'd like to come back and say hello to everyone, collect it yourself?" She smiled, and then the smile fell. "No, of course. OK. Sure. Hold on. She wants to talk to you." Sian held the phone out to Adrian.

"Hi," said a bright voice, "Adrian! Wow! This is strange. I mean, my phone. I don't think it was actually my phone. I'm pretty sure it was a work phone. When I was working for an estate agency, I had to give it back to them after I left. And now I think about it, that was the number I gave my mum, so that she wouldn't have a permanent way of contacting me. I knew I'd be leaving. Tell me though, what exactly did the woman look like, who left it in your flat?"

"Tall, blond, stylish, odd-colored eyes."

"Right, no. I just thought maybe she was the woman who replaced me at the agency. But that woman was Asian."

"Maybe she replaced the Asian woman? It would explain there being no numbers at all on the phone, if she was new?"

"Yes, but if it was still the agency phone, you'd have been

getting lots of calls. It sounds like the phone was out of commission. Sounds like this Jane character must have nicked it."

"Or found it?"

"Yeah. Maybe. Who knows? But listen, I wouldn't mind getting it back, if it's OK with you. Just in case my mum tried calling again. I guess." There was a short silence across the line. "How was she?"

"She was—"

"No, don't answer that. I don't really want to know. Enough to know that she's alive. Anyway. Could you leave the phone? With Sian? She can post it back to me."

"Sure. Of course. But where do you live?"

"Oh, yeah, south London, but honestly, let Sian post it. I'm crazy busy. It'll be easier."

"Sure," said Adrian. "Yeah. And I'll leave Sian my number. In case there are any problems. But listen, sorry, just before you go, what was the name of the agency you were working for? When you passed your phone over?"

"Oh God," said Tiffy. "It was in Acton. It was something and Cross. *Baxter* and Cross. That's right. On the High Street. But why do you want to know?"

"I'm not sure. This woman, with your phone. It seemed like she was stalking me for a little while, me and my family. I'd like to find out who she is. Or at least have a starting point, you know."

He felt curiously melancholy passing the phone across the desk to Sian a moment later. His last connection with Jane was now effectively snapped in half.

That was that. It was over. Whatever on earth "it" had actually been. That sense of hope, that feeling that his journey wasn't over, that there was another fork in the road. Now the wall was back, the road blocked. He was stuck once again in the moment of Maya's death, reliving and reliving and reliving until the thoughts rubbed his psyche raw.

12

———— ❧ ————

Luke moved in three weeks after Adrian's trip to see Susie in Hove. It was June, the first really hot day of the year, and Luke stepped out of Susie's car wearing tiny belted shorts, a fitted top and reflective sunglasses.

"You look very, er, cool."

"I think "gay as fuck" is the expression you're looking for," he said, pulling a holdall from the footwell.

"No, no, I was thinking more of those chappies in the nineteen twenties, the ones with pipes and tennis shoes."

"It's just fashion, Dad. Men these days are allowed to look cute."

"Well, then, mission accomplished. You look very cute."

Luke threw him a facetious smile and opened up the boot. Susie strode towards Adrian in a billowing purple linen dress and embraced him. "Hello, darling. And thank you. Seriously. I can't tell you how much I appreciate this."

"No problem," he muttered into her nest of hair.

Luke looked vaguely appalled as he always did when he stepped inside Adrian's modest flat. "You know," he said, "every time I come here it reminds me that you're not as big a dickhead as I think you are."

"What's that supposed to mean?"

Luke dropped his holdall at his feet and sank down into Adrian's sofa. He picked a cat hair off his shorts and let it drop to the floor. "Well, if it was me, I'd have kicked Caroline out of that bloody *mansion* and bought myself somewhere decent to live. So you can't be all that bad."

Susie sat in the armchair and Adrian looked from her to their son, slightly unsettled by their presence here on this humid June morning. He shook his head wonderingly at Luke's comment and then clapped his hands together and said, "Tea, coffee, water, beer?"

A moment later Luke took a cold beer from Adrian's outstretched hand and said, "So, how is this going to work out, exactly?"

Adrian sat on the arm of the sofa and said, "Well, we'll start off with a nice quiet weekend. Dinner with Cat tonight. Going to watch Pearl in a competition in Derby tomorrow . . ."

"Derby?" Luke sneered.

"Yes, Derby. Welcome to my world."

Luke said, "Well, I don't have to join your world to that extent, so I'll pass, thank you."

"No," said Adrian firmly. "I've told Pearl you're coming. So you're coming."

Luke shrugged. "Whatever."

"Then on Monday morning we're off to work. I've organized for you to work in the archives. Just for a month. Then we'll see."

"Mmmm," said Luke, "great. Old paper. Amazing."

Adrian stared at his son blankly. His chattiest child, the one who'd never stopped moving, talking, doing, thinking. They'd had him monitored for ADD and the therapist had said, "No, he's just happy." For more than three years Luke had been Adrian's only child. The sunshiny, miraculous center of his universe. Now he was a slightly fey, bitter-tongued young man who couldn't make eye contact with his own father.

Susie left after an hour or so and Adrian decided that with a long, plan-free afternoon ahead of the pair of them, there was only one thing for it. So they went to the pub.

❧

Adrian had often imagined visiting pubs with his sons once they'd grown into adults. Luke had been a burly, ruggerish little boy, and Adrian had pictured the pair of them ambling in together, two pints on the table, maybe a football match to pass comment on, a new job or girlfriend to chat about, a relaxed young man with his relaxed old dad, side by side, chips off the old block et cetera.

Instead it was like coming to the pub with a young Kenneth Williams. The interior of the pub that Adrian had chosen for their afternoon's drinking was clearly not to Luke's taste and he looked as though he thought he was in imminent danger of either physical attack or flea bites.

"So, son . . ." He said it on purpose and registered Luke's involuntary shudder with a wry smile. "What's going on?"

"It's not going to work like that," said Luke. "You're not just going to sit there and say: 'What's up?' and suddenly I'm going to say: 'Oh, Daddy! I'm so glad you asked! Finally I can open up and lay my soul bare!'"

"Fine. Well. Then how is it going to work?"

"I don't know," he muttered. "You tell me. This was your idea, after all."

"Well, actually it was your mum's idea."

"Whatever. The two of you. But not me. I was perfectly happy as I was."

"That's not the impression I was getting. From your mother."

He shrugged and picked up his gin and tonic.

"And for what it's worth," Adrian continued, "I was perfectly happy as I was, too."

"Yeah. Right. You've been in a state of unbridled existential *bliss* since Maya died. We couldn't help noticing."

"Nasty, Luke."

"Yeah, well, let's not make out that I'm the only one with an attitude problem round here."

"What's that supposed to mean?"

"You. You used to be the best dad in the world. Before Maya died."

Adrian felt something like a mule-kick to his solar plexus. The words were both soft, like words a toddler might have chosen, and hard as steel. Every bit of him ached as they sank in.

"Oh," he said. "God."

"Yeah," said Luke. "I know. And it's not your fault. Obviously it's not your fault. You didn't kill her. But, I don't know. It's like the old you died with her."

"In what way? I mean, I thought . . ."

"I know. You thought you were doing OK. I know you've got your, your *Board of Harmony*. That you never forget anything. But remembering things is not the same as *caring* about them."

"Jesus Christ. *Of course* I care! How can you suggest that I don't? All I bloody do is care!"

Luke sighed and his cheeks twitched and hollowed as he considered his next point. "No. You don't. If you cared you'd notice that Cat is stress-eating because she's so unhappy. You'd notice that Pearl has no life and no friends and everyone thinks she's weird. You'd notice that Otis is miserable and retreating into himself. You'd notice that I—" He stopped. "Nothing." His jaw set hard and his cheeks twitched again.

"How the hell am I supposed to know those things if nobody bloody well tells me?" said Adrian. "I take Cat out for lunch every single week. And yes, she does eat a lot but she seems happy enough to me. I have Otis and Pearl to stay every week and they seem fine. I mean, yes, Pearl's probably over-focused on sports, and Otis is a bit monosyllabic. I had *noticed* these things. But I hadn't *worried* about them. Kids are kids. They go through phases. Moods. It's normal."

"There is nothing normal about our family, Dad. I mean, what were you thinking? How did you think it was going to be OK just to keep building families and then leaving them? You know something—and you're going to totally hate me for saying this—but I'm glad you and Maya didn't get the chance to have a baby. Because seriously, Dad, that would have just been a joke."

Adrian sat very still in the wake of these words. He felt his hands ball up into fists but decided not to say anything.

"You don't know anything about me, Dad. All the stuff you'd know if you hadn't fucked off when I was nine. Fucked off and had more boys. Better boys. With a better woman. And lived in a better house . . ."

Adrian attempted to cut in but Luke stopped him. "No," he said, "you wanted me, now you've got me. Tell me something about myself, Dad. Tell me something that only a father would know."

"Oh Jesus, Luke . . ."

"Seriously. How hard could it be? Like, what was the name of my last girlfriend?"

Adrian sighed. "I have no idea, Luke."

"Scarlett. We went out for six weeks. Split up a year ago." Adrian nodded.

"So," said Luke, "ask me what happened. Ask me why I've been single for so long. Assuming you have any interest."

Adrian sighed again. "What happened? With you and Scarlett?"

"I dumped her," he said, leaning into the back of his chair and eyeing Adrian triumphantly. "Because I was still in love with someone else."

"Right. And who was that?"

"It was an unattainable woman. It was somebody else's woman. It was a woman I wanted more than I've wanted anything in my life and I couldn't have her. And since I lost her I have had no interest in anybody else."

"Wow."

"Yeah. Wow. I've spent the last year of my life trying to function with a broken heart. Not just broken, but fucking *smashed*." He looked down into his lap and Adrian saw his lip quiver. He wanted, suddenly, to touch his son. To hold him. Here they finally shared common ground. Months of heartbreak. Adrian knew what that felt like. "Let me get you a fresh drink," he said, getting to his feet. "Another G and T?"

Luke looked up from his lap. For a moment his dead eyes sparkled. "No," he said, "I'll have a pint."

"Pint of . . . ?"

"I don't know." Luke attempted a smile. "Whatever you're having."

"Good man," said Adrian, squeezing his son's bony shoulder, "good man."

13

The following weekend Adrian left Luke behind in his flat with precise instructions about feeding the cat, taking phone messages, locking the doors and disposing of rubbish, packed a small bag and headed to Caroline's to spend the weekend with his three youngest children.

It had been a strange week. Despite their rapprochement in the pub on Saturday afternoon, relations between Adrian and his eldest child remained strained. Luke and he were so completely different. Whereas he was rough and ready, Luke was vain and preeny. Whereas he liked to rise early and spend his mornings listening to the radio and eating toast, Luke liked to spend his fast asleep until precisely five minutes before it was time to leave, whereupon he would start shouting crossly about missing shoes and hair products. Luke had a horrible habit, also, of eyeing him fully from head to toe every morning when he stood to leave the house, half opening his mouth as though about to pass comment on something he'd found displeasing, and then shutting it again. Luke was fussy too, constantly rewashing things in the kitchen that had sat in drawers being perfectly clean for weeks. And sniffing things. Everything. Tea towels. Tubs of butter. The insides of mugs.

"Why do you keep smelling everything?" Adrian had asked eventually.

"I don't know," Luke had replied vaguely. "There's just this smell. In here. This whole flat. It just sort of . . . *whiffs*."

Whiffs, Adrian had thought disconsolately. All that money on private school, and that's what he got for it. A big posh, jobless streak of attitude who used the word whiffs.

On Thursday night he had opened a bottle of wine and attempted to reopen the channels that had closed so quickly after their chat in the pub. "So," he'd said, "this girl. The one who broke your heart. What was she like?"

Luke, staring blankly at the TV, had said simply, without looking in his direction, "I don't want to talk about it."

So it was with a sense of escape and liberation that Adrian left the flat that Saturday morning. The fine start to summer had dripped away into damp disappointment. The sky was limp and grubby and the pavement was full of old puddles from the previous night's downpour. But he was looking forward to a weekend in Islington: the leafy views from the narrow sash windows; the creak and bang of his children moving from room to room and charging up and down the stairs; the click and scrabble of Caroline's funny little dogs. Yes, he was even looking forward to the dogs.

Cat greeted him at the door. He was taken aback as ever by the sheer abundance of her. She had put on weight again and had crossed the line now from plumptious to unkempt, highlighted by denim hot pants and a black bandeau top that clearly came from her slimmer days. She hugged him tight and led him to his room for the weekend. Not Caroline's room. He understood why. It had been their room, where they had slept together, made love, made babies. And now, he assumed, it was the room where Caroline had sex with her toy-boy lover. He was to sleep in the study on a pullout bed thing, on the same floor as Cat and Otis. Otis was on the swivel chair in the study doing something on the PC that he clearly didn't want anyone to see as he rapidly switched screens when he heard them come in.

"Hello, handsome," said Adrian, scruffing his son's hair.

"Hi," Otis replied dully.

There was a time, he thought, when Otis would have been jumping about like a spaniel at the prospect of his precious dad coming to spend the weekend. Now his presence barely registered.

"Where are Pearl and Beau?"

"Pearl's skating. Beau's with them."

"Them?"

"Mum and Paul."

"Oh," said Adrian. "Right. When are they coming back?"

Otis shrugged. "Soon, I guess. They were out pretty early."

"And what have you been up to then, all alone?"

"Just on the computer. That kind of thing."

Adrian nodded, but felt quietly discomfited.

Cat stood in the doorway, one bare foot balanced on the other, and said, "He's an addict. That's all he ever wants to do."

"Not when he's with me," said Adrian.

"Yeah, well, there's probably more to do when he's with you. Round here it's all skating skating skating."

"Yeah," said Otis, without turning around, "and Paul Paul Paul."

"Come on," said Cat, "let's go down and you can make me a coffee. And make him a smoothie." She nodded at Otis, who allowed himself a smile and logged off the PC.

In the basement kitchen his daughter sat herself on a bar stool and watched him as he knocked old coffee grounds out of the coffeemaker. "So," she said, "how's it going with Mr. High Maintenance?"

"Jesus," he said, smiling. "I had no idea. He used to be so much fun."

"Yeah. He took a diva pill."

"What's that all about?"

She shrugged her shoulders. "I dunno. Some girl. And that posh-boy school you and Mum sent him to didn't help much."

Adrian sighed. The private school had been Susie's idea. She'd thought they'd be better placed to deal with Luke's high-octane personality and superior intelligence. Easygoing, model-student Cat had gone to the local comprehensive and still had a chip on her shoulder about it.

"I pity the woman who takes him on," he said, spooning fresh coffee into the machine.

"I don't think such a woman exists."

There was a commotion at the door and the dogs began to bark and clatter up the wooden stairs.

"I won't come in," they heard Caroline shout down the stairs, "but here's two more for you! Bye! See you tomorrow night!" The door slammed shut and the dogs stopped barking and Pearl and Beau ran down the stairs, both launching themselves into Adrian's arms with delight. Adrian made smoothies for all three children and handed them out at the dining table by the garden doors. He passed Cat her cappuccino and added a sugar to his own double espresso and sat at the kitchen counter, surveying the scene. So this was it, he thought. This was what he had missed every Saturday morning for the past four years. This is how it looked, the life he'd left behind. Pearl with cheeks still crimson from her training, Otis still in his pajamas at eleven a.m., Beau with a large pink circle around his mouth from the smoothie, kicking his legs under the table and smiling to himself. This was it.

He looked at Cat, adding sugar to her cappuccino, texting someone with the other hand, her enormous breasts barely contained by the skimpy jersey top, her black hair tumbling down around her olive face. And then he looked around the room, this family room he'd designed himself, from what had once been four dank basement rooms. He'd designed it for this, for exactly this, for lazy Saturday mornings, for smoothies and cappuccinos, children and their things in every corner; he'd designed it, built it, filled it with charming clutter and idiosyncratic personalizing touches. And then he'd left.

Beau had still been a baby.

He felt a lump pass up and down inside his throat.

If Maya were still alive he would still believe he'd done the right thing. But without her, doubt flowed through every vein in his body.

He opened his mouth to say the thing that was there, on the tip of his tongue, desperate to be released. *Would you all like it if Daddy moved back in? With Mummy?* And then he looked at his children again and he shut it.

14

Luke heard the front door bang shut in his father's wake and watched from the window as Adrian strode away from the house and towards the high street. He tutted at the state of him. He looked so old, so thin, so scruffy. Honestly, if he stood too long on a street corner someone would eventually throw money at him. Luke pulled his silk dressing gown around his own thin body and headed for the bathroom. It was nice, *so nice*, finally to have some space. This flat was doing his head in. There were no corners, nowhere to hide. His bedroom was a joke. Bunk beds! Bunk beds at twenty-three! And having no separate living space, the kitchen and the living room all squashed into one twelve-foot square. Luke had been happy living at home with his mum because the two of them never had to be in the same space together.

Luke peered at himself in the bathroom mirror. He examined his facial hair growth. He was growing a beard. It was coming in slightly dark and vaguely curly and he wasn't sure he liked it. He'd seen a guy the other day who looked a bit like him and he'd had a smooth, dark-blond beard and it had looked really cool. Luke was starting to look more like a tugboat captain than the cool city hipster he'd been hoping for. He sighed and decided to leave it two more days and if it didn't look any better, he'd shave it off.

It took him a further hour to shower and iron a shirt and some trousers and dress himself. And then twenty minutes to do his hair. He had tricky hair. It curled in places. Which could be a curse. Or a gift. Depending on how he'd slept on it. And the humidity. Today it was a curse.

Once he'd got the hair right, he spent a good fifteen minutes staring disconsolately at the contents of his father's kitchen and his fridge. He was hungry, kind of, but couldn't decide what he fancied. What he really wanted was a fresh-out-of-the-oven chocolate croissant from Prêt à Manger. The one on North Street in Brighton where his friend Jake worked. But that wasn't going to happen. His dad had left him with a dried-out whole-meal loaf and some rank jam. There was cereal too, for the kids. Some heinous organic stuff with "all natural sugars." But no fresh milk. There was a packet of eggs, but Luke couldn't be arsed to cook anything. Eventually he settled on a packet of Quavers and an overripe banana, which he ate at the counter, staring blankly through the window at the street outside.

And it was only then that his aloneness here really hit him. Properly. The sensation lifted his spirits momentarily, like a surge of fresh air. He poured himself a glass of grape juice and then he flipped open the lid of his dad's laptop and logged straight on to Facebook, straight into a world that hadn't changed, even when his had, beyond all recognition. There they were, all his friends, just as he'd left them a week ago when he'd moved away; posting from pubs and bars he used to go to, their arms around the shoulders of people he knew, smiling as if he were still there. His gut clenched with envy. He hadn't appreciated it when that was his life; he'd mooched about and moaned and gone to the pub under duress, talked to these people out of a sense of duty. He'd always felt there was somewhere else he was supposed to be, other friends he should be hanging out with, some amazing life he was supposed to be living. And now that he was living a different life, the one he'd left behind glittered in his wake like dropped diamonds.

Charlotte Evans had posted on his timeline. "Hey, gorgeous. Where've you gone to? Bumped into Austin last night and he told me you've moved to the smoke????"

Luke sighed. Of all the people to have noticed that he'd left town, Charlotte was the last one he wanted to open up a communication with. They'd dated on and off for a year or so back in 2010. She was hot beyond belief. He'd thought he was in love with her for one crazy week when the sun was shining. And then he'd cooled off and finally pulled himself out of it three months later than would have been ideal and she'd screamed and pounded his chest and called him names that left dark blots on his psyche even to this day. She'd got over it eventually, told him she'd like to be friends and he'd said, basically, *Whatever*, and she showed up at the pub sometimes and posted stuff on his timeline and tagged him on photos she posted of herself posing half-dressed. It was just one of those things, one of the many scourges of modern technology. It was so much harder to shake people off. He thought about ignoring the comment, but then sighed and thought: Throw her a bone, maybe she'll run off a cliff with it. He typed in: "Yes. Mum and Dad staged an intervention. I'm here until further notice."

He went back to his news feed and scrolled idly for a while. There was Otis, posting some crappy YouTube link. He'd changed his profile photo again; he seemed to change it every two and a half hours. This one showed him staring intensely into the webcam, his face slightly bloated by the lack of depth. He looked psychotic. Luke sometimes wondered if Otis wasn't a bit psycho. He found it quite hard to relate to his younger brother these days. He was a closed book, like Pearl, but the difference was that Pearl had always been inscrutable, ever since she was a tiny toddler, while Otis had started off easy to read and became inscrutable over time. And it didn't suit him.

Luke clicked on a few links, added to a couple of comment

threads, and then he got bored. He glanced up from the screen. His eye found its way to a framed photo of Maya further along the kitchen counter and he felt that familiar thump of despair, that kick of regret. He stared at the photo for a moment or two before opening up his dad's photo drive. He scrolled down until he got to folders dated earlier than April 2011. There was one: Cornwall '10. Luke had been there. All of them had been there. It was back in the days when they'd all done everything together, one enormous, multi-tentacled octopus of a family. It had been a blustery half-term week, sunshine and showers, gallons of wine and cooking rotas, pub lunches and kids and dogs running around everywhere. It had been back in the days when his dad had bent over backwards to make sure that nobody ever felt the sharp end of divorce. When he'd made it seem like an advantage to be part of a broken family. He'd almost felt sorry, back then, for people who only had one family.

Luke flicked through the photos. His father took good photos. He had an expensive camera and he knew how to use it. Luke smiled at the group shots; there were the little ones, so much littler then: Beau still a toddler, Otis smiling widely in a way he rarely did these days, funny little Pearl, wearing a dress. She did not wear dresses anymore. And there, on the far right of the shot, was Maya.

Luke sucked in his breath. It wasn't a great photograph of her. She was wearing some heinous professional walking gear, a blue shiny thing with a hood. That was his father's influence. He always favored practicality over style. But still her pure loveliness shone out. She had her arm around Pearl's shoulders and Luke could almost imagine that she was smiling at him. Just for him. And that had been the problem really. Maya had been one of those people who made everyone feel as though they were the most important person in the world. As though they were special. And like a total moron Luke had thought that he was more special than anyone. More special even than his dad. His flesh still crawled when he thought about that awful night at the pub, a few weeks after Cornwall, when she had stared into his eyes and hung on to his every word and brushed his arm gently with her fingertips and shared confidences with him and he'd thought . . . well, it didn't matter anymore what he'd thought. The fact was he'd been wrong.

Maya of course had been gracious and sweet. Had said she was "flattered." *Yeah, right.* Even now, coming up for two years later, Luke felt his skin flush hot with humiliation. He'd stopped hanging out with the family so much after that. So no, he couldn't blame his dad entirely for the fact that they rarely saw each other. But he could blame his dad for the rest of it: for never calling, for not arranging the big holidays anymore, for turning up to family gatherings looking thin and distracted. And for letting Maya go out one day and never come back.

He spent another hour looking at family photographs. His eyes swam with tears and he got up at one point to blow his nose. He peered at his face in the mirror, half relishing the melodramatic ugliness of it, half fearing that he wouldn't be able to leave the house today. He poured himself more grape juice and then went back to the laptop, patting at his eyes with the screwed-up tissue. He wanted more. He needed more. He searched the entire C drive and network for the word "Maya."

He read through her accounts, her marking notes, a recipe for chicken tagine that his dad called "Maya's Chicken," checklists, "Maya's passport." And there, strangely buried away in a folder called "Transfers" in a subfolder called "New Folder," was a file called "E-mails."

Luke clicked it open.

It was a Word document. Three pages of copied and pasted e-mails, all addressed to Maya. All unsigned. Dated from July 2010 to April 2011. And all beginning with the words "Dear Bitch."

PART TWO

15

JULY 2010

The sun shone too brightly through the living-room window, turning the screen of her laptop into a dark-glassed mirror. Maya swiveled it around and moved to the armchair. Billie looked at her, slightly affronted by her relocation, and then turned her attention to an itch on her hind leg.

Maya was looking for a cottage to rent for the October half-term. Adrian had asked her as a favor since she wasn't at work this week. It was a tall order. At least five bedrooms, but preferably six, walking distance from a pub so they wouldn't all have to haul themselves into three vehicles every time they fancied a pub lunch, near a train station so that Cat could get there and back on the train when she came for the weekend. It needed a good-sized garden for the kids and the dogs, possibly with a trampoline or some swings, but no dangerous water features or pools, as many bathrooms as possible and a "reasonable standard of décor."

Eighteen months ago Maya would have had a poor grasp of what constituted a "reasonable standard of décor" but after three such family holidays she now knew that she needed to avoid carpeted bathrooms, metal Venetian blinds, fake stained glass, dirty shower curtains, spider-filled anterooms and candlewick bedspreads, all of which had caused various members of the extended Wolfe family some kind of distress at various points. She had also been directed to avoid anything *cheap modern:* "You know, chrome, red leather, oversized canvases of the innards of orchids." This was from Caroline. Maya liked Caroline. She really did. But she was head of visual merchandising at Liberty and was all about the aesthetic. Susie on the other hand, dear who-gives-a-shit-as-long-as-it-smells-nice Susie, she would keep on smiling and saying, "I don't mind, really I don't, whatever you all think," and then she would arrive and immediately find the one thing wrong with it: "Oh, what a shame the sun goes behind those trees so early." Or: "Dear God, what are these mattresses filled with, mushroom soup?"

So Maya knew she needed to spend at least a day on the Internet, studying each page of information with forensic attention to detail, blowing up each picture and studying it for flaws, reading and rereading the descriptions for potential traps like "bedroom four is accessible only from the kitchen" or "the friendly owner lives on-site and is always available for assistance and sightseeing advice," before she could even begin sending out links for the others to look at.

She could never have imagined when she'd first set eyes on the shambling, scruffy form of Adrian Wolfe on her first day at Adrian Wolfe Associates two years ago that she would end up as his wife. She was a temp at the time, halfway through her summer break after teacher training college, brought in for a week as a "girl Friday." That was back when Adrian's practice was just seven people in a room above a pub in Tufnell Park. Everyone piled on top of everyone. A lowly paid, paper-shuffling temp had as much visibility as a partner back then. She'd stayed for nearly a month in the end, long enough to have been to the pub a few times, to have sat at the kitchen counter chatting over mugs of tea, long enough to have become one of the guys. And, by a matter of just two hours, long enough for Adrian to catch her forcefully by her arm as she passed him a drink in the pub at her leaving drinks and say, "Where are you going after? I'd love to buy you a thank-you dinner."

By that time, of course, Maya knew that Adrian had two families, that his life was a wobbling Jenga tower, one extracted brick away from toppling over. She had heard his late-night phone calls to Caroline explaining he'd be late again and the echo of Caroline's long-suffering sigh at the other end of the line. She'd met Caroline, once, one of the most intimidating women she'd ever encountered. Tall, naturally blond, unsmiling. She found it hard to imagine how Caroline and Adrian had ever found their way to one another. But then she'd met Susie a few months into their relationship, and it had all made perfect sense. She could see that Caroline had been nothing more than an inverse reaction to his first wife. She tried not to dwell too much on what that made her.

Adrian had assured Maya all the way through the two months of their illicit affair that it was all over between him and Caroline; that they barely spoke these days; that she was distant; that she was *completely out of love with him*. And, given how graciously and peaceably Caroline had let Adrian go, how kind Caroline had been to Maya from their first meeting and how few ripples their affair appeared to cause in the waters of Adrian's family, Maya could only assume that he'd been telling the truth.

And here they were, two years later, not just living in a flat together but married. She had a brilliant job as a year-two teacher in a posh girls' school in Highgate. Adrian's practice had exploded and was now based in a huge studio in Farringdon, employing thirty-eight people, most of whom did all the work—meaning he now took Fridays off.

Caroline liked her. Susie appeared to *love* her. She got on really well with all the kids. Everyone said that things were much better since Maya had come into Adrian's life. Everything was perfect. Truly perfect.

Except for the e-mail.

It had arrived in her inbox yesterday.

She'd had to leave the room when she saw it, as if it was a bad smell that she needed to escape from. She'd clasped her heart and then the kitchen counter. Then, a few moments later, she'd come back to it. She'd shaken the screensaver off with the mouse and there it was.

Dear Bitch

I can't believe it's been two years since you stole somebody else's husband. I didn't think you and Big Daddy would last longer than a couple of months. But for some reason you're still here! Have you not worked it out yet? You're not wanted. Everyone's pretending they love you so much but they don't. They hate you. So why don't you go now? Stop acting like the lovely little wifey and get your own life instead of crashing other people's.

The e-mail address was thelonevoice@hotmail.com.

An involuntary laugh had slipped from her body as she read.

Nervous laughter.

Then a wave of nausea had passed over her. *The Lone Voice*.

The e-mail was written in the tone of an objective observer, but the sentiment seemed entirely personal. She knew, instantly, and without a doubt, that it was one of them. It was a Wolfe. One of the children. One of the wives. One of the people who smiled so sweetly at her, who hugged her on greeting and kissed her on departing, who told her how happy she made Adrian, who praised her cooking, admired her shoes, played with her hair, sat on her lap, drank tea that she made, went on holidays that she booked. Told her that they loved her. The nausea passed and was replaced by tears.

The faces of Adrian's family passed through her mind like a police identity lineup. Each one she discounted immediately.

She was about to press forward to send it to Adrian at his work e-mail but then changed her mind. It might freak him out. She did not want to freak him out. She didn't want to worry him. And she didn't want whoever it was to get into trouble. Instead she moved it into her junk folder, where she wouldn't have to look at it every time she checked her e-mail.

She'd been bullied at school for four years by a group of blond-ponytailed girls who'd taken exception to her waist-length flame-red hair and freckled arms. Every day had been like a living nightmare. They'd called her *Red Rum*. Asked her about her pubic hair. Sent her cruel letters. Cornered her in the playground and terrorized her. It had only ended when she'd left school at sixteen. And it hadn't been character-building. All it had taught her was to appease and to please.

Which was why her affair with Adrian had been so out of character. The potential to hurt people, to piss people off, to make people *not like her*. It made her shudder, even now, to think how close she'd come to her own personal apocalypse.

She checked her e-mail account again now, flicking away briefly from a farmhouse in Fowey that was perfect in every way apart from a lethal-looking duck pond in the garden. It had been more than twenty-four hours now since the e-mail. With every moment that passed without a second e-mail, the more relaxed she became, the more convinced that the whole thing had been a bizarre one-off.

She sent an e-mail to the owner of the farmhouse in Fowey asking if they had any means of covering over the duck pond and then she made herself a cup of tea. She heard the ping of new e-mail landing in her inbox and she sat back down in the armchair. She assumed it was the owner of the house in Fowey. It was not.

Dear Bitch
  By the way, this will keep happening until you get the
message and get out of their lives. So you'd better get
used to it. Or get out.

Maya felt the corners of her consciousness begin to wrap
themselves around her eyes. She tried to control her breathing, but it was too late. She was back in the playground being
cornered by her tormentors. The panic descended and the
darkness took hold of her.

16

JUNE 2012

Adrian sat on a hard plastic chair in the waiting area of Kentish Town police station. He had a meeting booked with DI Ian Mickelson at 10:15 a.m. and it was currently 10:25 a.m. In his hands he had his laptop zipped into a rubberized envelope and a print-off of the e-mails that Luke had given him upon his breathless arrival at Caroline's on Saturday afternoon.

He had no idea what this might achieve. There had been no criminal investigation into Maya's death; the coroner's verdict plus two witness statements and a toxicology report had seen to that. Death by misadventure. She'd drunk too much. She'd fallen under a bus. *These things happen.*

DI Ian Mickelson finally appeared in the doorway. He was tall, as tall as Adrian, but young and remarkably good-looking. He apologized and apologized again; he shook Adrian's hand and then he led him to a small interview room, where he directed a younger plain-clothed policeman to get them both some tea.

"So," he began, glancing down at a notebook in his hand, "this is . . . cyber-bullying? Yes?"

"Well, yes, sort of. My wife, Maya, she died in April last year. She got knocked down by a night bus on Charing Cross Road."

"I'm very sorry to hear that."

"Yes," said Adrian, "and, well, the circumstances of her death always struck me as totally out of character. I mean, she was drunk, for one. Eight times over. Enough to kill her. She was tiny. And not only that but drinking alone, it appears. Or at least none of her friends ever came forward to say they'd been with her. So, we must assume . . ." He lost his momentum for a second, imagining again the sheer wretchedness of Maya drinking vodka shots on her own. "Anyway"—he brought himself back—"Maya died, we buried her, we tried to get on with our lives and then my son came to live with me, just over a week ago. He was using my laptop on Saturday. And he found a folder, hidden somewhere in the bowels of my home drive, filled with pages of these . . ."

He passed the papers across the table to DI Mickelson, who pulled them closer to himself with the tips of his big fingers and cleared his throat. Adrian watched him, silently, monitoring his facial expressions for signs of shock and distaste.

A few moments later, DI Mickelson pushed the papers away from himself an inch or two, again with his fingertips, and leaned back in his chair. He pulled a breath in through his teeth and said, "Very unpleasant. Very unpleasant indeed."

"So," said Adrian, "what do you think? Is there anything we can do?"

"Well, yes, we can certainly look into this. I assume you have the original e-mails?" He nodded at Adrian's laptop.

"Well, no," he replied. "It looks like Maya deleted them all. I'm not exactly a technical whiz kid but I've had a root about, and I can't find the originals anywhere. Just these cut-and-pasted copies. But it's all definitely connected. I mean, look"—he pointed at the last e-mail—"right there. April the eighteenth, that was the day before she died. And there were no other e-mails from this person. I went straight into Maya's e-mail account after her death, looking for clues, you know, and this person, this Dear Bitch person, never showed their face again. Clear evidence that they were involved somehow in Maya's death."

"Yes," said DI Mickelson, running his fingertips around a button on his bright white polo shirt. "I can absolutely see that there must be some connection. But I've looked at the files, Mr. Wolfe, and whichever way I look at it, nobody was directly responsible for killing your wife. Two separate people saw her fall into the path of the bus; it was three thirty in the morning; the streets were virtually empty. If there'd been another person involved, the witnesses would have seen it. The bus driver would have seen it. *Someone* would have seen it. So while I can look into this for you, open a file, see if we can track this person down, I'm not sure we'll be able to use it to open an inquiry into your wife's death. It would be a separate crime. *Assuming*"—he looked directly at Adrian—"we can get anything out of your laptop to lead us to this person. As it stands, without any hard data," he sighed, "these could just be a creative-writing exercise."

Adrian flinched at these words.

"Leave it with me." DI Mickelson tapped the edge of the laptop with his fingertips, signifying that the meeting had reached its natural conclusion. "I can get someone to have a look at this over the next twenty-four hours; you can come back for it tomorrow. We'll call you."

"Oh," said Adrian, clutching the arms of his chair, bringing himself up to standing. "Right."

"We'll just need your password, if you're happy to let us have it."

"Yes, yes, of course." He dictated it to the DI, who scribbled it down on his notepad. "I guess if I can't trust you lot with my password, we're all doomed."

Ian Mickelson looked up at him, half-amused, and said, "Yes. Indeed."

And then he left, emerging into an unexpectedly hot Kentish Town, feeling strangely euphoric. Something was happening. The events of April 19, 2011, were taking some kind of form. For so long it had felt like a sick joke, a hiccup in the space-time continuum. Maya, walking in front of a bus eight times over the limit when she should have been lying next to him in bed. It lacked context. It lacked depth. It simply was not supposed to have happened. And now, maybe, he could start to shade it in, make it look like something he could comprehend.

And he knew, he just knew, that beautiful, glittering, disappearing Jane had something to do with it.

17

Adrian went straight back to the office after his meeting with DI Mickelson at Kentish Town. He ignored the e-mails in his inbox, the Post-it notes flapping on his screen, the paperwork neatly arranged inside a clear folder with the words: "For the meeting with Brent. Please read and sign ASAP!!" attached to it. He brushed it all aside and he typed the words "Baxter and Cross Acton" into his search engine, sipping gingerly from an overly hot cup of tea as he did so.

He dialed the number on the estate agent's website and he asked to speak to the manager. The manager wasn't available so Adrian asked the man on the end of the line, "How long have you worked there?"

The man said, "Eight years."

Adrian said, "Great! Listen, do you remember a woman called Tiffy or Tiffany?"

"Yeah, yeah, definitely. I remember her."

"Well, she . . . sorry, my name is Adrian Wolfe. A woman left a phone at my flat some time ago. She didn't come back to claim it but I traced the phone back to a woman called Tiffany Martin. Your former colleague. She told me the phone was one she'd used when she worked at your agency. She said the phone would have been passed on to her replacement. Now, since all this happened it has come to light that the woman who originally left the phone at my house might know something about the, er . . ." He paused. "Sorry, what's your name?"

"My name is Abdullah."

"Great. Thank you. And sorry, this is a bit rambling, Abdullah. But it seems that she might know something about the death of my wife a year ago. Accidental death. Not murder or anything like that. But still, it was a very inexplicable death. Odd, you know, and I've never been able to make any sense of it. So, as you can imagine, I'm quite keen to follow any leads I possibly can. And if there *is* a connection between your agency and the woman, well . . . Anyway, I'm grabbing at straws, I know. I'm desperate. So . . ."

There was a suspended silence on the line. Adrian couldn't tell which way it was leading.

"God," said Abdullah eventually. "Is this for real?"

"Yes," said Adrian, "I'm afraid it is."

"Well, listen, the boss is out and I'm not sure how much info I can share, but I'm pretty sure Tiff's phone went to Dolly."

"Dolly?"

"Yeah. But let me talk to the boss. I really want to help you, but I don't want to get into any trouble. You know, these days, privacy, all that, I never know where the lines are drawn. It gets tighter all the time."

"Sure," said Adrian, feeling pretty certain that Abdullah would have given him Dolly's bra size if he'd thought Adrian was a potential house-buyer.

"But give me your number. I promise I'll call you straight back, minute I've got the all-clear. Yeah?"

"Yeah," said Adrian. "Thank you."

&

While he was supposed to be reading the notes for the big meeting with Brent Council and checking the final plans for the last-minute penthouse extension to the shared-ownership block on Goldhurst Road and signing off on the budgets for the last quarter and popping in to see Derek in response to Derek's scribbled note imploring him to "pop in to see me when you get back," Adrian read the *Dear Bitch* e-mails. Again. There were three pages of them and he'd read them all at least six times since Saturday afternoon. He kept waiting for some little turn of phrase, some lightbulb of recognition to jump out and make sense of it all.

The phrases danced in front of his eyes; he'd read them so many times now that they'd started to lose their shape:

> *Pathetic loser*
> *Home wrecker*
> *Selfish to your core*
> *The worst teacher in the country*
> *You think they all love you so much, but they don't, OK*
> *Even your own parents hate you*
> *Don't know what he sees in you, you're not all that*

This last comment hurt him the most. Sweet Maya. She'd been so insecure about her looks. I'm nothing special, she'd say, with an apologetic shrug as if she was somehow letting everyone down by not being more beautiful. She'd delete perfectly nice photos of herself from his phone and sigh over the cheekbones and hairstyles and buttocks of women she perceived to be more attractive than herself. He remembered the way her eyes would follow Caroline about when they were all together, as if she was trying to glean from her some essential trick about how to be beautiful. And he tried to imagine her reading these words, words that backed up all her insecurities. The thought of Maya dying thinking she wasn't beautiful enough made him want to weep.

He pulled a pen from the pot on his desk and began scribbling his thoughts down.

Knows she has two parents
Knows she is a teacher
Knows she is my third wife
Knows when she is at home
Knows what she looks like
Knows the names of people in her family
"Think they love you. They don't." Suggests someone on
    periphery of family
References to physical appearance sound bitchy. Suggests written
by a woman

He stopped and looked up. Would "Jane" really have known so much about Maya? Surely not. Adrian had known everyone in Maya's life: her headmistress, her weird best friend, her cousins in Maidstone, a couple of friends from teacher training college, the new friend from the posh school, what was her name? Holly. Yes. Holly Patch. He could even remember her surname. He'd met everyone. He was sure he had. Maya wasn't a great collector of people. She was fussy, like him. So if it wasn't "Jane," then who the hell else knew so much about his wife? One of his ex-wives? Could it be? No. No way. Not possible. Susie and Caroline were too clever, too secure, too wrapped up in their own lives to waste time sending poison e-mails. Cat? Pearl? Could it be? Could it be that these e-mails had come from one of his own daughters?

Could it?

"No." He said this out loud as if to ensure that his subconscious would hear it, too. "No." The thought was unpalatable to him. His girls. His angels.

His mobile phone rang. He sighed and put down the notebook and pen. "Yes," he said.

"Is that Adrian Wolfe?"

"Speaking."

"Oh, hi, my name is Dolly Patel. I was just talking to my colleague, Abdullah, about your problem with the phone. I'm not sure how helpful I can be. But it might be something, you never know . . ."

"Oh. Good. Great. Thank you." Adrian sat up straight and grabbed a pen and paper.

"My bag was stolen, from the hall table of a house I was showing clients around. I'd left the door on the latch for the next viewers. My phone was in it. Well, at least I think it was in it. I wasn't really using it then, I'd been given a smartphone. But I'm pretty sure it was. Apparently there've been loads of similar crimes on that street. Opportunists. They found my bag down a hedge around the corner. But the phone was gone, and my purse. So . . ."

"So . . ." Adrian's pen was suspended above his notepad, his breath drawn.

"So, that's it really. That was about two months ago. The phone never showed up. The police tried to trace the SIM but it wasn't being used. So. Game over."

"The police had the SIM number?"

"Yeah. But, like I said, the thief wasn't using it."

"I wonder . . ." He shuffled through the papers on his desk, looking for DI Mickelson's number. He found it and covered it over with his hands. "Good. OK. Thank you, Dolly. Actually, yes, that is helpful. Or potentially. Thank you very, very much."

"Good luck," she said. "I'm really sorry about your wife."

"Yes," said Adrian, "so am I."

❧

Within sixty seconds of Adrian's hanging up the phone to Dolly Patel, he was taking a call from Caroline.

"Hi, hello," he greeted her distractedly.

"Adrian. Listen. I've had a call from the school. From Otis's school. He's not there. He's not answering his phone." Her voice broke slightly. "I'm quite worried."

Adrian took his hand from the piece of paper and touched his heart with it. "What? Since when?"

"I don't know. They called about an hour ago. I've been phoning and phoning him ever since. I just thought, you know, he was bunking off. So I texted him, saying if he went straight into school, he wouldn't be in trouble. That was half an hour ago. No reply. And he's still not in school. I'm really scared. What shall I do? What shall I do?"

"But it's nearly lunchtime," said Adrian incredulously. "That means he's been missing from school for the whole morning."

"I know! I know! I was at . . . at an appointment. I had my phone switched off. And he's done this before, you know, he's bunked off before."

"He has?"

"Yes! Not much. Just a couple of times. About a year ago. After Maya died. You know. So I thought he was just, you know, *skiving*. But now I'm thinking . . . Christ, he's so beautiful. And so secretive. All those hours on the Internet. He could be talking to anyone! He might have met someone! You know. Someone pretending to be a cute fourteen-year-old girl. I'm shitting myself. I'm shitting myself!"

"Where are you?"

"At home! I'm at home!" Her voice had reached a pitch several octaves above her usual cool alto.

"Stay there. I'm coming. I'm coming right now."

18

By the time he got to the house in Islington, Otis was sitting on the armchair in the kitchen with a dog on his lap looking bullishly ashamed of himself.

"I'm sorry," he said before Adrian had even opened his mouth. His fingers plucked at the dog's fur and his eyes bored into the floor.

"Jesus," said Adrian.

Caroline was standing against the kitchen counter, flicking her thumbnail against her fingernail.

He leaned over Otis and tried to hold him. His son allowed this, but didn't reciprocate.

"So," he said, sitting opposite him. "What happened?"

Otis shrugged. "I just didn't want to go into school."

"And why didn't you answer your phone?"

"I left it at home. By accident."

Adrian sighed. "Christ," he said, "didn't it occur to you that me and your mum might be worried about you?"

Otis shrugged again, tossing his head slightly to get his pop-star curls out of his eyes. "I said I'm sorry. I won't do it again."

"Yes, but . . ." He looked up at Caroline. "Where did they find him?"

"They didn't. I did. Just happened upon him on my way home. Outside the tube. Sitting on a bench, like a tramp."

"What!" He turned back to Otis. "Sitting outside the tube? What on earth . . ."

"I just . . ." He pulled harder at the dog's fur. "I was just thinking. That's all. I can never think in this house."

"Oh Jesus Christ." Adrian ran his fingers through his hair. "Listen, mate—"

"Don't call me mate. It's not cool."

"Sorry. Son. If you were meeting someone, you can tell us. OK? We won't be cross."

Otis's brow furrowed and he said in that horrible deprecating tone of voice that all his children apart from Beau used when they talked to him, *"Meeting someone? Why the hell would I be meeting someone? I don't know anyone."*

"No, no, of course not. But you spend a lot of time on the Internet. There are people . . ."

"Yes. I know. I do know. Old men pretending to be teenagers so that they can stick their willies up my bum. I *know*. And I wasn't *meeting anyone*. I'm not an idiot."

Adrian exhaled, relieved and reassured. He and Caroline shared a look.

"So, what were you thinking about?"

He shrugged. "Stuff."

"What kind of stuff?"

Otis gently pushed the dog off his lap and got to his feet. "You know, actually, Mum, Dad, I think I'd like to go into school now." He said this less as a pronouncement of surrender than as an expression of disgust.

"Fine," said Caroline, looking at her watch. "But I'm walking you to the gate."

Otis shrugged. "Whatever."

"I'll come too," said Adrian.

Otis remained virtually silent as they walked the ten minutes to his school. Caroline said, "There'll have to be a punishment, of course, you know that?"

"Fine," said Otis.

They both hugged him at the gates and watched him skulking across the playground to the school office.

They turned to each other as the heavy swing doors banged shut in his wake and his dark head disappeared up the corridor. "Got time for a quick coffee?" said Adrian.

Caroline looked at her watch again. She sighed. "Yeah. Sure. Why not. But really quick. I've got a meeting at two p.m."

They went into a Starbucks and arranged themselves on armchairs set either side of a low table, the only free seats in the place. Caroline had an Earl Gray tea; he had a black Americano. He watched Caroline squeeze out her teabag with her fingertips, so measured, so elegant, her handsome face still unlined, exactly as it had been the first time he saw her. She brushed her damp fingers against the lapel of her jacket, unthinkingly tracing the outline of her breast as she did so, and Adrian felt a stirring of sexual desire. He closed his eyes, feeling wrong-footed, embarrassed by himself.

He had never been so long without sex before. He had, on average, taking into consideration the fallow periods that surrounded the gestation and emergence of five babies, had sex an average of once a fortnight since he'd left home. And now he was fourteen months down the line of unwanted abstention. Longer if you took into account the last few weeks with Maya, when she had been . . . well, anyway. He and Maya had been having sex pretty much every night before that. From 356 shags a year to nothing, virtually overnight. It was no wonder he was looking at his ex-wife inappropriately.

"So," said Caroline, holding her cup halfway to her mouth, oblivious. "Theories?"

"What?"

"Theories? About Otis?"

"God, no. Nothing. I mean, you said he did this before. After Maya?"

Caroline nodded. "Yes. Twice. We made all kinds of exceptions for him." She glanced at Adrian and read the question in his expression. "I didn't tell you. I thought you had enough to deal with. I protected you from a lot. *We* protected you from a lot."

Adrian nodded understandingly.

"But that was different," she continued. "He was with friends then. Doing what boys do. Mucking about. You know. None of this sitting-on-benches business, staring into space. I mean, if I hadn't come back on the tube, if I'd got a taxi, say, I wouldn't even have seen him there. He might still be sitting there now, for Christ's sake."

They sat quietly for a moment, thinking, and then sighed in unison.

"Is he doing all right at school?" said Adrian, already knowing the answer but asking the question out of a sense of desperation.

"Yes, yes." Caroline nodded. "He's doing so well at school. You know, his creative writing is amazing. I mean, I really think he has the potential . . ."

"Yeah, I know, I read that thing he wrote, you know, about the time-traveling girl . . ."

"Yes! Wasn't that incredible? So imaginative . . ."

"But so well executed too. I mean, he'd really thought it all through, hadn't he? All the complexities . . . And really getting into the mind-set of a girl."

"I know. I know."

Caroline rubbed her elbows and smiled up at Adrian. "Our brilliant children," she said.

"I know," he said. "Thank you."

She looked at him with barbed curiosity.

"I mean, for raising them. For letting me . . . for being so . . ." He swallowed hard as he realized with some horror that he was on the verge of tears. "Thank you," he said once he'd brought his emotions into check, "for being such a brilliant mother."

She gazed at him impassively. Then she looked at her watch.

He could feel that they were running out of time. Out of time for what? he wondered.

She drank half her tea and began to put things back into her bag. "I should . . ."

"Yes." He picked up his coffee.

"You don't have to rush off. You stay."

"No," he said, "no. I should go. I should probably . . ." He tailed off with no clear idea about what exactly he should be doing.

Caroline zipped up her bag. "Oh," she said. "The e-mails. I didn't ask. What happened about the e-mails? Have you managed . . . ?"

"No," he said, piling sugar wrappers into his empty coffee cup. "I've left the laptop with the computer-crimes unit. They're going to give me a ring at some point." He shrugged. "Don't suppose they'll find anything though."

"So strange," she said, "so incredibly strange. All that personal stuff. All that stuff that someone would only know if they were . . . *family*." She shook her head as though trying to dislodge a drop of water. "Weird."

"Horrible," he said.

"Yes. Completely. Anyway. I'll give you a ring later, OK, see if you've heard anything. Update you on Mr. Sitting-on-a-bench. We can have a proper chat then."

"Yes, thank you. That would be great." He smiled and let her go, his own hand on the back of his chair, readying himself to leave. "Oh," he said, a small concern from earlier leaping to the front of his mind, "your appointment, the one you were at this morning? Everything OK?"

She looked at him with surprise, one hand grasping the strap of her handbag, the other in the pocket of her jacket. "Yes," she said, "it is actually. Everything is OK." And then she smiled, a rare, beautiful thing, put her hand up to him as a farewell gesture, turned and left.

19

"Where's, er . . ." Luke stopped. "Adrian?"

He hadn't seen his dad since breakfast. Adrian had been working from home this morning because of that appointment at the police station. Freya on reception said that he'd come in at about 11:30 a.m. and then gone straight out again.

The woman who worked outside Adrian's office talked to Luke without looking at him as she hurriedly pulled together various pieces of paperwork. "No idea," she said. "He told me he was popping out for an hour, but as far as I'm aware he didn't come back. Have you tried calling him?"

Luke shook his head and said thank you. It was strange being here without his dad. Made him wonder why he was here at all. He walked across the open-plan area in the center of the office and through the doors to the stairs that took him to the ground floor, where the archives were. He took his phone from the pocket of his jacket hanging off the back of his chair and called his dad.

"Where are you?"

"I'm at home."

"How come?"

He heard his father sigh heavily. "Caroline called. Otis went missing."

"What!"

"Yes, I know. It's all fine now. She found him; he's gone into school. Everything's cool."

"God, where was he? What was he doing?"

"Sitting on a bench, apparently, outside Angel. Thinking."

"I told you!" said Luke. "Didn't I tell you? That boy's not right. Seriously, Dad, I knew something like this was going to happen. I tried to tell you."

"Nothing's happened."

"No. Not yet. But it could have. Who knows what's going on with him? It could be drugs for all we know."

Adrian pooh-poohed his theory and Luke groaned. "You're doing it again, Dad. You're assuming just because you live in the *best of all possible worlds* that bad things don't happen to people you love. But, Dad, Maya, *your wife*, she was hounded to her death by somebody. She jumped under a bus because someone was hurting her. These things *do* happen. You should be talking to Otis, following him, searching his browsing history. Not just sending him back to school and saying la la la, everything's fine."

He heard Adrian exhale. "Yes, yes, you're right. Of course you are. But he's not going to open up to me. He thinks I'm a moron." He paused. "Maybe you could try talking to him?"

Luke sat down, feeling struck by an unexpected wave of warmth. "I can try."

"He's sleeping over later this week," said Adrian. "I could work late? You could collect him from school?"

"School?" Luke felt vaguely horrified by the idea.

"Yeah. He'd like that. Showing off his big brother."

"But I'll be at work."

Adrian laughed. "I'll talk to the boss about letting you leave early."

"Right," said Luke, warming to the idea now that he knew it involved an afternoon off work. "Yeah. OK. I can do that. Maybe take him somewhere. Where do you normally take him?"

"He likes the Italian round the corner. You know, the greasy-spoon one. He likes their carbonara."

"Great. Carbonara. Yeah. OK. I can do that, but . . ."

"I'll give you cash."

"Right," said Luke. "Thank you."

He hung up feeling strangely substantial.

~∽~

There was a beautiful blonde sitting on the wall outside his father's office when Luke left work at five o'clock. He could see one-quarter of her in profile and was struck by the strong line of her jaw, the kick of her peroxide hair across her cheek, nice legs, the soft print of a summer dress, pink ballet pumps and a tan satchel. He peered curiously at her, wondering if he'd inadvertently placed an order at myperfectwoman.com during his lunch hour. Then she turned to face him and his heart fell. Instinctively he spun round and attempted to exit the building invisibly and in the wrong direction. But it was too late. She'd seen him.

"Luke!"

"Charlotte!" He tried to sound and look surprised. "Wow!" He kissed her on each cheek. "Wow, what are you doing here?"

"I was in town for the day," she said, "thought I'd come and see how you were doing."

Luke tried for a smile. "Right," he said, "cool. You look great." He gestured at her pretty dress, her suntan, her glowing skin, her amazing breasts. "Really great." He stopped, looked at his father's office and then back at Charlotte. "How did you know where . . . ?"

She beamed. "Google."

Luke felt something lurch uncomfortably within him. Hadn't he got rid of this girl? Wasn't she consigned to "my romantic history?" To the short but high-quality list of women he would one day remember having slept with before he met the woman of his dreams and settled into monogamy?

"Ah," he said, "right."

"So," said Charlotte, pulling at the strap of her satchel,

"lovely day. Do you fancy a pint? Just a quick one. Before I catch my train?"

Luke relaxed. A train home. Good. That sounded nice and finite. *Good-bye, Charlotte! Jolly nice to see you! Have a safe trip!* And it was a beautiful afternoon, the sort of rare London summer's afternoon when it felt almost criminal not to stand outside a pub with a pint in your hand.

"Yeah," he said, casually, not wanting to sow any seeds of hope, "why not?"

They walked around the corner to a pub on Cowcross Street with a courtyard set back from the road. It was heaving with the solid backs of men in crumpled shirts, and the gentle roar of coiled male tension released by beer boomed across the courtyard. He put a protective hand on Charlotte's back as they passed through the knot of men towards the doors and then snatched it back as he felt her body respond to his touch, her back arching slightly as she turned her neck to smile feelingly at him. No, he thought, absolutely not.

"So," he said, once they'd found somewhere to balance their drinks. "What brings you to London?"

"Nothing really. A couple of appointments, shopping for bridesmaid dresses . . ."

"Oh!" Luke brightened, imagining that Charlotte was about to share a happy, I'm-totally-over-you announcement. "So, you're . . . ?"

"No!" She laughed. "Not me! My cousin Nicky—remember her, with the black hair? Really pretty?"

Luke shook his head. Charlotte had a large family, he remembered that much, an unfeasibly large family whom she talked about all the time, expecting him to remember not only names and relationships but also physical nuances and personality traits.

"Well, anyway, she's getting married in August and always-a-bridesmaid muggins here is going to be chief bridesmaid, which makes me feel about a hundred years old, and she keeps showing me all these *elegant column* dresses in, like, *oyster satin*. And I am not built for satin column dresses; I mean, you need to basically be a stick for that to work. And I am not a stick. I have bumps. And you know, when you get to my age, you know what suits you, don't you? So I thought before she goes out and spends all her money on something that'll basically make me look like, like . . . fruit in a condom, I'd better find something *I* like and try and talk her into it."

Good, thought Luke, this was good. Neutral. Clothes. He liked talking about clothes. "So," he said, "did you find anything?"

"Yeah," she said, "but it's designer. Mui Mui? Something like that. I took some photos in the changing rooms. Want to see?" She pulled her phone out of her bag and started searching through it with her thumb. "I thought maybe I could get someone to make it up for me, you know, on the cheap. Here." She passed the phone to Luke, watching him eagerly for his response.

His brow raised and he nodded, passed the phone back to her.

"What do you think?"

"I think," he said, "that if you wear that dress you will be in danger of upstaging the bride."

She laughed. "I knew you'd say that. I did worry. Maybe I could get it made up with a sheer panel across here"—she passed her hand across her décolletage—"to avert the eye. You know?" She peered at him, all china-blue eyes and soft skin and simmering, deep-seated love.

Luke swallowed some beer and nodded tersely. *No*, he told himself again. *No no no no no.* "Good idea," he said.

She tucked her phone back into her bag and picked up her pint glass. "So," she said, "what's the deal with the 'intervention?'"

The conversational dogleg took him by surprise. "Oh,"

he said. "Yeah. That. I don't know. I think Mum was getting sick of me. Thought I could be doing more with my life. And my dad probably thinks he should be getting more for all the money he spent on my education."

She nodded, as though there was something she wanted to say but didn't feel she could.

"Not quite sure that sitting in the bowels of my dad's office folding up paper all day is really much of an improvement on working in a clothes shop, but there you go. And maybe . . ." He paused, forming his next thought, wondering if he should share it with Charlotte, if it would unblock sealed-up conversational vaults, and then feeling an uncontrollable sensation of opening up and saying it anyway. "It was almost predestined, I think."

She arched an eyebrow.

"I found something, on my dad's computer. Some old e-mails. To Maya."

"Right."

"Yes. Abusive e-mails. Telling her that everyone hated her. That she was ugly."

Charlotte's eyes widened and she clapped her hand over her mouth. "What! No way! Oh my God. Who are they from?"

"Nobody knows. They're anonymous. But there's this girl . . ."

She dropped her hand from her mouth and stared at him, gripped.

"She was kind of stalking my dad for a while, and Pearl. Nothing sinister. Well, we didn't think so at the time. But now we're not so sure."

"Oh Jesus, Luke! That is just awful. I mean, why would someone do that to Maya? She was such a nice person."

"I know. It doesn't make any sense. Although, in a way, it does help make sense of her death. That it wasn't just this random act of madness. That there was something behind it."

"So you think the two things are connected then?"

"Well, yeah, definitely. The last e-mail was sent the day before she died. So yeah, I think it's pretty certain that the e-mails drove her to it."

"So, God, is that, like, *murder*?"

"I don't know. It should be. But I don't suppose it is. I mean, anyone could drive anyone to killing themselves, couldn't they, if they were brutal enough? Bullies do it all the time, don't they? School bullies. Cyberbullies. And you know, Maya, she was so . . ."

"Immature?"

Luke threw her a look. "No," he said, "I was going to say: soft. Decent. I can totally imagine how badly this would have affected her."

Charlotte nodded and Luke lowered his face towards hers when he realized that she was crying. "Hey," he said, "what's going on? Are you OK?"

"I'm sorry," she said, "it's just, I still feel so sad whenever I think about her. She was always so lovely to me. Had such a sweet way about her. And the thought of her . . . and that bus." She sniffed and rubbed away the tears from under her eyes. "What's going to happen?" she said. "About the e-mails? And the stalker?"

"No idea," said Luke. "My dad's taken his laptop in to the police; they're going to have a look at it. But if that doesn't help, I guess we need to track down this stalker woman. See if she's got anything to do with it."

"Weird," said Charlotte after a short break.

"I know," said Luke.

"Who would want to hurt Maya?"

"Exactly," said Luke, "exactly."

20

Dear Bitch

So you and Big Daddy are trying for a baby. Aw. That's so sweet. Except, Bitch, for the fact that Big Daddy already has some babies. Lots of babies. Had you noticed? He's got a really nice little baby called Beau. He's fucking adorable. And the others, OK, they're not quite so adorable, but they're still his babies. Do you know what it does to a family, every time a new baby comes along? Everyone has to shuffle along a bit; everyone has to change. Don't you think Big Daddy's family have done enough shuffling and changing? Don't you think Beau would like to stay the baby? Don't you think you've caused enough problems? Don't you think you should just back off? Actually, don't back off, fuck off. Seriously, Bitch. You're nothing. You're just a silly little girl. You've bitten off more than you can chew. How did you think you could ever be a real part of this family? Seriously? Look at your predecessors, real women, proper women. You look like a sickly child in comparison.

So, keep taking that pill, Bitch, because nobody wants your sad excuse for a baby coming into their world. NOBODY.

Maya selected and copied the foul text, pressed shift and delete to take the e-mail permanently off the server. Then she opened the little document she kept buried deep in the entrails of the computer system and pasted it onto the end. The secret document felt a bit like one of those sanitary disposal units they had in public toilets. Something you tried not to look at, or inspect or linger over, a dark receptacle of unthinkable grimness. She wasn't sure why she was keeping these words. Her overwhelming instinct was to banish them from the cosmos. But it seemed prudent to have something to prove that these e-mails really had been sent to her. Just in case she lost her mind. Or did something stupid. Because that was clearly the intent behind the e-mails. To drive her nuts. So far this person had made no suggestion that they wanted to harm her. The language used seemed very deliberately chosen to encourage her to harm herself. Or disappear. Or both.

Maya still hadn't told Adrian. He'd won a massive bid for a huge new housing and retail complex in St. Albans and was growing the practice again. He'd taken on three new architects and another floor of the new building in Farringdon. He was stressed and distracted.

To save herself from the unpalatable truth that these e-mails came from someone she knew, Maya had invented an imaginary poison e-mail scribe. She'd made her almost comical: a middle-aged woman, wearing a harlequin-patterned satin blouse, wonky orange lipstick and a fascinator. With a parrot or some other kind of crazy bird on her shoulder. Both of them cackling, maniacally, as she typed.

It helped.

A bit.

But this now, today, this was a sinister development. Mrs. Crazy Parrot Woman knew that she and Adrian were trying for a baby. How could that be possible? She got to her feet and went to make herself a cup of tea. Whom had they told? She made a mental list as she opened and closed cupboard doors, switched on the kettle, pulled two tea bags apart down a perforation. She'd told Cat. When they'd spent the night down at Susie's in Hove last weekend. Cat had squealed and jumped up and down and said: "Have a girl! Have a girl! Balance it out! Please!"

She'd told Holly at work. Holly and her husband had just started trying for a baby, too. She hadn't told her best friend, Sara, yet, because, well, because she knew she'd be funny about it. Sara was funny about anything Maya did that didn't involve her. Well, actually, Sara was just funny, full stop, one of those "best friends" that had gone kind of past their sell-by date, but you can't quite bring yourself to throw away. And she'd told Caroline, in a girly sharing of confidences over white wine last week, when Maya had been in town looking for a birthday present for Adrian. She'd looked entirely unsurprised and rubbed at the nibs of her elbows in that calm, unflappable way of hers. "Lovely," she'd said, "another baby. That will be lovely."

And that was it. She hadn't told another soul.

She dropped her tea bag into the bin and took her tea into the garden. Ten more days, she thought to herself, ten more days of summer holidays, then it was back to school. It had been a long, dull summer. Adrian at work all the time, the sun barely coming out, these stupid e-mails all the time. She missed the schoolgirls and the camaraderie of her colleagues. She missed having somewhere to go every morning. She missed coming home tired and drinking wine she felt she'd earned. She missed the gossip and the cookies and the sense of living for the weekends.

Her phone rang and she looked at it to see who was calling. It was him. She smiled, pressed answer, her mood lifting at the sound of his voice.

"Hello."

"Hello, you."

"I'm in London."

Maya felt a rush of happiness flood her senses. "Oh, thank God. I'm dying here. Can you come? Can you come now?"

"I'm on my way. I'll be there in half an hour."

She turned off her phone and rested it on the table in front of her, smiling softly.

21

JUNE 2012

Lives on 214 bus route

Kickboxing

Date with man called Matthew

Possible bag thief?

Lives / works near post office?

May be called Amanda (prob not)

London accent

30–40

Adrian wrote down each fact on a separate square of paper and moved them around his desk. He was hoping, somehow, to use his architect's ability to break a pretty picture down into literal nuts and bolts and then build it up into something three-dimensional and functional. On another piece of paper he sketched out a visual map:

Ally Pally

UPPER STREET Strada

        North Finchley <——214 Bus stop

                                       Post office

Community hall HIGHGATE   ARCHWAY My flat

SOUTH LONDON (Bag theft)

He spread the pieces of paper around the map, cupped his lower face inside his hand and studied it for a while. The most helpful clue was the 214 bus route. But that might have been a red herring. She might just have jumped onto the first bus she saw to get away from Cat. And living in that direction made it less likely that she would have found her way to the post office in Archway where Adrian had put up the card about the cat.

His phone rang and he picked it up. It was DI Mickelson.

"We've been through your laptop with a fine-toothed comb and I'm afraid, as we both suspected, there's nothing there. All trace of the e-mails has been removed. And we've looked into the e-mail address they came from. Unfortunately the address was used by someone with a dynamic IP address. In other words almost impossible to track down, though we can say for a fact that the e-mails were sent from the southeast region, i.e., anywhere between here and the south coast."

Adrian sighed, waiting for the DI to say something else, the good news, after the bad news. But he didn't. "So that's that?"

"Yes, it does look like it. I'm very sorry."

Adrian sighed again. "Well, thank you for trying."

"It was no problem, Mr. Wolfe. I know it's hard, not knowing, when you lose someone. It would have been nice to have shed some light."

"I wonder," said Adrian, "could I just ask you a quick question? About stolen phones?"

"Yeah, sure."

"Well, it turns out that that woman I told you about, the one who was kind of stalking us for a while, used a stolen phone to get in touch with me. A stolen phone, but with the original SIM card reinserted. Have you got any theories about that?"

He heard the DI draw in his breath. "Hm," he said, "that's an odd one. How do you know it was stolen?"

"I traced it to the woman it was stolen from. She works

at an estate agency. It was her work phone. Got stolen a few months ago. In south London."

"Right. Well, maybe when you come for your laptop you could drop the phone off. We could take a look at it for you."

Adrian groaned. "Too late for that. I gave it back to the woman it originally belonged to. She wanted it back in case her mum tried calling her on it."

"Any chance you could get it back?"

"I don't know." Adrian thought back to sour-faced Sian at the children's home, edgy Tiffany on the phone. "Probably not."

"Well, usually with a stolen phone, the SIM card is destroyed before it's sold on or recycled or whatever. Otherwise it's traceable. Plus, of course, the end user will be plagued by phone calls from the original user's mates. So it's very odd indeed. Let me have a think about it. I'll ask some questions."

"Thank you. Thank you so much. And I'll come after work, for my laptop, if that's OK?"

"Sure. I won't be here, but I'll leave it on the front desk for you."

Adrian looked back at the paper map on his desk after he finished his phone call. He held the piece of paper with "Lives/ works near post office?" against the post office area of his makeshift map with the tip of his forefinger, sliding it back and forth gently, agitatedly. And then he jumped slightly in his seat. Of course. He couldn't believe he hadn't already thought of it. Another card. He needed to put another card up.

He left work early, collected his laptop from the police station in Kentish Town and made it to the post office five minutes before closing time.

He took a blank card from the pile next to the community noticeboard and he wrote down the following announcement:

DESPERATELY SEEKING JANE

YOU LEFT YOUR PHONE DOWN THE BACK OF MY SOFA!

PLEASE CALL ME!

ADRIAN

(AND BILLIE)

22

Pearl threw herself across the ice for the fifth time, finally nailing the double axel that had been eluding her for the past ten minutes. She looked up at her trainer, Polly, who was smiling encouragingly at her from the edge of the rink, her hands clasped together in applause. Cat whistled through her fingers from the bleachers and held her thumbs aloft. Pearl had got it. At least, she felt as though she had; her body told her she had in every neurological pulse passing through it. But she still needed that assurance. She allowed herself a small smile and skated towards the exit, grabbing a towel and a bottle of water.

"Nice one, Pearl," said Polly, hugging her gently. "Well done. I knew you'd crack it today. That's brilliant. We'll build on it tomorrow, yeah?"

Pearl nodded, pulled herself out of Polly's embrace, conscious of being damp and smelly. She waved to Cat, who was standing in the bleachers a few rows back, her hands tucked into the high pockets of a zipped-up cardigan, chewing gum and smiling at her. Cat waved back, and they walked together to the changing rooms.

"Totally awesome, Pearl," said Cat, her big eyes wide with wonder. "I mean, I totally don't believe I can be related to you sometimes, you know. Seriously."

"Where's Mum?" said Pearl.

"She's going out tonight. Said she was going to have a bubble bath. Or something." Cat shrugged and sat down on a bench, passing Pearl her shoulder bag.

Pearl nodded. Bubble baths and weekly waxes and dinners out and taxicabs and new bras and blow-dries. All for Paul Wilson.

She sighed. Once upon a time bubble baths had been something that she and her mum did together. A treat. Like ice cream. "I know," her mum would say, "why don't we have a *bubble bath*?" And Pearl would climb in behind her mum and marvel at every nook and cranny of her mother's naked body, put foam peaks onto her own flat chest and say, "Look, I've got bigger boobies than you!," spill water down her mother's back and sponge it dry for her, with the heat rising around their heads, steam blooming on the bathroom mirror, the tap drip-dripping into the still water. Just her and her mum.

"What are we doing? Are we going home?"

"Yeah. Sure. Or we could go for tea? Somewhere cheap? McDonald's?"

"OK."

Pearl stuffed her damp training kit into her shoulder bag and changed into jeans and a tank top.

"It's cool outside," said Cat, passing over her hoodie.

Pearl braced herself as she let herself into the passenger side of her mum's car. Cat was the worst driver in the world. She drove way too close to parked cars, two millimeters away from snapping off wing mirrors everywhere she went. If Pearl took an intake of breath, Cat would say, "What! What!" and then drive too close to the cars coming the other way. She also set off on journeys she'd never undertaken before with no forward planning, and would stop in the middle of the road to look for road names or turnings with no awareness of the queue of traffic building behind her until they started to hoot, at which point she'd get really cross and start shouting and swearing. And she did that thing that people usually only do on the television of turning to look at Pearl whenever she was talking to her. Pearl tried to keep conversation to a minimum when she was in the car with Cat.

Cat took her phone out of her huge bag and called Otis. "Hi, honey, it's me. We're going to Maccy D's. Do you want a takeout?"

"Takeaway," hissed Pearl. "*Takeaway*." Pearl liked things said the proper English way. Her mum said she was about the most British person she knew.

Cat tucked the phone under her ear and began maneuvering the car out of its space, still talking to Otis about Big Macs and Pepsi Max. She hit the brakes quite violently as a pedestrian passed behind them and Pearl tutted. She sometimes thought her mother shouldn't let Cat drive her around. She sometimes thought it amounted to neglect. She tried to imagine how guilty her mum would feel if she got killed or maimed in a car crash while she was lying in a bubble bath on her own with the door shut thinking things about Paul Wilson.

Cat got Pearl to McDonald's without any misadventure befalling them and ten minutes later they sat face-to-face across a table. "So," said Cat, half a Big Mac disappearing into her big, red-lipsticked mouth in one bite, "I had lunch with Dad today."

Daddy, Pearl wanted to hiss. *He's not* Dad. *He's Daddy*.

"He's put a card up in the post office. *Desperately Seeking Jane*." She made the shape of a card with both hands and laughed. "Not that it's funny, though," she said, hurriedly. "But still, you know, what are the chances of her replying? She knows where Dad lives. If she'd wanted to get in touch, she'd have done it by now. And she certainly wouldn't have run away from me outside her kickboxing class." She shook her head and stuffed four chips into her mouth. "He also said he's spoken to the police. And they couldn't trace the e-mails. All they could tell him was that they'd been sent from somewhere between here and the south coast. So, not particularly helpful."

Pearl pulled the gherkin out of her burger and let it drop onto the wrapping like a surgical waste product. She wiped her fingertips on a paper napkin and slowly arranged the burger between her fingers. She didn't really like McDonald's, but her mum had said something this morning about sausages and she really didn't fancy sausages, especially if Cat was making them. She brought the flaccid burger to her lips and took a small bite. Cat had already finished hers and was casting her gaze about the restaurant, as if she was looking for someone.

"Who do you think wrote them?" said Cat, her fingers hovering above Pearl's chips.

"I think it was the woman," said Pearl. "Jane."

"Yeah, but—why?" Cat took three chips from Pearl's bag and held them halfway to her mouth while she talked. "Why the hell would some woman we don't know want to hurt Maya?"

"We don't know everything about Maya," said Pearl. "When you think about it, she could have been absolutely anybody."

Cat stared at her for a moment and then nodded. "Yeah, I guess. I mean, she did just kind of appear from nowhere, didn't she? One minute the lowly office temp, the next minute our new stepmother. And her mum and dad are kind of weird. Don't you think? I always thought that. And that spooky friend of hers. What was her name?"

"Sara."

"Yeah. Sara. She always hated Dad. Was kind of jealous of him, jealous of all of us. Might have been her, you know." She shuddered before eating Pearl's chips.

"Yes, but why would she send Maya the evil e-mails if it was Daddy she hated?"

"To get her away from him? To make her leave? I dunno."

Pearl shook her head and took another small mouthful

from her burger. "It's that woman. Jane. I know it was. She was just . . . not normal."

"She's very pretty though. Prettier than Maya."

"Pretty isn't everything, you know," said Pearl sharply. She dropped a screwed-up paper napkin on top of her half-eaten burger and turned her bag of fries around to face Cat. "You want these?" she said. "I'm full."

"How can you be full? You just did an hour and a half skating. You should be starving!"

"I had a sandwich before training. I'm not hungry."

"Oh Christ, Pearl, you're not going all anorexic, are you?"

Pearl tutted. As if.

"You know you've got the most perfect body, don't you? An athlete's body. I wish I'd been an athlete when I was young. You know they say muscles have a memory. So if you train your body well when you're young, it'll be easier to keep your shape when you're older. That would have been really useful for me . . ."

Pearl nodded. She honestly didn't care about bodies or muscles or eating disorders. There were girls in her class who talked about being skinny and being fat, but she couldn't see what the big deal was.

They got home ten minutes later, and Cat gave Otis his takeaway, which he unwrapped and ate at the kitchen table with his homework at his elbow. The doors were open from the kitchen onto the garden and Pearl could hear the sound of adult conversation drifting through. She poked her head around the door and saw her mum and Paul sitting side by side in the sun, a bottle of wine on the table to their right, glasses in their hands catching the golden light of the lowering sun. Mum was wearing a pale-gold knitted dress, cap sleeves, just above the knee. It was the same color as her hair and her earrings and her strappy sandals. She looked, for a moment, in that golden light, like a goddess. She looked almost too beautiful, and it hurt Pearl's eyes to look at her.

Paul Wilson was talking quietly, directly into her mum's ear. Pearl couldn't hear what he was saying. Then Pearl's mum threw her head back and laughed at something, clasped her long throat with one hand and caressed it. Paul looked delighted to have made her laugh like that and squeezed her knee with his hand. They looked like film stars. Pearl, with her sweat-drenched hair, old jeans, half a cheap burger swilling about in her stomach, felt like an urchin peering through the windows of a gilded palace. She was about to head back indoors when her mother noticed her and called her over.

"Hello, darling," she said, gesturing for her to join her, circling Pearl's hips inside her outstretched arm, pulling her tight towards her. "I'm really sorry I didn't come to collect you, Paul surprised me with a last-minute dinner invitation and we'd been rebuilding all day at work so I was filthy. Really needed a good soak."

"Hi, Pearl," said Paul, smiling his easy smile at her. "Had a good day?"

She shrugged. "It was OK."

"How's the skating?"

"It was good." She wanted to tell her mum about nailing the double axel but the golden dress and film-star aura put her off her stride. If her mum had been where she was supposed to be, standing in the kitchen, in jeans and a top, prodding sausages in a frying pan, covered in a light film of plaster dust and lint from the rebuild, she would have told her. She would have told her everything. But this version of her mum didn't look like she'd care about double axels.

"You've had supper?"

"I had a burger. At McDonald's."

"Oh," said Caroline. "Good!"

"It wasn't good," said Pearl. "It was crap."

Caroline laughed as if Pearl had said the funniest thing ever. "Oh my God," she said to Paul, "I've created middle-class monsters!"

"I'm not a monster."

Her mum laughed again. "No, of course not, darling. I was just teasing. Have you got any homework?"

Pearl sighed. "Yes," she said. "I think so."

"Maybe Cat could give you a hand with it." She turned to Paul. "We've got to go soon, haven't we?"

Paul consulted his mobile phone, glanced up at Pearl, gave her a strangely inquiring look and said, "Actually, we've got about twenty minutes. What homework is it?"

"Maths," she said, "and some literacy."

Paul smiled. "You can bring it out here if you like?" he said. "See if I can help you out?"

Pearl looked at her golden mum, inhaled the jasmine scent of her, glanced at her freshly painted toenails. "No," she said, "thank you."

"Are you sure?" he said, smiling. "I'm pretty sure I can still remember all that stuff."

"Go on," said her mum, and Pearl knew she was just saying it to make Paul happy. "You do your homework with Paul, and I'll go in and make you some sausages."

"What sort of sausages?"

"Chipolatas."

Pearl thought of her mum tying an apron around her luminous gold dress and making herself smell of sausage grease. And then she thought of being on her own out here with Paul. She liked Paul but she did not want to be on her own with him. And Cat was rubbish at homework. She didn't focus, kept picking up her smartphone and playing with it halfway through a sum. Pearl's head swam with conflicting desires. In the end she said nothing, just shook her head and went indoors.

"Pearl?" her mother called in her wake.

"I'm fine," she called back, exchanging a look with Otis. "Don't worry."

Cat had already gone upstairs to her room and Beau was at Dad's. The kitchen was clean and tidy. Coming home usually provided the perfect counterpoint to the chill and the ice and the closed-minded focus of her training sessions. But today there were no toys anywhere, no dirty pans, no warm rumble of roasting food coming from the oven, no half-unpacked carrier bags of shopping on the counter. She switched on the TV, and found herself a suitably raucous and brainless show on the Disney Channel. Then she tucked her hair neatly behind her ears, took a stack of Marmite rice cakes from a packet in the bread bin, peeled open the Velcro fastening of her schoolbag and pulled out her homework.

23

The thing about being the childless third wife, Maya had found, was that you were always asked to take the family group photos. As far as pecking orders went, it was one step up from being the waiter in the restaurant. Who else could they ask on the banks of a babbling brook in the middle of Cornish nowhere? Who was the least related, the least attached? Whose connection to the family carried the least weight? So once again it was Maya standing with Adrian's huge camera, encouraging small children into position, telling everyone to smile, saying, "Just one more, Beau was hidden behind Otis!"

She handed the camera back to Adrian, who checked the screen and smiled and said, "Lovely," and put his arm around Maya's shoulders, bringing her fully back into his world.

The cottage in Fowey had been a success. Thank God. Even Susie hadn't found anything to complain about. The children were all having a ball, including Pearl, who had her arm in a cast; she'd fractured it falling down the front steps at home and hadn't been training now for two weeks. It seemed to do her good, Maya observed; she seemed freer, younger, more available. It was as though being fussed over for her frailty had brought out another side of her to being fussed over for her achievements. Maya had noticed her spending more time on her parents' laps, taking hold of proffered hands more readily than she usually did. The *Empress*, that's what Maya called her.

At first she'd found Pearl's froideur quite intimidating. But now she found it endearing.

Beau appeared at her side as they walked across the golden shorn cornfield towards the car park. "Can a-carry, Maya?" She looked down at him and smiled. It had been a long walk for a little person and Caroline had refused to bring the buggy, despite its being one of those proper off-road monster buggies designed precisely for a walk like this. She assumed he'd already asked Caroline for a carry, but Caroline would have said no. She would have said, "You're a big boy now. You don't need to be carried anymore."

Maybe it was different when they were your own, Maya mused, or maybe once you got to the third child you just ran out of steam, but when Maya looked down at Beau, in his chunky-knit, stripy sweater, with his mop of brown curls, his round cheeks full of color, his feet strapped into miniature leather walking boots, all she could do was think: My goodness, *of course* I can a-carry, and then scooped him up into her arms and held him good and tight.

Caroline was already unlocking her car, several meters ahead. She was shouting something at Otis, who was slouching in her wake. Beautiful Otis. If only Maya could get to know him. She sensed a kindred spirit behind those soulful eyes. Even with their weekend visits and weekly one-on-one nights, there never seemed to be the time to get to know these children properly.

She put Beau down onto the graveled surface of the car park and pulled his sweater down at the back, where it had ridden up in her arms, her eyes lingering on the loveliness of the pale dip in the small of his back before covering it up and watching him dash towards Caroline.

"You've got a leaf," said Luke, coming up behind her, removing something from her jacket. "There." He let it fall to the ground and smiled.

"Oh," she said, "thank you."

He nodded at her, looking at her strangely but softly with those pale eyes of his.

Maya had been quite taken aback the first time she'd met Luke. He was not at all what she'd been expecting of Adrian's oldest son. Having met Cat before meeting Luke, she'd been expecting more of the same: a Brighton lad, maybe a bit rough and ready, a bit of banter, a bit of a spark. But he'd been nothing like that; dry and scathing, thin as a rake, hair in a quiff, he wore thick-framed glasses which turned out to have normal glass in them, fashion-student trendy. She'd thought he was gay at first. He'd looked Maya up and down from head to toe at their first meeting, leaving her feeling horribly lacking in her Dorothy Perkins floral top and rather elderly black jeans. She'd subconsciously made an extra effort to dress better the next time she'd met him and felt strangely triumphant when he'd looked at her with faint approval.

It turned out he wasn't gay. Far from it. She'd heard him talk in passing about this girlfriend and that girlfriend but it wasn't until eighteen months after she first met him that she saw any real evidence of a girlfriend. And Charlotte was the kind of girl who made men crazy. Small and curvy and blond and bright, she looked at you as though nobody else mattered, she laughed like a child, she smelled of green meadows and rose bowers, her eyes were blue as summer skies and she dressed as though getting dressed was a casual afterthought. *Oh, this old thing.* Maya quite liked her; she was funny and sweet and good for Luke but possibly not quite clever enough for him and possibly not quite tough enough. But still.

He hadn't invited her to Cornwall. He'd said she was too busy to take time off work. She was glad. It was nice to have him to herself. Because that was the funny thing. Of all of Adrian's children, somehow, bizarrely, quite unexpectedly, Luke was the one who Maya had grown the closest to. Over the summer holidays he had come to see her on his days off. They went shopping together. They chatted on the phone. For some reason there had grown between them a comradeship, as though they were on the same side of some unspoken divide.

Maya didn't talk to Adrian about this connection. She wasn't too sure why. She'd actually lied once or twice in the past, about where she was going and who she was going with, if she was meeting Luke in town for a drink, or shopping on a Friday afternoon.

But in her situation, and God it was a hard situation to be in sometimes, being the third wife, she needed someone she could let off steam to. She couldn't let off steam with Sara because Sara would just say, "Well, what did you expect, marrying a man with all that baggage?" She couldn't talk to the little ones, obviously, and Cat, well, Cat was just so bloody lovely and so convinced that everything was perfect, that everybody was overjoyed about everything. Maya couldn't bear to put a pin of realism to her big pink balloon of optimism. Nobody else knew the terrain she'd found herself in as well as Luke did. Nobody else got it like he did.

Caroline had the three little ones strapped into her big black Audi station wagon, two dirty dogs peering through the back window, and was leading the way back to the cottage. Maya was in the back of Susie's little car with Luke. Adrian and Susie sat up front. She turned to Luke and smiled. "The kids," she said, referring to their configuration.

Luke smiled back at her. He was wearing his Sarah Lund sweater, with the collar of a pink shirt peeking over the neck, skinny jeans and brogues. His shoulders were slightly hunched over, to stop the top of his head banging on the roof of the tiny car. "Big kids," he said. "Horribly mutated, overgrown kids."

Maya grinned and stared at the backs of Adrian's and

Susie's heads, at the graying hairs and the runneled, cross-hatched skin. *Mum and Dad*. Then she glanced across at Luke's hands spread out beside him on the grubby, fabric-covered seats: young hands, soft-skinned, untouched.

She felt an urge to reach out, to cover his hand with hers.

She turned her head abruptly, fixed her gaze instead upon the moving scenery, at the big gold sun hovering above the horizon, at the closing moments of a perfect autumn day playing out like a symphony.

24

Luke cut into his ham and prosciutto pizza and eyed his brother's mountain of spaghetti carbonara. "Are you going to eat all that?"

"Probably not," said Otis.

Luke stared at the top of his head as Otis brought his mouth down to the bowl and slurped up a big mouthful of spaghetti. *His little brother.*

As arranged by his father he'd met Otis from school at four thirty, after a club of some description. He'd been talking to a girl, about his age. Not on a par with Otis, looks wise, but nice enough. From across the road he'd watched them say good-bye to each other. She was definitely more into him than he was into her. Her gaze had lingered on him desperately for a moment after their farewell.

Otis had been expecting him, greeted him shyly. Luke had felt shy too, not sure what to say to a twelve-year-old boy. They hadn't talked much, just fragments of dead-end conversation.

"Is that good?" Luke asked as Otis's head appeared again, his mouth ringed with Parmesan and sauce.

Otis nodded and reached for his Coke. "Do you want to try some?"

"No," said Luke. "You're all right."

"Are you sure? It's really good."

"No, honestly. You eat it. I've got plenty."

Otis nodded again and dug his fork back into the pasta.

"So, Dad brings you here a lot, does he?"

"Uh-huh."

"How do you feel about it all? You know, your nights at Dad's? Is it good?"

"Yeah," said Otis. "I like it. It was Maya's idea."

"Yes," said Luke, drily. "Like all the good ideas." They continued to eat in silence for a moment. "Do you miss her? Maya?"

Otis shrugged. "Sort of. Kind of half and half. You know."

"What do you mean, half and half?"

"I don't know. It was just like, basically, some things were better when Maya was around. And some things were worse. And obviously it was Maya who broke everything in the first place, so, you know . . ."

Luke looked at Otis in surprise. "Broke everything?"

"Yeah. Spoiled everything. Made Dad leave. So it kind of didn't matter how nice she was, really."

"Huh," Luke exclaimed. "That's interesting."

"Why is it interesting?" Otis coiled another bunch of spaghetti around his fork and put the whole oversized thing into his mouth.

Luke cut a neat square out of his pizza and prodded it with his fork. He could sense he was walking a delicate line with Otis, talking like this, and he didn't want to startle him into recalcitrance. "Oh, nothing really. I guess I just thought that you three were all fine about everything. You all seemed so cool when it happened."

Otis nodded and then looked up at Luke, making proper eye contact, and said, "Well, you know, we were really young. I guess we didn't really know how we felt back then. I guess, when you're little like that, you think you might wake up and it was all a dream. And it's only when the days go by and you wake up every morning and it's not a dream that you start to realize what really happened. And by then it's too late."

Luke stared at his brother for a moment, leaving him space to breathe.

"What about you?" said Otis eventually. "What was it like for you?"

Luke swallowed a mouthful, exhaled. "God, it was so long ago. It feels like another lifetime. But yeah, I suppose I felt a bit like you, like it was a bad dream, a bit like I must have done something wrong to make Dad go away, a bit like your mum was a good thing because she made my dad happy, and a bad thing because she took him away from us. I suppose I felt all sorts of things."

"And what do you feel like now? Now that you're grown-up?"

Luke wondered if he should lie, but then he looked at his brother and saw all the things he hadn't really noticed because he hadn't been looking: the new shape of his nose, no longer a formless protrusion but now taking on the substance of both his parents' noses. The hollows in his cheeks and the line of pimples around his jawline. The vaguely triangular heft of his torso and the size of his hands, almost as big as his own. He was half man, more than half.

"To be honest, I still feel angry," said Luke. "I still think he shouldn't have left us. That he let us down. But it's hard with Dad. Because he's so nice. So you kind of look around for someone else to blame. And I blamed my mum for ages. And then I blamed you lot."

"Us?" said Otis, his dark eyebrows rising in alarm. "You mean us children?"

"Yes. I know it's ridiculous. But I suppose I thought if he hadn't had all these other children then he might come back to us. And it all seemed so unfair, you know, when we came to stay, that we were the ones who had to go home at the end of the weekend and you all got to stay. With Dad. Not to mention the fact that you were all there in that amazing house, right in the middle of London. It was like you were all part of this beautiful fantasy world. And we were the poor relations."

"Do you still blame us?" said Otis, his eyes never leaving Luke's.

"No," said Luke. "Well, let's put it this way. I *try* not to. I *shouldn't*. Because obviously it's not your fault. But sometimes I still feel—" Luke stopped, pulled himself up short. "No," he said after a pause, "no. I don't blame you. No."

Otis nodded and turned his attention back to his food.

"So what was that all about then?" said Luke a moment later. "The other day? Bunking off school? Sitting on a bench? Was it anything to do with that girl?" He tried for playful but his tone came out interrogational.

"What girl?" Otis looked shocked; his spoon banged loudly against the rim of his bowl.

"That girl I saw you talking to just now, after school?"

"What?" Otis looked confused.

"Brown hair up in a bun, nice legs."

Otis wrinkled his brow. "Sienna?"

Luke laughed. "I don't know what her name was, but she looked like she was very into you."

Otis groaned, recognition dawning. "No," he said, "definitely not her."

"So? What was it then?"

"What was what?"

"You. Bunking off. If it wasn't that girl, then what was it?"

Otis prodded his fork into the batons of ham embedded in his pasta sauce, quite crossly. "It wasn't anything. It was just . . . I didn't feel like going into school."

"Dad says you're doing really well at school though?"

"Yes, well, I am. But that doesn't mean I want to be there, like, *all the time*."

"And you've got good friends?"

Otis stabbed more ham batons with his fork, his mouth set into a hard rectangle, and Luke could tell he was losing him. "I guess."

Luke sighed, put down his cutlery. "Listen, Otis," he said, "I know I've been a bit of a shit brother, especially since Maya died. I know we've kind of lost touch with each other. But I'm here now. I'm around. So, you know, you can talk to me. If you need to. I mean, we can do this again"—he gestured at the table and the restaurant—"whenever you like."

Otis raised his shoulders and made an unintelligible noise that sounded almost like an expression of interest. "'K," he said. Then he shoveled the remains of his pasta into a pile at the far end of the bowl with the back of his fork, leaned back in his chair and said, "Luke? Who do you think wrote those e-mails to Maya?"

Luke started. He hadn't known that Otis knew about the e-mails. "I have no idea," he said. "Some sicko."

"Do you think . . ." Otis began, then paused. "Do you think it was someone we know?"

"No," said Luke, "definitely not." He looked at the floor, not wanting Otis to see the doubt in his eyes. "Definitely not."

25

It was Adrian's weekend at the Islington house, but he'd come a night early so that they could all watch the Olympics opening ceremony together.

The whole family sat in front of the flat-screen TV, transfixed. Adrian, Pearl, Otis and Beau were stretched out across the big sofa, Cat was curled up in one armchair, Caroline was in the other with a dog on her lap. Luke sat on the floor, cross-legged, nursing a gin and tonic.

It occurred to Adrian that if Maya had still been alive, he'd have been at home with her right now, in his little flat, just the two of them. Luke and Cat would still have been in Hove. And Caroline would have been here alone with her three children. It pained Adrian to contemplate the possibility that Maya's death might have improved his situation, but sitting here right now, on a gray summer's evening, watching one of the most extraordinary televisual events of his lifetime with all his people gathered around him, he did wonder again why on earth he'd ever thought there was greater joy to be taken from life than this. And as the real, three-dimensional actuality of Maya faded from his consciousness with the passage of time, he was left with an unsettling sense of having spent the past few years on a diversion from his real life. As if Maya had been a dream holiday and now he was home.

"Why are they all dressed as nurses?" said Beau, turning to look up at Adrian. "And what's that big white baby for?"

Adrian smiled and stroked his hair. "I think it's supposed to represent the National Health Service."

"Why?"

"Because it's a very British thing. We all pay taxes so that if we get ill, we can go to the doctor or the hospital and be looked after. And it's free. In some other countries you have to pay to go to the hospital."

"It's weird," said Otis, staring at the screen. "It's just really weird. I don't get it."

"It is kind of off-the-wall," Adrian agreed.

"What does off-the-wall mean?" said Beau.

"It means—" started Adrian.

"It means weird," Otis cut in.

"Can't imagine what the rest of the world is making of this. They must think we're all nuts," said Caroline.

"We *are* all nuts," said Cat.

"Speak for yourself," said Luke. "I honestly think this is one of the most amazing things I have ever seen in my life."

Adrian smiled at his oldest child, at the rare delight of a shared opinion.

"I'm going to the toilet," said Adrian, getting to his feet. "Anyone want anything?"

Luke waved his empty glass at him without turning round and Adrian snatched it from him with a groan. "I need the toilet, too," said Beau. "Can I come with you?"

"Sure." He put out his hand for his boy and headed towards the downstairs toilet.

"Not that one," said Beau, tugging him back to the hallway. "Upstairs," he said. "Mummy's toilet."

"Er, why?" said Adrian.

"Because it hasn't got *spiders* in it. That one"—he pointed down the hallway—"has spiders in it."

"Oh, come on, buddy," said Adrian, who really couldn't be

bothered walking up the stairs. "I'll deal with the spiders, let's use this one."

"No!" cried Beau.

And Adrian, being a soft touch, especially where his youngest child was concerned, sighed and said, "OK, then, lead the way."

Caroline's en-suite was another of Adrian's indelible marks on this house. It had been a small bedroom when they bought the house; Caroline had wanted to put a baby in there but Adrian had insisted on knocking an opening through from the bedroom, and turning it into a massive luxury bathroom, with twin basins, twin showerheads, a double-ended bath. It had been designed totally, entirely, for him and Caroline to use as a couple. His and hers. And now there was just her. He sat on a linen box and watched his son pee, his little white bum cheeks clenched together, the sloped arch of his back, the concentrated focus on the toilet bowl.

His baby boy.

Adrian dropped his chin into his chest, suddenly subsumed by a wave of emotion.

If Maya had got pregnant over those months and months of trying, April 19 would not have happened. On April 19, 2011, Maya would have been at home, sober, stroking her swollen belly, or in bed, feeding her newborn baby. She would not have been careering around the West End with a belly full of vodka, seeking oblivion. And if Maya had had a baby, Beau wouldn't be his baby anymore; there would have been another baby. Another family. And that would have made everything legitimate. Because without the baby, without the new family, Adrian was just a selfish twat, abandoning a house full of children for the joys of lie-ins and loud sex with a woman with no stretch marks. Is that what it would have been? If Maya had lived? And never got pregnant? Just the two of them, getting older and older (particularly him), more and more set in their ways? While Caroline and Susie brought up his children for him?

Adrian sighed and then smiled as Beau turned to face him. "Wash your hands, baby," he said, and Beau, good, biddable, sweet Beau, smiled and nodded and washed his hands. Could he and Maya have made a better baby than this one? he pondered. He doubted it.

Adrian got to his feet and, feeling suddenly heavy with tiredness, sat on the toilet to pee. Beau dried his hands carefully on a hand towel and then turned and watched his dad. "Do you think we'll win?" he said.

Adrian blinked at him. "What?"

"The Olympics. Do you think we'll win them?"

"Well, you know, there's lots of events. We're bound to win something."

"Will there be skating?"

"No, not in the summer Olympics. They do skating in a separate winter Olympics."

"Pearl should be there then. She's the best skater in the world."

Adrian nodded. "That's true," he said, "she is. But she's a bit young still. Maybe one day."

"I'm going now," said Beau, suddenly bouncing to his feet. "I don't want to miss the skating."

"I don't think there's going to be any . . ." But Beau had already left the room, his small feet banging down the stairs two at a time.

Adrian dropped his head and stared into the lines of mortar between the tiles.

He couldn't bear it anymore. He needed to know. He needed to know who had sent those e-mails. He needed to know what all those murky allusions were about. He needed to know what was going through Maya's mind on April 19.

And he needed to know what the intriguing woman with the mismatched eyes had to do with everything. Because without answers he was lost, suspended halfway between grief and hope for the future, between guilt and absolution, between the beginning and the end.

He got to his feet and washed his hands, using, through sheer ground-in habit, *his* washbasin. He gazed at himself in the mirror, remembering the fuss he'd made of himself back in March when Jane was due to visit, the creams and the shampoos and the fresh green shirt. He hadn't looked at himself like that in the mirror again since. He'd lost interest. He pulled open a cabinet door, looking for a tube of something greasy to brighten up his skin, to imbue him with some of the same golden glow that emanated from Caroline these days. If he couldn't find it through having sex with someone five years younger than him, then maybe he could find it in Caroline's bathroom cabinet.

But instead of some miracle elixir, he found instead all the artillery of a woman in search of her next baby. Ovulation-testing sticks. Pregnancy-testing sticks. Folic acid. Black cohosh capsules.

He closed the door of the cabinet quietly and turned and left the bathroom, feeling faintly nauseous. And then he stood for a while in Caroline's bedroom, staring at the crumpled duvet cover, the loose arrangement of cushions, the fat feather pillows, imagining Caroline there, tall and strong and naked, with Paul Wilson. Trying to make a baby. Did Paul Wilson even know Caroline was trying to make a baby with him? Did he even know how old she was?

He thought with an ache of standing right here in years gone by, when this was his home, when Caroline was his wife, watching her breast-feeding first Pearl, then Beau, in that very bed. His bed. *Their bed*. And now she might have another baby to feed upon those pillows. A baby that had not come from him. A baby that was not fully related to his own children. An alien, other baby. He could not, absolutely *could not* imagine such a thing. It seemed beyond the laws of nature.

But, he thought, he was the one who'd created this vacuum in their family, who'd given this possibility the air to breathe. If this happened, he thought, it was of his own doing.

He pulled the door shut, went to the kitchen to make Luke another G and T and reentered the living room just in time to see the queen being helicoptered into the Olympic arena.

26

Maya tried not to question too deeply the fact that Luke had arranged to come to London on the first night of Adrian's business trip to Lithuania. There'd been a lot of discussion about the trip when they'd been in Cornwall in October. Adrian had been excited about it. A social housing seminar at which he was to be one of the keynote speakers. He'd spent a few hours in the cottage finessing his speech, showing his family photos on his phone of the amazing five-star hotel he'd be staying at. Telling everyone what a shame it was that Maya had to work, otherwise she could have come with him. It would have been hard for anyone in their party not to have picked up on the fact that Adrian was going away.

"I can meet you from school," Luke's text had said. "Take you to the Flask?"

She said yes. Of course she said yes. He was her friend. He was her stepson. They were *related*. Why would she say no? She didn't ask him why he was in London. She didn't ask him how long he was staying. She didn't ask him where he would be sleeping.

He was waiting for her, as arranged, on a bench outside the school on Highgate Hill. He was wearing another one of his Sarah Lund jumpers under a waxed jacket, narrow red trousers, black-framed glasses; his hair was in a quiff. If she hadn't known him—she allowed herself the thought briefly—she might have wondered who the lovely man on the bench was.

He looked her up and down as she approached, in that way he had. The way that made you desperately want his approval. She'd worn a pencil skirt today, dark green boiled cotton, with a mustard lambswool sweater with a cream lace collar, and tweed kitten-heeled shoes. Her hair was in a bun and she had on her reading glasses. Very schoolmarm. Very *him*. She'd tried to persuade herself that it was subconscious when she was choosing her outfit this morning.

"Hi!" Her voice came out high-pitched in her effort to sound breezy and stepmotherly.

He greeted her with two firm kisses, one on each cheek; she could feel the full imprint of his lips against her skin. "You look great," he said, eyeing her up and down again. "Like a real schoolteacher. In a good way." He smiled.

The day was dark already, the gnarled Victorian streetlights throwing amber apparitions into the light mist. Luke followed Maya's lead up the High Street, past tiny, bowed shop fronts, chichi boutiques, pinkly glowing cake shops, and down a dark lane towards a small green.

"I came here a couple of times when I was younger," said Luke as they approached the ancient pub.

"Really?" said Maya. "How come?"

"Oh, I had a girlfriend from Highgate. Ages ago, when I was a teenager. She was the sister of one of the guys in my year. She used to bring me here when I came to see her. We'd sit in a big smug row with all her rich smug north London friends. Like we were all that mattered in the world." He held the door open for her and they both bent their heads to duck the low beam. "I think," he continued, "if I'm honest, I was jealous of her, of all of them. A little bit."

Inside the pub was a rabbit warren of tiny rooms with low, nicotine-stained ceilings, sloping floors and rickety steps leading from area to area. They took a bottle of wine and two glasses to a small candlelit table hidden away behind a wall by the front window and sat side by side on a small settle. Maya stared at the tabletop as Luke poured the wine for them. She could not have poured wine; her hands were shaking.

Again she tried not to question herself, tried not to think too much about the situation. Luke was only just twenty-two. He was her stepson. So why—she tried her hardest to ignore the obvious question—were her hands shaking? Instead she thought about Charlotte, beautiful, young, blond Charlotte, with her doe eyes and her breathy voice and her particular way of filling out a simple jersey dress. She thought about Luke's hands on that body, Luke's mouth on that mouth, and she felt herself relaxing. This was fine. This was nothing.

"How are you getting along," said Luke, "home alone? Are you missing the old fart?"

Maya laughed. "Actually, yes, I really am." Adrian had left the day before, after dropping all the kids back at Caroline's. Normally on a Sunday night she and Adrian would watch a movie together, eat toast for supper, go to bed early. With the children around most of the week it was a rare night alone. But the flat had felt stark without Adrian; Maya had felt lost and slightly anxious and been glad to wake up this morning and head into work. "It's weird when he's not there."

"Yes," said Luke, stretching an arm across the back of the settle so that his fingertips hung loosely near Maya's chin. "I know the feeling."

Maya smiled uncertainly. Luke was never scared to let Maya know how it had felt for him, the years of hurt and disappointment wrought by his father's incorrigibility.

"When's he back?"

"Thursday," said Maya, aware of a certain breathlessness to her voice. She drank fast, wanting to feel different as soon as possible.

Luke nodded. "Will you be all right?" he said. "I could . . . I mean, I'm kind of between jobs, I think I told you." He threw her a slightly embarrassed look. "Sort of. Well, let's put it this way, I could stay in London for a few days and, truly, no one would really notice. Or care."

Maya cocked her head at him and smiled. "Erm, I think maybe Charlotte might."

"Charlotte Schmarlotte," said Luke. "It's got nothing to do with her." There was an edge to his voice that took Maya by surprise. He softened it with a smile. "Look, I only really see Charlotte at the weekends anyway so it's not as if she'd miss me." He shrugged. "It's just a thought. If you felt you needed the company. The big strong man in the house to see off all the burglars and the rapists. You know. It's up to you. Just—" he spread his hand over the table as if fanning paper, "putting it out there."

"Well, thank you. That's really sweet of you. I'll think about it."

Luke nodded at her and gave her a small smile. "Look," he said, pointing his chin over the top of his wineglass, his eyes focusing on a point on the other side of their small room. Maya followed his gaze. A procession of teenagers was filing through the room, all scruffy checked shirts, bird's nest hair, scuffed deck shoes, mustard trousers and ripped denim hot pants, clutching wineglasses and pints and mobile phones, shouting loudly to each other, as if trying to be heard over building works. "Nothing changes," he said. "All the north London poshies. In their Jack Wills finest. Shouting so the world knows they've arrived."

Maya smiled. She recognized the breed. She taught these young adults in the very early stages of their evolution. "So, are you still jealous of them, Luke?" she asked teasingly.

She expected him to laugh and pooh-pooh the suggestion

but instead he shrugged and said, "Yeah. A bit. I guess." His fingers played with bumps of melted wax on the candlestick.

"Really? But why?"

"I don't know," he sighed. "I suppose they're all . . . they're just . . . they don't know, do they? They don't know how it all turns out." There was a note of desperation in his voice. Maya looked at him, concerned.

"You know, they're all wrapped up in private school cotton wool, they're all bouncy and nurtured and they think it's all going to be this golden bloody staircase to the stars. And they shout to be heard because they think the world is always going to want to listen. And then if you're, you know, just a normal kid, if there's no rich mummy or daddy, nobody to buy you a flat or get you a job, five minutes later you're working in a clothes shop and five minutes after that you're not even working in a clothes shop anymore. And you've got nothing. Just a warped sense of entitlement and a posh accent. You've got no"—he turned his gaze from the blobs of wax he'd dropped onto the table and towards Maya—"*integrity*."

Maya didn't say anything at first. She was slightly shell-shocked. She'd always known that it had been a matter of some controversy that Luke had had a private education when none of Adrian's other children had. It was widely held to be a terrible mistake on Adrian's part. How could he? Such an injustice. Maya knew that Cat in particular found it galling. And now here was Luke telling her that he hadn't actually benefited from it in the least.

"Don't you think," she began carefully, "that life is what you make it?"

"Yes, yes, of course I do. I'm just saying that private school gives you a false sense of what real life might be like. If you don't live in a castle. If your dad buggers off and spreads himself so thin financially that there's no contingency. If you're just, you know, *normal*." He shrugged. "Could I sound like more of a loser?"

Maya laughed. "Oh, Luke, you're not a loser. You're a . . ." She put her hand out to touch his, but then retracted it, and the comment that was to accompany the gesture. "I just think that life is what you make it. Nobody owes you anything. That's what I believe."

"So, what about you? What kind of school did you go to?"

"Local comp," she said. "In Maidstone. Rough as shit."

"And now look at you. Teaching the fine young ladies of Highgate village."

"I know," she said. "Exactly my point."

He smiled and eyed her affectionately. Maya felt her stomach roll gently. His gaze was unflinching and full of secret, fascinating thoughts.

"What?" she said, smiling, knowing as she said it that she was inviting an escalation in the intimacy of their rapport.

He had a small dimple to the left side of his mouth. It only appeared when his smile was on full power. It was there now as he turned himself round towards her and said, "Nothing. Just . . ." He dropped his gaze. "Do you ever . . . ?"

The teenagers in the next room were all talking at the same time. The noise was alarming, overbearing. Shrieks of laughter, competitive shouting.

"What was it," he said, shifting his body language, changing tack, "about my dad? When you met him? What was it?"

Maya exhaled. "Well, nothing at first, I guess. I mean, he was just the boss. I didn't see him in that way at all." Her eyes misted over as she remembered. "I used to go home and tell my flatmate that he was the nicest boss I'd ever had. And as the days went by I suppose I just got to know him better and better and then one day I saw him walking into the office ahead of me and he was wearing this long gray overcoat and his hair was being blown about by the wind, and he stopped for just a moment, like this"—she angled her face into the air—"and the wind was wild, buffeting him about and he just closed his eyes and he smiled. He stood like that for about ten seconds, just, you know, *loving* the wind. And my heart kind of went flop. I thought, If he can love the wind, what else does he love?"

She looked at Luke, expecting a derisive laugh, a mocking sneer, but he simply nodded.

"And after that I started noticing other things about him. The way he spoke to people on the phone, always with respect, even cold callers. How he always held doors for people. Returned smiles. Left meetings to deal with his children in good grace. And believe me, I'd worked in a lot of offices before I worked with your dad, I've had a *lot* of bosses. That kind of stuff, it's rare."

He nodded again. "So you fell in love with him because he liked wind and holding doors open for people."

She laughed. "Yeah. Basically."

"I like snow," he said. "I like carrying prams upstairs for stressed-out mums. Why don't women like you go around falling in love with me?"

He was teasing. But still. There was something else there. "Women like me *do* fall in love with you. I believe there is one in Hove in that state as we sit here."

"She's not like you."

This was said abruptly. Almost sharply.

She blinked and stared at her fingers where they circled the stem of her wineglass. "She's beautiful," Maya said quietly.

"So what? How shallow do you think I am?"

"She's also really lovely."

He sighed, as though she were totally missing the point. "Yeah," he said after a moment. "Yes. She's lovely." It was a concession, that was obvious. Not what he really thought.

Two of the teenagers had left the next room and were sitting side by side in a cubby opposite. A boy and a girl, involved in a theatrically intense conversation. She was listening to him with wide eyes, stabbing the ice cubes in a glass of Coke with the end of her straw, then running her fingers through her thatch of uncombed hair. He said something deep into her ear and she laughed and as she laughed his arm came around her and pulled her into him, bringing her face straight against his mouth. There followed a prolonged and intense bout of French kissing, their chests pressed together, his hand pushed hard into the small of her back.

Luke and Maya watched, momentarily mesmerized, then they looked at each other.

"*Get a room,*" Luke muttered under his breath, and they both laughed nervously.

The interruption was Maya's cue to turn the conversation around onto neutral territory. But she couldn't help herself. It was something to do with those teenagers. So raw and underdeveloped. And here she was, thirty-two years old. Married to an older man. A stepmother. Trying to get pregnant. Yet *that*, that ridiculous, messy, glorious, overblown time of her life when a week felt like a month and boys put their tongues in her mouth for barely any reason at all, when she was touched and squeezed and ogled and used, when she held men in places she didn't want to hold them, wore clothes with holes in them and broke people's hearts as easily as dropping glasses, felt suddenly as if it was only yesterday. Was it really all over? Forever? She experienced a sickening swell of nostalgia and turned to Luke, seeing him suddenly as a man of her own age rather than her decade-younger stepson. "Who's your ideal woman, then?" she said, pulling the wine bottle out of the bucket and topping up their glasses to mask her nerves. "If it's not beautiful, lovely Charlotte?"

She watched a dozen thoughts come and go through Luke's mind. His strange pale eyes flickered slightly. He picked up his wineglass and then put it down again.

"You," he said. "Basically." He shrugged defensively.

She laughed, even though she'd almost expected him to say it. "Don't be silly," she said. "I'm old enough to be your—"

"Well, no, you're not," he cut in as though he'd already thought the whole thing through. "Not even nearly."

"Well." Maya put a hand to her throat, which had grown suddenly red and itchy. "Old enough to be your stepmother."

"Yeah." He ground the base of his wineglass against the tabletop. "That's for sure."

The teenagers had separated and were now caressing each other's hands and talking to each other in a seamless stream, their eyes locked together. It occurred to Maya that probably neither of them would even remember this night, this moment, this corner of the Flask that had once been the site of such fevered passion. They might not even remember each other's names. They certainly wouldn't remember the feel, the smell, the precise sensation of themselves, right here, right now. She felt another wave of sickness, felt again the need to catch hold of herself, to pin herself down into her own moment.

"I think you'll be an amazing husband to someone one day," she said. It was bullshit, but she needed to say something.

"Yeah," he said sadly. "Yeah." Then he turned towards her, very fast, and said, "Do you think you'll stay with him forever?"

"Adrian?"

"Yes. Adrian. Of course."

There was only one answer. "Of course I will," she said. "I love him."

He nodded. And suddenly his body language became

fraught with something tender and desperate. Almost as though he was about to cry.

The boy across the way had his fingers threaded up through the underside of his girlfriend's hair, his thumb rubbing against the skin at the back of her neck. She leaned into his touch and smiled and then blinked at him, slowly, catlike. Maya held back a groan of longing and despair and almost unthinkingly, comfortingly, put a hand over Luke's. His other hand immediately came down upon hers and then he caught her gaze with his, those eyes fixed onto hers, and Maya felt her heart pulse and burn with panic and watched his face come closer and closer to hers and she thought, I want this. Please let me have it. His lips came down upon hers and for one exquisite moment they were kissing each other and it was raw and teenage and damp and crazed and had nothing whatsoever to do with Adrian.

It lasted for all of six seconds, until Maya fought her way out of the moment and back into her real life.

"Christ," she said, holding him back with a hand against his chest, where she could feel his heart banging hard. "No. Oh God. No, Luke!"

She turned it into his fault. She had to. She wanted to apologize but she couldn't.

He pulled back from her, his fingertips over his lips. "I'm sorry," he said. He clutched the back of his neck and moved away from her. "I am so sorry. I don't—"

"It's OK. Luke. It's OK. Just don't—"

"No. Shit. It's not OK. That was . . . I'm such a twat. Christ. I can't believe—"

"Luke. Stop it. It's fine."

"Please." He gripped her hand. "Please don't tell anyone. What I did. Please."

She shook her head. "Of course . . ."

"Don't tell my dad."

"My God. No."

He let his head fall down onto her hand, rubbed his forehead back and forwards against her skin. She looked down into the youthful thickness of his hair and softly rested her other hand against it. She wanted to rake her fingers through it, feel it part beneath her touch. She wanted him to lift up his head and kiss her again. But for now, they sat like this, him prostrated against her while she stroked his hair and stared sadly through the window at the misty, sodium-stained Highgate night.

27

JULY 2012

Adrian let the curtain drop at the sound of Caroline's footsteps up the front stairs. He'd just watched Paul Wilson kissing his ex-wife in the front seat of his white minivan (it turned out that Paul Wilson was a purveyor of organic mushrooms and truffles, making him possibly the most Islington person in the borough of Islington. His van said "Shrooooom!" in diminishing typeface on the back doors) for approximately ten minutes. As if the entire preceding weekend hadn't given them both ample time for such things.

He heard the children upstairs stampeding to the door to greet their mother, and the dogs skidding about on the tiled floor in their desperation to see her face. As though she'd been gone for weeks, not since yesterday morning. Caroline appeared at the door of the sitting room a moment later holding a writhing dog and a wodge of mail, looking entirely like a woman who'd been having sex for thirty-six hours. Her lips were engorged and tender, her hair voluminous, her blue eyes burning bright as a hot summer sky. *Are you ovulating by any chance?* he wanted to ask.

As Much Sperm as Possible.

That had always been her mantra when they were trying to conceive. None of this timing it to the precise moment of the egg floating away from its moorings. Just quick and often.

"Hello," she said, dropping the dog and examining the letters in her hand. "Good weekend?"

"Yes," he said brightly. "Really, really good weekend."

She sat on the sofa and removed her sandals. Beau came in holding a certificate he'd been given that morning at a science show at the Business Design Center. "I made a firework," he said, climbing onto Caroline's lap and letting her look at his certificate. She peered at it over Beau's shoulder, pointing and making the appropriate parental noises. Adrian watched from the armchair. He imagined her sitting there, bursting at the seams with Paul Wilson's thirtysomething sperm.

Christ, he thought, is this what it was like when he and Maya had been trying to get pregnant? Is this what it felt like for the rest of them? He'd always assumed everyone would be delighted. A new brother! Or sister! A brilliant new addition to the large and wonderful family he'd brought into being. And everyone had seemed delighted. Cat in particular. At the time. But thinking of the venom in those e-mails from the mysterious poison penman or -woman, had the whole venture actually been shrouded in ill will and unhappiness? Had it upset Caroline? Susie? The little ones? He tried to remember what the others had said about it. But he couldn't. Is it possible, he wondered now, that he hadn't asked them? Hadn't discussed it?

"Miserable bloody weather," said Caroline, eyeing one of the letters cursorily and then sliding it back into its envelope. "Honestly, I can't remember a more depressing July. Makes me want to emigrate."

"What's emigrate?" said Beau.

"It means going to live in another country," said Adrian.

"I don't want to emigrate."

Caroline smiled and squeezed him. "We're not going to," she said. "Don't you worry. Did you watch the rowing?" she asked, addressing Adrian.

"No," he said, "no. Was it good?" He didn't care about the rowing. He imagined the rowing as having been a brief between-shag breather, watched in bed from under rumpled, sex-soaked sheets.

"Amazing," she said, "all those giant men. Backs like wardrobes." Her eyes glinted with lust.

"Can I . . . ," Adrian began. "Could we maybe meet up for a drink next week? Just the two of us?"

Caroline blinked at him. "Er, yeah, sure. I'll have to check with Cat, when she's in . . ."

"Or Luke could sit with them?"

"Yes, or Luke. Whichever. That's fine. But not Tuesday," she said. "I'm out Tuesday."

"Fine," said Adrian. "Good."

He got to his feet then and cupped Beau's soft, warm cheek inside his hand as he passed him, almost groaning at the tenderness of his skin. He went up to his quarters in the study, packed his bits back into his rucksack, kissed the kids, slung the rucksack over his shoulder and left the house. It was dreary and damp. He turned the collar up on his jacket and he headed for the bus stop.

There'd been a woman in his flat. Adrian could tell the moment he opened the front door. First was the smell, something sweet and floral, not like the spicy stuff that Luke slapped all over his chops every morning. Then there was Luke himself: lighter, softer, his hair not quite right.

He'd shaved off his experimental beard, too, leaving his face looking raw and exposed. He thought of Beau's cheek under his hand half an hour ago and wondered when he'd last stroked Luke's face. He was aware that there would always be the last time for these intimate nuances of his relationships with his children and that often that time would pass unnoticed. When, for example, had Cat sat on his lap for the last time?

When had he last kissed Otis on the lips, picked Pearl up in his arms, called Luke one of his childhood nicknames, held Beau up on his shoulders? He had no idea. He thought of crying at the leavers' ceremonies of his oldest children, knowing that he would never again see them in their primary uniforms, that they would never again be little. But there were no ceremonies for these other "lasts," no realization or acknowledgment that something precious was about to end.

"You OK?" he said, dropping his door keys into a bowl and removing his jacket. Luke nodded at him casually, his long legs hanging either side of the bar stool by the kitchen counter.

"Had a good weekend?"

"Yeah." Luke yawned. "Yeah. It was good."

"Do anything interesting?" He pulled yesterday's underpants out of his rucksack and put them straight into the washing machine, followed by socks and a T-shirt, dimly aware of the heat of the drum, of its having been recently used.

"Not really." Luke's gaze dropped back to the laptop.

Adrian headed into his bedroom, knowing already what he would find. New bedsheets. He wouldn't normally have noticed apart from the fact that his cleaner changed them every Friday and he'd left her out a brand-new sheet, still in its packaging, to replace an old one with a rip in it that he and Beau had used the week before to paint on. The new bedsheet had been pale blue. The one on his bed was blue chambray. He pulled open a drawer and found the pale blue sheet washed, pressed and folded into a freakishly neat square.

His cleaner did not iron bedsheets. Adrian certainly did not iron bedsheets.

He lifted the pillow to his face and sniffed it. There it was, that same sweet smell. And there, snagged on the corner of the bedside table was a blond hair. He smiled grimly. Fair enough, he thought, he couldn't expect his six-foot-two, twenty-three-year-old son to invite ladies into his bunk bed. But still. Sex. Here. In his monk's quarters. Sex all over his ex-wife. Sex everywhere. *As much sperm as possible.* He pulled his hands down his face. And then he sat down heavily on his bed. And through the grim conceptual fog of everyone but him having sex came suddenly and overpoweringly the thought of Maya. His perfect little Maya. Her neat, tidy body. Everything where it should be. The dimples in the small of her back, one above each pear-shaped buttock. The golden freckles on her shoulders and arms. Her eyes squeezed shut in the dark of night. The pale white nape of her neck like a beautiful surprise when he pulled up her amber hair.

"Oh *Christ*," he groaned. "Maya."

And then he remembered those last times. Those last months. When he'd look at her sometimes and wonder where she'd gone. She would be there, right in front of him, astride him, she'd be making the noises, pulling the faces, but he'd known she wasn't there. He'd thought it was because the baby wasn't coming. He'd thought it was because of him. He'd feel guilty, even while it was happening, guilty that he'd given everyone a baby but her. Guilty that he was too old. Guilty that his hair was thinning, that she'd got the tail end of him, not the golden beginnings. And the guiltier he felt, the more she'd looked at him with a kind of benign pity.

He hadn't thought about this. Not since April 19. He hadn't thought about how it had been then. He'd fixated on the years before. How perfect it had been. He'd fixated on the shock of her death. Here one minute, gone the next. *Completely out of the blue.*

But had it been? he wondered now. The e-mails had been coming for months. The baby had been failing to material-ize for months. The distance in her eyes had been there for months. Everything had been wrong for months.

Adrian rubbed at his eyes, holding back tears. Who had he thrown away his perfect family for? Who was Maya? He couldn't remember her anymore. What had it been? Him and her? Them? Had it been sex? Had he been having a midlife crisis? Was it nothing more than the joy of a sweet smile and perfect breasts?

His history was unraveling. For years it had been neatly filed, Rolodexed, Filofaxed. The linear progression of things. The stages and phases. Now it was as if someone had shaken everything out onto the floor in a pile. And there it was: his history. A bloody mess. And he didn't know where the hell to start.

PART THREE

28

JANUARY 2011

Dear Bitch

Happy New Year!

I hear you all had a lovely time at the big family Christmas. How magical it must have been for all your husband's children to have you there, the spare part, the moron who thought she could just waltz into someone else's family and play the queen bee. Apparently you contributed a homemade Christmas pudding to the party. Everyone pretended they liked it, but according to my sources it was inedible. Just you showing off, I suppose. Again. You really do think you can just bake a cake or remember someone's favorite TV show or give someone a piggyback or plait their hair and that everyone will fall in love with you. But they won't. They're not stupid. Not like your idiot husband. I can see right through you and so can they. It's just a matter of time, Bitch. Everyone will see you for what you are. In the meantime, do feel free to disappear.

Maya copied, pasted, deleted. She barely read them anymore. The e-mails had been coming for months now. Sometimes twice a week, sometimes not for a few weeks at a time. For a reasonably sensitive person, Maya had become pretty desensitized to the shock now. Yeah yeah, she'd think, inedible Christmas puddings, bring it on. *What. Ever.*

But the words, while they didn't sting at the point of attack, left a bruise on her emotions that ached dully over the hours and days that followed. She felt permanently tired. It was probably work, it was probably that bad cold she'd had the week before Christmas, it was probably just winter and the long nights and the dark afternoons. But often it felt more sinister than that, the heaviness in her limbs, the weight behind her eyes. It often felt as though she was being poisoned.

She'd promised herself she'd tell someone if the e-mails were still coming by the New Year. And here it was, January 1. And she already knew that she would never tell anyone.

She shut her laptop and surveyed her wardrobe. They were due in Hove at 1:30 p.m. for Susie's annual New Year's Day party. She pulled on a black knitted dress with a white satin collar and appraised herself. She patted her tummy. The little mound of it. In her heart she knew it was Christmas excess. In her heart she knew that there was no way, even if she was pregnant, that she'd be far gone enough to show like that. She pulled the dress off again. She didn't want to set people wondering today. She didn't want people looking at her in that infuriating, questioning way, their eyes lit with hope and delight.

Instead she pulled on a loose gray lambswool sweater and a pair of tight jeans. She dressed it up with diamond earrings, high-heeled boots and her hair up in a bun. She stared at herself hard for a moment, trying to picture herself objectively. What was she? Who was she? What would she be doing right now if she hadn't taken that temporary assignment from the agency back in 2008 and fallen in love with the boss? Was this where she was meant to be? Here, right now, standing in a tiny bedroom in a tiny flat in Archway, dressing herself for a rather dull drinks party at her husband's ex-wife's house in Hove? A party at which she was likely to see her husband's son for the first time since he'd kissed her on the mouth in a pub. Was this the correct turn of events? Or had something gone wrong along the way? She fixed her with a grim smile, this stranger in the mirror, and then she turned and left the room.

She and Adrian took the train down to Hove. London was quiet and slow. The tubes were half-empty and they had the train from Victoria to Brighton virtually to themselves. There was a stale flatness in the atmosphere, as though all the interesting people had stayed at home. They hadn't been out the night before; Adrian had cooked a lobster and they'd drunk a bottle of champagne, watched Jools Holland and the fireworks on the TV and then gone to bed at one a.m. and had barely conscious sex. Exactly the same as the year before.

Maya glanced across at Adrian. He was reading a broadsheet, one long leg crossed high up upon the other. He had some stubble around his face, salt-and-peppered, and heavy bags beneath his eyes. She conjured up a wave of affection for him. *Sweet Adrian*. Who could ever resist Adrian?

They took a taxi from the station to Susie's cottage. The sky above Hove was brilliant January blue and the shingled beach was full of people walking off the night before. Maya held herself straight at the front door as they waited for someone to open it. She patted her bun and forced her mouth into a smile.

"Hello!" It was Cat. She was clutching a glass of pink wine and the hand of a boy with tattooed arms. The boy with tattooed arms let go of her hand and headed towards the kitchen and Cat leaned in to hug Adrian and Maya, far too hard. "Hello, lovely, lovely people," she said, squeezing them again before releasing them. "Come in! Quick. It's freezing out there." Cat was wearing a black T-shirt with a sequined skull on the front and a tiny tartan kilt that barely covered her upper thighs. Her dyed hair was in a backcombed bun almost the same size as her head.

"Who was that?" said Maya, eyeing the kitchen and shutting the door behind her.

"That was Duke!" she said. "He's my boyfriend. Well, at least I think he's my boyfriend. He hasn't actually said he is but I figure if he said yes to this party—and I didn't put any pressure on him at all, I swear—then he must feel like he's my boyfriend. I mean, why would you come otherwise?" She gestured behind her at the vignette beyond the living-room door: Susie's ancient parents sitting side by side on Susie's sofa clutching paper plates of sandwiches and looking thoroughly confused.

They followed Cat into the kitchen, where they found Cat's boyfriend, Duke, making himself a vodka and tonic; Cat's best friend, Bonny, and Luke's girlfriend, Charlotte. Cat introduced Adrian and Maya to Duke, and Maya greeted Bonny and Charlotte with kisses on their cheeks. Maya suddenly felt powerfully that she did not want to be here. She let Cat pour her a large glass of wine and she started drinking it urgently. If Charlotte was here, then Luke must be, too.

The young people (Maya had no idea if at thirty-two she was still young. Being in your thirties was very confusing in that respect) were all hollering and laughing and pressing buttons on phones. Cat, Bonny and Charlotte took a photograph of themselves on Cat's smartphone, all pouting upwards into the lens. When had pouting replaced smiling, Maya wondered, as the natural response to having a camera pointed in your face? Susie burst in then, wearing a shapeless floral dress, tatty leggings and UGG boots, her pale hair held back from her weathered face with kirby pins. She looked a little like a day-release patient.

"I *thought* I heard your voices!" she announced, wreathing them in hugs and kisses. "Thank you both *so much* for coming! You've got drinks? Good! And there's food in the sitting room. Tons of it. Nobody seems to be eating for some reason, not

sure why, people are usually *starving* on New Year's Day. I hope
you two are, otherwise that's fifty quid's worth of M and S in
the mulcher. Have you met Duke?" She pulled Cat's boyfriend
towards them by the hand and squeezed his shoulder.

Adrian and Maya said that they had and Susie said, "Isn't he
just *gorgeous*? Look at all these lovely tattoos! I do love a man
with tattoos."

Susie led them into the sitting room. There was Luke, sitting on the piano stool talking politely to a large, waistcoated
man whom she did not recognize. Luke didn't notice Maya
walk in at first. But when he did, he did a full double take
and then pulled an expression halfway between a smile and
a grimace. Maya returned the smile and mouthed hello. She
watched as Luke tried to refocus his attention on the man,
tried to find the thread back into the conversation. But his
body language had changed and he looked trapped, self-con-
scious, a red flush inching up his pale neck.

Maya turned away and focused instead on the buffet table at
the far end of the room. She wasn't hungry. She and Adrian had
had baguettes from the station. But she needed something to
do. She piled a Cath Kidston paper plate with things she had no
appetite for and turned back to the room. Luke had gone and
Adrian called to her to join him in a conversation with "an old
friend." The old friend was a too-thin man in his fifties wearing
a Clash T-shirt and battered black Converse. There was something slightly unnerving about the aspic-set look of him, like a
kind of punk Miss Havisham. Maya did not want to talk to him.
She knew already that she would have nothing in common with
him and nothing to say to him and that he would inevitably at
some point bore her to tears with some hilarious anecdote
about the things that he and Adrian had got up to when they
were young. They all did that, Adrian's friends. They dug deep
for their best selves to impress the *young girl*. They were never
quite natural and always too eager either to grimly overplay

their ancientness or to ensure that she was made aware of the fact that they too had once been young.

She thought of the young ones in the kitchen, with their tattoos and their piercings and their smartphones and their pouting, and for a moment she stood there in the center of the room, clutching her paper plate, swaying gently in the terrible, squalling realization that she did not belong here. She had been so desperate to be a part of this, had watched the machinations of this life from a distance all those months, marveling at the magical glow of it all: the Islington town house, the trophy wives and darling children, the weekends away en masse, the ramshackle parties, the legends, the traditions, the glittering story of them all and their sprawling mass of friends and people. She'd seen it, she'd smelled it and she'd wanted it. And now it was hers. And, like a shiny thing seen and coveted through the plate-glass windows of a fancy shop, now that she had it in her hands it had lost its allure.

She drew in her breath and smiled at Adrian. She gestured that she was heading back to the kitchen and saw the old friend's face drop slightly with disappointment. She took her plate and left the room. She hovered at the cusp of the kitchen, but couldn't quite bring herself to walk in. She could hear the screech and overwrought hilarity of the youngsters and she suspected Luke was in there too. She opened up the door to Susie's snug, a tiny room off the hallway where Susie had a desk and a sofa and a huge collection of vinyl records housed in reclaimed cubbies. She sat on Susie's chair and rested the unwanted plate of food on the desk. The walls in here were covered in photographs, a mosaic of vintage mismatched frames, barely a gap between them. And there it was, yet again, a physical reminder that she was an interloper in this world. The decades of life that had been lived before she'd arrived, the children born and raised and grown, the holidays and birthdays and Christmas mornings without her. And the only thing that could possibly bring her truly into this world was a baby of her own. And the baby would not come. It refused to come. It was almost as if the baby knew that it was only wanted as a golden ticket. Because Maya didn't really want a baby. She wasn't broody. There was no clock ticking. Just a desperate urge to belong to this club of which she felt like an off-peak member.

The e-mailer was right. She was nothing. She was a shadow in the wings.

She ran her finger along the frame of a photograph of all four of them: Susie, Adrian, Luke and Cat. Susie was California pretty in faded jeans and a checked shirt, her pale hair long and plaited, a crescent of creamy cleavage showing at the V of her shirt. Adrian was full-cheeked and handsome, his arms draped around Cat's neck from behind. The children were chunky and small, around four and six, Maya estimated, much more similar to each other than they looked now that they were adults. Behind them was a range of golden sand dunes and a puffy blue and white sky. Where was this taken? Maya didn't know. She would have been a teenager when this photo was taken. She would have walked past this young family at the beach and thought nothing of them.

She jumped slightly as she heard the door hinge creak slowly.

"Hi." It was Luke.

"Hi." She felt her face fill with color.

He joined her alongside the photograph. "Norfolk," he said.

She nodded. "I've never been."

"We used to go every summer. My uncle had a cottage there."

"I didn't know you had an uncle."

"Yeah, Mum's brother, Pete. He killed himself. A couple of years after that photo was taken."

"Oh God." She grimaced. "How awful." How did she not know about Uncle Pete? Who else did she not know about?

"Yeah. And then Dad left. A year later."

Maya glanced at him. He was like a walking wound sometimes.

"Was it hard for your mum?" she asked. "When he left?" Adrian had always talked fondly of the transition from wife one to wife two. Almost as if it had been a wonderful piece of serendipity that had led him from Susie to Caroline, from Hove to London.

Luke looked at her as though she was dim. "Of course it was," he said. "I mean, *look at us.*" He directed his gaze back to the photograph. "Look how happy we were. Three years later he'd gone. I was nine."

"But your mum, she was OK about it?"

"Well, yeah, kind of. But that's only because she was off her tits all the time."

"Susie?"

"Yeah. She knew what was happening. She knew about Caroline long before my dad told her. She was always leaving us with our grandparents and going clubbing, raving. I think she thought it was better than staying at home and waiting for Dad to get back. I think she was just getting ready, you know, for the big revelation, so she could make out that she didn't care either way. But she did. She didn't used to be like this, you know"—he gestured towards the living room—"scatty and scruffy. She used to be quite cool." He looked back at the photo and sighed. "Anyway. How are you?"

"I'm fine," she said. "You?"

"Yeah. I'm OK. I'm sorry I haven't been writing or calling or anything. It's been a bit . . ."

"That's OK," she replied hastily. "I understand."

"I really need to apologize," he said, turning to face her. "For what happened. It was . . . it was totally out of order."

"It's fine," she said, glancing anxiously through the crack in the door, listening for footsteps. "Really, Luke. I was flattered."

He issued a dry bark. "I wasn't trying to flatter you, Maya. I was . . . oh God. I shouldn't have said anything. Look. Let's just . . ."

"Yes," said Maya. "Yes. Forget it happened."

"Yes," Luke agreed. "Yes. Thank you." He sounded relieved.

Maya smiled sadly. She did not feel relieved. She felt sad and anxious. She felt as though she was smothering something tiny and precious, something that had barely drawn its first breath. She clutched his hand, squeezed it hard, and then dropped it at the sound of the door hinge creaking again.

"There you are!" It was Charlotte. She glanced from Maya to Luke and back again. "What are you two doing in here?"

"I was just showing Maya some old family photos," said Luke, pulling Charlotte towards him by the waist and kissing her on the cheek.

Maya tried not to look, tried not to feel anything. She forced a smile and said brightly, "Look! Look at the cuties!"

Charlotte followed her pointing finger to a photo of Luke and Cat sitting one on each end of a seesaw, both in brightly colored anoraks and woolen hats. Her face scrunched up and she said, "Oh. Adorable! Look at how adorable you were!" She kissed Luke on the cheek and rested her head against his chest.

Maya picked up her plate of uneaten food and turned to leave the room. The last thing she saw as she did so was Luke's blue eyes fixed upon her over the top of Charlotte's head, meaningfully and desperately.

29

JULY 2012

Adrian didn't listen to the voice mail from the unknown number until he got home from work on Monday. The voice mail icon had been flashing at him since nine o'clock that morning but he simply hadn't had a free moment. He was shutting the office early during the Olympics, so that his employees wouldn't have horrible nightmares getting home on London transport and miss dates and bedtimes and hot suppers. In theory his employees would be working remotely once they got home and nothing much was going to change. But in practice it appeared that his employees were all going home and planting themselves straight in front of the TV with a can of lager, and Adrian kept finding himself in the office at nine p.m., answering phone calls and desperately trying to pull various issues together with no backup.

It was almost ten o'clock by the time he got home. Luke was watching the Olympics highlights with a lager in his hand and gave Adrian his customary greeting involving the use of approximately three facial muscles. Adrian joined him with a heavy sigh and his own can of lager and finally dialed up his voice mail service.

Hello, Adrian, this is Dolly Patel. I spoke to you a while ago about the mobile phone? Listen. Funny thing. I found my phone. Or at least my little girl found the phone. It was in her toy box. Right at the bottom. Completely flat, of course. So it wasn't actually in my bag when it got stolen. Which means it can't be the phone that woman left in your flat. So, listen, I just spoke to my boss and he says he thinks he knows what happened to Tiffany's phone. I told him about your wife and he'd like to help. So maybe you could give him a ring? His name is Jonathan Baxter. Here's his number: 07988 033460. Take care. Bye.

Adrian sat up straight, staring hard at his phone as if it had just spoken to him.

"You all right?" said Luke.

"Er, yeah. Yeah, I think. Hold on, just got a call to make." He stopped and glanced at the time on his phone. "Is ten o'clock too late, do you think?"

"Too late for what?"

"To call someone."

"Depends who you're calling."

"An estate agent."

Luke raised an eyebrow.

"No, not for anything like that. It's the phone. You know, the stalker's phone? There's a man who thinks he might know who's got it. He's an estate agent."

Luke sat up straighter, too. "Yeah, yeah," he said. "No, it's not too late. Call him. Call him now. He won't answer it if he doesn't want to."

Adrian swallowed down a wave of nervous excitement and dialed in the number.

"Hello?" said an uncertain voice.

Adrian leaned forward, his knees touching the coffee table. "Hi, is that Jonathan Baxter?"

"Yes, speaking."

"Hello. I'm so sorry to be calling you so late. My name is Adrian Wolfe and—"

"Ah, hello, yes, I've been expecting your call."

"Is it OK to talk now? I can call tomorrow if that's more convenient?"

"No, not at all. I'm just here watching the sports. It's

easier to talk now than when I'm at work. So, this phone?"

"Yes, Tiffany's phone."

"I gave it to my son," said Jonathan Baxter. "About four months ago. He said he needed it for his business. He's a . . . Christ, I'm not sure actually, something to do with the Internet. Anyway. He said he needed a couple of cheap phones and I had a load of them rattling around in a drawer at work; we upgraded everyone to smartphones a few months ago, so they were kind of redundant. I handed them over to Matthew, didn't think another thing."

A flash of blue-white clarity exploded through Adrian's consciousness. "Sorry, sorry. Matthew? Your son is called Matthew?"

"Yes. Why? Do you know him?"

"Well, no, not exactly. But the third time I met the woman who left the phone in my flat, she was with a man called Matthew. On a date."

Jonathan Baxter grunted. "Not my Matthew then. My Matthew is gay."

"Well, I assumed they were on a date; she was holding a rose. But is he tall and dark, your son? Short hair? Very good-looking?"

"Yes, I guess that does kind of describe him."

"Youngish, about thirty?"

"He's thirty-one."

"Does he live in north London?"

"Yes. He lives in Highgate."

There was a short silence. Then Adrian said, "Does your son have a friend called Jane?"

"Not that I'm aware of."

"Or Amanda?"

"Again, not that I'm aware of. But he does have a lot of female friends. He shares a flat with a girl. Has a lot of girls working for him. I'm not sure I could identify one from the many."

Adrian sighed. "This one," he said, "she is remarkably beautiful."

"All Matthew's female friends appear to fall into that category."

"This one," he continued, "has odd-colored eyes. One is blue and the other is blue with an amber section."

Now Jonathan Baxter sighed. "Really," he said, "I wouldn't know. I might well have met this woman but I honestly wouldn't remember. They all kind of blend into one amorphous beautiful young woman."

"Well, would you . . . do you think you might be able to give me your son's number? Maybe I could have a word with him?"

"Oh, now, I don't know . . ."

"Or at least give him my number. Ask him to call me?"

"Yes, yes, that I can do. Of course. But remind me, what exactly did this mysterious woman do, this Jane? Dolly gave me the rough outline but . . ."

"It's all very strange," said Adrian. "She seemed very keen to track me down, stalked my daughter, purposely bumped into me on the street that night and then disappeared. Mine was the only number on that phone. And I would have let the whole thing lie, but since she came in and out of our lives, we've uncovered some poison-pen e-mails that were sent to my late wife. E-mails that appear to have contributed to her death. And I can't shake the feeling that she had something to do with it."

"Something bad?"

"Well, yes, I suppose so."

"In which case, and assuming my son knew why he was giving her the phone, he might not be too keen to give her up. Listen. I won't say anything just yet. But let me have a word with my ex-wife and Matthew's sisters. They would probably have more of an eye for detail. They're more likely to remember something like odd-colored eyes. Leave it with me, Adrian. I'll see what I can do."

"What was that all about?" said Luke once Adrian had switched off his phone.

"I think," said Adrian, "that that man might just be able to help me track down the mysterious Jane."

30

Adrian stared intently at the menu, glancing from time to time at the clock on his phone. Caroline was ten minutes late. Caroline was always ten minutes late. It had been one of the many things about her that had started off beguiling (always being ten minutes late clearly meant that she was better than him and Adrian did want to be with a woman who was better than him) and ended up infuriating (what made her think she was any better than him?). Sitting here now he felt the fresh thrill of it again, that *will she/won't she turn up* edginess that had reeled him in so effectively thirteen years ago.

Finally, at eleven minutes past eight, Caroline appeared at the door. She shook out an umbrella and passed it to the waiter who greeted her. She was wearing a navy Pac-a-mac which she pulled over her head and folded into a ball. Adrian felt a stab of disappointment. A Pac-a-mac. He felt fairly sure she didn't wear Pac-a-macs when she was out with Paul Wilson. Under the Pac-a-mac she was wearing a classic Caroline outfit of jeans and a Liberty-print shirt with the sleeves rolled up. Probably what she'd been wearing all day, he mused. She arrived at their table smelling of the street, of London rain and wet umbrella. No aroma of freshly washed hair or just-spritzed perfume.

"Sorry I'm late," she said, hooking her bag over the back of her chair and sitting down elegantly. "Cat was running late."

Adrian knew this was a lie. Cat was never late.

"You need a haircut," she said, resting her smartphone on the tabletop and pulling her reading glasses out of a Liberty-print pouch.

"Yes. I know." He passed a hand down the length of it at the back. He hadn't had a cut since the end of March. It was almost long enough to tie back.

"It's something I'm starting to come to terms with. The older you get, the neater your hair needs to be. Bedhead only looks sexy when you're under forty. After that it just makes you look deranged." She picked up the menu and opened it. "Take Susie for example," she finished, looking at Adrian over the top of her reading glasses.

"Oh, bless Susie," said Adrian, who knew that Caroline bore Susie no ill will.

"I know. God bless her soul. She really doesn't care. I wish I had her confidence." She moved her gaze back to the menu and said, "Have they given you the specials yet?"

"No," said Adrian, "but I heard them talking them through to the table behind. Something to do with sea bass. A prima-vera risotto. And a rib eye. I seem to recall they do a great rib eye here."

They'd come here a lot when they were married. It was their easy local.

Caroline closed her menu and removed her glasses. "Rib eye then, yes, I could do with the iron. Been feeling a bit dizzy lately."

"That'll be all the sex," said Adrian, before he had a chance to censor himself.

Caroline rolled her eyes but didn't rise to it.

They placed their order and Adrian noted Caroline's reticence to order a bottle of wine. Whether this was related to her efforts to get pregnant or merely because she had no interest in having a fun night with her ex-husband he did not know. Instead they ordered a glass of wine each and a bottle of water.

"So," said Caroline, "to what do I owe the honor?"

Adrian smiled. He wasn't going to go to the crux just yet. Caroline had been known to walk out of restaurants if the turn of events displeased her and he wanted at least to have first had a nice meal if that was going to be the case.

He shrugged. "Nothing special. Just a catch-up really. About Otis. About the kids generally. Luke gave me the impression that there were some issues?"

"Issues?" Her expression grew defensive, clearly anticipating a strike on her parenting skills.

"According to Luke, Pearl is lonely and weird and Cat is stressed and overeating."

Caroline tipped her head back and laughed. "What a load of crap," she said.

"Yeah. I thought as much. I assumed it was just Luke hamming it up to make me feel shitty. But after the Otis thing, I thought I should check in on it."

"I promise you," said Caroline, pushing up the sleeves of her blouse, "everyone is doing incredibly well. Given the circumstances."

He looked at her quizzically. "Circumstances?"

"Yes, you know. Us splitting up. Maya dying. They've had a lot to process the last few years. And Otis, you know, he's twelve. It's a tricky age. But I do think, everything taken into consideration, they're all doing brilliantly."

Adrian nodded, only partially reassured. "Although," he said, "Cat has been piling on the weight."

"Well, yes. That is true. But she spends a lot of time with the kids now and it's hard when you've got a big appetite like Cat, hard to resist the chips and the leftovers. She'll work it out. She'll work out that she doesn't want to be fat and then she'll work out how not to be fat. She's so young. She's still got such a lot to learn."

"And Otis? Is he any more forthcoming? Any more ideas yet about what he was doing outside the tube station that time?"

"No." Caroline sighed heavily. "No. Still none the wiser. I'm putting it down as an aberration. He's been quite clingy actually, since it happened, quite needy. Spending much more time downstairs, keeps asking me if I love him and how much I love him and will I always love him. Like, you know: if I hurt someone, would you still love me? If I did something really bad, would you still love me? And he's started asking for bedtime stories." She shrugged. "A tiny bit of regression. But nothing to worry about. It happens sometimes."

"And Paul," said Adrian, trying to make the name sound normal on his tongue, "are they all OK about him?"

Caroline glared at him. "Paul," she said, "has no impact on their lives. I am very sure of that. He is just a friend as far as they are concerned and they barely see him."

Adrian bit his lip. It was still too early to launch into the main event. But she had, with that last wholly inaccurate comment, given him a perfect launching point.

"I promise you," she said, "I would not do anything to threaten the children's stability right now. They've had enough to deal with. They deserve a nice quiet life."

"Where does he live, Paul?"

"Highbury."

"On his own?"

"Yes, on his own."

"What is it, a flat or a house?"

"It's a maisonette, two floors, a garden."

Adrian nodded again.

"What?" said Caroline.

"Nothing," said Adrian. "I'm just curious. Do you think . . . do you feel like it might be a long-term thing? With Paul?"

Caroline tugged at the sleeves of her blouse again. "Christ," she said, "I have no idea. I hope so."

Adrian laughed drily. "Well," he said, trying to keep the disdain from his voice, "you do appear to have changed your tune. What happened to 'smelly men' and 'snoring'?"

She raised an eyebrow at him and said, "Paul is not smelly and he does not snore."

"Bollocks," said Adrian. "All men snore."

"I promise you," said Caroline, "that Paul does not."

Adrian felt his resolve begin to break down, the weight of his anger and jealousy pushing at the doors of his self-control. He was peaking too early but he could not help himself.

"So if you're hoping it might be long-term, where do the kids fit into this?"

Caroline flared her nostrils. "Sorry?"

"I mean, are you planning on moving in with each other? Getting married?"

"God, Ade, I really don't know. We've only been seeing each other for a few months. He's young. Well, *younger*. We haven't really talked about it."

Adrian felt a fire of indignation starting to build beneath him. He saw the waiter approaching with two large steaks. He dampened himself down.

"Oh, wow," said Caroline, appraising the plate in front of her, "look at that. Amazing."

Adrian asked for mustard. Caroline asked for another glass of wine. They chatted genially about mutual friends, about Caroline's upcoming holiday in France, about the Olympics, about the weather. As Caroline talked, Adrian watched her. She was such a cool customer, formidably so.

He'd met her when he was working on a rebuild of a shopping center on the King's Road. She was in the window of the clothes shop opposite putting in the Christmas display and he'd been on-site with the landlord talking through some alterations to the plans. He and the client were meant to be talking face-to-face but in reality he was talking to the view over his client's shoulder, watching the statuesque blonde single-handedly drag a five-by-five-foot square of chipboard into the display, climb a ladder to hang a weighty mirror ball and assemble a mannequin in ten easy movements. He had been mesmerized by her, by her strength and agility, the elegance of her movements, the lack of vanity.

The client had turned eventually, aware that he was not the prime focus of his architect's attention, and said, simply and with conviction: "Goddess."

Ultimately, of course, it transpired that Caroline was not a goddess. She was simply a rather impressively designed human being with all manner of annoying habits and foibles. She was emotionally stunted, forgetful, tardy, hard to impress, impossible to beguile; she had no time for losers or stragglers; she was impatient and demanding and she talked in her sleep.

The waiter removed their plates and they both agreed to look at the pudding menu although Adrian already knew that Caroline would read it in great detail, mmming and yumming, and then put down the menu and say, "Actually, I'm not sure I can manage a pudding." Adrian ordered a plate of fresh fruit and an affogato.

"So," he said, "Paul . . ."

Caroline groaned and rolled her eyes.

"Does he want children?"

"I have no idea," she snapped.

"How old is he?"

"Thirty-nine. It was his birthday yesterday."

"Oh, well, happy birthday to him. So even more *of an age* then. Nearly forty. He must want a family of his own."

"Yes. I'm sure he does. Probably."

"So? How is that going to work?"

"Oh God, Adrian. Will you stop this? Seriously. Paul is just my boyfriend, OK? We like each other. We enjoy each other. End of story."

Adrian tried not to take too much pleasure from his next statement, the pleasure wasn't his to take, but he couldn't help but feel a tiny thrill of satisfaction when he said, "Is it? Is it the end of the story? Caroline, I saw the stuff in your bathroom cabinet. I saw the ovulation sticks."

"What! What were you doing snooping around in my bathroom cabinet?"

"I wasn't snooping around, I was looking for moisturizer."

"Moisturizer?"

"Yes. I was waiting for Beau to finish going to the toilet and I looked in the mirror and I looked old and dried out so I thought I'd use one of your amazing cream things. I figured they seem to work for you . . ." He added a twinkle to his smile to soften her defenses. "And I saw all the *stuff*, you know, the folic acid and that herbal stuff you took when we were trying."

"Oh, for God's sake." Caroline tutted and folded her arms. "It's nothing," she said. "Just . . . nothing."

"What kind of nothing?" He could sense an opening here.

"Urgh, God. It's just . . . Paul wants a baby. There. OK. He hasn't said he wants a baby with me, but he's always banging on about this friend's baby and that friend's baby and he thinks I'm . . ."

Adrian watched her dispassionately, not wanting to say or do anything to make her stop talking.

"He thinks I'm forty. So." She sighed. "He probably thinks I could still get pregnant. Anyway . . ." She broke off to call over a waiter and ordered herself a large brandy. Adrian followed suit. "My friend at work just met this guy, she's forty-two, never had any kids and she went to Harley Street for one of those tests, to see how fertile you are, to see if they were going to be able to get pregnant. So *just for fun*—I didn't even tell Paul I was doing it—I went with her and got myself tested. That's what I was doing that morning, when Otis bunked off school. And it turns out I have the fertility of a thirty-five-year-old. According to my test results I should still be able to conceive without assistance." Caroline glowed proudly at her announcement.

"Wow," said Adrian. "And what did Paul say?"

"I haven't told him," she said. "I've just been mulling it over. And then I was in Boots and I thought, you know, good to have it all there. Just in case. And of course once you get the idea of a baby into your head, it's almost impossible to get it out again. I'm already thinking about names. I'm already working out how to reconfigure the bedrooms. You know. It's nuts, Ade. It's absolutely nuts."

"Have you stopped using contraception yet?"

She threw him a brief, defensive glance, then swirled her brandy violently round the bottom of the glass.

"Jesus, Caroline."

"Look," she said, "I've been on the pill for decades. You know how long it took my body to adjust every time I went off it when we were trying to conceive. I figure . . ."

"Caroline. Caroline." He shook his head, appalled.

"Oh, come on, Ade, I'm forty-four. Really. How likely is it?"

"Well, the test you had done seems to think it's very likely."

"It took us thirteen months to conceive Beau. And I was only thirty-eight."

"Caroline! You know that's irrelevant. Totally irrelevant."

She exhaled and leaned her head down, resting her forehead against the rim of her brandy glass. "You're right," she whispered, slowly bringing her head back upright. "You are right."

"If you want another baby, Caroline, at least tell the man."

"No, but that's the thing. I don't think I do want another

baby. Not really. I *don't* want to be standing in the reception playground, fifty years old, everyone thinking I'm a glamorous granny. I don't want to do night feeds and buy another buggy and sing 'The Wheels on the Bus' and all that. I just want . . . Oh, I don't know, I want a baby that doesn't change anything. You know. A baby that comes along and makes everyone really happy without anything having to change."

"If you don't mind me saying, it doesn't really sound like you've thought this through."

"No. I haven't. I'm just acting on pure animal instinct and every time I try to engage my intellect, the whole thing falls apart into an indecipherable mess and my head feels like it's going to explode. I mean, Adrian, you've done this. And you were going to do it again, with Maya. How did you reconcile yourself with it?"

"With what exactly?"

"With . . . with making all this mess."

The words sat suspended between them, frozen and harsh.

"I never thought of it as a mess," he said. "Children aren't a mess."

"No, that's not what I meant. It's just, you know, it was just me and my mum growing up and I'd look at what other people had: two parents, two children, this neat square. And that's still, in spite of everything, my intrinsic definition of family. I still feel like I've broken some fundamental law of nature by making a family with a man who already had a family. I'm not sure I could do something like that again. Add another spoke to the wheel. Another line to the grid. You know? How do you do it, Adrian? How do you make yourself feel OK about it?"

Adrian stared at her. It had never occurred to him that he needed to feel OK about anything. It had never occurred to him that he had made any decisions he needed to reconcile himself with. Life had brought him to these women. Fate had delivered him these children. Love was the name of the game. You woke up, you ate, you worked, you loved, you slept. And if one day it turned out that you were loving the wrong person, then you rectified that by loving somebody else. He had no Catholic guilt. His wives still liked him. His children all loved him. What on earth was there to feel bad about?

"How could anyone ever feel bad about making beautiful families?"

Caroline blinked at him. "Seriously?" she said, the withering ice maiden back.

"Yes. Of course. There's no right way. No wrong way. As long as nobody gets hurt. As long as nobody dies."

Caroline's gaze did not waver. She put a hand upon Adrian's arm and said, firm and quiet, "But somebody did, Adrian. Maya died."

Adrian drew a small, painful breath. "That wasn't my fault."

Slowly she pulled her hand away from his arm and leaned back in her chair, her eyes not leaving his. She looked as though she had thirty things she wanted to say to him. But she didn't say any of them.

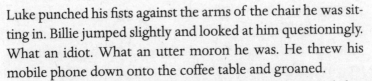

31

Luke punched his fists against the arms of the chair he was sitting in. Billie jumped slightly and looked at him questioningly. What an idiot. What an utter moron he was. He threw his mobile phone down onto the coffee table and groaned.

He had no idea why he'd allowed it to happen. And that was exactly what he had done. Allowed it to happen. He certainly had played no part in the series of events that had brought Charlotte into his bed (or, more accurately, into his father's bed) on Saturday night when his father had been at Caroline's with the kids. It had been the result, purely, of a series of submissions on his part, a succession of accessions.

She had messaged him on Facebook on Friday night saying she was going to be in London again the following day, would he like to meet up? He had replied fairly quickly in the negative, an attempt to nip it in the bud, said something about family commitments, thought that would have been the end of it. Until the doorbell had rung at half past midday, while he was still in his lounging gear and had yet to brush his teeth, and there she'd been, all gleaming blond hair and chatter and determination.

She insisted on coming in and making him a salad and uncorking a bottle of chilled white wine, all unpacked from a raffia basket, with a running commentary of news and gossip and tedious tidbits from her life. At no point did she express surprise that he was at home and not involved in his fictional family commitments. At no point did she express any concern that her visit might not be welcome or convenient.

She had sent him away to wash and dress, which he had done as compliantly as a pet dog, and then served him lunch in the courtyard, Maya's cat purring on her lap, words and words and more words pouring from her soft, pretty lips between mouthfuls.

Luke had ascertained, from the small amount of information that had got through his defensive deafness, that she was back in London shopping for this fabled bridesmaid dress, a little concerned that the stress of it was causing her to lose weight and that even if she found a dress she liked it would not fit her by the time the Big Day came. That it would be *falling off her*.

The salad had been delicious, as had the wine. Halfway through his second glass Luke had started to soften up. The strap of Charlotte's sundress had kept slipping down. Each time she hooked it back up with a delicate forefinger his pulse would quicken a little. Everything about her was soft and female. And Luke's reaction to a soft, feminine woman with a loose dress strap and a purring cat on her lap was not, in retrospect, something he was very proud of.

So, they'd spent the afternoon and the evening and the night in bed. In for a penny, in for a pound. He had not had sex since he and Scarlett had split up last year. In one way it had been good to get back into the saddle with someone familiar. But in a hundred other ways it had not been good at all.

And now of course she would not leave him alone. Kept tagging him in photos of herself on Facebook. Kept texting him. Nothing in particular. Just the rolling minutiae of her life. Because that was the thing, the main thing about Charlotte, the thing that had taken him so many months to pin down and determine when they were going out together—she was so bloody boring. That was why he hadn't wanted to stay friends with her. That was why he groaned every time he saw her name in his inbox or her face in the doorway of the pub. And for over a year he'd managed to hold it all at arm's length. And now the dam was compromised and he was being flooded with Charlotte.

There had been five texts tonight alone. The last one had said, merely, "Bored bored bored." He had replied to none of them. But still they came. She needed no oxygen to breathe, it seemed.

But there was something more sinister bothering Luke this morning. A terrible thought plaguing him. It was something Charlotte had said, at one in the morning, when they were lying naked and splayed across the sheets after their third round of sex. Luke had asked her why she'd come, why now, after all these months. And she'd said: "Because I was waiting for you to stop grieving."

"What do you mean?" he'd asked, turning to face her, propping his head up on his elbow.

"You know exactly what I mean."

"No," he'd said. "I don't."

"Maya," she'd said, almost bitterly. "I was waiting for you to stop grieving for Maya."

"What made you think I was grieving for Maya?" he'd asked tentatively.

She'd shrugged. "I just knew you were. I know how you felt about her. I know that you . . ." She'd pulled the sheet up to cover her nakedness as she formed the next sentence. "I know that you and she were more than just stepson and stepmother. More than just friends."

He'd scoffed at the idea. "What on earth are you talking about?"

"I'm talking about the looks and the cozy chats and the

springing apart when I entered the room. I'm talking about my female intuition."

"Oh, for God's sake. What a load of crap. There was nothing between me and Maya. Nothing whatsoever."

"My friend saw you both in Oxford Street a couple of summers back. When you were supposed to be in Brighton. When you said you were at work and couldn't see me." She pulled the sheet high up towards her chin.

"Big deal," he said. "I had the day off. She was bored. We went shopping. So what?"

"She said you looked really into each other."

He'd snorted and got out of bed. "Maya was a friend," he said, "a good friend. That is all."

"Whatever," she'd said with another shrug.

"Yeah," he'd said, "whatever."

His phone pinged again. He sighed, leaned forward, picked it up and switched it on. "Going to bed now. Sleep tight xxxxxxx."

He switched it off.

Charlotte had always been, in his opinion, disproportionately attached to the Wolfe family. She would ask after the children, ask after his father, pass comment on the various storylines occurring in the family as though she were somehow an intrinsic part of it all. And now it transpired that she had been secretly theorizing about his relationship with Maya, too. That she had her suspicions. And what was it she'd said? The sighting of him and Maya in Oxford Street? That was the summer, he realized, the summer when the e-mails had first been sent to Maya.

Was Charlotte the poison-pen writer? Was that possible? Sweet, boring, sexy, silly Charlotte? And in that case, had he just had sex with the person responsible for Maya's death?

He felt relieved to hear the sound of his father's key in the lock just then, to hear him clearing his throat in the hallway. A warm and genuine smile came to his face when Adrian walked in. "Hi," he said brightly.

"Good evening," said Adrian, "everything OK?"

Luke looked at his father strangely. He seemed drained, bruised. "Yeah," he said. "You?"

"Hm, yeah. I think."

"Good night?"

Adrian sat down heavily on the sofa. "A good night?" he said. "I wouldn't say it was a good night. No. I would say it was an *interesting* night."

"Ah."

"Yes. Ah. Exactly." Adrian breathed in heavily and then breathed out again. "Do you think it's my fault that Maya died?" The words left his mouth in one solid lump, as though he couldn't bear to utter them separately.

"What?"

"Look, Luke, you've always been my greatest detractor. You've never been shy about letting me know what you think of me. And my decisions. So now I'm asking you straight. Do you blame me for Maya doing what she did?"

Luke needed to allow himself a moment of silence before replying. "Well, I suppose," he said eventually, "if you look at the narrative arc of Maya's life and put little crosses by the bits that directly correlate to the moment she walked in front of a bus, you would probably feature quite heavily. Yes."

Adrian deflated slightly, his stomach seeming to go concave as he absorbed the impact of Luke's words.

"But what could I have done?" he said. "She didn't tell me. So what could I have done?"

"It's not about what you could have done, Dad. It's about what you did do. It's about everything you do. It's like, you brought Maya into your world, your shiny new toy, and then you didn't know what to do with her. So you just kind of let her get on with it. It was really hard for her, dealing with all of us. She was so young. She was *so young*, Dad."

"Well, not that young, actually, Luke."

"Young for her age. Not ready for all of this." He spread his arms about him. "You know we used to be quite close, Maya and I?"

Adrian looked at him with surprise.

"Yes, for a while. I used to come and see her sometimes when you were at work. We used to go shopping or for a drink." He shrugged, as if to say: *There it is, deal with it.*

"What? When?" Color leached from Adrian's face.

"Every now and then. We texted a lot. Talked a lot."

"But how come Maya didn't tell me?" His father sounded injured.

He shrugged again. "I don't know," he said. "Same reason she didn't tell you about those nasty e-mails, I suppose. Same reason she didn't tell you how hard she found it, being the spare part in your great dynasty. She obviously didn't feel like she could talk to you."

"But we talked. We talked all the time."

"Yes," said Luke, "but not about the stuff that really mattered."

"And she wasn't a spare part. She was my wife."

"Listen, Dad, in a family like this, the wife without a child is at the bottom of the heap. Everyone comes before them. Everyone."

His dad stared at him, mutely, as though still processing his words. "Did she ever tell you," he said eventually, "how she felt about not getting pregnant?"

Luke nodded. "Sort of. I know she found it difficult."

"But why didn't she tell *me*?"

"Because she didn't want to sound greedy. She didn't want

to make a fuss. Because she felt so guilty about you not living with your children anymore. She didn't want you to ever regret your decision. That would have killed her."

An echo of silence followed these words.

"I never did," Adrian said quietly. "Not for a moment. I never regretted it. Not then. Not when she was . . ." He trailed off.

"But now?"

Adrian sighed. "I don't know. Those e-mails. The way things turned out. Looking at the whole thing from this end of it all, I do wonder . . ."

"You should have settled with Caroline, Dad. That's what you should have done. You should have stuck with her. Just stuck with her."

32

MARCH 2011

There it was. Her fourteenth period since she and Adrian had started trying. It wasn't a surprise. She'd been feeling it coming for days. But still, the disappointment registered like a mule-kick to Maya's soul. Red, raging disappointment followed by a single heartbeat of relief. With each passing day her life lost more focus, her feelings became more oblique, her whole reason for being became cloudier and cloudier. She had somehow arranged to see her weird friend Sara tonight. She'd been trying to get out of it for so long that she'd used up all her excuses. And in a funny way, given the murkiness of her current state of being, it would be quite nice to see someone from her "before" days, someone who'd known her when she was normal. So she was meeting her in Soho for drinks (Sara didn't eat, or at least, if she did, it was something she did in the privacy of her own home).

Maya had come home from work first and now had exactly eighteen minutes before she needed to leave again, enough time to discover her period had started and to check her e-mail and find the latest missive from her charming friend.

Dear Bitch

Still no baby? That must be gutting. Such a huge disappointment to find you're less fertile than the first two wives who just popped them out like cherry pips. Looks like it's just the two of you then, forever, you and the old man. Are you looking forward to the passing years? To him getting older and you getting more bitter and twisted? Ooh, I bet you are. What fun you'll both have together. *Not*. So, why don't you get out now? While you're still young. No one will miss you. It will be like you were never there . . .

By the way, that new haircut? Nobody likes it. Caroline says it makes you look masculine and Cat thinks you look like the ugly one in a boy band. Yet another bad move, Bitch . . .

Maya instinctively moved her hand to her hair. All the girls at school had said they loved it. "Ooh, we like your hair, miss!" they'd said. "You look like Emma Watson!"

Adrian had loved it too, stared at her as if she were the loveliest thing he'd ever seen and gently cupped the bare nape of her neck.

She got to her feet and gazed at herself in the mirror. She fluffed at the fringe with her fingers, slapped on a smile, struck a pose. It suited her. It did. She was sure of it. And Caroline had been so nice about it when she'd seen it at the weekend. And Cat? Had Cat even seen it? How did Cat know what her hair looked like? And then she remembered that she'd texted her a photograph of it, just after she'd had it done, because Cat had asked to see it. She grabbed her phone and searched for the text. There it was, the photo she'd taken of herself, and there was Cat's response, in black and white: "You look STUNNING babe! Wish I cd get away with a cut like that! What does Dad think?"

She'd replied, "He likes it!"

To which Cat had replied, "Of course he does. You're so gorgeous. He's soooo lucky xxxxx."

Maya frowned. How was it possible that the same person

who had sent her that lovely text could also have said such a horrible thing about her to somebody else? Of all of Adrian's children, Cat was the simplest, the easiest to win round. She hadn't had to work on Cat at all. Even Beau had needed some persuasion and even now occasionally looked at her as though he wasn't sure what she was doing there. But Cat had accepted Maya into her life like the friend she hadn't realized she was waiting for.

The tone of the e-mailer's messages was getting more and more personal; there was more and more detail each time and now this, a supposed quote from Cat. Something completely out of character but with the ring of truth about it. She looked at the time. She had two minutes. She cut and pasted the e-mail into her secret document, deleted the original and then quickly composed a text to Cat, before she could decide whether or not it was the prudent thing to do.

"Hi there. Just wondering if you showed the photo of my haircut to anyone else? Just looking at it again and thinking I look so ugly!! Please delete!"

She pressed send, stuck the phone into her bag and headed out to meet Sara.

⌒

"My God, your hair," were Sara's first words when Maya walked into the bar on Frith Street that Sara had chosen for their meeting.

Maya touched it and smiled. "Yes," she said. "Seemed like a good idea at the time."

"No! No! I really like it. It suits you."

"Yes, well, the jury's out on it for now." She smiled at her oldest friend and said, "You look great. It's been ages!"

"Thank you. And yes, I know, but not for lack of trying on my part."

"I'm really sorry. It's just work. The days are so long . . ."

"As are the holidays." Her left eyebrow arched slightly.

"Well, yes, true. I know. I'm useless." Maya put up her hands and smiled.

They ordered expensive cocktails. Sara was one of those people who earned tons of money and appeared to have no grasp whatsoever of the concept that other people might be poorer than her. She was slick and smart in her City clothes, her hair pulled tightly away from her face, makeup freshly reapplied. They'd been best friends at school, slightly less best friends as they both headed off to college and barely friends at all these days but still clinging on to the idea that they were intrinsically linked.

"So," said Sara, slipping off her silk-lined jacket, "how are things going?"

Maya said, "Fine. Yes. Things are good."

"And how's Adrian?"

"He's great," she said, "busy, you know, but great."

Sara looked at her penetratingly. Sara had made it clear from the beginning that she did not approve of Maya's decision to marry Adrian. She'd said: "Why come third when you could come first?"

Maya had not really understood what she meant at the time, but now she could see that her friend had been keenly prescient.

"And how are you?" she asked brightly, moving the subject along.

"Oh God, the usual. Stressed, ill, lonely."

"Are you still in Clapham?"

"Yes, still there, rattling around that huge flat, all by myself. Too busy to even buy myself a sofa. Not that I need a sofa since I'm never actually there long enough to sit down."

"Why do you do it? Why don't you retire?"

"I'm going to," she said. "I'm giving myself until thirty-five and then I'm getting out. Going to get out and find myself a lovely soft husband who wants to stay at home and look after babies, and while he's looking after the babies I'm going to do what you did. I'm going to retrain as a teacher."

Maya's jaw fell open.

"Thought that might take you by surprise." Sara smiled smugly.

"Well, yeah, I mean, I just never saw you as the marrying type, let alone the baby type or the teacher type. Christ."

"Yes, well, I can't keep doing this. I've got tons of money in the bank. And I look at the women at work who are older than me, the ones who sacrificed everything, or worse, the ones who tried to have it all and ended up with children they never see and husbands they barely know anymore. And I don't envy them. I don't aspire to that. I want to be normal. You know, I want to be like you."

Maya smiled uncertainly. Before Sara could order another round of expensive cocktails, she called over a waiter and asked for a bottle of house white. Sara looked at her in horror. To which Maya responded, "You'd better get used to it if you're planning on living on a teacher's salary."

Sara nodded and laughed. "I suppose so," she said, and she already seemed like a different person to the brittle, humorless woman she'd become across the years.

Sara's pronouncement had softened Maya's feelings towards her old friend. They had drifted away from each other at such a sharp angle over the years that she couldn't imagine how she could ever feel close to her again. But as the minutes ticked by in the bar that night and the cheap wine made its way through her bloodstream, she found herself feeling strangely restored to herself. It was as if the Maya who'd married a twice-married man and turned herself inside out to accommodate other people's children and the women who'd made them, the Maya who had sex out of a sense of duty, who fell asleep at night and dreamed about her stepson and then felt disappointed when she woke up in the morning and the dream fell away, leaving behind a snoring middle-aged man with a bald patch, the Maya who was sent venomous e-mails from a stranger who knew too much about her to really be a stranger, the Maya who had lost so much sense of her own identity that she had gone to a brand-new hairdresser and asked him to do whatever he wanted, that Maya seemed to fade away, leaving in her place the original version of herself: young, fresh, silly and free.

Their conversation turned to old times: to school days and old boyfriends and strange people they had known. Another bottle of wine was ordered and delivered to their table and shortly after that two champagne cocktails sent over by a pair of men standing at the bar looking at them meaningfully.

"Do you think either of them wants to be a house husband?" Sara said through her hand.

Maya turned and looked at them. "I don't know," she said. "Why don't we ask them? Excuse me," she said, beckoning to the two men, "do either of you want to be a house husband?"

The men smiled at each other and then joined them at their table. "What do you mean by a house husband?" said man number one, who was tall and fair with a small but not offensive belly bulging above his waistband.

"You mean a husband who doesn't leave the house?" said man number two, who was dark and small but perfectly formed.

"No," said Sara, "we mean a man who cleans the house and shops for the house and cooks food for the people who live in the house."

"And babies," Maya added, "a man who looks after babies."

"While his wife goes to work."

"And doesn't complain about it."

"Or feel like less of a man."

"And what's in it for us?" said the fair man.

"A grateful wife. Job satisfaction. A happy family."

"Blow jobs?" said the dark-haired man.

"Yes, blow jobs."

They both put their hands up and all four of them laughed.

The two men stayed and chatted for a good hour. It was harmless and silly, leading nowhere. They exchanged numbers at the end and Maya immediately lost hers.

"So," said Sara, her face flushed with exhilaration, "I suppose you need to be heading home like a good married girl." It was eleven thirty. The last two hours seemed to have sped by in twenty minutes. Maya shook her head and said, "No way. The night is young. How about another glass each for the road?"

And so they stayed for another hour and each drank a glass of wine that neither of them really needed and it felt as though they'd both shed a few layers, and when Sara leaned in towards Maya and said, very close to her face, "So, tell me, are you really happy? Like, really and truly?" Maya had barely missed a beat to say, "No. I'm not. Not really. Actually, I'm miserable."

"I knew it," said Sara, banging the tabletop a little too hard. "I knew you weren't happy. What is it? Will you tell me?"

"Oh, you were right, you were right all along, Sara. They all hate me. The whole family. I try so hard. I do everything right but still I can't do enough. And Adrian is so sweet. He's so kind and so nice to me but he just doesn't get it. He thinks everyone is so happy just because he is. And . . ." She hesitated. She'd been about to tell Sara about the e-mails, but even with a bottle of white wine and two strong cocktails in her system, she lost her nerve. She would never tell anyone about the e-mails, she knew that without a doubt. "And it gets worse, Sara." She bit her lip and threw her friend a nervous look. "I think I'm in love with someone else."

Sara clapped her hand over her mouth. "Oh. God. Who?"

"His son," she said. "Adrian's son."

"Not the tall snooty one with the bad smell under his nose?"

"Yes. That's the one."

"But, Maya, he's a child."

"Well, no actually, he's twenty-two."

"Twenty-two! Oh good God."

"And he's not snooty. Well, at least, he's not as snooty as he looks. Under the surface he's a big softhearted fool."

Sara looked at her skeptically. "Have you . . . ?"

"No! God! No! We've barely kissed."

"So?"

"So, I don't know. He has a girlfriend. I'm married to his dad. He's ten years younger than me. It's ridiculous."

"I'd say it is."

"Sara, seriously, whatever happens, you have to swear that you will never tell anyone what I've just told you. Will you? Swear?"

"Of course I will," said Sara. "It will never pass my lips. But what are you going to do about it?"

"Nothing," said Maya. "I'm not going to do anything about it. I'm just going to keep going through the motions until I go completely numb."

◦⌒◦

Maya got home at one a.m. Adrian was sitting up waiting for her, some plans spread out about him, an anglepoise desk lamp throwing a perfect circle of light around him, a cup of green tea at his elbow and the laptop open at his side.

"Look at you!" he said, genially. "Pissed as a fart!"

She smiled and hooked her arms around his neck. Lovely lovely Adrian.

"Good night?"

She tipped off her boots and left them where they stood on the living room floor; then she picked up the cat and brought it to her face, breathing in the wonderful scent of clean fur. "It was really fun," she said.

"I can tell." He looked up at her fondly. "How was Sara?"

"She's going to retire in two years and retrain as a teacher."

"Wow," said Adrian, raising an eyebrow. "Didn't see that one coming."

"My period started," she announced.

He looked up at her again and she could see the machinations beneath his flesh, his brain trying to decide how to make his face look. He settled on sympathetic. Which was entirely wrong. She wanted him to look devastated. "Oh," he said in his sweetest voice, "darling. I'm so sorry."

"What are we going to do?" she asked, more dramatically than she'd intended. "What are we going to do if we can't have a baby?"

"Of course we're going to have a baby."

"No," she said firmly. "We might not. I've never been pregnant in my life. And I've taken risks. There might be something wrong with me."

"Well, then," said Adrian, pinching the bridge of his nose after removing his reading glasses, "we'll have to investigate. We'll have to do whatever it takes."

"But is that what you want? I mean, how much do you want another baby? Enough to go through fertility treatment? Enough to spend thousands of pounds? And then it might not even work? And supposing I do get pregnant? What then? How would that work? There'd be no more weekend sleepovers for the little ones—"

Adrian interrupted her. "Why ever not?"

"Well, where would they sleep? There's barely room for them all as it is. And how would that make them feel? Elbowed out by the new crown prince or princess. I'm just thinking . . ." She paused for a moment. "Maybe it's not such a good idea. I mean, maybe if no baby comes we should just be philosophical about it?"

Adrian switched off the anglepoise lamp and joined her on the sofa. He cupped his hands around hers and looked at her in that way of his, that *you have my full and undivided attention* way, that *I'm listening* way. She looked back at him, at the softness of his hazel eyes, the gentleness of his face, and it hit her with full force, hard, right at the very core of herself, that she did not love him anymore. She gasped, almost silently. He was talking, something about *let's see how you feel in another month or so, we can keep having this conversation as long as you need to have it, we'd find a way if necessary, we'd find a way,* and she nodded mutely and tried to reason with herself; *it's just the alcohol, it's just my hormones, it's just the e-mails warping my emotions.* But the more she tried to reason with herself, the more certain she became.

It was over.

She didn't want to have a baby with this man, another suitcase to add to his towering pile of baggage. She didn't want to live here, in this guesthouse for other people's children; she didn't want to be the cause of more angst and more reorganization; she didn't want to be whispered about behind her back, to have her haircuts and her Christmas puddings judged by a panel of self-justified critics; she didn't want to *sit in the backseat of the car.*

She twisted her wedding ring around and around her finger as he talked, the conviction of her realization flooding her body with adrenaline. Then she took Adrian's hand back in hers and she looked at him and she said, with a certainty that took her completely by surprise, "You know what. Actually, I think we should stop trying for a baby, Adrian. Because"—she squeezed his hand, a little too hard—"I'm not so sure about us anymore. I'm not so sure this is working."

The silent moment that followed this pronouncement spanned millennia and galaxies. It reached every corner of the universe and wrapped itself around every inch of everything that had ever existed across all of time.

Outside a single car passed by, throwing a pale gold curtain of light across the pair of them, highlighting the numb terror in Adrian's eyes. The silence stretched on further and Maya began to wonder if she had even said it out loud.

Then, slowly, without rancor, Adrian pulled his hand from Maya's, got to his feet, kissed the top of her head and said, "I'm off to bed, sweetheart, I'll see you in the morning. Love you."

"Love you," Maya repeated unthinkingly.

She watched him shut down his laptop, pull his plans into a neat pile, pick up a glass of water and leave the room. It was like watching a ghost. She shook her head, questioning what she had just seen, what had just happened, or failed to happen. She made herself a coffee, poured herself a glass of water, then she sat back down and drank both, efficiently and robotically. She took her phone from her bag to charge it and saw that she had a new text message. It was from Cat. She clicked it open and read it: "You FREAK! How can you not think you look gorgeous! But I'll delete it anyway. And don't worry, nobody saw it, just me and Luke! ☺."

There. There it was. The final, crushing nail. It had sounded like exactly the sort of thing that sharp-tongued Luke would say: campily cruel, designed to elicit guilty laughter. She fought back a sob of indignation and headed towards bed.

She could hear Adrian behind the bedroom door, opening and closing the wardrobe, brushing his teeth. She stood there for a while, her head spinning slightly, her hand upon the doorknob. And then she exhaled quietly, turned, and made her bed for the night in the bottom bunk of the children's room, her head facedown on a pillow that smelled bittersweetly of Beau's scalp.

33

"Where's the Board of Harmony?" said Otis, peering at the white space on the hallway wall through his fringe.

"I took it down," said Adrian, swinging bags of groceries through the doorway to the living room and resting them on the kitchen counter.

Otis followed behind him and added his bags to the pile on the counter. "But why?"

Beau was still standing in the hallway staring at the bare spot on the wall with his jaw hanging open as though the missing whiteboard was a spectacle on a par with a holy miracle.

"Because," said Adrian, "it made me sad. Because she did it to make everyone like her and it doesn't seem to have worked."

"I liked her," said Beau indignantly.

"Yes," said Adrian. "Of course you liked her."

"Well, mostly I liked her," he continued. "But also sometimes I didn't like her."

Adrian looked at his baby curiously from the corner of his eye. "Oh yes?"

"Yes, like when she told me to *do the right thing*. Because she was a teacher, but she wasn't my teacher. And she wasn't my mummy."

"No," said Adrian, "she wasn't your teacher or your mummy."

"But mostly I liked her."

"Good," said Adrian, rolling a net of satsumas into the fruit bowl.

"Well, I'm glad," said Otis, hunting through the bags for the packet of Maoams he had somehow persuaded Adrian to buy for him. "The Board of Harmony was basically a really, really bad idea."

Adrian threw him a curious look.

"Yeah, it was like I almost preferred it when you forgot things because at least it was *you* forgetting things. You know. And the crappy presents you used to get us. At least you chose them yourself."

Adrian draped a hand of bananas over the satsumas and frowned. "But you lot were always moaning because of that kind of thing."

"Well, I wasn't moaning. I was happy. You were doing your best. You were just being . . . you."

"And I got the distinct impression from all and sundry that me being me was not good enough."

Otis shook his head and ripped open the Maoam packet. "It was good enough for me," he said. "I didn't see why you needed someone to come along and change everything for you."

"I think the idea was that Maya was *improving* things, not *changing* things."

Otis shrugged and put a sweet into his mouth. "Whatever," he said, "I'm just glad it's gone. I hated it."

Adrian flinched. There was a darkness and a heat to his words, unexpected and unsettling. He looked at his son, his middle child, this mysterious boy of his who appeared so often to have no opinions at all, suddenly expressing one—with such vehemence. And the thought occurred to him, like a small electric shock to his consciousness, that maybe it was Otis who had sent the e-mails to Maya.

He didn't allow the thought to grow roots. He busied himself with the preparation of a meal for his two boys. He chatted with them both about all manner of interesting topics. He arranged food onto plates in pleasing patterns with bits trimmed off and separated from each other to request. And then, halfway through loading the dishwasher, while the boys sat at the kitchen counter, eating their dinner and watching something shouty on the TV, Adrian's phone rang. The number was vaguely familiar so he took the call. It was Jonathan Baxter.

"Hi, Adrian, listen, good news. Or at least I think so. According to my wife and my daughter, Matthew has a flatmate with mismatched eyes. Not only that but she also works for him so she might easily have had access to one of my old phones."

Adrian stood up straight, a plastic cup still clutched in his other hand. "What's her name?"

"She's called Abby. They're very close-knit apparently. Best of friends."

"God, OK . . . What do we do now? I mean, does she know I've been looking for her?"

"No," said Jonathan. "No. We haven't said anything to Matthew or to her. I wanted to let you know first. Find out how you wanted to handle things."

"Well, right, I'd like to talk to her ideally. As soon as possible. Can you give me a number?"

Jonathan sighed. "Well, personally, *I* would be very happy to give you the number but my wife is being very cautious about this. A bit paranoid. You know. So we thought we could give you Matthew's e-mail address instead; you could write to him, and take it from there. How does that sound?"

"Well, yes, it sounds better than nothing, I guess." He put down the plastic cup and sifted through some paperwork on the counter looking for a scrap of paper and a pen.

"I hope you understand. I mean, you hear so many bizarre stories these days, you know, stalkers, identity theft. For all we know you could be an ex-boyfriend with a grudge."

"Well, no, that I most definitely am not. Most definitely. But I do understand. And that will be fine. Fire away."

"OK. His e-mail address is matthewbaxter@retrotech.co.uk. Got that?"

"Yes, yes, I have. Thank you so much."

He hung up and smiled, feeling suffused with relief. Because he had a much better idea than e-mailing Jonathan Baxter's son and getting some flannelly response because clearly this woman was very close to him and clearly this woman had no desire to see Adrian's face again and clearly Matthew Baxter would do whatever he needed to do to protect his friend from Adrian's appearance in her life. Instead he flipped open his laptop and Googled "Matthew Baxter" and "Retrotech" and there it was, in under five seconds, an office address on the City Road.

"Who was that?" said Otis, a piece of roast chicken speared on his fork.

"That," said Adrian triumphantly, "was a man who is going to help me find Jane."

"Jane who came here to take Maya's cat?"

"Yes. That Jane. Except she's not Jane. She's Abby. And I'm going to find her tomorrow. It's my turn," he said, studying the Google map on his screen and writing down the address, "to stalk her."

∽

The following afternoon, Adrian found himself outside the offices of Retrotech, which were housed in a scruffy art deco block halfway between Old Street and Angel. He pressed the buzzer and shouted into the intercom, "Is Abby in today?"

"Yes, but she's not here right now. Who is this?"

"Just a friend. Just passing, was going to see if she was free for lunch. What time are you expecting her back?"

"She's gone to a client's in Soho; she should be back within the hour. Can I give her a message for you?"

"No, no, don't worry. I'll try again next time I'm passing. Thanks for your help."

"You're welcome."

Adrian walked slowly away from the office doors and glanced from side to side. He saw a bench diagonally across the street and ran through the traffic to get to it. Then he phoned the office and asked the receptionist to reschedule the three p.m. development meeting, pulled on a pair of sunglasses and waited.

34

It was a relief for Cat to see Luke's face when she pulled the front door open that afternoon. It was the second week of the summer holidays and she was done. Done with kids, done with rain, done with picking up dog crap, done with cooking fish fingers, done with Caroline's increasingly late returns from work. She had not had time to do her hair properly for, like, three days and it was currently in a ponytail that she knew would stay in place even after she released the elastic band.

"You look like shit," said Luke, taking in her appearance from head to toe.

"And you look gay," she retorted, not for the first time. It was often true and it was always satisfying. "You try looking after three kids and two dogs every single day for two weeks. What happened to your beard?" She squinted at his baby-soft face.

"I took it off," he said. "I didn't look gay enough with it on."

"I quite liked it," she said, letting him into the house, where he was greeted like a long-lost son by the dogs. He patted them and then brushed nonexistent dog hair off the front of his immaculate cream drainpipe trousers.

"Yes, well, the day I take sartorial advice from you, dear sister, is the day I turn myself in to the fashion police."

He headed automatically down the stairs to the basement, the dogs running behind like footmen. "Jesus Christ," he said, looking at the carnage in the kitchen and the TV area. "You should totally not be in charge of children. Or houses."

Cat looked at what he saw: a halfhearted attempt to tame the kitchen post lunch and cookie making, one chocolate-faced child watching the Olympics on the floor in a pile created from every cushion in the house, another chocolate-faced child stretched out on the cushionless sofa eating yogurt from a pot balanced on its chest and a third child, dark-eyed, still in pajamas, banging a tennis ball off the exterior wall in a state of near psychosis.

"I agree," she said. "This was not a vocational decision, I can assure you. And I will not be doing this again next summer. I will be somewhere else entirely."

"A hundred pounds you won't. Hello, small siblings!" he shouted across the room to the children, only one of whom turned at the sound of his voice and raised a feeble hand.

"What are you doing here, anyway? Why aren't you at work?"

"Oh, Dad's doing these early finish days, to beat the non-existent Olympics traffic nightmare. Everyone is totally taking the piss. Dad wasn't there this afternoon, he's gone AWOL again, so I thought fuck it—"

"Language . . ."

He raised his eyebrows. "So I thought *to hell with it*. And then I thought I hadn't seen you for a while . . ." He shrugged.

"You are a love," she said drily. "Coffee?"

He shook his head.

"Wine?"

"What time is it?"

"It's . . ." She pretended to look at a watch. "Oh, look, it is wine o'clock. Actually, it's ten past." She beamed at him, pulled open Caroline's booze fridge (she did love Caroline for having a booze fridge) and took out something with a screw top. "I totally deserve this," she said. "And I'm never having children. Or actually, if I do, I'll emigrate to Hawaii or something, somewhere where it never rains. It's so *fucking boring*." She mouthed the words silently. "Seriously, every time I suggest something, some activity, you can guarantee there'll be one who says *no way*. And then I can't be arsed to talk that person round so I end up having to placate the ones who *did* want to do the thing, which takes just as much effort as it would have taken to talk round the person who *didn't* want to do the thing and then we're all stuck here in the rain in bad moods. Making mountains out of cushions *for the thousandth time*." She rolled her eyes.

She offered Luke a plate of slightly misshapen cookies decorated with Team GB emblems printed onto rice paper. "Olympics cookie?"

"No," said Luke, as she'd known he would. She wasn't sure she'd ever seen him eat anything that had been baked in a real person's oven. "Thanks all the same."

Cat looked at her brother properly, over the rim of her wineglass. He looked pensive and uncomfortable. "So," she said, "what are you *really* doing here?"

"I told you," he said, "I came to see you."

"No," she said, mock-sternly, her head cocked to one side, "you did not."

"No," he conceded. "Well, yes and no. I've done something really stupid."

"Oh, goody!" She rubbed her hands together.

"Oh, fuck off," he said sardonically.

"Shhh!"

He grimaced. "Anyway, listen, remember Charlotte?"

"Of course I remember Charlotte. We used to be quite close, remember?"

"Well, anyway, *I slept with her*," he whispered.

Cat looked at him inquiringly. She had no idea if this was a good thing or a bad thing.

"I bloody well slept with her. After it took me so long to get her out of my life. And now she's . . . she's . . ."

"She thinks she's your girlfriend again?"

"Yes. Exactly."

"And you don't want that?" She eyed the plate of Olympics cookies from the corner of her eye. She'd already had two; they weren't even that nice, but she couldn't stop thinking about them. She plucked one from the plate delicately and nibbled at the edge of it as though the cookie were neither here nor there to her, a mere prop, something to do.

"Of course I don't want that. She's a pyscho."

"Then why did you sleep with her?"

"Well, no, obviously. Obviously I shouldn't have slept with her. But I did. And now she's all over me. Talking about moving up to London, getting a flat together."

"Oh, you total idiot."

"Yes. Thank you. I know. What shall I do?"

"Why are you asking me?"

"Because you're a woman; because you used to be friends with her. I thought you might have some insight."

She nibbled another strip off the cookie and fiddled with the crumbs left in its wake. "Sorry, mate. No insight whatsoever. But maybe some honesty wouldn't go amiss. Just tell her that it was a mistake. Tell her you don't want her to be your girlfriend."

"I've tried."

"Trying doesn't come into it, Luke. Just do it. Just say: Charlotte, you're so hot that I couldn't control my tiny little penis, but now, in the cold light of day, I've decided that this isn't what I want. I'm sorry I'm such a total cocksucker. Please forgive me."

"Please don't talk about my penis, it makes me feel dirty."

"Well, don't go around putting your penis inside scary girls and then asking me what to do about it afterwards." She forgot to be delicate with her cookie and stuffed the remaining third into her mouth in one piece.

Luke threw her a strange look. She thought it was disgust at first, at her gluttony. But then she saw he was nervous. "Listen," he said, "there's another thing. About Charlotte. She said something a bit weird."

"What, like, *My, what a huge penis you have?*"

He tutted. "No. About Maya. It sounded like, I don't know, like she might have had a grudge against her. It made me wonder if maybe it was her who wrote the e-mails."

"Wonder if it was *who* who sent the e-mails?"

"Oh." Cat turned at the sound of Otis's voice. "Nothing," she said dismissively. "Nothing at all. You really should get dressed."

"No point getting dressed now, it's closer to bedtime than it is to getting up this morning." He shrugged. "Who were you talking about?"

"Nobody," she said. "Just a woman at Dad's office. That's all."

She gave Luke a warning look and mouthed *later* at him.

"Hi, Otis," said Luke.

"Hi, Luke." He didn't make eye contact but he smiled gently.

"Having a good holiday?"

Otis shrugged. "It's OK," he said. "Pretty boring."

Luke looked at Cat and then at Otis and then at the two children buried in cushions at the other end of the room and he clapped his hands together and said, "Shall we all go out for tea?"

Otis looked up at him suspiciously. "Where?"

"I don't know," said Luke. "You choose."

"Nando's," said Otis.

"No," said Pearl, "sushi!"

"No," said Beau, "I want pizza!"

Cat looked at Luke and rolled her eyes. "See?" she said. "Constantly. Every single time I try to suggest anything. It's so boring."

"Right." Luke pulled a piece of paper from a memo pad and tore it into three strips. He wrote the name of a restaurant on each strip, screwed them up and then tipped them onto the counter. "Cat chooses," he said.

Children started to complain. Luke pretended to put the balls of paper into the bin. They stopped complaining. Cat picked a ball of paper. "Nando's," she announced. "Come on, then. Clothes on!"

～

Five little Wolfes, sitting in a row. Cat wondered if anyone was looking at them, if anyone was wondering how they all fitted together. There was little connecting them physically. It was family lore that each one had been fathered by a different milkman.

"Everyone happy?" she asked across the table. Beau nodded effusively. Pearl smiled enigmatically. Otis grunted. Cat smiled and turned to Luke, who was sitting opposite her. "So," she said, tucking into a pile of chips and half a medium-hot chicken. "How are you getting on, living with Dad?"

"Not too bad actually," said Luke, picking over the contents of a spicy chicken wrap. "He's not so bad."

"I know," said Cat. "I've been trying to tell you that for years."

"He is a bit of an old fart though."

"He's only forty-eight. He's not that old."

"No, but he is, you know, fart-like."

"In what way is he fart-like?"

"Oh, you know, wearing the same old clothes, all that weird organic stuff he buys, the radio droning on all the time. You know, there are forty-eight-year-old dads who listen to cool music, wear cool clothes. I mean, hard as it is to believe, he was actually a teenager during punk."

"Oh, come on, you don't really want a dad like that, do you? A trendy dad? An *old punk* dad?" She tipped some ketchup onto the rim of Beau's plate. "Your problem," she said, "is that whatever Dad does, it's never good enough for you. You've been like that about him since you were tiny. It's like . . ." She paused and screwed the lid back onto the bottle. "It's like you were expecting someone else. And he turned up. And you never quite got over it."

Otis turned at these words and eyed Cat and Luke curiously. "Are you talking about Dad?" he said.

"No," said Cat.

"Yes," said Luke.

He looked at them both in confusion.

"Yes," said Cat, with a sigh.

"What are you saying?"

"Just that we all have a different view of him. That's all."

"I have the same view as Luke," said Otis.

"Oh," said Cat, slightly taken aback. "Right."

"Yes. I think he's an idiot."

"I never said he was an idiot!" said Luke.

"No, but you think he is one. It's obvious."

"Obvious, how?"

"The way you talk to him. The way you talk *about* him."

"Nice one, Luke," said Cat, under her breath.

"You know, all the shit choices he makes. Leaving Susie for Mum. Leaving Mum for Maya. For, like, no apparent reason.

Then making Maya so miserable she walked under a bus on purpose."

Cat rocked back in her seat at her brother's words. "Whoa now, Otis, we don't know that she did it on purpose. It's more likely it was an accident. And blaming that on Dad is *really* unfair."

"Why is it unfair? He was married to her. It was his job to keep her happy."

"Yes, but we know why she was so unhappy now, don't we?"

"I don't think that was the e-mails," he said mysteriously. "I think those are a red herring. I think it was something else making her unhappy. So unhappy that she didn't even want to *be* with Dad anymore."

"Beau, sweetness," Cat said nervously, "do you need the toilet? Pearl, can you take Beau to the toilet?"

For once the two younger children did as they were told without complaint, and watching them disappear through the door to the toilets, Cat turned angrily to Otis and hissed, "Otis! What are you doing? Stop it!"

"I'm just telling the truth. It's time to tell the truth now. Maya hated being married to Dad and then she fell in love with somebody else. And it was someone she shouldn't have fallen in love with. And *that's* why Maya killed herself."

"Oh, come on. Seriously—"

"It's true. It's totally true!"

"And where exactly did you pick up this red-hot nugget of information from?" said Luke, his voice calm and even.

"From a woman. Just from a woman."

"What woman?" said Cat.

"The woman who knew the man that Maya was in love with!" he barked impatiently, as if it was startlingly obvious, as if they were idiots.

"Right," said Cat, "and this woman was who exactly?"

"I can't tell you," said Otis. "I promised."

Cat and Luke stared at each other blindly across the table.

There was a moment's silence, muddied by the sound of the restaurant around them, of piped world music and cutlery and chatter.

"Have you told Dad?" asked Luke, his face deathly white. "Have you told him what you've been told?"

"No," he replied, almost in a whisper. "How could I?" He looked up then, properly, and stared desperately at both Cat and Luke. "Promise you won't tell him?" he pleaded. "Promise?"

Cat looked desperately at Luke. Of course they would have to talk to their dad about this. Of course they would. Otis saw the look pass between them and got to his feet, panicking. "No," he said, loudly, seriously. "No. Promise. You have to promise." His big brown eyes flashed with terror.

Still Cat and Luke stared at one another.

"Well . . . ," Luke began, circumspectly.

"Fuck," said Otis. "Fuck."

And then suddenly he was heading away from them, sprinting out of the door, towards the High Street. Luke jumped to his feet and gave chase. Over his shoulder he shouted to Cat, "I'll see you at Caroline's. Wait there for me!"

Beau and Pearl returned from the toilets. Cat forced a smile.

"Where are Luke and Otis?" asked Pearl.

"Oh, they've just gone for a walk," said Cat. "We're going to meet them back at the house."

Pearl looked at her suspiciously.

"It's fine," said Cat. "Come on. Finish your tea. We can go home via Costa if you like, get you one of those giant Bourbons."

Pearl shook her head. "No," she said quietly, "I think we should just go home."

"Fine," said Cat. "Eat up."

Cat regarded her own plate of food. There was over half a portion of chips left and all the best bits of the chicken, but suddenly she didn't have the stomach for it. She concentrated, instead, on collating the children and their possessions, including, hidden beneath a crumpled napkin, Otis's phone. Otis normally guarded his phone like a Rottweiler. It was always in his hand, in his pocket, under his pillow. She slipped it into her handbag and led the children home.

35

There. There she was. My God. It was actually her, after all these months.

She was wearing a fitted white cotton dress, black wedge-heeled sandals and a denim jacket. Her golden hair was combed straight and worn down, pushed back from her face by a pair of oversized black sunglasses. She was chatting to someone on her phone as she approached her office, laughing and strolling, clearly a personal call, not a business call. Adrian got to his feet and threaded his way through the traffic. She didn't see him at first; she'd pulled over by the entrance to her office to finish off her call, leaning backwards against a wall, her legs crossed in front of her, a sudden blast of sunshine illuminating her, causing her to lower her sunglasses and twist slightly away from him. Adrian pretended to use his own phone while he waited for her to finish her call and then, as she turned back, a smile still on her face, he stood before her, smiled and said, "Hello, Jane."

She clutched her chest. "Shit," she said, "you made me jump."

She pulled up her sunglasses and there they were, those remarkable, peculiar eyes of hers.

"Sorry," he said, "I've just been waiting for you to finish your phone call. I didn't mean to startle you."

"What on earth are you doing here?"

"I've been following the trail of your phone. The phone you left in my flat."

"Oh," she said, "right. Well, I really don't need the phone. It wasn't mine anyway, I borrowed it from someone. They're really not bothered about it."

"Well, that's just as well since I ended up giving it back to the woman who had it three owners back."

She smiled nervously, clearly struggling to make sense of the situation.

"So," she began, her eyes turning constantly to the office building to her left, as if to make her intentions obvious. "What can I—?"

"I'd like to talk to you," he said. "About Maya."

He watched her carefully, looking for signs of recognition. And he saw it, a flicker of her eyes, a parting of her lips, a mental recalibration. "Who?" she said feebly.

"Maya," he repeated. "My wife? The one who died?"

"Right," she said, feigning confusion.

"Have you got time," he said, "for a quick drink? A cup of coffee?"

"Look," she said, "I really don't understand. I didn't know your wife . . ."

"They're not expecting you back just yet. And honestly, I only need five minutes. We could sit over there if you like." He pointed at the bench on the other side of the road.

She looked at the bench and then back at her office block. He could see her hand inside her bag, her fingertips tracing the edges of her cigarette packet. He could see her resolve separating into two parts: the part that wanted a cigarette, that wanted to get rid of whatever it was she'd been wanting to do or say to him when she first came to his flat back in March; and the part that wanted to disappear into her office block and defer this thing indefinitely.

He stared at her impassively. He didn't want to scare her away. "Five minutes," he said again.

Her hand came out of her bag and onto her hip. "No," she said. "I'm sorry. I really do need to get back to work. But listen . . ." She stopped and softened. "Your family, how are you all? How are your beautiful children?"

"They're OK," he said, feeling that there was a right and a wrong answer to this question and that the key to opening up Abby's secrets rested in answering it correctly. "But there's been some unsettling developments, regarding Maya. I think we're all feeling a bit, you know, shaky."

Bingo. Her hand left her hip and hung loosely at her side. Her shoulders slumped. Her face lost its stiff mask of defensiveness. She sighed. "I could meet you later. If you like."

"How do I know you'll turn up?"

"I will. I promise you."

"So, you do know something?" he said. "About Maya?"

"I didn't say that."

"But you're agreeing to meet me. Why would you unless you knew something?"

"I am agreeing to meet up with you. You obviously want to talk to me. We'll work out the rest later. OK?" Her voice was soft and her hand rested on his sleeve. He was reminded of the impression she'd made on him all those months ago, her warmth and wisdom, her kindness and beauty.

"Yes," he said, his hand squeezing her upper arm. "Of course."

"Meet me at seven, at the Blue Posts in Rupert Street. Do you know it?"

"Yes," said Adrian, "yes, I'm sure I've been there before. I'll find it, anyway."

"I'll see you later," she said.

"Thank you," said Adrian. "I'm very grateful."

"Well," she said, her smile faltering, her hand going to the strap of her handbag, "maybe you should wait to hear what I have to tell you before you feel too grateful to me."

She smiled again, uncertainly, and then turned and headed into the office block, the door opening and closing behind her with a buzz and a click.

36

Luke kept the shaggy helmet of Otis's hair in his line of vision for a short while after he disappeared from the restaurant. Otis had started out at a brisk pace and then, as he neared the corner of the road, he'd begun to run. Luke picked up his pace to keep up with him and tore around the corner, nearly knocking over an elderly couple as he did so. He saw Otis's head bobbing, weaving urgently through the crowd. All the way up the road and around the corner he kept Otis in view. And then suddenly he was gone. Just like that.

He rounded the next corner, his heart pounding now with dread. It was Charlotte. That's who Otis had talked to on the bench outside Angel. It was the same day that Charlotte had turned up outside his office, unannounced, when they'd gone for a beer and she'd showed him photos of the bridesmaid dress she liked. Mere hours earlier she'd been telling his little brother that Maya had been in love with another man. Why? Why was she telling a twelve-year-old boy? And more importantly, had she told him who the other man was?

Luke found himself in a street of terraced houses, empty apart from a woman pushing a pram, and two teenage girls heading in the opposite direction. He stood at the junction, looking all around him. It was the summer holidays. There were children as far as the eye could see. But none of them was Otis.

He kept to the High Street. He didn't think Otis would take

a side turning; this wasn't his immediate locale, not an area he would be familiar with. He would be more likely to stick to the main roads.

Luke turned right figuring that Otis would be unlikely to cross a busy junction in a hurry. He called Cat to tell her that he couldn't find him, to tell her to phone him on his mobile, but Cat said Otis had left his phone in the restaurant, that she had it with her. Then he told her to log on to Facebook and put a message on Otis's wall asking his friends to look out for him. And then to send a text to everyone in his address book. "Shall I call Caroline?" she asked.

"No," Luke said, "let's wait a while. He's bound to head for a friend, or for home. Let's see what happens when the messages go out. Let's not freak her out just yet."

Luke walked for over two miles during the course of the next forty-five minutes. He walked until the soles of his feet had started to chafe against the insoles of his deck shoes because he was wearing no socks. He walked until he was lost and had to call Cat again to find out how to get back to Caroline's. When he finally got there he was sweating so much that he had dark ovals under the arms of his shirt.

"Well?" he said as Cat opened the door to him. "Anything?"

Cat shook her head and started to cry.

"Come on," said Luke, guiding her into the front room by her elbow and lowering her into the sofa, "come on. Don't cry. It's OK. He's twelve years old; he's not a baby. He'll be fine."

"Yes, but he was really upset. What if he makes a bad decision? Or what if he does something stupid?"

"He won't do anything stupid. He's a bright boy. He's just keeping his head down until the storm blows over."

"I think we should call Caroline now," she said. "It's been an hour. Oh God, I feel sick." She made the call and then switched off her phone.

They both turned at the sound of Beau and Pearl running down the stairs together. "We've been trying to hack into his Facebook page but we can't," said Pearl.

"We've tried about a hundred different passwords," breathed Beau.

"Loads of people have replied to your post on his wall though," said Pearl, "everyone's really worried about him."

"But nobody knows where he is."

"Although a girl in his class called Hannah said she reckons she saw him in Swanage about an hour ago."

"Which is completely stupid, because he was in Nando's with us an hour ago."

"And I looked up Swanage," said Pearl, "and it's about three hours on the train."

"Good work," said Cat, squeezing the back of Beau's leg. "Keep at it. Let me know the minute someone says something helpful."

They both nodded and ran back up the stairs to the study.

"Dad!" said Cat. "I haven't told Dad."

"I'll call him," said Luke.

Cat nodded.

"Dad," said Luke, when his father answered his phone. "It's me. Listen, Cat and I took the kids out for tea. We got into a bit of a row with Otis and he stormed off. I tried to follow but I lost him. He's been gone for over an hour. And he didn't take his phone with him."

There was a dead silence on the line.

"Dad?"

"Sorry. I mean— Shit. Does Caroline know?"

"Yes, she's on her way home right now."

"Jesus. What were you arguing about?"

"Well, it wasn't an argument exactly."

"Well, what was it then, exactly?"

Luke paused. "Where are you? Can you come over?"

Now Adrian paused. "I was just leaving the office." He sounded strangely reticent.

"Then get over here."

"Yes"—a beat too slow—"yes. Sure. I'll see you in thirty minutes."

"Yeah," said Luke sourly, "if it's not too much trouble."

"It's not that, Luke. It's . . . it's that Jane woman. I've found her. I'm supposed to be meeting her in an hour. She's going to tell me what she knows about Maya."

"Ah," said Luke. "Can you reschedule?"

"No. I haven't got her number. She hasn't got mine."

"Ah," said Luke again. "Well, I'm here. Cat's here. Caroline's on her way. But make sure you've got a good signal. OK? If I call you and you don't answer I'll break both your arms. Seriously."

"Of course," said Adrian urgently, "bloody hell, *of course*. If there's no signal I'll make sure we go somewhere where there is a signal. OK? Call me constantly."

Luke was about to say good-bye and then he stopped and said, "Dad, do you have any idea where Otis might be? I mean, he's your son. Does anything occur to you?"

He could hear the almost silent exhalation of disappointment on the other end of the line. "No," said Adrian, "no. I truly do not have a clue."

"Don't worry," said Luke, "I didn't really think you would."

37

APRIL 2011

Another holiday, another carefully chosen cottage in one of England's picture-perfect corners. It felt more like summer than spring. The temperature had been in the midseventies for days; the tender spring grass was already frazzled and brown; Maya had a tan mark under her wedding band.

The drive up to Suffolk had been a tonic; the sight of London fading away through the windows of a rental car had brought about a sense of release. The thought of not being in that flat, of not going through the motions, of breaking the weird patterns of the past few weeks since the drunken pronouncement of her night out with Sara. She hadn't thought too hard about the prospect of what lay ahead, about seeing Luke and being watched and being judged, about the as yet uncommitted faux pas that would be reported back to her in cruel, exacting detail upon her return to London. For now she was just glad to be getting away.

She sat now, reading, upon the grass outside the French windows of her and Adrian's ground-floor bedroom. She was wearing a black halter-neck bikini top and black shorts. In the distance she could hear the smaller children dashing around with the dogs, and behind her she could hear the sound of people arriving, the crunch of gravel, the banging of car doors. She put her book down by her side, folded open against its spine, and sat up. She recognized the sound of Luke's voice. She hadn't heard his voice for a long time. It filled her with something mad and stupefying. She heard Susie's voice, too, loud and enthused. Then she heard another voice. A shrill voice. A silly, carefree voice. She recognized it and immediately stood up, slid her feet into warm flip-flops, pulled on a T-shirt and headed around the walls of the rambling house to the front door. Adrian and Susie greeted each other warmly and then turned to smile at Luke and his companion: *Mum and Dad*. It always surprised Maya how right her husband looked when he stood side by side with one of his ex-wives, how each woman complemented him in some unique and distinctive way. With Susie it was the scruffiness, the slightly shabby clothes, the outgrown hair and large feet and hands. With Caroline it was the height, the substance, the imposing presence. And with her? Well, they both had two arms and two legs. But that was about as far as it went.

"Hello!" She swallowed her discomfort and walked towards Luke. Then she turned to his companion, to the unannounced and unexpected guest. "Hello, Charlotte," she said, leaning in to kiss each shiny, puppy-fatted cheek. "We weren't expecting you! How lovely!"

She tried not to look at Luke but couldn't help a brief sideways glance, just enough to theorize that maybe Charlotte's being here wasn't quite what he'd had in mind himself. According to the family grapevine Luke and Charlotte had split up last month. *Again*. Sources reported that Charlotte had taken it very badly. Sources also reported that this was it, over for good. No more off and on. Luke was adamant and his mind was set.

"No!" said Charlotte, echoing Maya's forced jollity. "It was all a bit last-minute! I literally walked into the pub last night and there was Luke, completely out of the blue, and literally a few hours later he'd invited me up to Suffolk! I mean, literally!"

Susie, Adrian and Maya all nodded at Charlotte and made noises of muted wonder.

"Well," said Adrian, "that's great. Really lovely to have you here, Charlotte. Really."

"I promise I'll pull my weight. I'll wash up and cook and all that business. I'm not just here for a free holiday!"

"No!" said Adrian. "No. Of course you're not. And even if you were, nobody would particularly care. We're pretty easygoing."

"Yes, I suppose you need to be to have these kinds of holidays. Especially in your circumstances. I mean"—her face fell—"you know, this big extended family. Hard enough to make it work when you're all apart, let alone when you're all squeezed into a house together." Her face fell again. "I think I'll stop talking now," she said.

Adrian and Susie laughed and said, "Nonono, don't be silly, of course, you're right." Maya managed a smile. Charlotte was just adorable. Look at her, in her little pleated shorts with rosebud sprigs, her tight white Aertex polo shirt, shiny white Converse, vanilla-cream hair pinned back on each side with kirby grips. Just adorable. But what was she doing here? Where was she going to sleep? Luke was supposed to be sharing a room with Otis and Beau. The only spare bed in the house was in an anteroom, just off her own bedroom. A camp bed. Charlotte couldn't sleep in there. It was too weird. And what about Luke? Was he expecting to share a bed with her? Were they having sex again? Why hadn't he phoned ahead to say he was bringing her? *What was she doing here?*

"Where are you going to sleep?" she asked, more forcefully than she'd intended.

"Oh, I'll sleep anywhere! A sofa. The bath. Anywhere that I don't get in the way."

"I'm sure we can rejig things," said Susie. "Don't you worry. It's just lovely having you here."

Susie looked at Adrian and Maya as though checking that

they shared her sentiment. They both smiled back tightly and nodded.

It was another two hours before Maya was able to corner Luke by himself. She found him moving a mattress from one room to another on the first floor. Charlotte was in the garden playing croquet with Pearl. She took the other end of the mattress and said, "Where is this going?"

"The girls' room," he said, pointing his head in the direction of a door on the other side of the landing. "Beau's going to sleep with Caroline, so we have a spare mattress."

"Didn't he mind?" Beau usually loved sharing a room with both his big brothers.

"You know Beau. World's most obliging child."

"So you and Charlotte, you're not . . . ?"

A twitch of Luke's left shoulder told her all she needed to know.

"Oh, Luke." She sounded like his mother and she didn't care.

"Don't," he said, pushing the bedroom door open with his back.

They positioned the mattress on the floor next to Cat's bed and let it drop. Then they regarded each other across the bed-sized space between them. "I was already drunk when she got to the pub. She was being all sweet and lovely. I wasn't thinking straight. Seriously, I was so drunk. She had to take me home. Back to hers. It's all kind of a blur from there . . ."

"Fine," said Maya, feeling that she was in no position to cast judgments on other people's poor decision-making skills, "but why the hell did you have to invite her?"

"I *didn't*," he hissed. "She invited herself. This morning. She asked me what I was doing today and I was too messed up to think of a lie. Well, actually, I didn't think I'd need one, I thought me going away *with my family* might be enough of a deterrent for her."

"She's quite something," said Maya drily.

"Hm." Luke puffed up the pillow and tidied the bedclothes.

He straightened up and put his hands into his pockets. His hair had grown longer since she'd last seen him, and flopped over his left eye. He was wearing his non-prescription glasses, a gray T-shirt and pale blue seersucker shorts. There he was, so young and half-formed. She looked for the memory of their kiss in his eyes and found it there. She flushed and looked away.

"So," he said, "you had your hair cut?"

She put her hand to it as she did instinctively every time someone mentioned it.

"I really like it."

Maya laughed gruffly. "Really?" she said. "You don't think it makes me look like the ugly one in a boy band?"

He laughed as though she'd cracked a joke. "Absolutely not! It makes you look really feminine. And delicate."

She smiled at him gratefully. She believed him. Which meant that someone else had seen the photo of her hair and someone else had made the spiteful observation. "I'm growing it, anyway," she said. "It was a mad moment. Not sure what I was thinking."

"You have to do those things sometimes. You have to give in to them. Surrender to whim. Otherwise how would you know what suited you?"

He was talking about fashion. He was talking about hair. But he could just as easily have been talking about her life. She stared at him for a moment, taking in the angles and the lines of him, taking in the unsettling eyes, the just-so hair, the thin legs and arms, the exquisite loveliness of him. Would he be just another bad haircut? Because that's exactly what Adrian had been. She could see that now. She remembered the moments of prevarication in the early days of their romance. The mental pros and cons lists she'd run through in the dark of night. All the stuff she'd finally convinced herself wouldn't be a problem because she was *surrendering to whim.*

He has too much baggage.

He's too old for me.

His family will never really forgive me.

Other women have already had the best of him; I will get the dregs.

He doesn't really seem to see me when he looks at me.

I'm not sure I really love him.

She'd looked at all these things and decided that they didn't matter. What mattered was this: She'd been single for two years. She wanted to change her life. She'd just left teacher training college and had to find a first job and she wanted some security while she did that. Adrian was lovely. Adrian was kind. Adrian made her feel safe and protected. She knew he was lying when he said the children would be fine. She knew he was lying when he said everyone would understand. But she'd been prepared to take that risk. She'd had a master plan. She would be not only the sweetest, least-threatening person she possibly could be, she would actually make things better for everyone. She would find the weaknesses in Adrian's family life and fix them. Adrian's family would be grateful to her! They would wonder how they had ever managed without her!

Essentially, she saw now, she had gone into her marriage to Adrian with the same mind-set as she'd had going into that hair salon to ask them to cut all her hair off. I *can always grow it back if it doesn't suit me.*

Stupid girl.

She ran her hand over her too-short hair again and said, "Well, I can safely say that this haircut does not suit me."

"Well," said Luke, "I disagree."

"Thank you," she said.

"I've really missed you."

"I know," she said. "It's been too long."

"Three months and nine days."

She looked at him strangely.

"I'm not being a freak." He smiled. "It was the first of January. Easy maths."

She smiled. "Are we cool now?" she asked. "You and I? Can we be normal?"

He laughed. "I thought we *were* being normal."

"No, you know what I mean."

"I do know what you mean. And yes, we can be normal. If you want us to be normal, that is?"

No, she thought, I don't want us to be normal. I want us to be fabulously abnormal and twisted. I want us to be all over each other with tongues and toes and lips and teeth. I want us to climb naked over each other's bodies while my aging, oblivious husband, *your father*, sleeps on in the next room. I want us to announce to the family that we are *in love* and watch their faces contort with incomprehension and hurt. And then I want us to suck each other dry until there is nothing left of us, until we are all done and desiccated and then I can move on and surrender to the next whim, commit the next heinous misdemeanor.

She couldn't look at him. She didn't recognize herself anymore. She felt like a soap opera villain: breaking up families on a whim, falling in love with handsome young stepsons, pretending to be so nice when really she was a scheming bitch. *Dear Bitch*. Her poison pen pal was right about her. Her poison pen pal had recognized her for what she was before she'd even recognized it herself.

She dropped her gaze to the floor and she said, in as bright a voice as she could muster, "Yes. I want us to be normal."

"Normal?" said a voice from the doorway.

They both turned as one, the fading shadows of guilt still there in Maya's eyes. It was Charlotte.

She smiled uncertainly from Maya to Luke and back again. "What are you two talking about?" Her tone was playful but sharp.

"Oh, God, nothing," said Luke. "We were just . . ." He looked to Maya for assistance.

"Talking about work," she said hopelessly. "Just stuff at work. New head of department. You know. All the changes."

Charlotte nodded. "Right," she said. Her eyes found Luke's and Maya saw her study him closely.

"Your bed!" he said, with a flourish of his hands. "Will you be OK in here?"

Charlotte nodded again. "Sure," she said, "I'll be fine. Thank you. Both of you." She looked again from Luke to Maya and then slowly she left the room.

❧

Adrian was sitting at the table in the kitchen when Maya came downstairs. He had Beau on his lap and they were playing Snap together. Beau's face was streaked red with dried tears and there was a crumpled tissue in his hand.

"Everything OK?" she asked, sitting down next to the pair of them.

"Oh, just some sibling rough and tumbling got a bit out of hand. Elbow in the eye. But we're fine now, aren't we?"

Beau nodded bravely and turned his next card over.

"Brave boy." Maya ran her hand down the thick mane of Beau's hair and felt it there as she'd felt it more and more often these days: the almost imperceptible shake of his head. He immediately tried to compensate for the head-shake by smiling at her. But the smile was brittle and forced. In her raw emotional state she was almost tempted to stalk into the garden and have a little weep of self-pity. But no, she'd done this, she'd broken this family *on a whim*, she needed to deal with all the messy bits she'd left in her wake.

Beau was like her. Such an anxious little people-pleaser, so keen to do the right thing, to be accepted and adored. But deep down inside he was just as full of bad thoughts and dark feelings as every other child in the world.

"Snap!" said Beau.

"You are a *legend*," said Adrian, giving Beau a high five.

Beau beamed at him. Not the funny, crooked little smile he'd just given her, but a big, loving punch of a smile.

"One more?" Beau asked, his face upturned to his father's.

"One more," said Adrian. "And then back out into the garden."

"OK." He was already dealing out the pack.

"You all right?" Adrian asked Maya over the top of Beau's head.

She nodded.

"Bed situation all sorted out?"

"Umhm." She nodded again.

He smiled at her. It was that same smile he'd been giving her ever since her night out with Sara. That injured smile. That *please don't hit me again* smile. It didn't make her feel sorry for him though. It made her want to scream.

This, she'd realized, *this* was how he reconciled himself to the terrible compromises of his life. He simply pretended that things didn't happen. He edited them out. Blacked them out. Carried on regardless. It was quite disconcerting and she longed now to talk to Caroline, to talk to Susie, to find out how it really was when Adrian left. Because she'd only ever heard Adrian's side and she could see now that Adrian's side was a crime scene stripped bare of even a shred of real evidence.

"Where is everyone?" she asked.

"Caroline, Susie and Cat have gone to the supermarket; everyone else is in the garden. I think." He smiled pitifully at her again. She resisted the urge to slap him and damped down the familiar sense of irritation that she had not been included in a "wives' outing," had not been consulted on a shopping list, had once again been relegated to the status of unpaid au pair girl.

"OK," she said, her voice deadened with resentment. "I'll go and see what the kids are up to."

Otis was throwing balls for the dogs. Pearl and Charlotte were playing croquet and shouting at Otis for allowing the dogs to run through their croquet pitch. Charlotte looked up at Maya as she approached. "Hi!" she said brightly. "We're just starting a new round. Want to join in?"

"Sure," said Maya.

Charlotte walked across the lawn to the croquet bag and pulled out a mallet for her. "There you go. We'll play in age order, youngest to oldest. So Pearl, me and you. Oops, not to say that you're old, obviously." She squeezed Maya's arm and grimaced and Maya truly could not decide whether she was being genuine or disingenuous.

"Well, that depends who you're comparing me to, really," she said, lightly.

"Ha, yes. It's quite a spread in this family."

"Yes," said Pearl, counting on her fingers, "it goes four, nine, eleven, eighteen, twenty-two, thirty-three, forty-three, forty-seven, forty-eight. Like lottery numbers."

"Which one is forty-eight?" Charlotte asked Pearl.

"Susie. She's the oldest, then dad, then Caroline, then Maya, then Luke, then Cat, then Otis, then me, then Beau. And then whoever comes next." She smiled at Maya.

"*If* someone comes next," Maya replied.

"*When* someone comes next."

"Oh!" said Charlotte. "Are you and Adrian trying for a baby then?"

Maya forced a smile. "Sort of," she said. "But not very successfully so far!"

Charlotte's face fell and she squeezed Maya's arm again. "Oh God, I'm sorry," she said. "That must be really tough."

Maya arranged her face into an expression of terrible sadness. Her ongoing inability to conceive had gone from being a matter of worry and unhappiness to a matter of relief and marvelous good luck. And, now that she and Adrian had stopped having sex altogether, to a matter to which she no longer gave any thought at all.

"I'm sure it will happen for you," said Charlotte, her hand still on Maya's arm. "I'm sure you and Adrian will find a way. It must be hard, though," she said, her cornflower eyes boring into Maya's, "to be surrounded by all these children, if you think you might not have one of your own.

"Sorry," she went on. "Christ. Sorry. That was tactless. Sorry. I just meant, you're so good with the kids. You'd make a lovely mummy. You *will* make a lovely mummy."

"Thank you," Maya said. "I'm being philosophical."

"Best thing to do," said Charlotte, and gave Maya's arm one last squeeze.

Pearl stood at the other side of the croquet pitch, having got her ball clear through the first eight hoops while they'd chatted. "I just got thirty points," she said. "Your turn, Charlotte."

"On my way," Charlotte called out with a smile. She turned back to Maya. "By the way," she said, "I really like your haircut! It suits you."

"You think?" said Maya, her hand upon the bare nape of her neck.

"Yes. Totally. But then, you're so pretty, you could get away with anything."

"Oh."

"Yes. I was just saying to Luke in the car on the way here, I don't think you really know how pretty you are."

Maya smiled awkwardly. "Nowhere near as pretty as you though."

"I wasn't fishing for compliments," said Charlotte, her voice suddenly edgy.

"No, I know you weren't. I was just—"

"This isn't a competition." She lingered over the break between her words. "Is it?"

"What?"

Charlotte stared at her coldly. Then the frost thawed and she smiled. "My turn," she said brightly. "Better get back to the game."

38

The "real wives" had decided upon a dinner menu of pasta bake and garlic bread for the children and mushroom risotto and tomato salad for the adults. The kitchen, from four thirty until dinnertime, was a hive of adults chopping, pouring, stirring, drinking, talking, shouting, arguing, laughing, nibbling. Children came and went, the windows misted up, Cat played music using her iPhone and a portable speaker, and this was it, the best bit of these family holidays.

Maya still remembered her first country weekend with Adrian's family. She'd been so nervous but it had been like a beautiful dream. The banter and noise, the warmth and the laughter. She'd compared it to her own upbringing, the neat house just outside Maidstone where she'd lived with her much older brother—who was gone, anyway, by the time she was eleven, leaving her an only child for the next seven years—her very proper parents and a mute cockatiel called Penny. There had been no variation to her lineup of family members. No stirring up of the basic familial ingredients. And until Maya met Adrian she'd believed that hers was the only form a family could happily take.

But now she looked at this mess of people from a different point of view. She saw them not as a family, not as enchanted and magical, but as a group of survivors, a support group almost: Adrian Anon. Each one wore an invisible scar, some deeper than others, but a scar nonetheless.

Susie, for example: Maya had always suspected that if Adrian hadn't left her, she'd have left him eventually. They'd been so young to get married and have children. They would have grown out of each other. Yet how had it been for Susie to know that she had been lied to for so long? By the father of her children? How had it been to put her children to bed at night by herself, to explain to them that no, Daddy wasn't going to read them a story tonight, that Daddy was in London reading stories to some other children he'd had with some other woman? How had it been to live with fragile, angry Luke through the years of his blighted adolescence and beyond?

And Caroline, so cool and unemotional. She must have known, going into a relationship with someone else's husband, that she too would get burned one day. Or maybe she hadn't. Maybe she'd thought that she was the fabulous, glittering end of Adrian's road, the answer to all his prayers, capable, independent, on a par with Adrian himself. She'd probably felt sorry for Susie. She still had that air about her when she talked about her predecessor: *poor Susie*. How had it really been for Caroline to be toppled from her position of superiority? To be shown to be no better than *poor Susie*? And Caroline's children—her perfect children—shown to be no less disposable than the ones Adrian had left behind in Hove?

Though these scars should have been visible, should have been *glaringly obvious* from the very first touch of Adrian's hand upon her arm in the pub that night, they had not been. Because Adrian had blinded her to them with his talk of fate and long-dead love.

And now, like one of those laser beams that picks out the sun damage on an apparently blemish-free complexion, the falling away of her love for Adrian had revealed the damaged truth of his perfect family. And buried deep inside this group of survivors, all clinging together for dear life, there resided a truth-teller. Someone shouting and waving. But only at her. Her poison-penned correspondent. Someone who knew what she was finally coming to understand: that Maya was a step too far. That a third wife and third family was too much for this family to take.

She looked around the table again, from happy face to happy face, trying to imagine which one it might be, which person was already planning their next written assault. And then it hit her, horribly, violently.

It could be any one of them.

Like guests at an Agatha Christie–style weekend house party, each one had a motive. And, apart from Beau, each one had the means.

She caught Pearl's eye across the table. Pearl smiled at her in that inscrutable way of hers. Pearl wasn't one for loud displays of affection, but Maya was fairly certain that Pearl was on her side.

She smiled back at Pearl. And then she sighed. Because, really, she was in no position to feel certain of anything.

～

Maya went to bed early that night. She wasn't tired but she had run out of the particular type of energy required to go the distance with the Wolfes. She couldn't be bothered with it all. Once upon a time she'd have done whatever it took to prove herself equal to this exclusive group of people, to show them her best side, but now she saw them for what they were and she wanted no part of it. So she said her good nights and nobody said, *Oh, Maya, don't go, stay up!* And she took her wash bag through to the tiny shower room around the corner from her room and brushed her teeth in water that tasted of being away from home and then she put on her pajamas and laid herself under the overfilled duvet that a hundred other people had already lain under and she stared at the dusty beams in the ceiling and wondered what she was doing here.

The noise of laughter passed around the twisty corridors of the ground floor and in through the crack of her door. She could hear Susie; she could hear Caroline. Is it one of you two? she wondered. Is it one of you two who hates me so much that you want me to *disappear*?

The thought filled her with dismay and also with contrition.

And then she heard the sound of Adrian saying good night, his steps along the corridor. She reached for the table lamp and switched it off, pulled the thick duvet over herself, turned onto her side and closed her eyes.

"Are you awake?" she heard him whisper loudly into the darkness.

She made a noise, a moan suggestive of being disturbed in half slumber.

"Are you OK, darling?" She heard his voice closer to her ear and repeated the same noise, this time adding a hint of annoyance.

"You were very quiet tonight." She felt him lower himself onto the other side of the bed. "We're all a bit worried about you."

"I'm fine," she said groggily, her body wriggling with irritation at the suggestion that they'd all been talking about her.

"Is it . . ." He had his therapist voice on, soothing and mellifluous. She gritted her teeth. "Is it to do with the baby?"

She turned now and opened her eyes. She could just make out the dark outline of him in the gloom. "What baby?"

"You know, the baby we're trying to have. *Were* trying to have."

"What? No!" she snapped. "Of course it's not about babies. I told you, I'm fine. I'm just really tired. And I was drinking red wine. That always makes me sleepy."

He reached over and squeezed her shoulder avuncularly. "You would tell me, wouldn't you?" he said. "If you were worried about anything?"

She stared at him in the dark, her mouth opened but no words coming out. Did he really not remember, she wondered, did he really not remember her saying that she didn't want to have a baby with him? That she was having second thoughts about their marriage? Maybe he'd put it down to her being so drunk when she said it? Or maybe he was choosing not to recall? Because that's what Adrian did. He repainted his world only in colors that he found palatable. That way, whatever happened, whatever bad decisions he made, he would always look out upon a perfect world. She needed to break down this wall. She needed to scream into his face in a way that nobody had ever screamed into his face. She needed to paint out his world in different colors and force him to confront it.

But she couldn't do this now, not here, not surrounded by his family. "Of course I would," she said, as softly as she could. "Of course I would." And then she pretended to fall back into the deep sleep she'd been pretending to be in when he arrived.

39

AUGUST 2012

Adrian entered the pub, his phone held tightly inside his hand. He'd just spoken to Luke. There was still no sign of Otis. Caroline was hysterical, apparently. He promised he would be at the Islington house as soon as possible, that he wouldn't spend one more moment with Abby than he needed to. His pulse was fizzing with adrenaline. His heart raced so fast that he'd had to stop for breath at the top of the steps out of the tube station. The thought of it, the thought of something horrible happening to his beautiful boy.

He saw her immediately. She was sitting at a tiny table for two just behind the door, looking every bit as fresh and magnificent as she'd looked earlier in the day. Her sunglasses were folded up and resting on the table in front of her and she was reading a book.

"Hi," he said, pulling out a small stool and sitting down.

She smiled and folded away her book. "Hi there," she said.

"Look," he began. "I'm really sorry but I can't stay. My son, Otis, he's gone missing and I need to get back to my family. Is this something we could do really quickly? Or maybe we could do this another night?"

"Oh no," she said. "Christ. How long has he been missing?"

"Since five o'clock. Two hours."

"And how old is he?"

"He's twelve."

"Oh." She looked relieved. "So probably just gone off with a friend or something?"

"I don't know," said Adrian. "We've been in touch with pretty much everyone he knows, but apparently nobody knows where he might be."

"Well, it only takes one," she said. "Someone's probably keeping schtum. And I speak from experience. I was a serial runner-awayer when I was a teenager. I once disappeared for two days. I came home when I needed to do a number two." She smiled wryly and Adrian would have laughed if he hadn't been so distracted.

"I don't think this is just teenage angst though," said Adrian. "Apparently he had a row with his older brother and sister, said something he shouldn't have said and thinks he's going to get into trouble."

"What did he say?"

"I don't know," said Adrian, exhaling loudly. "Nobody will tell me. It's 'not important,' apparently. Which makes me think it's probably very important but not something that anyone wants me to hear." He shrugged.

"Well," said Abby, pushing her blond hair behind her ears. "Why don't I give you the rough outline of what you want to know and then you can decide if you want to talk now or another time. It's possible . . . ," she began, and then paused. "It's possible that what I have to tell you might have something to do with your son's disappearance."

Adrian checked the signal on his phone, as he had done approximately every forty-five seconds for the last hour. Seeing that he had all five bars he turned his attention back to Abby. "Yes," he said. "Please. But first of all, why did you pretend to want my cat?"

"Because," she said, "I saw you putting the card up in the post office and I knew it was a way of getting into your flat."

Adrian blinked at the bizarre notion of Abby watching him pin his card up on the post office wall. "And why did you want to get into my flat?"

"Because I wanted to talk to you."

"Why couldn't you talk to me in the post office?"

"Because I wanted to see where you lived."

"And why did you want to see where I lived?"

"Because I needed to know what damage I might do sharing what I know. I wanted to see family photos, hear you talk about your wife, watch you in an intimate setting. I watched your daughter ice-skating; I watched your son walking home from school. I watched your adult daughter walk your little boy home from school. I was there, for days, just trying to get a feel for you all. Because, you know, when someone tells you about a man who's had three wives, who's left two families behind, you know you're either dealing with a pathetic sociopath or a misguided fool, and I needed to know which one you were."

"And . . . ?"

"You were neither, really. You were just broken. And I couldn't be the one to make it any worse."

"And how could it be worse?" Adrian almost shouted the words.

"Because . . . See that table over there?" Abby pointed at a rectangular table close to the bar.

"Yes," he replied impatiently.

"Well, I sat at that table with your wife on the night that she died."

Adrian locked eyes with Abby, his attention finally undiluted. And then, at the tail end of the ponderous silence that followed, he felt the tabletop fizzing under his elbows. He grabbed his phone. It was Luke.

"He's just called," said Luke breathlessly. "Reversed charges from a phone box. In Holloway. Caroline's on her way to get him."

Adrian felt his torso concertina itself flat with relief. "Is he OK?"

"He's fine," Luke continued. "Apparently he was trying to find a friend of his who he sometimes sleeps over with. He was going to hide out with him, but he didn't have his phone with him so he couldn't call him and then he tried to remember how to walk there and got massively lost. Some old woman found him sobbing on a bench and showed him how to make a reverse-charge call. She's waiting with him now."

"Oh God, oh God. Thank God."

"I know," said Luke, his voice holding not a shred of its usual acid sarcasm.

"Right, well, that's brilliant. Totally brilliant. Tell him I'll be there in an hour or so. Tell him to stay up and wait for me. Tell him I love him. In fact, get him to call me the moment he gets back so that I can tell him myself."

"How's it going with stalker woman?"

"I'll tell you all about it later," he said.

"OK, but be quick."

"I will. I will."

He turned off his phone and let his face fall heavily into his hands. Then he looked up at Abby. "They've found him."

She smiled. "Thank God."

"Thank God," repeated Adrian.

"And he's OK?"

"He's fine."

"Do you want to go?"

He almost laughed. "No," he said. "No. Of course I don't. Jesus." He stood up, put his hand into his trouser pocket and pulled out his wallet. "What can I get you to drink?"

He went to the bar and got Abby a glass of white wine and himself something much stronger. When he came back to the table he started talking before he'd even sat down. "So," he said, looking behind him at the table where Abby claimed to have talked to Maya on her last night on earth, "tell me. Tell me everything."

Abby pulled her wineglass towards her by its stem and then turned it in slow circles between her fingertips.

"It was about ten o'clock," she said. "I was here with an old friend; we'd been drinking for a couple of hours, here and there around town. I don't really remember how we ended up in here. Not our usual style. Anyway, she had a train to catch so it was going to be one last drink before she had to run and we noticed this girl, this tiny red-haired girl, standing by the bar, drinking vodka by herself and crying. Not, like, sobbing. Just tears rolling down her cheeks. And really, the only reason we noticed her in the first place was because my friend said she looked like me. I couldn't see it myself." She shrugged and picked up her wineglass, took a sip. "But anyway. We were quite drunk and feeling sisterly so we asked her if she was OK. Asked her if she'd like to come and sit with us. She said no at first but then I bought her a cup of coffee and kind of forced her to. So she sat down with us and then my friend had to go so I decided that I'd stay with this girl—Maya—until I thought she was sober enough to get home."

Adrian continued to stare at Abby.

"You mean," he said, "you were there with her? That night?"

She nodded.

"So, what? What happened? Did you see her get hit by the bus? What did you see?"

"No." She shook her head forcefully. "No. I spent about an hour with her. She said she was going home. She spoke to you on the phone. She seemed to be sober. She seemed to be feeling much better. So I let her go . . ."

Her face fell. She took another, larger gulp of wine and put down her glass. She looked at Adrian and there were tears in her eyes. "She said she was going home. I thought she was going home. And then I picked up a newspaper two days later and read this terrible story about the night bus and the girl . . . There was no name. But I just knew it was her. The age was right. The location was right. I just knew it was her."

Abby had started to cry now. Adrian leaned across the table to take her hand in his. She looked into his eyes and said almost silently, "I'm so, so sorry."

"Oh no," said Adrian, "no. It's not your fault. You did what you could."

"No. I could have done more. I could have brought her home myself. I could have at least put her into a taxi. It took me ages to find you. I used to run Google searches all the time: 'Maya Night Bus.' And then finally a story came up. About the coroner's report. And there was your name. And I found you easily enough. Waited outside your offices from time to time, even followed you home. But I was too scared. Too scared to approach you. Until I saw you in the post office that day." Her eyes dropped and she pulled her hand from his. "I thought I was ready to talk to you then. But I wasn't."

"And you are now?"

"Well, no, not really. But you kind of cornered me." She smiled tightly.

Adrian smiled back and picked up his gin and tonic. "So," he said, "you spent an hour with Maya that night. Did she" —he paused, rolling his drink around his glass—"did she give you any idea about . . . I mean, what did you talk about?"

"We talked about you," she replied simply. "About your children. About your ex-wives. We talked about everything."

"And did she tell you about the poison-pen e-mails?"

Abby nodded. "Yes, she did." She sounded surprised. "How did you know about those? She told me she'd never mentioned them to anyone."

"My son found them, in a hidden file on our network at home. A couple of months ago."

"So you know who sent them then?"

"No," he said, his eyes widening. "No. I have no idea. Why?" He stared right into the heart of her odd-colored eyes. *"Do you?"*

"Yes," she said. "Yes. I think I do."

Adrian gulped and waited for her to talk.

PART FOUR

40

APRIL 2011

It was nearly a week before her poison-pen friend got in touch after the Easter holiday in Suffolk. For a while Maya thought maybe she'd got away with it, thought maybe the family sociopath hadn't found her irksome enough during the week, or hadn't gathered enough juicy tidbits to pass on to whoever it was on the outside compiling these missives of bile.

She had kept herself very much under the radar in Suffolk, gone to bed early at night, not tried to impress anyone, not attempted to ingratiate herself in any way. She'd been like a ghost, a vague presence on the periphery of things, a shrunken child in the backseat of the car. She had surrendered entirely to the authority of the first two wives and their adult children and just counted down the hours until it was time to come home.

Never again, she'd vowed to herself, staring at the view from the window of the rental car as urbanization reasserted itself. *Never again*. Next time she would feign *alternative commitments*. Or *contagious unwellness*. That's if, she'd thought to herself, there ever was a next time.

Adrian was back at work and Maya still had a week before school started again. Caroline had asked her if she would sit with the children for a couple of days because her normal babysitter was away and she had back-to-back meetings she couldn't reschedule. The request, which had come on the last day of the Suffolk holiday, had taken her by surprise, but not unpleasantly so. She had never been given full in loco parentis charge of Adrian's children before. She'd occasionally taken Beau out for an ice cream or collected Pearl from ice-skating practice. But to be left alone with all three of them in an empty house for a full day was a huge development.

Just before she left the house that morning she decided to check her e-mail. And there it was.

Dear Bitch

Not quite the golden girl anymore I hear. Apparently you were a shadow of yourself, skulking about like an abused child. Is it finally starting to get to you? The magnitude of what you've done? The impossibility of there ever being a proper happy ending for you and Big Daddy? Well, hallelujah, praise the Lord. According to sources on the ground, you're much more palatable when you're not sticking your oar in, trying to make everyone happy. Because everyone is sick to the back teeth of you and your pathetic attempts to be one of the gang. You're not one of the gang and you never will be. So, follow your instincts, Bitch. You know it and I know it. It's time for you to disappear, to let this family heal without you.

I hope I don't have to write to you again.

Please don't make me.

She sighed heavily. Ah, well, there it was. Nothing had changed, after all. She was still under surveillance. She fed the cat, found her travel card and headed for the bus stop.

～

Caroline was being unnervingly pleasant. As she showed Maya around the house—the dog biscuits, the garden-door key, the things the children were allowed to eat, the things the children

weren't allowed to eat, the remote controls, the password for
the PC—she kept turning to Maya and smiling at her, resting
her fingers on the sleeve of her jumper, telling her over and
over *how much she appreciated this*. It seemed to Maya that Caroline smiled at her more times during the ten-minute tour of
the house than she had in the preceding three years.

The children were scattered about the basement. Beau was
on the sofa at the far end of the family room watching TV, Otis
was on the laptop at the kitchen counter and Pearl was in the
garden combing the dogs. The breakfast things were piled up
around the sink.

"Just ignore that," said Caroline, seeing Maya's eyes stray to
the mess. "I'll sort it out when I get home. Please do whatever
you want today. Totally ignore them if you like. I feel terrible
making you look after children during your precious holiday."

"Honestly," said Maya, already mentally planning to leave
the place cleaner than she'd found it, "it's fine. It's only a couple of days and you know how much I love your children. It's
genuinely a pleasure."

Caroline smiled at her and said, "Thank you, Maya. You're
so, so kind."

There was something vaguely melodramatic about her
demeanor and it occurred to Maya that maybe Adrian had
been talking to Caroline about her again. It wouldn't have
been the first time. Caroline had virtually chosen Maya's
engagement ring for him, after all. Adrian saw Caroline as a
peerless arbiter of good taste and the font of all emotional
intelligence. She was his go-to friend if a client needed advice
about interiors, if one of his junior partners was having
personal problems that were affecting their performance
at work, if he needed to choose something nice for Cat's
birthday—or if his new wife had fallen out of love with him
and he wanted to know how to fix it.

"Are you OK?" Caroline asked, widening her pale blue eyes.

"I'm fine," said Maya brightly.

"You know, Maya, that if you ever need to talk to me . . . about Adrian. About anything . . ."

Maya did not want to talk to Caroline. Not now. It was an offer that should have come a lot earlier to have held any substance. She shook her head and smiled. "Thank you," she said.

Caroline gave her one last compassionate smile before checking the time on the clock above Maya's head and snapping back into scary Caroline mode. "Shit," she said, "I need to run. Kids," she called out, her eyes and hands inside her handbag, searching for something, "Mummy's going now! Come and kiss me!"

Beau raced from the sofa and threw himself into Caroline's arms. She squeezed him hard, kissed Otis on the top of his head and blew a kiss to Pearl, who was blowing her kisses from the garden door, a dog held under her arm.

There was a false exit, followed by the sound of Caroline crashing back down the basement stairs, grabbing a file of paperwork, and then finally the sound of the front door slamming shut in her wake, a whistle of air being syringed through the house and sudden stillness.

Maya looked around, nervously. A whole house. Three whole children. Two whole dogs. A full eight hours. And she had responsibility for all of it. She smiled at Beau, who was standing looking over Otis's shoulder at whatever he was doing on the laptop. "So," she said to him, "fancy helping me to load the dishwasher?"

Beau looked at her as though she'd just suggested a bonus day at school.

"I *never* load the dishwasher," he said. His sweet face was a study in frosty affrontedness. It wasn't one of Beau's own faces. He'd picked it up from elsewhere and was trying it on for size.

"That's OK," she said. "I'm sure I can manage it by myself."

She peered surreptitiously over Otis's and Beau's shoulders at the screen as she collected bowls and cups from the surfaces, trying to work out what they were both looking at, checking that it was age-appropriate. It looked like some kind of virtual world peopled by colored blobs with black eyes and a variety of interesting hats. Each blob appeared to be in charge of a smaller blob and there was lots of whizzing about and things coming up in speech bubbles, much too fast for Maya to read them. It looked perfectly harmless.

As she stacked things into the dishwasher she looked out across the basement and into the garden, where Pearl was still combing a dog. Pearl looked up and caught Maya's eye and she smiled, very briefly, before returning her gaze to the dog. Between them the TV was still on, *Go, Diego, Go!*, lots of shouting in Spanish. She closed the door of the dishwasher and walked over to the coffee table, found the right remote and turned it off.

"Why did you turn it off?" cried Beau, looking at her in horror.

"Because nobody was watching it."

"*I* was watching it!"

"No, you weren't," she said gently. "You were playing on the computer with Otis."

"I am *not* playing on the computer. I'm just standing here. *Otis* is playing on the computer!"

"Well, whatever you were doing, you weren't watching the TV. And it's really loud."

"Turn it back on!" he cried.

Maya looked at Beau in surprise. Otis looked at Maya in surprise. It was the first time Maya had ever heard Beau shout at anyone. She had recently started to notice the small flashes of resentment behind his eyes, the tiny shrugs of his head, but this was the first time she had seen him submit properly to his urges.

"Please don't talk to me like that," she said. "It's not very nice."

"Well, it's not very nice for you to turn off the TV without asking me." He was softening. The devil was climbing back into its box.

"OK, Beau," said Maya. "I'm sorry, I should have asked. Would you mind if I turned off the TV until you're ready to start watching it again?"

He shook his head.

"Thank you."

Maya breathed in deeply, just once, and carefully placed the remote control back on the table. Pearl was watching curiously through the garden doors.

"I didn't know you were a professional dog groomer as well as a champion ice-skater," said Maya, joining her in the apple-blossom-heavy garden.

Pearl shrugged. "I just watched some tutorials on YouTube," she said. "It's really easy. They used to get so stressed out at the dog parlor. Now they really enjoy it." She pressed the palm of her hand hard into the stomach of the dog and it was clear that every muscle in the animal's body was relaxed. "Was that Beau shouting?" she asked.

"Yes, it was," said Maya, "believe it or not."

Pearl pulled up one of the dog's legs and tackled some matted hair with a small metal comb. "That's not like him," she said.

Maya sat down. "No," she sighed. "No, it's not at all."

"He said something weird the other day," said Pearl, picking apart the matted fur. "He said he wished he'd been a big boy when Daddy left because then he would have stopped him."

"Oh." Maya felt an emotional blow to her middle section. She cupped it subconsciously.

"Yeah. It's weird. I mean, he was only one when Daddy left so as far as he knows it's always been like this." She shrugged and rolled the dog away from her, pulled up the opposing leg, started the process again.

"That is kind of strange," said Maya. "I wonder what brought that on."

"Maybe it's something he's picked up from nursery? You know? The other kids living with their mums and dads? Maybe he's just worked out that he's different?"

Maya wriggled awkwardly in her seat.

"He seems quite cross, you know? When we got back from Suffolk he was saying, 'Why can't Daddy come and sleep here? Why does he have to go to that other place?' And he was asking me and Otis about what happened when Daddy left; he kept saying, 'Why did you let him? Why didn't you stop him?' And acting like it was all our fault, or something."

"Oh God."

"It's not *your* fault," said Pearl. "It's Daddy's fault. He's the one who thought it was OK to go."

"Are you cross with him?"

"Not really," said Pearl. "I do miss him though. I liked how he used to wake up really early, like me. So all the lights used to be on down here when I came down. And he'd be sitting there, in his dressing gown. He used to make me breakfast. And ask me about my dreams. Before everyone else got up. Just the two of us . . . I miss that."

A smile had set itself hard onto Maya's face. She thought of her own unexceptional childhood and the mundane details she'd taken for granted: the double humps in her parents' bed in the morning, the tweed overcoat hanging by the door, the beers in the fridge, the football on the TV on Saturday afternoons; the strong arms to carry her to bed when she'd fallen asleep in the car, the two heads in the front seats of the car on drives to visit friends, and yes, she remembered it now, her father up first, sitting in the kitchen every morning in his trousers and a T-shirt, his business shirt hanging on the back of his chair, stirring leaves around a teapot and greeting her with puffy eyes as she appeared in the doorway with a gruff: "Good morning and how are you today?"

"What about your special nights at Daddy's flat?" Maya asked tenderly. "Do they help? Do they make it better?"

Pearl shrugged. "I guess," she said. "But it's not the same."

"No," said Maya. "No. I don't suppose it is."

They sat in silence for a while. Pearl let the dog go and wiped hair from the palms of her hands.

"What would you think if Daddy said he was coming back to live here?"

Pearl turned and threw Maya a look of hope and wonder. "What?"

"No, I don't mean he is. I just mean, would that be nice? Would it be good? Or would it be weird?"

"Well, it would be weird in one way because it would mean that he'd split up with you and he'd be sad and stuff." She rolled the excess hair into a tiny ball between her hands and let it fall to the ground. "But in another way it would be really great. Although . . ."

Maya waited for her to speak.

"In a way it would be weird because I'd just be scared, you know, waiting for him to do it again."

"You think he'd do it again?"

Pearl gave her a withering look. "Dad?" she said. "Yes. Of course he would. He's addicted to love."

Maya laughed.

"It's not funny," said Pearl. "He is. Mum told me. She said

that's why he left us. Because he's addicted to being in love and he's not mature enough to deal with real life. You know, people being grumpy and boring and stuff."

"Your mum said that to you?"

"Yes. My mum treats me like an equal. She doesn't tell me stupid fairy tales about things." She shrugged. "It's better that way. It's like, when I'm grown up, I'll know what to expect. And I won't marry a man who is addicted to being in love. I'll marry a man who likes it when I'm grumpy."

Maya smiled. And then, feeling the softness of intimacy in the air, the openness of their mutual channels, she said, "Do you ever hate me, Pearl?"

"No," Pearl replied, rather suddenly.

"Really?"

"Why would I hate you?"

"Because I let your Daddy leave you all."

"I told you. That wasn't your fault. If it wasn't you, it would have been someone else."

"What about your mum? Does she hate me?"

Pearl looked up at Maya through her pale eyelashes and then looked down again. "I don't think so," she said, quietly. "I think . . ." She paused. "I think she just feels sorry for you."

"*Sorry* for me!"

"Yes, because . . ." She stopped again, checking herself for the sake of damage limitation. "Mum just thinks he'll leave you, too." She shrugged apologetically. "That's all."

Maya nodded. Of course that's what Caroline would think. She would have to think that to make everything more palatable. "And Otis. What do you think Otis thinks? About me?"

"I don't know what Otis thinks about *anything*. He's not the chatty type." She sucked her lips together and raised her brow. "But I don't think he hates you. I don't think *anyone* hates you."

Maya laughed gruffly. "You'd be surprised." She let a silence fall, because here it was, a small window of opportunity and she didn't want to miss it. "Have you ever heard anyone say anything? About me? You know, nasty stuff?"

"No."

"I don't just mean family. I mean, like, other people. You know, maybe family friends."

"No," she said again, shaking her head forcefully. And then she opened her mouth, as though to say something before shutting it again.

"What?"

"Nothing."

"I don't mind. Honestly. I'd rather know."

Pearl sighed and said, "Well, Charlotte said something. In Suffolk, that was a bit horrible."

"Oh," said Maya cautiously, "really? Like what?"

"Oh, just something about your hair. I can't even remember what it was."

Maya caught her breath. "Did she say I looked like the ugly one in a boy band?"

"What? *No*." Pearl looked mystified by the question.

"Right, so, what exactly . . . ?"

"Oh, I can't remember, just that you looked much prettier with it longer. That you looked a bit manlike. Something like that."

Maya thought of the chat she'd had with Charlotte while playing croquet in the sunshine. She remembered how effusive Charlotte had been about her hair. How sweet. Yet the moment Maya was out of earshot she'd been bitching about her behind her back.

And then she thought again of that strange moment, when Charlotte had walked in on them making up her bed, her and Luke, and the tail end of their conversation that she'd overheard. It wasn't the first time Charlotte had walked in on

Luke and Maya having an intimate conversation. There'd been that time at Susie's New Year's Day party too. Did she suspect something? Did she know? Could it be sweet, silly Charlotte trying to oust Maya from the Wolfe family? Could it be her sending those horrible e-mails?

She sighed. The e-mail situation was spinning around her head like a top gone crazy, ricocheting off the walls of her consciousness, dizzying her to the point of nausea.

"Sorry," said Pearl, mistaking Maya's silence for hurt feelings.

"No," said Maya. "No, don't be silly. It's fine. I don't like my hair either; I'm growing it out."

"Good," said Pearl. "I like it longer."

"Thank you for your honesty."

"You're welcome," said Pearl. "I'm a very honest person."

"Yes," said Maya. "Yes, you really are."

41

After the rather explosive start, the rest of the day passed quietly enough. After lunch someone arrived to take Pearl to the rink. Beau asked to go for his afternoon nap shortly afterwards and then, for an hour or so, it was just Maya and Otis in the kitchen together.

Otis was listening to music now, through the laptop. His eyes never left the screen, while his overlarge feet tapped irritatingly against the plinth of the kitchen counter. Maya looked around her. She had tidied the basement, plumped every cushion, put away every bowl, every felt-tip pen, every piece of paper. The sun had gone behind a bank of clouds and the house felt big and deserted. Maya had only ever been in this house when it was full of people, children and noise. It felt strange and slightly unsettling to be here alone, like being on the set of a popular TV show when all the actors had gone home.

She offered Otis a drink, a snack; he politely but monosyllabically declined both. And then she passed from the basement and up the stairs towards the upper levels of the house. She looked at the art on the stairs as she passed: the fluid pencil sketches of the children at various stages of their development, the pop art that clashed so perfectly with the watery representations of favorite holiday locations, photographs arranged together in multiple-aperture frames. She stepped into the hallway, towards the oversized dresser bearing more photos and a huge glass vase of plonked-in peonies. A fan of mail had been deposited on a worn-out polka-dot doormat. She reached down for the mail and placed it on the dresser, next to a glass paperweight filled with swirls of aqua-blue and green, and a box of pebbles and shells gathered from beaches on breezy half-term holidays.

To the left, through double doors, was the formal reception room: button-backed sofas in teal velvet, peacock-print cushions, white floorboards, gilt-edged mirrors, hardbacked books arranged in piles on a mirror-topped coffee table. More and more and more photos. More and more beach ephemera. At the other end was a battered piano overhung by a huge canvas of abstract streaks of paint, a large chrome floor lamp with an arced neck and glass doors out onto the wrought-iron spiral staircase. Everything just so, yet conversely looking as though nobody had given any of it so much as a moment's thought.

Maya exited this room and continued up the stairs. On the next floor was the study, Caroline's bedroom and en-suite and up a short flight of steps a palatial bathroom with an antique chandelier hanging at its center.

She remembered some of the things that Adrian had told her in those early days of their affair about this house, about this marriage. He'd told her that he hated this house, how it was all that he and Caroline had talked about for the five years it had taken to renovate it from its former state of dereliction. He told her how much happier he and Caroline had been in their scruffy house-share, just the two of them and baby Otis.

"It's always the house," he'd said, "that's where the rot sets in. When women start to care more about cushions than they do about love."

Maya had nodded at the time and felt herself a cut above, being as she was a woman who had never given a moment's serious consideration to a cushion in her life. She had understood him—yes, she had—understood how hard it would be to live with a woman that shallow and uncaring. She had pictured this house then, this perfect prison of cushions and custom-made cabinetry, of lights that had been obsessed over to the point of madness and bathroom tiles that had been discussed and dissected to death. She had imagined it soulless and harsh, the product of a horrible woman and her lack of affection for her poor neglected husband.

Maya had tried to ignore the kick of surprise to her gut the first time she'd been here. When she'd seen for herself the sweetness of the place, the little touches that shouted family and love: the children's art and the scribbled portraits, nothing showy, nothing there just for the sake of it. The clutter, the mess, the dents both made and left in the cushions on the sofa. It was, she had realized, the perfect family home, created out of love by a woman who had thought she would live here as part of a family forever. Nothing more, nothing less. He had lied to her. But she let it pass.

As she let so many things pass in those first few months.

Caroline's bed was unmade and strewn with her discarded nightwear. The curtains were still drawn, and in Caroline's en-suite, the toilet remained unflushed. She would have no time for anything in the mornings, Maya supposed, not even to flush a toilet. Three children to prepare for the day ahead. A full-time, high-powered job to get to. And no husband to pick up the slack.

Maya stood in the doorway between the bathroom and the bedroom and stared at Caroline's bed. That had been their bed. Caroline and Adrian's. In that bed two children had been conceived, babies had been suckled, nightmares had been chased away, secrets shared, intimacies whispered, a future imagined. She remembered the morning after the children's first sleepover at the flat. She remembered the bedroom door being nudged open by a clutch of small fingers, two scruffy heads appearing in the doorway and Adrian sitting up, smiling, bleary-eyed, patting the bed and saying, "Come in, little ones." Then she remembered the two heads disappearing, the door being slowly pulled shut behind them, little footsteps receding into the distance.

They never came into Adrian and Maya's room in the mornings. They knew it wasn't their nest.

What had she done? Whatever Pearl might think about the likelihood of Adrian's having left eventually anyway, he had left for *her*. For whatever false promises and hollow dreams she had inadvertently offered up to him in her desperation to be with the sort of man to have accumulated such high-quality baggage.

She approached the bed and sat down gently on the edge. She looked at the photos of the children in mismatched frames on the bedside table, the Space NK hand cream, the reading pile of book-group clichés, a cocktail ring, a strip of ibuprofen and a dead rose in a shallow silver bowl. On the opposing bedside table was a pile of children's picture books, an iPad set to charge and a bowl full of Lego pieces.

She stood up and peered through the clothes hanging in the open wardrobe, at Caroline's tailored jackets and Liberty-print blouses, soft knitted cardigans and washed-out chinos, scuffed Chelsea boots and lace-up brogues in untidy rows on the base.

Meeting Caroline for the first time had been a shock to the system too. Although every bit as statuesque, icy-blond and unsmiling as she'd been led to believe, what Maya hadn't been expecting was the soft hands, the small child held tenderly against her bosom, the bitten-down nails, the fusty floral print, the moth holes in the cardigan and the air of vulnerable confusion. Adrian hadn't told her about that. Adrian had implied a woman in killer heels and leather trousers, lips stained red, mobile phone nailed to her temple, children ignored in the periphery of her priorities.

She'd let that pass, too.

She'd let the never-replied-to texts he sent to his oldest son pass. (*He's fine with it, he really is. Luke is such a cool boy.*) She'd let the shock of meeting poor, demoralized Susie pass. (*I think I did her a favor leaving her. She's blossomed since I set her free.*) She'd let the expressions of numb disillusionment on the children's faces pass. (*They're so young; children don't really know what's going on at that age. They're very flexible.*)

She'd ignored it all and questioned nothing. And she was as complicit in the scorched battlefield of disenchantment in which she now lived as him. Not a victim. But a perpetrator.

She pulled something towards her from the far end of Caroline's wardrobe: a soft gray garment bag with a clear front. She turned it towards her and saw with a shock that it was Caroline's wedding dress. A lovely lace thing, low-cut at the front, empire line, timeless. Slowly she unzipped the edges of the carrier and pulled a length of the dress towards her, to her nose, where she breathed it in. It smelled different to anything else in Caroline's house. It didn't smell of Caroline or of the fabric conditioner she used on her family's clothes or the jasmine-scented candles that sat on surfaces throughout the house. It didn't smell of warm, dusty floorboards or Space NK hand cream or dogs. It smelled, Maya realized with a jolt, of a time and a place before any of this. A time and a place that had been surgically excised from Caroline's personal continuum. It smelled of Caroline's happiness.

"What are you doing?"

Maya jumped and let the dress fall back into its bag. Her heart thumped about in her chest and she clutched it hard. "Oh God."

"What are you doing?" Otis stood in the doorway and eyed her with hostility.

"I'm just . . . I'm . . . Nothing. Just nosing about."

"Why?"

"I don't know," she said.

He frowned at her.

She stared at him.

"You probably shouldn't." He put his hands into his pockets and continued to stare at her.

"No," she said. "I shouldn't. I suppose," she began, her emotions temporarily upended by the shock of Caroline's wedding dress, "I'm just trying to understand things."

"*Things?*" said Otis, caustically. "What kind of *things?*"

"Oh, I don't know. Just all *this.*" She spread her arms about. "All this kind of . . ."

"Mess?" suggested Otis harshly.

"Yeah. I guess. Just trying to work it all out."

"Bit late for that, isn't it?"

Maya felt the hard pressure of tears behind her eyes, pushing at her temples. "Is it?"

He shrugged. And then he turned and walked away. She stood and listened to the soft padding of his feet up the floorboarded stairs to his room on the top floor. She heard his bedroom door closing and the springs of his bed as he lay down upon it. Now the house was truly still. She flicked a stray tear from the bridge of her nose and breathed herself back to a state of calmness.

She tucked Caroline's wedding dress back into the wardrobe and headed downstairs to the basement. The dogs milled hungrily around their food bowls and she fed them on autopilot. She dropped the meaty fork into the dishwasher and then she jumped slightly at the sound of an electronic alert. Not her phone. Not any of the kitchen appliances. She knocked the mouse of the laptop with her hand and watched the screen light up. A Skype message from Cat.

What's she doing now?

She stared at the message a moment longer, wondering with a sudden chill if it was about her.

Hello? Little bro? U still there?
K. I'm going now. Love ya.

Maya continued to stare at the screen. She was wondering if there was any way for her to look at the earlier section of this conversation without anyone noticing. And then suddenly another message fell onto the screen with a loud plop:

I'm back! In my room now. On phone. Just caught her going thru mums clothes.
No way!
Yeh. She said she was trying to understand things.
!!!! WTF does that even mean?!
Yeh. I know.
She's a freak.
Yeh.
You gonna tell your mum?
Maybe.
You totally shuld.
Yeh. Maybe.
Anything else?
Oh, yeh, actually. Beau shouted at her before.
No way! What happened?!
She turned off the TV without asking him. He went mental.

OMG! What did she do?
Nuffing.
Stupid bitch.
Heh.

Then, after a moment's silence, from Cat.

I fucking hate her.
Me too.
I wish she'd disappear. Like, forever.
Yeh.
Bitch.

Another moment's silence and then, from Otis:

GTG.
Yeh. Me too. Skype me later?
K.
KK.

And then, the longest silence of all.

42

"So, the e-mails," said Adrian, "they were from *Cat*?"

The noise of the pub had been sucked away down a black hole. All that existed in Adrian's head were Abby's mismatched eyes staring at him across the table, and her words echoing inside his head.

Abby shook her head. "She didn't know for sure. But she strongly suspected."

"But, Cat—she *loved* Maya."

"Well, I can't comment on that," said Abby. "Obviously I can't. People can be complicated. Especially in a family like yours."

"And *Otis*."

"Yes. But it sounds like it was a kind of bonding thing. For the children. A coping mechanism. I don't think it was truly personal. It sounds like whoever you'd brought into their world at that precise moment would have suffered the same fate."

"But Maya didn't know that."

"I think she did," said Abby gently. "I think the way she was feeling that night was about much more than those Skype messages. I think it was a combination of all sorts of things. Guilt mainly. Fear."

"Fear of what?"

Abby sighed. She uncrossed and recrossed her legs, tugged down the skirt of her dress. "The reason she was drinking that night . . ." She paused. "The reason she got so drunk. It wasn't because of the Skype messages. Or the e-mails. It was because she was planning on—urgh, I'm really sorry, Adrian. But she was planning on leaving you. That night."

Adrian rocked back in his chair with the power of her words.

"That's why she was crying. That's why she kept putting it off and putting it off. She told me that's where she was going. After our conversation. She was so filled with resolve. I was so sure she was going to do it."

"So, she didn't seem suicidal? She didn't seem like she wanted to die?"

"No! She was emotional. She was scared. She was sad. She was nervous. She was very, very drunk. But not suicidal. Not at all."

"So, then, why?" he said. "Why did she do it?"

Abby sighed. "I truly think it was an accident," she said. "Honestly. A split-second thing. You know. Happens to everyone. One of those moments where if you'd stepped off the curb a second later you'd have been run over, if you'd changed lanes you'd have gone straight into that car in your blind spot, if you'd waited for the next train you'd have been blown up by a bomb. That kind of thing. I don't think she wanted to die. I think she just wanted to make everything better. Give you back to your family."

They sat in silence for a moment. Adrian rubbed and rubbed at the twenty-four-hour stubble on his chin until he became aware of the repetitiveness of the gesture and dropped his hand into his lap.

"What would you have done?" Abby asked. "If she'd made it home? If she'd told you she was leaving?"

Adrian didn't answer for a few seconds. His thoughts were spinning. "I think she'd already tried to do it," he said, almost in a whisper. "Before. She tried to leave me before. And I didn't hear it. I didn't let her say it."

Abby stared at him, kindly.

"She told me she didn't think it was working. Us. I told myself she'd only said it because she was drunk, because she'd been out with her single friend, because she was sad about not having a baby. Anything but accept what she was trying to say. I persuaded myself that if I just ignored it, it would go away. And it did. I thought it had worked . . ."

"She did love you, you know. But she was very cross with you."

"She was?"

"Yes. She told me that you'd misled her. That you'd let her believe she could make everyone happy. She said you'd 'mis-sold' your life to her."

Adrian was about to jump to his own defense but stopped. First of all he could not reasonably shoot the messenger, and secondly she was right. He had given Maya entirely the wrong impression of his home life. Possibly not deliberately. But certainly subconsciously.

"She also—" Abby stopped abruptly. She closed her mouth and shook her head. "No," she said, "nothing."

"No," said Adrian, greedy for more insights, however unpalatable they might be. "Please say it."

"She was, at least she *told* me she was, in love with somebody else. Someone you know."

"She was having an affair! Oh my God. Who with? Was it a teacher? From the school?"

"No. No. Not that. No. It was your son."

Adrian closed his eyes. *His son*. Of course.

"But nothing ever happened. No affair. Just feelings."

"Feelings?"

"Yes. Mutual feelings. I wasn't going to tell you, but now we're here, it seems pointless not to get it all out there."

"And what—my God! Was she planning on *being* with him? Once I was out of the picture?"

"No," said Abby quietly. "No. Far from it. She just wanted to leave you all to heal. To be a family. She just wanted to be out of it all. As if it had never happened. She was going to get a flat with her friend."

"Sara?"

"I can't remember. Her friend who was going to do teacher training. She had it all planned."

"Christ." Adrian hit the wooden table with the heels of his hands. The glasses clattered together. Where had he been? Where on earth had he been? His son in love with his wife. His children sending poisonous e-mails. His wife desperate to leave him and talking to strangers in bars. Everyone so angry and unhappy. And where had he been? Sitting cross-legged in the middle of this toxic tornado of human emotions humming la la la with his hands over his ears?

"Look," he said to Abby, "is there more? It's just . . . I have to go. They're all waiting for me."

"No," said Abby. "There's no more. Just that. Except for something she told me. She said it was the thing that really made her mind up for her. Something your little skater girl said that day. About missing you in the mornings. In the kitchen. Asking her about her dreams."

Adrian looked at Abby for a moment, searching for the memory. And then there it was. Suddenly, like a flashbulb in his head. The dark, unstirring basement, the drip and gurgle of the coffee machine, the footsteps down the wooden steps and his girl, standing there in her pajamas, dirty-blond hair in disarray, sometimes with a soft toy under her arm. Just the two of them in the morning gloom. The sound of Pearl's spoon against the china bowl, the swing of her bare feet under the kitchen counter. His eyes upon her, asking her what she'd dreamed about, only half listening to her reply, but drowning sweetly in the seawaters of his daughter's voice. Every morning, of every day. How could he have forgotten? And how could he have taken himself away from that?

"Thank you," he said. "I really need to go now. I really need to be with my family. Right now. But thank you. So much."

"I'm sorry," said Abby, half rising to her feet. "I'm sorry I didn't tell you before. In March. I just . . . you were so raw. I couldn't do it."

"No," said Adrian. "I understand. I needed to be ready to hear it. I wouldn't have been ready then. I wasn't ready then." He stopped and looked at the door of the pub. "She was a lovely person, wasn't she?"

"I only knew her for an hour," she replied softly. "But yes. She seemed a lovely person. Not the sort of person to tear a family apart."

"*She* wasn't the sort of person to tear a family apart," said Adrian sadly. "*I* was."

43

He took the tube to the Islington house. He couldn't face the thought of a cab journey, of being trapped in a vehicle with someone wanting to talk about the bloody Olympics for twenty minutes. The Piccadilly Line was August quiet and he found a seat without any trouble. He sat, his chin pressed into his chest, his feet planted solidly on the floor, his head filled with it all. Not a suicide, after all. Not an inexplicable act of inner turmoil unrelated to himself. Instead, if Abby's theory was to be believed, a terrible misstep *entirely* related to himself. To himself and to his family.

Lovely, soft, pliable Maya.

If only she'd been harder. She would have dealt with the issue of the e-mails before it had got under her skin; she would have come home from Caroline's house that night filled with righteous anger about the behavior of his children and she would have thrown her few things into a bag and gone and made a life for herself, a nice flat-share with Sara, a nice boyfriend eventually, who would have married her and made a baby with her without anyone paying a price.

But instead she'd lost her nerve, walked the streets of late-night London with a belly full of vodka rather than come home to do what she needed to do. And then there, that blighted curbstone on Charing Cross Road where the bloodstains had long since faded away, she'd slipped from the pavement, either by accident or by design, but certainly without properly thinking about what she was doing.

He thought about Abby's question earlier in the pub. What *would* he have done if Maya hadn't fallen from the curb, if she had made it home, drunk and disordered, and told Adrian she was leaving? How would he have reacted? And he knew the answer, well and good. He would have talked her round. He would have pooh-poohed all of her objections; he would have convinced her to stay. And if she'd told him about the e-mails? About the Skype chat? About the disgraceful way she'd been treated by his own daughter? He would still have found a way to make her believe that it could all be OK. And what, he wondered, would he have said if she'd told him about Luke? About their platonic affair of the heart?

He sighed and tipped up his head. Even then, he knew, even then he'd have thrown platitudes at her, told her that everything was going to be fine.

And why? Why would he have thrown a smokescreen over everything? Why would he have ignored the alarm bells, the signs of impending doom? Why would he not have said, *My God, Maya, what a terrible, terrible mess this all is, and how are we going to fix it?*

Because there was nowhere else for him to go. There had always been somewhere for Adrian to go before. The next woman. The next house. The next family. The next chapter. But he was only halfway through the book of Maya and himself. And he wasn't prepared to put it down until he'd finished it. Maya didn't get to choose when it was over. No woman had ever got to choose when it was over with him.

He thought again of Pearl's bare feet swinging beneath the kitchen counter. And then he thought of the Sunday morning, after he'd gone. He'd woken up in bed with Maya in their new flat and he'd turned to her and smiled and said, "The rest of our lives has officially begun." He had not thought of Pearl padding down the stairs in her pajamas; he had not pictured her walking into a dark empty kitchen with nobody there to ask her about her dreams. Instead he had pressed his face into Maya's soft flame-red hair and breathed in her fresh, new smell, told her again and again how happy they would be, how wonderful this new chapter would be, how everyone would love her, how she'd made his life complete.

He'd expected everyone to be happy, just because he was.

Who the hell did he think he was?

Did he think he was *God*?

And Cat? And Luke? He'd left them too, maybe not in an empty kitchen, but what other tender spot had he ripped himself away from? What other horrible gaping hole had he left in their worlds? Why had he never asked? Why had they never told him?

"You're just a child, Adrian."

That's what Caroline had said to him more than once during the process of their breakup.

"You're just a little boy."

"You exist only in the world according to you."

"You think the rules are for other people."

"You think anyone who tells you the truth is being mean."

"You have this innate belief in your own fairy-tale narrative."

Caroline had said many things to him over those months, in that deep, calm voice of hers. He had not listened to a word of it. Instead he had stroked Maya's hair and held Maya's hand and talked to Maya about the baby they would have and rushed home from work to Maya, and met Maya at cinemas and pubs and dreamed about the bright blue future with Maya. Everything else had been aural interference.

He'd thought himself so very reasonable. He'd given Caroline the house. He'd let her choose the terms of their shared custody. He'd carried on paying the bills for over a year without any fuss. He hadn't once raised his voice or thrown blame at anyone but himself. He had conducted himself impeccably.

But really, what was impeccable about leaving your children and their mother because you liked another girl better?

He changed trains at King's Cross onto the Northern Line towards Angel. In the corners of his consciousness Pearl's pale bare feet swung back and forth and back and forth with every footstep he took.

He climbed onto another half-empty train and took another empty seat. His thoughts turned to Caroline and her half-baked ideas about having a baby with Paul Wilson. He tried to imagine it. He tried to imagine there being a child in the world who was inextricably bound to him but was not his. Another face at the Christmas dinner table, another "Daddy." The thought made him cross. Then he thought of Pearl coming down for her breakfast in her pajamas and Paul Wilson sitting in the half-light, Paul Wilson asking her about her dreams, Paul Wilson maybe holding a baby in his arms who would be Pearl's new baby brother or sister, and he felt a red heat of injustice spread through his entire anatomy.

Yet he'd expected his family to be happy with his plans to do exactly the same. He'd expected them to embrace Maya and their theoretical child. He'd assumed that everyone would go with the flow, get on with their lives, unscathed.

One more person to love.

The train pulled into Angel. He stumbled onto the platform and made his way up the soaring escalators towards Upper Street. He started to run as he got closer to the house. The air was humid and gray and his shirt stuck to his skin with sweat. His heart was racing. He shouted into his phone as he ran, to Caroline, "I'm on my way. I'll be there in five minutes. Don't let Otis go to bed. Don't let anyone go to bed."

He took the steps up to the front door two at a time and hit the doorbell urgently. Luke opened the door and stood back to let him pass. "Everyone downstairs?" he asked.

Luke nodded and Adrian ran down the stairs, nearly breaking his neck over the two dogs as they ran towards him to find out who was at the door. He found his family in the kitchen. Caroline was standing over the hob, stirring hot chocolate in a pan. Cat and Pearl sat side by side on the bar stools at the counter and Otis was on the sofa next to Beau, who was fast asleep in his clothes. Luke came from behind Adrian and stood next to Cat.

He looked at them all. He had a hundred things he wanted to say. "I'm sorry," he said. He put his hand against his racing heart, feeling the sweat cooling on his shirt. "I'm really sorry," he said again.

And then, quite unexpectedly, he began to cry.

44

Luke stood pressed up against the wall, his arms pinned behind his back, as though there was a lunatic with a loaded weapon in the room. He stared fearfully at the various members of his family as they played out the next scene: Pearl holding his father in her arms, Caroline patting his back, Cat fetching him water, Otis staring at them all from the sofa. He had no idea what was about to happen. A few hours earlier Otis had confessed to a revelation from a strange woman about Maya's being in love with another man. And now his father was standing five feet away from him crying about a meeting with another strange woman in a pub in central London. Somewhere between the two meetings, he feared, lay the truth about him and Maya. Was it about to be revealed? That the whole thing was his fault? That he'd taken Maya's love away from his father? That his failure to finish his relationship with Charlotte properly had led Charlotte to write Maya those terrible e-mails? That he was duplicitous and weak, as bad as his father? His breath was red-hot, his heart a beating hammer. He waited to hear what his father had to say, waited for his just desserts.

Otis sat on the sofa, watching his father's dramatic entrance with fear and awe. What had that woman said to him? It was his fault. He knew it was. It was all his fault. And it was all about to come out. He thought back to that last day, when Maya had babysat them all, when he and Beau had been really horrible to her. He remembered finding Maya in Mum's room, touching her dresses, and he remembered her looking so confused, telling him she was trying to work things out. He could have said something different; he could have helped her. He'd replayed it in his head, time after time, day after day, imagined himself sitting down with her on his mum's bed, asking her if she was OK. Maybe she wouldn't have opened up to him about being in love with somebody else, but she might have felt a bit better about things. Instead he'd gone up to his room and had that really mean Skype chat with Cat. Said things he totally didn't mean. Forgotten that he'd left Skype running on the laptop downstairs. And then five minutes later—BAM—Maya was dead.

He watched as Cat passed his dad a glass of water. She was looking at Adrian really strangely, almost as though she was feeling as scared as him.

He hadn't told anyone about the Skype thing. Only Charlotte. It was weird how he and Charlotte had become kind of friends. She'd PMed him on Facebook a couple of weeks after Maya died, just to say she hoped he was OK, that Cat had told her he was feeling bad, that she was always there for him if he wanted to talk. He'd felt kind of proud having her as a Facebook friend. She was so pretty. And also, you know, his big brother's girlfriend. It was like a link to Luke somehow. Because up until recently there hadn't been much of a link between them. So he'd written to Charlotte a lot, told her how he was feeling, how he hated himself, how he held a pin next to his skin sometimes and thought about dragging it through his flesh. But he never did, because he was a coward.

Then Cat had moved in and he hadn't needed Charlotte so

much; they'd kind of stopped writing to each other. Until the thing about the e-mails had exploded in the family and he'd started feeling bad all over again. Not that he'd written the e-mails. But he had a feeling he knew who had. And that he was part of the whole stinking thing. Charlotte had written back and said, No, no, Otis, it was nothing to do with you. It was nothing to do with those e-mails. I know what it was. *I know why she died.* She wouldn't tell him online so she'd met him outside the tube one morning, told him about Maya's being in love with somebody else. Someone she couldn't be with, could never tell anyone about. And that was why she'd got drunk and walked into a bus.

It hadn't made any sense at first. Otis had sat on the bench outside the tube for ages, he didn't know how long, just watching the people and trying to make sense of it all. It had made him cross. Really cross. Why had his dad left their whole family to go off with a woman who wasn't even in love with him? Surely, he'd thought bitterly, surely if you were going to do that to all the people you loved you should at least be sure it was, you know, *forever*.

And now his dad was standing in the kitchen crying and nobody knew what he was going to say and Otis knew, he just knew, that it was all about to go down. It would all come out. And it was all his fault. All of it.

∽

Cat passed her father a glass of water and then stepped away from him, as if he were radioactive. He was crying, hysterically, and it was freaking her out. He hadn't even cried like that at Maya's funeral. Pearl had her arms around him and was holding on to him tight. Otis was sitting on the sofa looking wide-eyed and terrified and Luke was standing pinned up against the wall, watching their father through narrowed eyes.

And still Adrian hadn't said a word. He was crying too hard to talk.

Cat wanted to go. She wanted to pick up her jacket and her bag and just run. Anywhere. It didn't matter where. She just wanted to be away from here. Because it was obvious to her that whoever the hell that woman was, the woman with the phone and the odd-colored eyes, she had just told her father something revelatory and deeply distressing. And she suspected that it was something to do with her. And what she'd done.

Killed Maya.

That's what she'd done. She'd killed her, as sure as if she'd stood behind her on Charing Cross Road and given her a little shove. Cat hadn't been a human being these past sixteen months. She'd been a murderer. When she looked in the mirror she saw a murderer. When she heard her name being called she heard a murderer's name. When people stared at her on the street, when they caught her eye for longer than a second, she felt like they were thinking, Look at that murderer.

She'd been an animal, hiding away from the world in the bosom of Caroline's family. Eating. And eating. And eating some more. From the moment she'd sent that very first e-mail back in 2010 she'd been waiting for this. She remembered the breathless rush of adrenaline as she pressed send, the sense that she was about to change everything, forever. But then the days had passed and nothing had happened. No reply. No accusations. No consequences. So she'd sent another. And then another. And then another. She'd become addicted to the feeling of power and control. To the euphoria of getting away with it. And then she'd watched with sick satisfaction as Maya had grown smaller and smaller, quieter and quieter, less and less of the person she'd originally been, until that last holiday in Suffolk when it was almost as if Maya wasn't there at all.

She'd seen the distance between Maya and her father and the coldness in Maya's eyes and she'd thought, *Any minute now, any minute now, she'll be gone, it's just a matter of time.*

She'd sent one more e-mail, just after they got back, just to be sure, just to give Maya that final kick towards the exit doors. And then she'd gone and got herself killed. And the happy ending that Cat had dreamed about, the one where Maya left and her dad moved back in with Caroline and everything went back to the way it had been before—which wasn't exactly conventional, but which she had been happy with—had been ripped from beneath her feet. Instead of being the anonymous, conquering heroine, the one who'd saved the family from the dark compromises of a three-family existence, she had become instead an unspeakable monster.

Her father was beginning to calm down now. She could hear his breathing leveling itself out. She risked a glance in his direction. He was forming his first words. She caught her breath, clenched her fists and waited to hear what they would be.

45

Adrian placed the glass of water on the kitchen counter and pressed the paper towel that Caroline was offering him against his eyes. He hadn't been expecting the wave of emotion that had hit him like a shovel to the head as he'd walked into the kitchen and seen his family all there, all safe, all in one place. As his tears subsided and his vision cleared he could see fear in their eyes.

He crossed the room towards Otis and sat down next to him. "So," he said, "how was your little adventure?"

Otis tutted. "It wasn't an adventure."

"Well, whatever it was. Are you feeling OK?"

He shrugged. "Bit tired," he said.

"I bet." He drew himself closer to Otis and tried tentatively for a hug, but his son's body stiffened against his touch. Adrian looked up and saw everyone looking at him. There was a strange wariness in their expressions.

Adrian smiled. All he wanted to do now was to make everyone feel OK. "Listen," he said, looking from child to child. "I've heard something tonight that changes everything. Maya didn't kill herself." He looked around again, saw heads slowly rising, eyes finally meeting his. "That woman, Abby, she was the last person to see Maya alive. She spent an hour with her, in a pub, talking to her. About everything. And she told me: so now I know. It was nothing to do with not being able to have a baby and it was nothing to do with those e-mails. She didn't walk out in front of that bus on purpose. She fell. She slipped. Because she was drunk. And she was drunk because she was too nervous to come home. To come home and tell me that she didn't love me anymore and that she wanted to leave me."

"So it wasn't about the e-mails?" said Cat, her full, open face etched with fear.

Adrian took a breath. Here was where it ended. All of it. No more blame on anyone apart from him. "No," he said carefully. "Abby said that Maya didn't take the e-mails very seriously. She said that Maya had no bad feelings towards anyone in the family. It was all about me," he said, looking at Cat, making sure she looked at him. "All of it. Nothing to do with anyone else. At all."

A sob caught in the back of Cat's throat, loud enough to make Pearl jump. By his side, Adrian felt Otis's stiff little body slump and soften and suddenly Otis's arms were around Adrian's chest, his head buried beneath his arms, tears soaking through his shirt. Adrian felt his heart swell at the earnestness of the gesture. He had not felt his boy's arms around him for a very long time. Otis pulled away after a moment and stared up at his dad through tear-streaked eyes. He rubbed them away with the heels of his hands and said, "I love you, Dad."

Cat walked towards Adrian and Otis, tears spilling down her face, "Dad," she began, "those e-mails . . . those e-mails . . ."

"We're not going to talk about the e-mails," said Adrian. His tone was firm, final.

He saw Luke staring at him desperately from the other side of the room, still pinned to the wall. He saw the terror in his eyes and directed his next words at his eldest son: "We're not going to talk about any of it. OK? What we're going to do is this: we're going to blame me for everything. What happened to Maya is my fault. Every bad feeling any of you has ever had is my fault. Any bad thing any of you has ever done is my fault. OK?"

Nobody said anything.

"OK?" Adrian repeated.

Everyone nodded their heads.

"A fresh start. Yes?"

More nods.

"I am so sorry." He held his hand out to Caroline, who took it and squeezed it uncertainly. "I'm so sorry that I've spent my life putting myself first. I just always thought that if I was a 'nice guy' then people would be happy for me, whatever I decided to do. That's what my mum always said to me: 'As long as you're happy, darling, that's all that matters.' But she didn't teach me that happiness should be dependent on the happiness of people I loved. But now," he said, "I want you lot to decide what I should do." He rubbed Otis's hair and smiled at Pearl. "I want you all to write me a letter, from the heart, no holds barred, and tell me how to be what you want me to be. It can be as stupid as you like. You know"—he smiled at Luke—"maybe you'd like me to dress differently." He looked at Pearl. "Or maybe learn to skate. Or maybe take a vow of celibacy." He squeezed Caroline's hand. "Just anything you can think of. And I'll try to do it."

Beau stirred from his sleep and looked up and around in awed shock. "What?" he said. "What's happening?"

Adrian looked down at his youngest child and smiled. "We're all just talking. About what we want Daddy to do so that we can all be happy again."

"Are you coming home? To live?"

Adrian smiled. "I don't know about that. But I'll do whatever anyone wants me to do."

Beau nodded. "OK," he said, yawning. Then he turned his

big eyes to Adrian and he said, "Can you carry me? Up to my bed?"

Adrian was about to say: *Oh no, big boy, you're too heavy for that now.* But he stopped himself. He thought of all the nights when Beau had been small enough to be carried to bed and he'd been watching TV in a flat two miles away with another woman.

He got to his feet, turned around and said, "OK then, big boy, up you jump."

Beau hooked his arms around Adrian's neck and his legs around Adrian's waist and tucked his chin into Adrian's shoulder.

"Night night, everyone," said Beau.

Adrian carried this boy-giant, the tallest in his class and the heaviest, carried him up three flights of stairs and placed him in his bed, as if he was no more than a bag of air.

He put him into his pajamas and he kissed his cheek and tucked him in under his duvet.

"Night night, my baby boy," he said, "I'll see you tomorrow."

And under his breath, too quietly for Beau to hear, he said: *And hopefully all the tomorrows after that.*

46

The following morning Adrian answered a knock at his front door. He was expecting a postal delivery or a local politician but instead he found a beautiful blonde.

"Carrie," he said, his eyes taking in the statuesque lines of her, the warmth in her eyes, her scruffy red car double-parked in the street with its hazards flashing. "Do you want to . . . ?"

"No"—she gestured at the car—"I'm in a terrible rush. I just, er, the children—they wrote their letters. Here." She pulled them from her handbag. "One from Cat, from Pearl, one from Luke and this one is Beau's. Otis was still working on his when I left." She shrugged.

Adrian took them from her and smiled. "Thank you," he said.

Caroline craned her neck to check her car and then turned back to Adrian. "Listen," she said, "we should talk. You and I. What are you doing tonight?"

"Nothing," he replied.

"Can you meet me for a drink? At the Albion? Seven thirty?"

Adrian smiled uncertainly. He could not begin to imagine what Caroline might want to say to him. But he knew that his entire future rested on it. "Sure," he said. "I can be there."

A horn sounded in the road behind them and Caroline turned anxiously. "Got to go," she said. "I'll see you later."

He watched her dash towards her car, wave apologetically

at the driver of the waiting car, strap herself in quickly and speed away. And then he took the letters into his flat and he opened them.

Dear Dad,

First of all I want to say that I'm not perfect either. I've spent a lot of my life blaming you for my shortcomings, but I think a lot of that was because I felt like everyone was just letting you get away with it. Like I was the only one who could see the truth. But no, it's not your fault that I'm doing nothing with my life. It's not your fault that I have nothing important in my life and no focus. You did everything you could, you paid for my education and I do appreciate that so much, especially as you didn't pay for anyone else's. I know you and Mum thought I'd be prime minister by now! And I'm aware that I've let you down, but I'm young still. Hopefully there's still lots of time left to make you both proud of me.

As for what you can do for me now? Well, first of all I hope you'll forgive me. It was shit what you did: leaving me and Cat and Mum down in Hove when we all needed you so much. But if Mum can forgive you, then I can be a bigger person and try to forgive you, too. I've been waiting for fourteen years for you to say sorry and you finally did. So now it's just onwards and upwards, I hope.

I also think you should move out of that flat. You're only forty-eight but since Maya died you've aged about ten years. You need a fresh start. You're an architect, for God's sake, living in a crap conversion with no light and no space! That place is dragging you down.

I also need you to not have any more children. Seriously. You always said it would be "another person to love." But I don't agree. I think it would be another person

to take you away from us, especially the small ones. Don't
do it. You've got five totally amazing children. Enough.
Stop. Move on.

But mostly I'd like us to try and be friends, instead of
two spoilt boys sharing a house.

I really love you, Dad. I'm glad we're getting a chance
to start over.

Yours, always,
Luke

Dear Dad,

I know you said not to talk about the e-mails. But I
have to talk about the e-mails. If I don't talk about the
e-mails I'm going to end up in a nuthouse. It was me, Dad.
I know you probably already know that. That woman in
the pub probably told you because I'm pretty sure Maya
worked it out that night. She saw a Skype chat that me and
Otis were having. It wasn't very nice. She probably put
two and two together.

Dad, when I saw those e-mails again after all that time
I actually couldn't believe I'd written them. They looked
like they'd been written by a psychopath, by someone evil
and twisted. I felt like there must have been some monster
living inside me. I hated myself. I still hate myself. I truly
can't believe I was capable of such a thing.

The last year and a half has been like pure torture.
When I heard about Maya I was on my way to work
and I literally threw up into my own hands on the bus. I
thought I'd murdered her. Christ. I wish I could explain
how I was feeling, what made me do it, but it's hard.

I was so angry with you when you left Caroline. If
you'd had any idea how hard I worked to accept you leaving Mum, leaving us, how hard it was to carry on loving

you when my heart was broken. I couldn't have done it without Mum. She was so forgiving. So gentle. I totally took my cues from her. I couldn't let my anger out, for her sake, so I focused instead on being a part of your new family. I never blamed Caroline and I made her a friend. And I loved each and every one of those babies as if they were fully my own flesh and blood. I took the "if you can't beat them join them" approach. AND THEN YOU FUCKING LEFT!!! I wanted to kill you!! I hated you! Much more than I did when you left us. And then I met Maya and she was so sweet and so young and so *bleugh*. I just totally didn't get it. You know, you left Caroline— for *that*. Sorry, that makes me sound like such a bitch. Clearly I am a bitch. But I wasn't the only one. Nobody understood what was going on. The children said things to me that they couldn't say to you. And I just thought that maybe for the sake of all the children I could get her to leave. I thought I was doing it for everyone, you know, for the greater good. Nobody knew I was sending them. Not even Otis.

I don't really feel I'm in any position to ask you to do or be anything, apart from forgiving. I know that woman in the pub said that Maya didn't kill herself, but really, how can she know? How can anyone know, apart from Maya herself? I'll take it with me always and forever. I just wanted her to disappear. I was an idiot. I have learned. I am a better person. I just hope that one day you'll be able to look at me again the way you always have done, like I'm the loveliest girl in the world. But I wouldn't blame you if you didn't.

I love you, Daddy. Please come home.

Your Cat xxxx

Dear Dad,

I haven't written my letter yet. I'll give it to you soon.

Love,

Otis x

Dear Daddy,

I want you to be happy again. I want you to cut your hair. I want you to go on a date with Mummy. I want you to get rid of Paul Wilson. I want you to do my homework with me. I want you to sleep in Mummy's bedroom. I want you to stop buying me ice skates for my birthday and buy me something surprising that you thought of yourself. I want you to have a fat tummy again. I want to be part of a normal family, like we used to be. I want you to have tomato soup and bread with me all the time, not just once a week. I want you to be downstairs in the mornings. I want to tell you all my dreams, always, until I'm too old to tell my daddy about my dreams.

I love you,

Pearl

Dear Daddy,

I want you to come home. And tickle my feet. Please.

Love from,

Beau

47

Caroline wasn't wearing a plastic Pac-a-mac when Adrian met her in the vine-draped beer garden of a heaving Islington pub that night. She was wearing one of her "Paul Wilson" dresses: tight and swooping down into a V-neck towards her cleavage. Her pale hair was tied back into a stubby ponytail, her blunt fringe swept across one eye. She wore eyeliner and silver earrings and strappy sandals. She looked about twenty-eight.

Adrian stood up when she walked in, greeted her as he always did, with fulsome kisses to each cheek. But the gesture carried more substance than usual. "You look lovely," he said.

She did not return the compliment. Instead she pulled her phone out of her bag, switched it on, looked at it, switched it off and placed it neatly on the table in front of her, next to her sunglasses.

In the corner of the beer garden there was a huge screen showing the Olympics. Adrian sat with his back to it, not wanting to be distracted for even a second. He poured Caroline a glass of wine from the bottle on the table. His hand shook slightly. Caroline gave him a look that he translated as meaning: *Good, you should be nervous.*

"How are the kids?"

"They're good," she said. "The mood seems lighter after last night. Otis, in particular, seems like a different boy."

"And how's Pearl?"

"I don't know," said Caroline, running her fingertips up and down the arm of her sunglasses. "She's quiet. I think she suspects that Cat might have had something to do with those e-mails." She threw a questioning look at Adrian and he nodded.

"Are you ready?" he said. "Shall I tell you?"

Caroline nodded nervously. "I guess," she said.

And then Adrian told her everything: about the Skype chat, about Cat's e-mails, about Luke and Maya.

He stared at Caroline afterwards and said, "How do you feel now, about Cat?"

Caroline shrugged. "I don't know," she began. "I feel lots of things. But mainly sad. I can see what she was doing. But she's just, well, no offense, but she's not the brightest star in the sky. She's not very mature for her age." She shrugged. "It was schoolgirl stuff. It was cruel. And idiotic."

"You know," said Adrian, "I was talking to Susie about it last night and she reminded me of something. Something I'd completely forgotten about. When Cat was a teenager she was excluded from school for a week for bullying."

Caroline raised her brow.

"Yes. When she was about twelve, thirteen. Same age as Otis. A new girl started at her school, partway through a term. Everyone really liked her, apparently. She was a real hit with the boys and the girls. And she started to impinge on Cat's territory. So Cat pretended to befriend her, and all the while was spreading rumors about her and turning everyone against her. The girl in question told her mum what was happening and her mum happened to be a school governor and so knew exactly how to deal with the situation. It ended up with Cat being excluded and having to write an apology to this girl. It seemed quite petty at the time. Or at least, that was my understanding of the situation from my position in bed with you dozens of miles away from the action." He raised a sardonic eyebrow. "I just put it down to girls being girls. You know. It never occurred to me that it meant she was a horrible person."

"You think she's a horrible person?"

"No." Adrian sighed. "No. Of course I don't. I think she is just yet another victim of her runaway serial adulterer juggernaut of a father."

He and Caroline exchanged a look.

"Do you think she'll stay with you?" said Adrian.

"She hasn't said anything about moving on." She shrugged again. "I guess she'll stay for a while."

"Are you OK with that?"

"Sure. Totally. You know how I feel about Cat. I love her as though she was my own. Also, I'd be totally lost without her. So . . ." Caroline smiled a tight, sad smile and lifted her glass towards Adrian's. "Anyway," she said, "cheers. Here's to getting it all out there. All the grubby stuff."

Adrian smiled drily and knocked his glass gently against Caroline's.

Caroline topped up their wineglasses and then she turned her eyes up to Adrian and said, "Off you go then. You have the Talking Stick."

"The what?"

"You know, the Talking Stick. It's what they use in therapy. While you're holding it, nobody else is allowed to talk."

"Oh," said Adrian. "OK then."

Caroline looked at him expectantly and Adrian felt something at the core of himself soften and then bubble up. Then he felt a thought rise up through the molten flow of his emotions like a golden phoenix. A big dazzling thought that threatened to burst from his head and out of his lips. *You are the love of my life.*

He swallowed it down, no longer able to trust himself or his own feelings. Because the one thing that had become blindingly apparent to him over the course of the last twenty-four hours of self-reflection was that he really was a total blithering idiot. He'd found himself replaying sections of his life in almost lifelike detail and at nearly every juncture he had seen, as a spectator, that he had been blowing through life without a clue of what he was doing. It was almost as though he was going from golden light to golden light, blindly, like a moth. The moment a light lost its golden glow he would turn away from it and start looking for the next golden light.

Yes, after many hours of contemplation the dazzling conclusion that Adrian Wolfe had reached about himself was that he was a human moth.

But how could he explain that to Caroline? He had no idea. So he sighed and smiled at her and he said, "I am a moth."

She said nothing, but raised an eyebrow at him and sipped her wine.

"I am a moth," he said again. "And I need to be a cow."

Caroline slanted her eyes at him over the rim of her wineglass.

"You know, a cow. It stays in its field. It eats the same grass all day long. It doesn't think about the grass over there, or the daisies over there, or the possibility of clover in the field across the way. It just stays and it eats the grass and the grass tastes good. And when all the grass has gone, it waits for more grass to grow. Because there will always be more grass. And possibly clover, too."

Adrian looked at Caroline and saw the impatience in her eyes. He was losing her.

He sighed and leaned across the table towards her. "What I'm saying, in a completely ridiculous way, is that I left Susie because I couldn't be bothered to wait around for the grass to grow again. And I saw you and . . ."

"I was full of clover."

"Well, yes. Kind of."

"So I could have been anyone?"

"Have you got the Talking Stick now?"

"Oh, fuck the fucking Talking Stick. Just tell me. Could I have been anyone? As long as I was shining brightly enough?"

"No," said Adrian. "No. You . . ." And there it was, the perfect opening for his revelation, but how would she take it? He breathed in deeply, turned his hands palms up and said, "You were the love of my life."

He watched her eyes while she absorbed this pronouncement, trying to gauge what her response might be.

She looked first surprised, then pleased, and then furious. "Oh, you fucking arsehole," she said.

"I know," he said.

"No, really. You are the fuckingest arsehole in the universe. *Love of my life.*" She rolled her eyes. "If I was the love of your stupid fucking life, then why did you bounce off to Maya? Don't tell me," she said, "because you couldn't be bothered to wait for the grass to grow?" She tutted loudly and swallowed down some wine.

Adrian had spent a lot of time the previous night revisiting the days and weeks around his affair with Maya. He had looked at it, like an exhibit in a Perspex box, from every conceivable angle. And then he'd finally seen it. The precise moment he'd made the decision in his big, stupid head to fall in love with somebody else.

"Do you remember," he said, "the summer after your fortieth birthday? When I booked us that night in Paris?"

She rolled her eyes again and groaned. "Oh God," she said, "not that again."

"No, honestly, hear me out. It wasn't that you didn't want to come. It wasn't that you didn't want to leave Beau. It wasn't even that you said it was a really thoughtless thing to do. Because yes, in retrospect I can see that it was quite thoughtless. You were breast-feeding. You were tired. You'd said about a million times that you didn't want to do much to celebrate. But that Monday, I went into work and Maya was there and she said, 'How was Paris?!' Because she knew I'd been planning it. Everyone in the office knew I'd been planning it. And I said, 'We didn't go to Paris.' And she said, 'Oh.' And her face fell. And I could tell she was hurting for me. And she didn't say anything else. Just that. *Oh.* And a hand on my arm. And that was it, Caroline. That was the moment that it went from her being this bright young girl in the office to me thinking she was the answer to all my woes. Because, *arsehole* that I am, I thought that anyone who could hurt on my behalf like that would never do anything to hurt me."

"And what," said Caroline, "I was hurting you, was I?"

"I thought you were going to leave me."

"Oh, don't be ridiculous."

"I'm honestly not being ridiculous. I thought that you were going to leave me."

"Based on what?"

"Based on many things, but mainly on the fact that you are completely out of my league."

"What?"

"Completely out of my league," he replied. "Cleverer than me, prettier than me, a better parent than me, a better person than me. And if I couldn't buy your adoration with impromptu trips to Paris, then I was out of ideas. I had no idea how to keep you. So I left you."

Caroline stared at him avidly. "You do realize that's the most stupid thing any person on this planet has ever said since the creation of language, don't you?"

"I'm not sitting here trying to persuade you of my superior emotional intelligence, Caroline. But you asked me why I left, and I'm telling you. And I agree, from this vantage point it's ludicrous, but there and then, it made total sense. I left Susie because I had fallen out of love with her and I left you because I thought you'd fallen out of love with me. That you'd turned the lights off."

"Are we back to moths again?"

"Yes. We're back to moths again."

Caroline sighed and appraised Adrian coolly. "It's all well and good talking about moths, Adrian, it's all very good talking about fields of clover. But what glows more brightly than children, Adrian? Huh? How did you do it? How do you square yourself with that?"

"Well, you know, I can't, obviously. Of course I can't. But I can tell you that I honestly thought . . . well, thought is the wrong word, because I wasn't thinking, was I? But I honestly just assumed that as long as the children had their home and their mother, they wouldn't miss me. I mean, I was never there anyway."

"Oh, that's crap. You were there all the time."

"Well, not as much as you. I suppose that's what I thought. So long as they had their constants: their house, their school."

"Oh, Adrian. That's pathetic."

"I know it is. That's the thing, Caroline, there is no longer anything you can say to me about my behavior or my . . . my motivations over the last few years that I could disagree with. When I look at myself, objectively, without the obfuscations of *being in love* or, you know, the grieving process, I find it hard to believe I could have made the decisions I made. Did the things I did. Walked out on a baby."

"You walked out on five babies, Adrian."

"Yes. Yes. I did."

"Have you read the letters?"

"*Of course* I've read the letters."

"And?"

"And they are all amazing."

"What did they say?"

"You didn't read them?"

"No, of course not."

"Not even Beau's?"

"Not even Beau's." She glanced at him. "Anything interesting?"

"Pearl wants me to choose more imaginative birthday presents. Luke wants me to be friends with him. Cat wants me to forgive her. And Beau wants me to tickle his feet. Oh, and . . ." Adrian smiled and then glanced up at Caroline. "He wants me to move home. Actually, so does Pearl."

Caroline didn't respond. Instead she pulled her handbag onto her lap and took a letter from it. "Here," she said, sliding it across the table towards Adrian. "From Otis."

Adrian pulled it towards himself. This was the one, he thought, the one he had no idea about at all. "Shall I . . . ?"

Caroline nodded. "Why not."

Adrian opened the envelope and pulled out the letter, typed onto a word processor.

Dear Dad,

I don't really know what to say. I've been trying to write this letter all night and all day but it keeps coming out wrong. First of all I'm really sorry that I wasn't nice to Maya. That thing with the Skype—that wasn't really what I was thinking. It was just a thing, with Cat. It made me feel close to her. I didn't hate Maya. I liked her. I thought she was really nice. I miss her.

I've really hated myself since Maya died. Totally despised myself. But I think I'd rather hate myself than hate you. Because you're the best dad in the world. I know I don't show it much. But that's just me. It's hard being the middle child. It's hard being the oldest child. And I'm kind of both. I sometimes don't really know how I'm supposed to be.

I'm trying to think of things I want you to do, but I

can't. I guess I just want you to be you. Because you're
nice. And you're generous. And everyone likes you. I'd
like to be like you when I grow up. Except I would just
choose one woman to marry and I'd stick with her. I don't
really like change. I like things to stay the same. It took a
lot of getting used to when you left, but I got used to it
eventually. I'm not like you in that way, I suppose. You
obviously like change.

I'm still not happy with this letter. It's not really saying
a lot. But then maybe I haven't got much to say. Except
I'm sorry if I've let you down. I'm going to try harder
now. At everything. At school and at home. And maybe if
I can be a better person you might want to come and live
with us again.

I love you, Dad. You're the best.

Otis x

Adrian passed the letter to Caroline and wiped a tear from
the side of his nose.

She looked at him curiously.

"Read that," he said.

She took the letter from his outstretched hand, her eyes
still on his. Then her eyes dropped to the letter. He watched
her reading, his chin balanced on top of tented fingers. He saw
a judder of emotion pass through her body. He watched as a
tear coalesced at the rim of her lashes and dropped onto the
back of her hand; then he watched her wipe it away.

Their boy.

When she'd finished reading she slid the folded letter back
into its envelope and handed it back to Adrian. He caught
her fingertips inside his and squeezed them. "OK?" he asked
quietly.

"OK," she said.

"He's right, you know. I should just choose one woman and stick with her."

"But he's also right when he says that you like change."

Adrian sighed. "You know, I think I'm too old for change now." He ran a fingertip up and down the back of Caroline's hand.

She didn't move her hand, just left her gaze on his and waited for him to finish talking. But he had nothing left to say. He pulled her other hand across the table towards him. For almost a minute neither one of them spoke. In the background a Chinese swimmer was winning a gold medal on the giant screen. Around them the young, smooth-skinned hipsters of London N1 sat and talked about things that seemed important to them in their nebulous world of media jobs and marriage engagements, clubs and flat-shares and broken hearts. Their world was all about change. All about the next golden glow and the next field over. And there, in their midst, sat Adrian and Caroline, halfway through their lives, if they were lucky, five children, two careers, three homes, two dogs, one cat, a dead wife and a fresh-faced boyfriend between them.

But as they looked at each other across the table, their hands entwined, as they studied the familiar angles of each other's faces, read the silent messages behind each other's eyes, it was as though some invisible bellboy had been to collect all their baggage. It was as though they were starting over, with hand luggage.

"I really like you," said Adrian, picking up one of Caroline's hands and holding it to his lips.

Caroline laughed. "You fool," she said, her eyes still on his.

"Shall we go home?"

"Yes," said Caroline.

EPILOGUE

The energy was still there in the London air, like a lingering perfume. The Olympics were over but their scent remained. As Adrian walked from his empty flat through the back streets of north London towards Highgate Road, he felt the warmth of strangers, the connections built over weeks of communal screen-staring and eruptions of national pride. He knew it wouldn't last but for now it enhanced his already heightened sense of rightness with the world.

The box he was carrying was much heavier than he'd thought it was when he'd first picked it up twenty minutes ago and he needed to keep transferring it from hand to hand as he walked. Each time he did so the contents slid from the back to the front and complained quietly. Halfway to Highgate he felt the need to sit for a while. He brought the box up onto the bench next to him and peered through the holes in the front.

"You all right, girl?" he said to the anxious-looking cat crouched inside.

Billie meowed at him and he stuck his fingers through the holes to tickle her nose. "Nearly there," he said. "Not long now."

He took a bottle of water from his backpack, had a good long sip and then carried on his way.

The flat was in a converted Victorian house, just like his own. He rang on the doorbell and passed a hand over his newly trimmed hair.

A moment later the door opened and there she was.

"Hello!" she said. "Hello! Come in!"

She greeted him with a kiss on each cheek, her golden hair brushing against his face, her perfume clean and floral. He followed her into an open-plan living room, vintage, bohemian, tidy, clean, done out from trendy markets and eBay. The man called Matthew sat at a small desk in the corner on an Apple Mac, wearing the sort of colorful, tight-fitting clothes that Luke liked to wear, an earpiece connecting him to his smartphone. He pulled out the earpiece when he saw Adrian walk in, got to his feet and smiled.

"So we meet again!" He shook Adrian's hand firmly. "Sorry about the last time. Blame her," he said, pointing at Abby, who stood behind him smiling. "And who do we have here?" He dropped to his knees and peered through the holes in the cat box. "Hello, you!" he said. "Aren't you lovely!"

Adrian unclipped the front flap of the box and let it fall open. Billie emerged, one leg at a time, her face full of fear and excitement.

Matthew offered Adrian a cup of tea and Adrian requested a glass of water. "Welcome to your new home," said Abby, kneeling down to address the cat. The cat appeared to recognize Abby and greeted her fondly, rubbing her face against her hands.

"So," she said, smiling up at Adrian. "You're leaving your flat?"

"Yes. Yes. Today, in fact. The builders start today in Islington. Building me my man-shack."

"Ah, your little house in the garden?"

"Yes, my monk's quarters. I need to be on-site to oversee the works. But until it's built, I'm in the spare room. With the computer."

"So, she didn't take you back?"

"No. She did not take me back. But I'm allowed in the house. For mealtimes. Like a dog. And she hasn't ruled out a reconciliation at some later date. But for now I have to prove myself."

"Prove what exactly?"

"That I am able to be alone."

"Chastity?"

"Yes. That." He exhaled. "I would have moved out earlier but I still had a little problem to deal with." They both looked at the cat. "But now, thanks to you . . ."

"No, no, seriously. This is a pleasure. I feel honored to have her. It's like destiny. Don't you think?" She looked up at him and he felt that kick to his gut he always felt when he looked at Abby, that kick of sheer red-blooded appreciation. She was wearing a cream camisole top, with a bra visible above the fabric, a slim chiffon tie around her narrow waist, tight denim jeans and yellow flip-flops. Her toenails were painted pale rose and she was looking at him as though he was interesting to her. Not like he was an old man, not like he was *Dad* or *idiot* or *silly old fool*. She was looking at him as though he was a man. And he could see right down her bra to two swells of young, tanned flesh.

"I like your hair," she said, getting to her feet, tucking her hands into the pockets of her jeans.

He touched it and flushed pink. "Yes," he said, "my daughter's idea. As was this." He patted his tiny paunch, just visible now above the waistband of the trousers Luke had forced him to buy in the Reiss sale last week.

"You look good," she said appreciatively.

"For an old man."

"No, not for an old man. For you. Compared to the man I saw half-dead with grief six months ago."

"Thank you," he said. "It's been quite a journey."

"And now it's over?"

"Well, it will never be entirely over. There's still the ghost of Maya. There's still the scars. There's Cat. Not *this* cat"—he pointed at Billie, who was sniffing curiously at the skirting boards—"*my* Cat. She's still suffering. Obviously. She's going to therapy. Trying to get to the root of the whole thing. That will take time. And lots of little bridges to build here and there. But, on the whole . . ." He shrugged. "Yes, the journey's over. I'm home."

"And you're happy?"

Adrian smiled at the question. "Yes. I'm really happy. I can't really believe I ever thought I could be happier anywhere else. Than there. With them. You know."

Matthew appeared with a glass of water for Adrian and two cups of tea for himself and Abby. But Adrian didn't drink the water. This was it. The final moment of the transition. He wanted to go home now. He took one last look at Maya's cat and smiled fondly. "Bye bye, Billie." He crouched down to stroke her. "I hope you're very happy here."

"Oh, she will be," said Abby, eyeing Adrian in that eviscerating way of hers. "We'll make sure of that."

She would fall in love with him. It wouldn't take much. A few drinks. Some charming self-deprecation. He hadn't imagined the chemistry between them from that first meeting in March.

Adrian absorbed the look and held it inside himself. This is what he would do now with compliments and loaded moments with beautiful women who weren't his wife. He would absorb them and hold them inside. He would keep them like souvenirs, reminders that he was once a man who could choose his path in life according to the wiles and desires of beautiful women. But that he was now a man who'd found his sticking point.

He kissed Abby hard on each cheek, inhaling the unfamiliar, giddying smell of her, basking one last time in her golden aura, and then he left. As the door closed behind him, so did the memory of a weaker man than him.

He turned the corner and he headed home.

ACKNOWLEDGMENTS

This book was conceived, written and rewritten almost entirely alone. Every time I tried to explain what it was about, people would look at me strangely and say: Oh. Right. So I stopped talking about it, shut all the blinds and just got on with it.

So my thanks really must go to Adrian, Maya and the rest of the fictional Wolfe family for making me care about them so much that I was compelled to keep going until I'd found a story good enough for them.

And, back in the Real World, a huge thank-you to my wonderful editor Selina Walker for writing me "that" blurb when I was nearly at the end which allowed me finally to see the book I had been writing and make sense of it all. Thanks also to all the magnificent team at Arrow; to Jen and Najma and Beth and Sarah and Jenny and Susan and Richard. And thank you to Richenda Todd for the top-notch copyedit.

Thanks to Jonny Geller and everyone at Curtis Brown. And in the US, thanks to Deborah Schneider at Gelfman Schneider. I am so lucky to be represented by the best in the business both sides of the pond.

Thanks to all at Atria, my US publishers. Especially thanks to Sarah Branham, Ariele Fredman and Daniella Wexler.

And, closer to home, thanks to Jenny, Jojo, Mike, Jascha, Sacha, Tanya, Grace, Nic, Yasmin and Sarah, who are always there to talk writing even though they don't get paid for it.

Lastly, Amelie and Evie, my girls, who don't help me write books in any way. But they do provide a very helpful counterpoint to the process. And they're really lovely. Thank you.